ROGUE STATE

ALSO BY STEVEN KONKOLY

THE FRACTURED STATE SERIES

Fractured State

THE PERSEID COLLAPSE SERIES

The Jakarta Pandemic
The Perseid Collapse
Event Horizon
Point of Crisis
Dispatches

THE BLACK FLAGGED SERIES

Black Flagged Alpha
Black Flagged Redux
Black Flagged Apex
Black Flagged Vector

WAYWARD PINES KINDLE WORLD

GENESIS SERIES

First Contact
Last Betrayal
Sanctuary

ROGUE STATE

BOOK TWO IN THE FRACTURED STATE SERIES

STEVEN KONKOLY

f THOMAS & MERCER

Text copyright © 2017 by Steven Konkoly

Published by Thomas & Mercer, Seattle

www.apub.com

Amazon, the Amazon logo, and Thomas & Mercer are trademarks of Amazon.com, Inc., or its affiliates.

ISBN-13: 9781503940338

ISBN-10: 1503940330

Cover design by Cyanotype Book Architects

Printed in the United States of America

To Kosia, Matthew, and Sophia, the heart and soul of my writing

PART I

PART I

CHAPTER 1

The dune buggy carrying Nathan and his family slowed with the rest of the convoy as they drew even with a dense stand of trees several hundred feet to the left of the road.

After bypassing a lifeless town along one of the few paved roads they had encountered, they'd driven at breakneck speed down this unimproved dirt path for the past fifteen minutes. This was the first time they'd slowed since emerging from the tunnel under the border.

The mix of tall Mexican elders and low, sprawling mesquite surrounded a modest, hacienda-style home, mostly concealing it from view. Some kind of rendezvous point, Nathan suspected.

The synthetic daylight image provided by Nathan's helmet-mounted night-vision goggles confirmed his suspicion. Two military transport trucks with covered cargo beds appeared beyond the far corner of the hacienda as their dune buggy continued down the road. A few SUVs were parked behind the military trucks. Nathan looked over his shoulder; the last compound they had passed was a speck on the horizon behind the last dune buggies on the road.

"What is this place?" yelled Nathan.

The driver half turned his head. "One of our staging areas. We'll swap the dune buggy for a more comfortable ride. We have a long drive ahead of us."

Keira looked at him from the front passenger seat. He couldn't see her expression beyond the night-vision goggles pulled over her face, but he could guess what she was thinking. Where the hell was Jose taking them?

The first dune buggy in the column turned sharply toward the hacienda, and the rest of the squat vehicles followed. Looking across the empty expanse of sparse scrub brush between the road and house, Nathan wondered why they followed one another so closely. Then he noticed the signs. Yellow background with a black skull and crossbones on the top; black with the yellow words **DANGER—MINES** on the bottom half. Either the signs had been posted as a deterrent, or Jose wasn't messing around.

"Dad. Look." Owen was pointing at one of the signs less than twenty feet from their vehicle.

"I see it," said Nathan. "I'm sure the driver sees it, too."

"We're good to go," said the driver.

The signs ended once they reached the trees, and the dune buggies headed toward the group of trucks and SUVs parked next to the hacienda. As soon as the buggies stopped, the soldiers that had hitched a ride with Jose's team jumped to the hard-packed ground and began unloading their gear. They were loading their spent parachutes and packs into the military vehicles before Nathan got Owen unbuckled from the dune buggy and lowered him to the dirt. The trucks' diesel engines roared to life moments later, carrying the soldiers back down the same path through the middle of the minefield.

"Almost like they didn't exist," said Keira, standing next to him.

"Not 'almost,'" said a voice to their right. "As far as anyone here is concerned, they don't exist."

Nathan and Keira turned to face Jose, who walked briskly toward them.

"You're working for the Mexican government?" said Nathan. "I suppose that makes sense."

Mexico stood to gain from an independent California, particularly in terms of trade agreements. Federally imposed trade restrictions with Mexico had hit California hard, severely limiting the amount of petroleum the state could import. Even worse, the new antitrade laws rendered California's plan to fund the construction of several nuclear triad plants in Baja California impossible. The deal surrounding the nuclear plants would have guaranteed a significant source of fresh water and electricity for California.

"Nathan. I guarantee you I'm not working for the Mexicans. I can't wait to explain everything to you, but it can't happen now. I need to get you on the road immediately. Grab your gear and follow me," said Jose, gesturing for them to move toward the SUVs.

"Where are we headed?"

"Let's walk and talk. I seriously need to get you moving."

Nathan helped Keira shoulder her backpack, then grabbed his own. They walked as a family with Jose to the running vehicles.

"I'm sending you about four hours south to a coastal town called Puerto Peñasco, where you'll take a boat to Cabo San Lucas."

Keira beat him to his question: "How long will we be on that boat?"

He held queasy memories of more than a few spur-of-the-moment, beer-fueled Friday-night road trips to Cabo in college. The prospect of spending twenty-plus hours in a car driving through Mexico had sounded far less appealing the next day, nursing a hangover. If the trip to Puerto Peñasco took four hours, that still left them with a lot of distance to cover—on a boat.

"Admittedly, the transit will take about twenty-four hours," said Jose. "But it'll take you completely off the grid for a full day. We'll sneak you ashore in Cabo."

"That's a long time in a boat," said Nathan.

"It's a luxury yacht," said Jose. "Trust me, it won't be uncomfortable, and you'll be completely safe. Same with your accommodations in Cabo. Totally secure. You'll have a private beach—the works."

"Whoa," said Owen.

"It really is a nice place, and you guys deserve a break," said Jose.

Nathan almost started to tell Jose about their plans to travel north and meet up with his parents, but decided to keep that to himself. Jose had snatched them from the jaws of death, but he was still a complete stranger whose ultimate motivations were unclear. With Nathan's parents safely hidden in Idaho, there was no reason to turn down Jose's offer. Not that he really had a choice.

Jose ushered them to a white SUV and opened the rear gate so they could off-load their backpacks and rifles. While Nathan swung his pack into the cargo compartment, he saw a man carrying a body over his shoulder toward the next SUV in the column. He felt a hand on his shoulder and turned his head. Keira stood next to him, watching the somber event.

"I'll see you in a few days," said Jose.

"You're not coming with us?"

"Unfortunately, I have to tend to a few things before I can break free. I'll explain everything in Cabo."

"What happens after Cabo?" said Nathan.

"That's completely up to you. I promise."

Nathan shook his hand. "Thank you."

"My pleasure, Nathan," he said, accepting Keira's hand next.

"We owe you for this," she said.

"You don't owe me anything," said Jose.

"Where's Mr. Quinn?" said Owen.

"He'll be in a different SUV," said Jose.

"Why?"

"Well, he . . . uh . . . ," Jose faltered.

"He's riding with Alison," said Keira.

"Oh," said Owen.

"I'll see you guys soon," said Jose.

Less than a minute later, they had threaded their way out through the mines and were headed south on the dirt road that had brought them to the hacienda. Their dune buggy driver had assumed the same role for their transit to Puerto Peñasco. A second heavily armed and body armor–clad operative sat in the front passenger seat, his head panning back and forth as he scanned the sides of the road ahead with night-vision goggles. Nathan craned his neck between the rear bench headrests, examining the compartment behind them. His rifle and Keira's weapon were within easy reach if needed.

Nathan squeezed his wife's hand. Her arm was draped around Owen, pulling him tight against her vest, as the SUV bounced on the rough dirt road. She squeezed back and smiled under her night-vision goggles.

"You should close your eyes and get some sleep," said Nathan. "We're in good hands."

Their vehicle was squeezed between two SUVs loaded with Jose's people, heading rapidly away from the border.

"What about you?" she whispered back.

"I'll rest when we're on the boat."

"All right."

Keira raised her goggles and looked through the windows before leaning her helmet against Owen's and closing her eyes.

"It's dark out there," she said.

"There's nothing to see, really."

"I love you," she said.

"I love you more."

Nathan surveyed the landscape, seeing little more than scrub and the occasional tree. A line of utility poles appeared in the distance ahead of them, growing closer as the convoy sped down the road. When they reached the tall wooden posts, the SUVs turned right onto a paved two-lane road.

"What road is this?" said Nathan.

The driver responded, "It's part of the Highway 2 bypass. We'll take this south for about ten minutes, then use an old farming road to cross the Colorado River and intersect with Highway 40. Forty takes us most of the way to Puerto Peñasco."

"Thank you."

He had more questions, but he didn't want to distract Jose's people from the critical task at hand—safely transporting his family south. That was the only thing that mattered right now. Getting them as far away from Cerberus as possible.

The convoy navigated through the lifeless expanse of land that had long ago given up its fertile soil. Every half mile or so they passed a derelict irrigation well on the side of the road, recognizable solely by the concrete footing that had once supported a pump. Thirty years ago, the hardscrabble ground flanking this road would have held lush green fields of cotton or vegetable plants. The water fight north of the border had destroyed the Colorado River Valley in Mexico.

Their SUV dipped in and out of a shallow gulley.

"You just crossed the Colorado River," said the driver. "Hard as concrete. You can cross anywhere south of the border at any time, outside of flash flood season."

Soon after crossing the dry riverbed, they turned south on another two-lane paved road that his driver identified as Highway 40. They'd follow this road along the eastern banks of the Sea of Cortez until they reached their destination. Nathan had just contemplated shutting his eyes when the SUV slowed. He leaned over Owen, peering between the front seats at the road ahead, unable to determine why the driver had decelerated.

"What's happening?"

"Lead vehicle spotted a checkpoint ahead," said the driver. "They'll check it out and report."

Their SUV came to a gentle stop while the lead vehicle continued down the highway.

"Will it be a problem?"

"Depends. We have agreements in place with federal and state police authorities, and the local cartel, but the situation is fluid. Nighttime checkpoints are pretty rare."

"Is that a good or bad thing?"

"Usually bad. You might want to grab your rifle and wake your wife."

"I'm awake," said Keira.

Nathan reached over the seat and retrieved Keira's MP-20, placing it in the foot well between her legs before grabbing his rifle.

"Windows down," said the front passenger, lowering his window and unlocking the SUV's doors. "Keep the hardware out of sight for now."

Nathan pressed the button to lower his window, breathing in the cool night air. He glanced at Keira, who fumbled for the button with her one free hand.

"Lower your night vision," said Nathan.

"I got her window," said the driver, the glass next to Keira dropping quickly.

She flipped the goggles in place and gently moved Owen off her shoulder. Pulling the MP-20 into her lap, she faced the door and asked Nathan if he could see anything.

Nathan leaned his head out of the window, staring down the road. The lead SUV had traveled about several hundred yards, approaching three military-style vehicles arranged in a roadblock. At least one of the vehicles had some kind of turret-mounted machine gun. He lifted his goggles, weary of the bright synthetic daylight image, taking in the scene with the naked eye. The cluster of vehicles blocking the road was little more than a shadowy silhouette.

"Shouldn't we find another way?" said Nathan. "This looks serious."

"Highway 40 is the only easy way south. When the river started to dry out, they built a maze of concrete irrigation canals here. No way to get past those. We might be able to buy our way through if this is a group of bored *federales*."

"What if it isn't?"

"We could backtrack a little and work our way west to Highway 4. That would take us south through a shithole of a town called Estación Coahuila. Jose wanted us to steer clear of it."

As if on cue, a sudden explosion due west of the SUV exposed a distant town—the shithole in question, Nathan guessed. Streams of green tracers floated across the horizon between the low buildings, answered by red tracers headed in the opposite direction. Nathan couldn't guess the distance, but it felt uncomfortably close. Dozens of tracers ricocheted skyward, arching into the flat landscape surrounding the town. He lowered his goggles, changing the scene to daylight. Colored tracers continued to race back and forth through the distant town.

Their driver addressed the lead vehicle over the radio net. "Alpha, this is Echo. You seeing this? What's going on up there?"

"What did they say?" said Nathan, after waiting a few seconds.

"There's some kind of serious military operation going on in Estación Coahuila."

"Maybe we should get behind the vehicle," said Nathan. "Ricochets are going everywhere."

"The town is more than a mile away," said the passenger. "We're fine here."

"I don't know about that," said Nathan.

A line of green tracers zipped over the highway ahead of them, passing above the vehicles at the roadblock. The nearby sound of rapid gunfire followed moments later.

"Contact. Right!" yelled the driver. "Outbound from the town!"

Nathan aimed his rifle through the open window next to him, searching for the source of gunfire. A pickup truck, followed closely by a sedan, raced toward the roadblock from the west, in what appeared to be a desperate attempt to flee the military forces converging on the town. A machine gun mounted to the roof of the pickup truck unleashed another long burst of green tracers, which appeared to strike the cluster of military vehicles blocking their escape.

"Grab Owen and get down next to the SUV!" said Nathan.

Keira reacted swiftly, opening the left passenger door and pulling Owen onto the pavement. Nathan followed, dropping to the highway next to them and pushing them toward the back of the SUV. He raised his head high enough to look through the rear passenger windows, then lowered it immediately—the two vehicles had turned off the road, trying to bypass the roadblock. The evasive maneuver pointed them directly at Nathan's SUV.

Nathan suddenly felt very exposed hiding behind the vehicle. He'd witnessed the effects of armor-piercing ammunition firsthand and had no intention of taking any chances with his family.

"Quick. Follow me!" He took Owen's hand and pulled his family across the road into a shallow ditch next to the highway, hearing a torrent of bullets tear into their SUV—some snapping directly over their heads.

"Stay down!"

A few moments later, after the inbound tracers stopped flying over them, he risked a look over the side of the ditch. A maelstrom of return gunfire from both the Mexican soldiers at the roadblock and California Liberation Movement, or CLM, operatives hiding behind their own vehicles pounded the off-road convoy, bringing it to a stop a few hundred yards from the vehicle Nathan had just abandoned. Before Nathan could raise his rifle to join the fight, one of the soldiers fired a rocket at the halted convoy, exploding the pickup truck and flipping it backward onto the sedan. Two figures scrambling away from the flaming wreckage were instantly cut down by gunfire. The greater battle for Estación Coahuila raged in the distance.

Their driver, crouching next to the SUV, turned toward the ditch and motioned for them. "Get everyone back in the vehicle! We're turning around! The soldiers expect more trouble from the town."

Nathan brought his family back to the SUV, shocked to see that several bullets had penetrated the vehicle, exiting where he had moments ago crouched with his family. Turning around made no sense. Mexico was a free-fire zone, at least near the border. He wanted nothing more than to get his family out into the middle of the Sea of Cortez, away from this insanity.

"Can't we go off-road to the east and bypass the roadblock?"

"It's impossible with the irrigation canals," the driver said. "West is our only option, and that's not looking good."

"Where the hell are we going?"

"Anywhere but here," he said. "They're talking to Jose right now."

Once Nathan's family settled into the vehicle, their driver executed a three-point turn and passed the SUV that had been behind them, settling into the northbound lane. Moments later, the lead SUV raced past on their left, and they picked up speed until all of the SUVs were in a column speeding back the way they came.

"What did Jose say?" said Nathan.

"We try again tomorrow."

"Tomorrow? Jose sounded pretty sure he wanted to get us out tonight."

"He thinks it's too risky to proceed. We're heading back," said the driver.

"To the hacienda?"

"Somewhere more secure."

He couldn't imagine what could be safer than a house in the middle of nowhere—surrounded by land mines.

CHAPTER 2

A powerful gust of wind shook the SUV, pelting its bullet-resistant windows and heavy armored frame with pebbles and light debris. Mason Flagg clenched his fist. The damn Russian was insufferable. Of all the places Petrov could have chosen for the meet-up, he'd picked the middle of the Salton Sea—a dried-up, toxic lake bed in the middle of nowhere, east of the Anza-Borrego Desert. The perfect place for an unobserved meeting, if you didn't mind walking away with a lungful of arsenic and selenium dust.

As the wind squall died, the view returned, leaving him with the same featureless expanse of wasteland he'd observed a few minutes earlier. To his immediate right, roughly twenty-five yards away, the SUV carrying his security team waited for orders. He'd equipped the team with the latest shoulder-launched surface-to-air missile system, capable of acquiring and destroying any helicopters and drones that closed to within seven miles. They also carried the same variant of Javelin missiles used in the previous night's ambush, giving them a three-mile buffer against a ground attack. Not that anything could sneak up on them in the middle of this dried-up seabed. The windshield's muted green heads-up display gave no indication that any vehicles, traveling by ground or air, had entered the area.

"Thirty-five minutes late," said Flagg. "And still no sign of that arrogant ass."

"He'll show," Leeds said from driver's seat. "It's in his best interest to be here."

Flagg grunted. The trick would be convincing Petrov that it was more than just in his best interest. Flagg needed to sell this as critical to the survival of AgraTex—the Russian's agricultural empire. Falling short of that, Flagg would likely land on Cerberus's black-flagged list, his lifespan suddenly measured in hours. Nick Leeds faced a similar fate if Petrov rejected their proposal. The fact that Leeds hadn't gone behind his back to report the ambush's failure amounted to a tacit collaboration.

He leaned the side of his head against the cool passenger window and peered skyward, wondering if Petrov's answer would arrive in the form of a Cerberus-delivered guided missile.

"I know what you're thinking," Leeds said. "We'd already be dead if he wasn't interested."

"Don't make any assumptions when dealing with the Russian."

The HUD displayed an alert: CONTACTS DETECTED. EIGHT MILES. Three tightly spaced green icons appeared in the center of the windshield, staying together for several seconds before rising a few degrees above the horizon. CONTACTS CLASSIFIED AERIAL.

"Helicopters," said Leeds. "I don't like this."

"Neither do I," said Flagg before ordering the security team to lock on to the helicopters with the SAM launchers.

Cerberus operatives spilled out of the adjacent vehicle, racing to open the rear cargo door and retrieve the compact missile systems. He briefly considered ordering Leeds to turn the SUV around and flee east. The frequent gusts of wind might conceal them long enough to reach the crumbling boat ramps at Salton City. But what would be the point? Leeds was right. If Petrov had told the One Nation cabal about this meeting, Flagg and Leeds would never have made it out of San Diego County alive. Their fates would be decided here. They'd either drive out of the desert with a temporary lease on life, or they'd water the cracked, toxic lake bed with their blood.

The security team vanished in a crunching explosion that rocked Flagg's vehicle. Metal fragments smacked the armored exterior, cracking his side window in place and keeping him hunched over in his seat until pieces of the obliterated SUV stopped raining down on the roof.

"I can't see the security vehicle," said Flagg, trying to catch a glimpse through the shattered window.

Leeds turned his head and peered through the rear passenger window.

"It's gone. Shall I take evasive maneuvers?"

"Like you said earlier. If he wanted us dead, we'd be dead."

Flagg's satphone beeped, the SUV's HUD displaying UNKNOWN NUMBER. He muttered a few obscenities before instructing the vehicle's smart system to answer the call.

"That wasn't necessary," said Flagg.

A few moments passed before a thick Russian accent filled the cabin. "I get a little nervous when I see surface-to-air missile launchers."

How the hell could he know that? He couldn't, from seven miles out. The real question was: How did the missile arrive undetected? It hadn't come from the helicopters.

"Check behind you, Mason."

Flagg twisted in his seat, scanning the dusty terrain visible through the lift-gate window, while Leeds checked the rearview mirror. A tan vehicle materialized several hundred yards directly behind the SUV, veering left to reveal a second vehicle, which moments later fanned right to form a rapidly approaching column. Impressive. Adaptive camouflage technology applied to entire vehicles. He'd seen a few in-house demonstrations at the leading high-tech defense technology companies, but had never seen it used in a real setting.

He checked the windshield HUD, finding no warning about the vehicles. The system remained fixed on the helicopters, one of which was moments away from a right-to-left, low-level pass. Petrov had either jammed Flagg's system, or his vehicles employed an equally impressive stealth technology. Possibly both.

"I have to give you credit. That's a neat trick," said Flagg.

"An expensive trick," said Petrov. "Well out of your price range."

One of the helicopters thundered overhead, rattling the SUV and kicking up a dust storm. Flagg couldn't tell what kind of helicopter, or more importantly, what kind of armament it carried. Not that it mattered anymore.

"Your idea of a private meeting is a little different than mine," said Flagg.

"I think you've confused the concept of private with secret . . . or perhaps not. Step out of your vehicle and approach the center SUV. Alone."

He didn't like the idea of broadcasting his identity to Petrov's security team. If Petrov didn't sell him out immediately after the meeting, what would stop one of his mercenaries from cashing in on the information?

"Don't worry yourself," said Petrov. "We can talk both privately and secretly in my SUV. I trust the people I hire implicitly. They understand the consequences of betrayal."

"Be there shortly," said Flagg. He disconnected the call and shook his head.

"This should be interesting," said Leeds.

Flagg reached for the door handle. "I don't know if you'll get any warning if things go south."

"They won't. Petrov won't burn the chance to take advantage of our contacts in Mexico."

"Cerberus's contacts."

"Easy to spin," said Leeds. "And you own those contacts."

Flagg grinned. "I own every Cerberus asset in the Southwest."

"Exactly. See you in a few minutes."

Outside, the deep buzz of Petrov's helicopters dominated the lake bed, their dark shapes circling in the distance. The nearby SUV had been turned into a charred heap of twisted metal. Thick black smoke rose skyward from the mess, quickly diffusing in the strengthening wind.

Flagg glanced over his shoulder at the eastern horizon. Another wall of caustic dust approached, drawing strength from the dry Santa Ana winds that had swept across Southern California most of the year now. He took off for the line of SUVs fifty yards to the west, hoping to beat the approaching wind gust. The helicopters ascended rapidly, the pilots no doubt just as eager to elude the rolling cloud. Fine sand and helicopter engine parts didn't mix well.

Petrov met him on the passenger side of the middle vehicle, ushering him through the rear door as a wave of debris-filled sand washed over the SUV. The wind slammed the door shut seconds after Flagg pulled his legs into the foot well, blasting a swirl of foul, chemical-smelling dust across the pair of leather captain's chairs.

"Hot diggity damn it!" whooped Petrov from his chair. "Yippee-ki-yay and all that American Wild West shit. Right?"

Flagg brushed the rust-colored sand off his light khaki tactical pants, examining the two shadowy men seated in the front seats. Close-cropped hair, thick necks. Private security types.

"This isn't exactly the best place for a meeting, especially after the stunt you pulled with my security detail. We're less than seventy miles away from last night's convoy ambush point."

"The area has been quiet for most of the day," said Petrov.

"It doesn't take long for a flight of Marine F-35s to arrive from Yuma. God knows you've attracted enough attention."

"You didn't have to show up."

Flagg stared through the curtain of sand beyond his heavily tinted passenger window, seeing little aside from an occasional dark speck hurtling past. "We both face an uncertain future."

Petrov laughed heartily, slapping Flagg's thigh and causing his fists to clench. The Russian was truly intolerable. "That is very dramatic talk," Petrov said. "Such intensity! Maybe though we cut BS, huh? What do you want from me?"

Flagg twisted in his seat to face the Russian. He looked anemic, the fluorescent glow of the vehicle's interior lights playing the worst possible trick on his pale Muscovite skin. Despite all his boisterousness, the man's bitter mask of a face regarded Flagg with the same skeptical look he cast on everything around him, regardless of the circumstances. Even while laughing, he looked both disgusted and mildly displeased.

"It is imperative that we enter into a temporary strategic partnership," said Flagg. "To survive the upcoming days."

Petrov's face remained impassively rigid. "You know where to find Fisher and the others?"

The question caught Flagg off guard. Did Petrov know they'd eluded him? How could he? Maybe he was fishing. While his mind whirred, Flagg tried to mirror the other man's flat affect, but Petrov's faint grin indicated he'd failed.

"Don't worry. Your secret is safe with me—for as long as I remain convinced that you can deliver Fisher's whereabouts. I assume you have extensive contacts south of the border?"

"How did you—what exactly do you know about Fisher?" said Flagg.

Petrov drew out a folder he'd kept hidden beneath his legs and held it between the captain's chairs. Flagg took the file and flipped open the cover, noting the red top-secret seal. He didn't need to thumb past the Bureau of Reclamation cover page to know what he held.

"I didn't know he was still alive until my reconnaissance assets confirmed that you had indeed showed up without a small army to take me out," Petrov said. "If you hadn't arranged this meeting to assassinate me—why else drag me into the open and insist I keep it secret from the rest of the group? No other scenario made sense. The only thing you could possibly need from me is a little off-the-books help solving a problem. Or in this case, a lot of help.

"As for this file? I did a little digging when Fisher's name first appeared in your memos a few days ago. I do a lot of my own digging these days. Looks like my concerns were well founded. Fisher possesses more than enough knowledge about the Colorado River's dam system to threaten my company's share of the Upper Basin's water, if his knowledge fell into the wrong hands—which I assume it has."

Flagg nodded, allowing a faint smile. "You appear to have a very good handle on the circumstances," he said. "And to answer your original question, yes, I have the contacts necessary to find Fisher."

"And these contacts won't raise alarms with your corporate dog handlers?"

"Doubtful, since I have direct access to the contacts at my level."

Petrov stared at him with his unchanging face, which yet somehow conveyed a range of feelings. Or did this blank slate simply reflect the observer's state of mind? In any event, to Flagg right now, the Russian looked doubtful.

"In the highly unlikely event that word got back to Cerberus," Flagg said, "I can explain my sudden interest in Mexico as an expansion of intelligence-gathering efforts against CLM."

"You have proof that Fisher is in Mexico?"

"One of my surveillance drones remained on-station long enough after the ambush to make that determination. My guess is they made their way to Mexicali or San Luis Rio Colorado, the two largest cities in the area."

Flagg neglected to mention the mysterious platoon of paratroopers that took part in the rescue. He figured this would raise too many alarms with the Russian, who appeared far more perceptive than he'd initially assumed.

"That's cartel land," said Petrov, raising an eyebrow slightly in a rare expression of curiosity.

"Exactly," he said. "Nothing goes unnoticed by the cartels. I expect actionable intelligence within forty-eight hours. Possibly sooner. How quickly can you deliver assets to the area?"

"Why don't you use the cartels to kill Fisher and company?" said Petrov. "Why involve me?"

"There's only one cartel—the Sinaloa—but they're fractured west of the Colorado River. Factions controlling the Baja Peninsula, directly below California, make very little money compared to the syndicates operating south of the wide-open borders of the Wasteland states. If the CLM pays them rent to hide in Baja California, which is very possible, they'd be unlikely to give up the income source without a fight."

"Offer them more money! Enough to cover the rent for years to come," said Petrov. "I'd be glad to make a donation to that cause."

"Money is a slippery slope with the cartels, and quality is always an issue. I'd prefer to use professionals, guided by our network of trusted contacts."

"I know a team based out of Mexico City that would be perfect for the job," said Petrov. "Former SVR and GRU Spetsnaz types. Not cheap either, in case you think I'm cutting edges."

"Corners," said Flagg.

"Corners?"

"It's nothing. This group sounds more than adequate for the job. Move them into Mexicali as discreetly as possible, while I work on finding Fisher. I'll send a few trusted operatives down to join your group on the raid, to recover any intelligence, if this turns out to be a CLM safe house."

Petrov extended a hand. "It's good to be in business with you! I feel much safer with you on my side. And just to be clear. We are on the same side now. Locked at the hip, as you Americans say."

"Joined," said Flagg, taking his hand.

"That's right. We've joined the same team. And our fate will be the same. Don't forget that."

"How could I?" said Flagg.

They shook hands vigorously for a few moments before Petrov nodded toward the front seat of the SUV. The bulky shape on the passenger side muscled the front door open, filling the cabin with sediment and dust.

"He should wait until the winds die down," said Flagg, shielding his eyes from the sand. "Another minute or so."

"Sorry, but I need to get moving. We've been out in the open for long enough," said Petrov as the bodyguard wrenched open Flagg's door.

"Another minute won't make a difference. Not in this," said Flagg.

"Time to go, Mason."

A hand-size piece of dried wood hit the front of the door frame and ricocheted inside the SUV, barely missing his head.

"You're fucking crazy, Alexei!"

"Without a doubt. And don't you forget that either."

I won't, thought Flagg, fighting against the gale-force wind and random debris strikes on the return trip to his SUV. The wind eased when he reached the back of the dust-caked vehicle, a quick glance over his shoulder confirming that the dark shape of Petrov's convoy was gone. He opened the front passenger door and dumped his body into the seat, feeling wasted.

"Jesus!" said Leeds. "I didn't even see you coming. What happened?"

"Don't ask."

Leeds put the vehicle in drive, easing them forward into a wide U-turn. Flagg emptied the half-consumed bottle of spring water in the door cup holder over his sand-blasted face, saving the last swig to rinse the sand out of his mouth. He spit the grainy water into the foot well between his legs and took a deep breath.

"We have a deal with that crazy motherfucker, but mark my words, Nick. I will kill that son of a bitch as soon as he no longer serves a purpose."

CHAPTER 3

The aroma of deep-roasted coffee greeted Jon Fisher as he opened the coffee shop door for his wife. As she passed through the door, he nodded appreciatively at Scott Gleason, who saluted Jon and drove around to the drive-through line in his tan Jeep Wrangler. He'd make sure to tell the barista to charge whatever Scott ordered to his own tab. It was the very least he could do for a friend who had opened his home to them under risky circumstances, asking for nothing in return.

Leah turned to him. "Why don't you get our boy on the line? I'll get your usual."

"Give them an extra ten and tell them Scott's drink is on me," said Jon.

"Great idea," she said, kissing him. "Be right back."

He watched her walk to the counter, every bit as deeply in love with her as ever. She had been a trouper during his long Marine Corps career, enduring his extended absences and extended work hours as a senior enlisted Marine without complaining. Well—she could complain with the best of them, but she never made him feel guilty for the time he missed with her or Nathan. She'd struggled to eke out a career as a special education teacher, making inroads at one school just in time to be ripped away by one of his mandatory career transfers.

She'd been able to settle into a longer-term position at an Oceanside, California, elementary school during the final eight years of his career, when he bounced around between sergeant major positions at Camp

Pendleton. He'd been gone a lot, but she was the happiest he'd ever seen her. With his retirement looming, he'd left it up to her to decide whether they'd stay in California or head north. If she'd wanted to stay and build on her teaching career, he would have supported the decision wholeheartedly. Decision time yielded a surprising turn of events—unknown to Jon, Leah had given the school district notice of her departure a few months before his retirement.

As much as Leah wanted to stay and continue teaching, the realities of transitioning from a comfortable, military-subsidized lifestyle to being a full-fledged member of California's oppressed citizenry didn't appeal to her. Sure, they would have been able to skirt a number of regulations and social controls by shopping and gassing up their cars on base, but they would still be subject to the same travel restrictions, home water-use limits, and utility caps. Not to mention the fact that they'd only had two viable options for housing due to the insane cost of California real estate.

They could rent an apartment in the federally sponsored military retirement community adjacent to Camp Pendleton, a sprawling mess of high-rises built by the VA to address the retiree income issue. Two tiny bedrooms, one and a half bathrooms, a kitchen that flowed into the family room and a glorious view of Interstate 15—all for the price of his monthly pension, plus part of Leah's paycheck. Not exactly what either of them had in mind after giving thirty years to the Marine Corps.

Their other choice involved sinking everything they'd saved outside of his guaranteed pension in a modest home twenty to thirty miles east. The state would cut them a break on travel back and forth from the military base of their choice and any VA medical facilities, but that would be it, beyond Leah's authorized drive to work and back. They'd be lucky to get a thousand square feet of home, on a desert scrub lot, in the middle of nowhere.

In the end, there hadn't really been a choice at all. Jon still felt terrible about it, even though Leah had called the shots from day one of their retirement. She'd chosen the land in central Idaho, the building site and the house plans. Everything. He was along for the ride, and a smooth ride it had been—until a few days ago. It had killed him to see the despondent but accepting look on her face when she understood that they might drive away from this house forever. That once again, Leah's life wasn't her own.

She'd said very little on the drive up to Montana, and he couldn't blame her.

Jon settled at a small table next to the front plate-glass window, opening his laptop case and placing the thin, silver laptop on the table. They had a few hours to kill in Starbucks while Scott ran a few errands. More than enough time to get in touch with Nathan and check on their house in Idaho. He was dying to know if Cerberus had paid it a visit. Part of him wished he had taken the time to rig up some kind of trap. He had a sawed-off, double-barrel shotgun that would have made one hell of a greeting for anyone entering his workshop through the ground-level door.

He smiled at Leah, who stood facing him by the counter, waiting for their drinks. She put a hand to her ear, gesturing for him to call. He wasn't sure who was more anxious to hear from their son. The strict but completely understandable rules enforced by Scott on behalf of the survival community had prevented them from making contact with Nathan while they were holed up with them. Neither of them had spoken with him since the night they'd left Idaho.

Jon took the phone out of his jacket, eyeing it apprehensively. The screen showed no new voice or text messages. Part of him didn't want to make the call. There was no guarantee that good news awaited him on the other end of the line. He stared at it for a few more seconds before selecting the right number and pressing "Send." Encryption protocols negotiated the satellite transfer as Leah gathered their drinks. She'd made it halfway to the table when the call forwarded to a voice mail box assigned to the number.

The phone was powered down—or worse.

He waited for the digital voice to finish before leaving a message in the agreed format. "June tenth. Seventeen fourteen hours. No change in status," he said, pressing "End."

He shook his head at Leah when she arrived. "No answer. Sorry."

Her face deflated for a moment before she forced a thin smile and nodded.

"Hold on," he said, getting up to pull her chair out.

"Thank you."

They sipped their drinks in silence, staring at nothing in particular beyond the window.

"I'm sure they're fine," she said, putting her warm hand over his on the table.

He took a deep breath and let it out. "I know. I just want to hear it from Nathan."

"Me, too," she said, squeezing his hand. "He's in good hands."

"I know. I just thought he would have called by now. At least left a message," he said.

"They're probably being extra cautious. The longer Cerberus thinks they're still on Pendleton, the better," she said.

"You're right," he said, placing the phone on the table.

With Cerberus focused on Camp Pendleton, Nathan could slip away from the Marine Corps base in Yuma, eventually joining Jon and Leah to the north. He took a long sip of his coffee, savoring the dark roast flavor.

"Do you want to read the stories with me?" he said, scooting his chair a few inches toward the window.

"No. You go ahead for now," she said. "It's all lies anyway."

"All right," he said, opening the laptop.

Jon was kind of glad she didn't want to look. He wanted to check on their house first but didn't want to do that in front of her.

After connecting with the Starbucks wireless signal, he navigated to a password-protected site, granting him access to his home security system's page. A flagged message indicated activity deep within his home. He clicked on the message, reading the time and date of the activity. The infrared sensors had picked up movement in both his workshop and the first-floor hallway between 11:35 and 11:42 on June 7. Barely two hours after they left. Sons of bitches! His left hand gripped the table next to his coffee cup.

The system ceased transmitting at 11:42, suggesting that the team had finally discovered the security system. He released the table and drank his coffee, signing out of the remote security server. They could have burned the house to the ground for all he knew. Even more infuriating, he might never know. They couldn't safely return to that house until this business with Cerberus was settled once and for all. The thought of what it might take to get to that point was beyond his grasp at the moment.

"Anything interesting?" said Leah.

"Not really," he said. "Do you want me to grab you a paper? They have the *New York Times* and a few local ones."

"I'm fine," she said, casting a distant, depressed look out the window.

"We may be here awhile."

"I may grab one in a minute," she said, nodding.

Jon typed a few keywords guaranteed to bring up the latest news, surprised to see that the manhunt for their son had been extended nationally. He found no mention of David Quinn, which was a relief. Stuart's son had risked everything to help Nathan and his family. He would have hated to see his name dragged through the mud, too. Reading the articles about his son stoked a rage he hadn't felt since Afghanistan. Cerberus had framed Nathan for two murders, one of which occurred while he was hiding at Camp Pendleton. Now the police were investigating unusual bank deposits. What a crock of shit. He wished he hadn't bothered to check.

"You're turning red, Jon," said Leah.

"I think you had the right idea," he said, closing the laptop. "Bunch of bullshit lies. He's a federal fugitive now."

"Of course he is. He'll be on Interpol's watch list next," said Leah. "Have you heard from Stuart?"

"No. I told him I'd call with an update once we got into town," said Jon. "At least David's name is still out of the news."

"He might appreciate hearing that, and maybe he's talked to them already through some other means. He seems to have a few tricks up his sleeve."

"True. I'll grab a refill and check in with him. Need anything?" he said, scooting his chair back.

"I'll take a blueberry scone," she said. "And a chocolate chip cookie. Why not?"

"I can't think of a reason," he said, kissing her on the forehead before he left.

Chapter 4

Chris Riggs took another sip of lukewarm coffee from the Best Western mug and stared out of the suite's wide sliding door at the pine tree–covered slopes of Mount Baldy. A few white lines of snow zigzagged between the seas of green, showcasing the remnants of Sun Valley Ski Resort. At least the room had a view. He'd been stuck in Ketchum since Thursday night. Close to three days babysitting the Cerberus tech-support team flown out by Flagg. The evidence team had done their work in less than twenty-four hours, finding nothing to indicate where Jon Fisher might be headed. That left him with the goth gang.

Nissie Keane, the lead computer tech, wasn't too hard on the eyes—if you didn't mind an unhealthy number of facial piercings, tattoos up her neck, and a partially shaved head. He wouldn't turn down a go at her in one of the bathrooms if she were up for it. So far, she hadn't shown any interest outside of the computer screens in the dining room and the playlist of god-awful music seeping past her earphones.

The rest of the group fit the same mold, which led him to suspect they were a contract team of hackers brought in from the outside. A group that had probably worked together for a long time on highly questionable projects—like his own crew. Disappearing the parents of a sanctioned Cerberus target must fall outside approved company boundaries—a first, in his experience.

"Got him!" yelled Nissie, spinning in her seat to face him. "He logged into the Protekt server at Aegis Solutions from an IP address corresponding to a Starbucks in Missoula, Montana—5750 Grant Creek Road. Total activity time, thirty-nine seconds."

"He knows we paid his house a visit," said Riggs, who had already arrived at the dining room table. "Is he still online?"

"His computer is still connected to the Starbucks Wi-Fi signal."

"Then we better get our asses up there right away. It's a thirty-minute flight from the Ketchum airport," said Riggs, pointing at his operatives. "Tex, call the crew and make sure they can take off as soon as we climb on board. Ross, load up whatever gear we need that isn't already stowed on the plane. We walk out of here in three minutes."

"You don't need to move that fast," said Nissie. "Missoula has city-wide Wi-Fi coverage. I'm already pinging his laptop. We can follow him anywhere."

Both of the operatives stopped, looking at him to see if her statement changed anything.

"What the fuck!" he yelled at them. "Is she in charge now?"

The two men started mumbling apologies.

"Get moving!" he screamed before speaking calmly to Nissie. "What do you need to track this guy?"

"My laptop rig, power source, and a broadband satellite connection."

"Do you need another tech?"

"No," she said, shaking her head.

"Good. I'm taking you on the aircraft. You have two minutes to get the gear you need," he said. "I want the rest of your team driving up to Missoula within fifteen minutes. Can anyone here even drive?"

Only one hand out of the five remaining techs shot up.

"That's what I figured," he said. "We'll leave you the keys to one of the Suburbans."

"I've never driven anything bigger than a minielectric," said the tech.

"Then it's time to grow up and drive a real car. You'll thank me for it later," said Riggs.

He walked to the master bedroom, where he kept the duffel bag with his personal weapons kit. One the way, he dialed Flagg.

"We've located Jon Fisher in Missoula. I have the jet spooling up for takeoff. We're out the door in less than three minutes. Travel time—"

"Twenty-seven minutes. I know all of this. I'm patched into the tech team's feed. He's using a Starbucks on the northern outskirts of Missoula, stuck in between several chain hotels. It's less than two miles from the airport."

"Perfect," said Riggs. "With a little luck, we'll nab him before he finishes his coffee."

"Don't count on it. He's likely staying at one of the hotels, in a room paid for by someone we haven't connected to him."

"The computer bitch is pinging his laptop. We'll find him wherever he hides."

"That computer bitch is one of the best in the business," said Flagg. "I'd like the option of employing Miss Keane again, so don't piss her off."

"Copy that," he said, lifting the duffel bag onto the bed.

"Remember, Riggs. I want Mr. and Mrs. Fisher alive. Don't jump the gun on this. You bring me the Fishers, and I'll let you burn their house down."

Riggs grinned. Flagg knew how to make him happy. "Kidnapping is one of our specialties," he assured him. "We won't fuck this up."

"That's why I hired you. Notify me the moment you land in Missoula," said Flagg. "And Chris?"

"Yeah?"

"Be careful up there. Stuart Quinn remains off the grid. Jon Fisher's his best buddy. Quinn could be anywhere in the country by now."

"Understood," he said, seeing that the call had already disconnected. "Hot damn," whispered Riggs, shouldering the bag and returning to the two-story great room.

Nissie zipped her black leather jacket when he arrived and grabbed her laptop case.

"Miss Keane. See you in the parking lot shortly."

He paused for a moment before walking toward the front door—wanting nothing more than to burn that smug look off her face.

CHAPTER 5

Stuart Quinn squinted at the upcoming highway sign, still unable to read the words. He waited a few seconds. **ST. JOSEPH 28 MILES.** Three days ago, he could have read that sign from twice this distance. Exhaustion was taking a cumulative toll on his senses, which came as no surprise. He'd been running nonstop since the night he'd unearthed the sordid details linking the international conglomerate the Sentinel Group to Cerberus International, the secret paramilitary group hunting down his son and Nathan Fisher.

Disappearing from the grid and mustering the initial resources necessary to help his son in the short term had taken more time and effort than he'd expected. Acquiring a vehicle with no link to him hadn't been easy, or cheap, and stepping into a clean identity had been no less complicated or costly thanks to the recent proliferation of state and city government–installed facial recognition systems (FRS). It was no longer good enough to hit the streets with a shiny new set of source-quality, undetectable counterfeit IDs. You had to emerge looking different enough to fool FRS, and the deception had to be consistently maintained in public if you wanted to remain hidden.

Federal law enforcement agencies devoted significant funding to co-opting municipal and state FRS feeds, posing a significant detection risk. The Department of Homeland Security maintained a massive persons-of-interest FRS database, reportedly tracking the real-time movements of nearly a million people. He'd be surprised if his profile hadn't been added to the database—flagged top priority thanks to patrons of Sentinel.

Thanks to a longtime friend and former CIA identification counterfeiter, he could roam the streets freely as Devlin Rhoades, as long as he followed a few rules. He had to wear opaque, color-changing infrared contact lenses to foil a quick eye scan, one of the most common detection methods. A pair of microbattery-powered sunglasses that modified the bridge of his nose and matched any alteration of his body temperature attacked the second most common identification marker. A mouthpiece raising his cheeks and widening his jaw distorted the skeletal framework markers. On top of this, they'd waxed and reshaped his eyebrows, covered his bald head with a surprisingly stylish hairpiece, and taught him a few subtle makeup tricks. It now took him longer to get ready than his late wife had.

He sensed someone staring at him. A quick glance at the driver's seat confirmed it.

"What?"

"I can't get over your new look," said his son-in-law, smirking. "The eyebrows are a little over-the-top metro, but uh . . . man, I wish Carlie could see this. She'd laugh her ass off. They should have made your hair blond. That would have been the icing on the cake."

"You done having fun?"

"It's gonna take a while to get used to the new you," he said.

"I knew it was a mistake to get in touch with you."

"You kind of look like a Cro-Magnon man slash alternative rock band promoter. Or maybe like—"

"I'll give you to St. Joseph, Missouri, to get this out of your system before I consider pushing you out of the car—while it's moving."

"Just busting your chops. They could have put you in blond curls and pink lipstick as long as it keeps you off the radar."

"You'd like that, wouldn't you?" said Stuart.

"Might be a little easier on the eyes," he said, laughing up a storm for several seconds.

Stuart stared at the road ahead, hoping his overt lack of interest would put an end to the jokes. Normally he appreciated Blake's sense of humor, but he was exhausted to the point of grumpiness. He'd arrived at a crappy, no-questions-asked motel west of Kansas City around one in the morning to catch up on some sleep before Blake arrived, but his siesta was cut short by dozens of anxious thoughts rattling inside his head, the most important being his son's convoy. It was no coincidence that he woke up minutes before the convoy was scheduled to leave Camp Pendleton. He knew sleep wouldn't come until David had confirmed they had safely arrived at Yuma. That call had never come either.

He'd spent the next four hours fading in and out of consciousness, loosely plotting a more permanent solution to the Cerberus problem. His biggest challenge was finding people with the right connections that he could trust. His list of people with the right connections was long. No problem there. Identifying people he could trust was a different story. At the moment, he was seated next to half of that list. Sentinel's reach was extensive, and he needed to do some more digging before he could risk approaching some of his more powerful connections.

His satellite phone beeped.

"About time," he said, snatching the phone out of the center console.

"David?" said Blake.

"No. Jon Fisher," he said, accepting the call. "Will this be pickup or delivery?"

"Delivery. With a smile."

It was an easy-to-remember, effective code. Anyone guessing had a one in two chance of getting the question right, but that wasn't what mattered. The follow-on sentence obeyed a simple protocol. Always three words.

"Have you heard from the boys?" Stuart asked.

"No. I just tried a few minutes ago," said Jon. "Wait. You didn't talk to them yet?"

"I talked to David a few hours before the convoy left. I haven't heard from him since."

"They're probably being extra cautious about leaving any electronic trace. I'm sure they'll get in touch once they make some progress north."

"I don't know," said Stuart. "David was pretty clear about contacting me. I'll call Major General Nichols and shake the trees at First Marine Division. How are you and Leah holding up?"

"Pretty well. Scott let us out of the yard for a few hours while he runs errands. I just checked my account at Protekt. It appears you were right about getting out of the house right away. Someone broke into my house no more than two hours after we left."

Protekt? That's right. Home security monitoring. He'd recommended the service to Jon a few years ago. Shit. "I forgot about Protekt. Can you step away from your laptop? Preferably a few tables over. And please whisper."

A few seconds passed before Jon spoke in a hush. "Did I screw up?"

Stuart might not have the time to explain. "How did you log in?"

"From my laptop, through a Wi-Fi signal."

"How long ago?"

"A few minutes."

"Good. Where are you, precisely?"

"At a Starbucks in Missoula. I screwed up, didn't I?"

"It's not a matter of you screwing up. It's a matter of Cerberus having unlimited resources and zero scruples. If they discovered the security system, they probably hacked into Protekt and installed a log-in trace, which would give them the Starbucks IP address."

"I'm pretty sure they discovered the system," Jon said. "Protekt stopped receiving data several minutes into the break-in."

"That was sloppy of them."

"Not as sloppy as me."

"Maybe we can take advantage of this. They know you're in Missoula. We know where to find them."

"That doesn't sound like good odds."

"I brought an associate."

"Someone you can trust?"

"I let him marry my daughter, so that puts him at the top of that list," said Stuart, glaring at Blake. "Though he's been getting on my nerves, and we're barely an hour into the drive."

"Does he have the skill set necessary for this kind of thing? I'd hate to get your son-in-law killed. I feel bad enough dragging David and you into this."

"He spent six years in the Marine Raiders, followed by a two-year stint with the CIA's Global Response Staff. I introduced him to Carlie when he got out of that line of work."

"Hell. We might slow him down."

"I suspect we will," said Stuart.

The Global Response Staff was a little-known CIA unit recruited exclusively from the special operations ranks. They provided on-site security for CIA case officers and installations located in high-risk locations worldwide. The work had a burnout rate close to 50 percent, with most members leaving voluntarily within a year. Two years was a long tour of duty with that outfit. Too many of Blake's friends left involuntarily—in body bags.

"Here's what I need you to do, Jon. Leave the laptop on the table and get out of there. If they traced the laptop, they'll ping the Wi-Fi antenna, turning it into a homing beacon. I'd say you have forty-five minutes to an hour before they arrive, unless they already have an associate in Missoula. Then you've got between five and ten minutes. Call Scott and find a clean place where he can pick you up."

"What do you mean by clean?"

"No surveillance cameras. The side of a road or the back of a parking lot would probably be your best bet. Stay out of sight until he's close to picking you up."

"Got it," said Jon.

"Give me a quick call when Scott picks you up, so I know you didn't get nabbed. I'll plan to meet with you tomorrow morning— nowhere near Starbucks."

"I don't know how Scott is going to feel about that. I might send Leah back with him and stay at the town house. I can't ask him to drive me back into town tomorrow. Not with Cerberus around."

"Sounds like the right thing to do," said Stuart. "If we drive straight through, you can expect us around zero eight hundred hours. We'll come straight to the town house."

"Drive safe, Stu, and thank you again for all of this. I can't . . . uh—" Jon sounded like he was choking up.

"Don't get soft on me, Jon. I need Sergeant Major Fisher in the game for this one."

"He never left the game, my friend."

"Good to know. Now get the fuck out of there," he said, ending the call.

Blake's expression had changed from mischievous to pensive. "You think they made it to Yuma?" he asked without taking his eyes off the road.

Stuart shook his head slowly back and forth. "No. I don't."

CHAPTER 6

Jon Fisher held Leah close, taking in faint traces of her favorite lavender-scented shampoo. They pressed tightly together, motionless except for the synchronized rhythm of their breathing. He tensed at the sound of the slow approach of Scott's Jeep, the parking lot gravel crackling under its oversize tires, then melted back into his wife's arms. Jon hadn't felt this way since his last wartime deployment. Like he needed to drag out the farewell as long as possible, because the homecoming might involve an honor guard delivering his casket. Leah squeezed him tighter. She understood the stakes, too.

"I guess this is it for a little while," he said.

"I suppose so," she responded, looking around them. "Not exactly your best send-off."

They had walked a few miles south of Starbucks along Reserve Street, taking temporary refuge in a massive parking lot attached to Retz Brothers RV and Marine Showcase. Scott had directed them to the business, seemingly well aware that cameras didn't monitor the place. Rows of recreational vehicles and motorboats swarmed the lot, creating the perfect barrier from prying eyes. The tan Jeep appeared between two nearby mobile homes.

"Do you have everything you need?"

"Satphone. Pistol with three mags. Wallet with cash. I'm good," he said, kissing her forehead.

"What's the plan?"

"Get our boys and their families to safety," said Jon. "That's it for now. We can worry about the rest later."

She nodded, a painful smile on her face. "Can you try him one more time?"

"Sure," said Jon, taking the satphone out of his pocket.

As Scott's Jeep turned into the wide aisle created by two rows of side-by-side parked motor homes, he dialed David Quinn's number. The Jeep pulled even with them as the call went to voice mail. He shook his head, about to disconnect the call, when Leah grabbed the phone. Jon met Scott in front of the Jeep, giving his wife some privacy to leave Nathan a message.

"You sure about this?" said Scott.

"It's the only way. You keep her there until we're done with this thing."

"I can't keep her prisoner, Jon."

"She understands what's going on. If things go well, she'll be out of your hair in a few weeks—"

"She's no bother at all, my friend."

"I know, and I can't thank you enough, but once we find our own safe haven, I'll be back to reclaim the love of my life," he said, turning to smile at Leah.

"Sounds like he's ass kissing," she said. "What are the two of you conspiring over?"

Scott laughed. "I was just telling your obstinate husband that his wife is welcome to stay as long as she'd like."

"I'll be back before you know it," said Jon. "We better get moving."

When Leah turned to open the passenger door, Scott leaned closer to Jon. "If things don't go well down south, she has a home with us."

Jon took a deep breath and exhaled. "I have every intention of returning—but thank you."

"More conspiring?" said Leah before climbing into the backseat.

"Good luck with that one," Jon said, patting Scott on the shoulder. "I almost feel bad teaming her up with Kim. You don't stand a chance with the two of them on your case."

"Shit. I gave up pretending I had any say in things years ago."

"I never tried to pretend," said Jon.

They both enjoyed a quick laugh.

"Hey," Scott said, walking to the rear gate of his Jeep, "I keep a little never-know bag locked in the back." He opened the gate, reaching inside to move a dirty blanket and expose a low-profile safe box extending from one side of the Jeep to the other. He entered a code into the keypad and lowered the safe's door.

"That's a neat contraption," said Jon.

"It's the only way to keep shit from being stolen out of your car up here," he said, hauling a heavily laden duffel bag out of the hidden compartment and heaving it on top of the safe. He unzipped it, then took a step back to let Jon get a look.

"Looks more like a never-know-when-it's-going-to-be-World-War-Three bag," said Jon.

"I'll leave this with you at the apartment, because—"

"You never know."

CHAPTER 7

"Park here," said Riggs, pointing at an empty parking spot facing Grant Creek Road.

Tex squeezed the silver Yukon into the space, backing out once to readjust the oversize SUV dead center between two smaller vehicles. "You got enough room to get out?" he asked.

Riggs examined the space along the side of the SUV through the side mirror. "I think we're good to go. We're not taking them down here, anyway. This is strictly surveillance. You still tracking them inside?"

"On two different Wi-Fi networks—citywide and Starbucks," said Nissie from the third row of leather seats.

"Just yes or no will do it," said Riggs.

"Ahhhh-firrrrr-maaaa-tive," she replied. "Is that better?"

"Way better."

"Is one of us going in?" said Tex.

"You in a hurry?" said Riggs.

"No, I just thought—"

"Can I run the show for a second? We just fucking pulled in."

"All right," said Tex, taking his hands off the steering wheel and shrugging his shoulders.

"Obviously, this is a shitty stakeout location," said Riggs.

"Just slightly," said Ross, twisting in his seat and looking through the lift gate window, or at Nissie. Riggs couldn't tell.

"The other choice was parking right up against the building, nose in. Wouldn't take James Bond to figure out we were up to something."

"If they're paying attention, this will still look funny," said Tex. "Big-ass truck with tinted windows. Nobody getting out."

"You're killing me, Tex," said Riggs. "I'm going in to buy us all some coffees. I'll locate our targets, make sure they're not sitting with a bunch of FBI-looking goons, then we'll park somewhere else where we can watch from a distance. As long as we can track the laptop, we can make ourselves look inconspicuous. Good enough plan for you?"

"Didn't mean to jump the gun," said Tex, which was as close to an apology as Riggs could expect.

"What does everyone want?" said Riggs.

His team stuck to straight coffee. Nissie ordered a drink requiring more than six words. He'd already forgotten three of them.

"I'm not ordering queer drinks," said Riggs. "You want soy milk, I can live with that."

"Can't remember the order?" she said.

"I can remember the order," he said, lying. "I'm just not ordering froufrou drinks."

"I can repeat the order," insisted Nissie.

"What did she order?" said Oz, elbowing Ross.

The two smirked at each other before Ross joined in. "I didn't catch it either. What was it, Tex?"

"I don't know, but I'll have what she's having," said Tex.

"You get coffee. That's it," said Riggs, opening the door hard enough to bump the car next to them. "Fucking assholes. You're lucky I didn't set off the car alarm."

"I'll have what she's having, too," yelled Ross.

"Fuck you," he muttered, shutting the door on their nonsense.

Riggs shook his head, ignoring the repeated knocks on the windows. He didn't care how much Flagg appreciated Miss Keane's talents—that bitch needed to be taught some manners. In fact, his whole team could benefit from an attitude adjustment. Crossing the parking lot, he glanced back at the Yukon, imagining flames roaring from the windows as charred arms flailed inside. Or he could get a new team. He shook the image and focused on the mission.

Inside Starbucks, he didn't immediately spot anyone fitting the description of either Jon or Leah Fisher. Without obviously panning back and forth over the customers, he ordered four caramel Frappuccinos, having heard at least two of the words spoken by that stupid bitch, and a regular coffee. While he waited, he pretended to check his phone and scanned the tables for laptops again. He spotted several but was unable to match any faces to the pictures on his phone. She said the computer was here!

A few minutes later, still not seeing the Fishers, the last drinks in his order were placed on the counter. He packed them on the tray as an idea hit him. Riggs checked his phone again and gestured for one of the baristas.

"Sorry to bug you. I was messaging a friend who lost his laptop. He doesn't think he left it here, but he can't be sure. Do you guys keep a lost and found? If it's here, he'll head over and grab it."

"Sure. What kind is it?"

"I think it's a Dell. Let me check," he said, pretending to send a text.

"Hold on," she said, disappearing into the back office and reappearing.

A few moments later, a thin woman emerged from the room carrying a silver laptop. She identified herself as the manager. He could tell right away that the computer she held was not a Dell. It looked more like an Apple product. Could Nissie tell what kind of computer she was tracking?

"He said it was a Dell Inspiron. That doesn't look like a Dell," he said, feigning a disappointed look. "Bummer. He's been without that computer for three days, if you can imagine."

"This looks like a Mac Pro. An older couple walked out without it maybe an hour and a half ago," she said. "Sorry. Hope your friend finds it soon."

"I'm sure he will. Thank you."

When he got back to the SUV, he removed his coffee and handed the tray to Tex.

"What the fuck is this?"

"It's your froufrou drink! I got everyone whipped cream because I didn't want any of you to miss out on the full bitch experience," said Riggs, slamming the door shut.

He took a sip of his black coffee while the froufrou tray made its rounds.

"The Fishers walked away from their laptop about ninety minutes ago. It was sitting in the manager's office. They were using a Mac Pro, correct?"

"Affirmative," said Nissie, taking a sip. "Is this made with nonfat milk?"

"It's a caramel Frappuccino. Everyone got the same thing."

"Thank you for trying," she said, causing some laughter.

"This tastes like shit," said Ross, the straw still in his mouth.

"You have no idea how you look right now," said Riggs, staring at Ross until he lowered the drink. "Miss Keane. What are our options? Cameras?"

"The Starbucks security cameras would be a good start."

"Can you do that from your computer?"

"Yes, but I'll need the full system to access facial recognition networks. In case we discover someone helping them. Never know."

"All right. You work on what you can with your magic laptop, and we'll get set up in one of the hotels. The rest of your team should be here by five. We also need to rent one more vehicle, preferably a sedan. I haven't seen too many luxury SUVs up here."

"My team has hacked into most of the nearby hotel systems from the road. They obviously haven't found a couple named Jon and Leah Fisher, but they're combing for irregularities. I'll have them start compiling and preparing security feed data. May as well run it all through the facial recognition networks. That'll save us from sifting through hours of footage."

"Sounds good," said Riggs, turning to Tex. "You enjoying your Frappuccino?"

"Actually, it's kind of growing on me," he said, turning the drink toward him. "Want to try?"

"I ain't sipping coffee through a straw. What the fuck is wrong with you?"

CHAPTER 8

Stuart Quinn kept the satphone pressed to his ear, leaning his head against the seat's headrest. He'd been on hold for close to forty minutes, waiting for Major General Nichols to get out of a staff meeting. Not that he was complaining. Nichols had already gone way beyond the call of duty on this, and he hated to bother him again—but David's check-in was long overdue. He'd run every possibility through Blake, as a sanity check, and neither of them could come up with a serious scenario that didn't involve Cerberus.

"Colonel Quinn, they just broke camp. I'm gonna hand this phone to the general when he walks by. He said he'd take your call, but things are pretty tense around here, so I can't guarantee anything."

"Major, I appreciate you sticking your neck out like this."

"Don't mention it. We've been eyeballing your son for a division billet for some time now. Just looking for a way to steal him away from Lieutenant Colonel Smith. Hope everything's all right."

"I'm sure it is. Thank you again."

"Here he comes."

A few seconds of silence passed before the general spoke.

"Stu. I'm running to another meeting. San Diego County PD has intensified their blockade around the base."

"Sorry to jump you like this, Larry. I haven't heard from David."

"I should have reached out to you earlier," said Nichols. Stuart's stomach clenched as the major general continued. "I assumed he got in touch."

"Not since before the convoy left," said Stuart, afraid to ask what had happened.

"Here's what I know. All four vehicles were hit simultaneously by Javelin missiles, about twenty-five miles east of El Centro."

"Jesus. Javelins?"

"David survived, along with the Fishers. The details are sketchy, but I don't think David's wife made it."

"Shit."

Blake muttered an obscenity, pounding the steering wheel.

Stuart turned his head and whispered, "David's fine."

"The platoon supporting the convoy lost more than half its Marines."

"I'm sorry, Larry. Jesus, I'm really sorry," said Stuart, the general's words sinking in. "What do you mean the details are sketchy? Is David in Yuma?"

"No. Apparently, a group of mystery soldiers arrived by dune buggy and—get this—parachute, turning the tide. The platoon sergeant in charge of the convoy said this group saved their asses."

"Parachutes? No idea who they were?"

"None, but David and the rest left with them voluntarily—last seen headed south."

"With Alison?"

"All we know is that she was hit at some point during the ambush. Witnesses say she went down hard, but we can't confirm. David took her body when he left with this mystery group," said the general. "Some of the Marines reported hearing fluent Spanish, so I'd say Mexico is a good guess."

"This is unbelievable. All of it," said Stuart. "Smith's Marines aren't talking?"

"We're still sorting through their limited statements. They're very protective of your son. He was well respected and admired throughout the battalion."

"Right. Thank you," he said, understanding how the Marines would be hesitant to share information that might get David into trouble. "Did your Marines take any Cerberus operatives alive?"

"The recovery and removal operation was handled by Marine Corps Air Station Yuma. They're processing the scene for now. I'm told they have taken a few unknowns into custody, along with a dozen or so unidentified bodies. We'll be taking a hard look at these folks. You can rest assured of that."

"This radically changes things," said Stuart, his mind swirling with scattered thoughts. "Thank you, Larry. I'm racking up one hell of a debt here. I don't know what to say about your Marines other than I'm sorry."

"It's an inevitable part of war, and make no mistake, Stu—we are at war with whoever did this," he said. "I'm accelerating First Marine Division's deployment to Yuma and points east of the Colorado. Lieutenant Colonel Smith's battalion will be the tip of this spear. I anticipate armed reconnaissance missions ranging into western Arizona by late tomorrow night."

"Sand Devil? I thought we were a still a few months from pulling the trigger on that."

"Someone pulled the trigger on First Marine Division, so I'm bumping up the timeline."

"This wasn't the Sinaloa cartel," said Stuart.

"Nothing goes down near the border without the cartel's knowledge. Smith's Marines are going to make some noise out there. See what he can scare up. You never know how things are connected. *When you get in touch with David, let him know he has friends in western Arizona.* Keep me posted. Sorry to cut you off, Stu, but I have to run."

"Copy that, General. I'll make him aware of the battalion's presence. That's good news."

"Semper Fi, brother. Good luck with whatever crazy-ass plan you have brewing."

"You know me too well," said Stuart. "Semper Fi."

He lowered the phone and turned to Blake, who shook his head solemnly. Stuart felt helpless, sitting in a car more than a thousand hostile miles away. He knew about loss and the slippery slope it left behind. Stuart's wife, Liz, had been taken from him prematurely but not unexpectedly. Her cancer had moved fast, but they'd made their peace with it by the time she passed. A reluctant, tenuous peace on his part, but the acceptance they had built together kept him from sliding off the deep end during the dark months that followed. Alison's sudden death would take a catastrophic toll on David, smothering him in darkness. He needed to get in touch with his son as soon as possible.

They drove for few more minutes, Blake giving him some mental space to let everything sink in. Stuart could use more time, but that was the one thing they couldn't afford to waste.

"Mexico?" said Blake.

"Sounds like it," said Stuart. "I'm not sure where that leaves us."

"Leaves us with a road trip to Meh-hi-co."

"Did you understand what I meant about making David aware of the battalion's presence?"

"More guessing than understanding."

"Major General Nichols is sending David's battalion into Arizona, and he implied they could be counted on to help."

"That could come in handy, considering there's only three of us. I assume this deployment is part of a legitimate military operation. Sand Devil?"

"Constitutional scholars might shy away from the word *legitimate*, but yes, Sand Devil has been in the planning phase for over a year. Long overdue, if you ask me," he said, stopping to stare at the flat expanses of land beyond the SUV's windows.

"You gonna tell me about Sand Devil, or is that classified?" said Blake, taking a hand off the wheel to make an air quote.

"Hold on," said Stuart, picking up the phone.

A few seconds later he had connected with Jon Fisher, verifying his identity with their code.

"The boys are safe," Stuart said. "So are your daughter-in-law and grandson."

"Thank God," said Jon, continuing after a noticeable pause. "What about Alison?"

"Doesn't sound like she made it. According to Major General Nichols, details are a little sketchy. David's platoon is tight-lipped about what happened. They lost a lot of Marines out there."

"Son of a bitch," said Jon. "I'm really sorry to hear about Alison."

"Me, too. This is going to crush David."

"I don't doubt it. All the more reason to get our asses down there. Please tell me the Marines are getting involved. This is getting out of control."

"Nichols is moving part of First Marine Division into Arizona, ahead of Operation Sand Devil."

"Sand Devil? Never heard of it."

"Few have. The name and full scope of Sand Devil haven't trickled any lower than division-level commanders, though nearly every major military unit based in the continental United States has prepared for it under one guise or another. The White House has directed our military to eject the drug cartels from the United States soil. Several US-based combat divisions will participate in the invasion. First Marine Division will spearhead the western front."

"Wow," added Jon. "Sounds like our boys should sit tight in Yuma."

"They're not in Yuma." He explained the uncertain report passed by Nichols.

"Why isn't David communicating with us?" said Jon.

"I don't know. Maybe this mystery group is following the same set of security rules your friend Scott is observing. They sound serious enough."

"Any idea who we're dealing with?"

"I'd say a group with an interest in keeping Nathan alive. I can't think of any other reason they would have intervened. Your son has been at the center of this from the start. If I had to guess, I'd say the group was tied to the California Liberation Movement, and they've been aware of him for a while."

"Well, they haven't exactly done a stellar job watching over him."

"It's all pretty baffling. Hopefully we'll get some answers soon. David will reach out when he can."

"We should direct them west, into First Marine Division's protective umbrella."

"I agree, though I'm not sure how effective that will be. Nichols plans on sending Lieutenant Colonel Smith's battalion well ahead of the division, but it sounds like the battalion will be scattered. Mostly conducting armed recon. I think their best strategy is to head north and hide, veering west if practical."

"This is all assuming they're free to travel," said Jon. "Sounds like someone went through a lot of trouble to snatch them out of the jaws of death."

"I was thinking the same thing. All we can do is keep moving forward. I'll let you know if anything changes."

"Same here," said Jon. "See you bright and early."

Stuart nestled the phone into an empty drink holder, contemplating the hours of empty landscape that awaited them.

"When does any of this start to look different?" he asked.

"Billings, Montana," replied Blake.

"How far away is that?"

"Twelve hours with food and gas breaks, but you'll only have to stare at this mind-numbing shit for about half of that. The sun sets around nine in these parts."

"Is there anything you don't know?"

"I don't know. Does that count?" said Blake.

"Have I told you you're a knucklehead?"

"Surprisingly, you haven't mentioned it today." Blake tapped the wheel with his fingers. "It's gonna be fine, Stu. I can feel it."

"I know," he said, unable to shake the sinking feeling that everything was far from fine.

PART II

PART II

CHAPTER 9

Nathan squeezed his eyes shut against the bright light probing his eyelids—as if keeping them closed could somehow prevent his disastrous reality from materializing. He knew the thought was irrational on every level, but there he lay, like a frightened child rejecting the existence of monsters by refusing to see.

The acrid smell of chemical smoke attached to Keira's hair reminded him that denial wouldn't make this nightmare go away. He rolled on his back and rubbed his dirty, unshaven face with both hands, trying to regain some memory of his surroundings. He didn't have much to work with.

His family had been politely but firmly asked to place breathable hoods over their heads upon arriving at the unlit outskirts of a city he assumed to be Mexicali. Run-down buildings and businesses sprawled in every direction. Had to be Mexicali. It was the only Mexican border city of consequence between Tijuana and Nogales that had survived decades of drought and drug cartel violence.

They'd experienced a long, bumpy ride into the depths of the city, followed by an endless walk through a maze of subterranean passageways tight enough to scrape against both arms at once in several points.

Their rescuers had removed the hoods in front of the door leading to this room before stuffing them inside with a few gallon jugs of water.

Jose, the group's de facto leader, had told them to get some rest and promptly closed the door.

When Nathan tested the door a few moments later, he was surprised to find it unlocked. A weathered, middle-aged Latina woman dressed in military-style gear sat on a folding chair in the tight hallway outside the door. A tan battle rifle leaned against the earthen wall behind her, but she made no move to retrieve it when he appeared. She glanced at him and nodded with a neutral look. Farther down the dirt corridor, in the direction they had come, another sentry stood outside an open door, cradling a rifle.

He closed the door and helped Keira arrange the dusty mattresses they'd found stacked against one of the walls. They spent the next few minutes removing their boots, tactical gear, and body armor, piling it on the room's one table. Nathan barely remembered pulling a pile of colorful serape blankets off a roughly hewn wooden table next to the door and pulling them over his family.

He'd obviously been too tired to turn off the LED bulb hanging from the wooden-beam ceiling above them. Now, in an effort to escape the light's glare, he shifted toward the edge of the creaky bed.

"What time is it?" croaked his wife.

He lifted his wrist above his face. Shit. They'd been out for close to thirteen hours. In and out, really. It was hard to sleep soundly with a price on your head.

"Four forty-seven," he said.

"Are you serious? We need to get out of here."

"We don't know where here is yet. Mexicali, I'm guessing. Though why Mexicali? Seems like an odd place for the California Liberation Movement to keep a safe house."

"Is it possible we crossed back into California?"

"I don't think so, but anything's possible at this point."

"It doesn't matter. All I know is that this isn't far enough away."

She was right. The brazenness of the ambush against the Marine vehicles carrying their family to safety revealed the extent of Cerberus's desperation to kill Nathan. To kill all of them. He wasn't sure anywhere in the world was far enough away, but they could certainly do better than a lawless, dilapidated city less than thirty miles from the ambush site. This was a far cry from the luxury yacht in the middle of the Sea of Cortez that Jose had originally intended.

"I'm sure Jose is working on it."

"I don't know if Jose's boat trip is a good idea anymore," said Keira, rolling over to face him. "He's not the only one with money to wave around in Mexico. Cerberus has to know we're down here. I think we should consider going back to our original plan."

"Head north?"

"Why not? It might be the last thing Cerberus would expect."

"Let me talk to David about it. He might have a better sense of what we're up against."

"All right," she said.

Nathan knelt next to the mattress and put a hand on her shoulder. Her hair was a tangled, matted mess, her face caked in dust, but he didn't care. He leaned over and kissed her dried lips, tasting the desert grime.

She held him close for a long moment. "I love you," she whispered, letting go.

"I love you, too. I'm going to poke around and check on things."

"Can you start by finding us a bathroom and something to eat?" said Keira.

"Of course."

"And I could use some coffee."

Nathan nodded at the gallon jugs of water next to the mattress. "I wouldn't get your hopes up."

"We had some coffee in our packs. What happened to those? Once they put hoods over our heads, I lost track of everything except Owen."

"The backpacks made it into the SUVs. That's about all I know. How's he doing?"

"Nightmares," she said. "He was burrowed into me all night. Kicking and twitching."

He nodded, not finding the words to express his regret for inadvertently putting Owen through this disaster. Standing up and stretching his arms, he found the ceiling a lot lower than it had looked from the mattress. His head cleared the wooden beams by only a few inches. He was accustomed to the three or four feet of clearance in their house; even the bedroom hallway gave him plenty of space. Not that they'd ever see it again. Their house in California felt as far away as the house in Tucson. Everything behind him felt inaccessible. Wiped clean by Cerberus.

He put on his boots and opened the door to the hallway, which was just as cramped. A different guard rose from the chair outside their room. The thick-bearded, pale-skinned man in his early twenties was dressed in khaki cargo pants, brown hiking boots, and a desert camouflage tactical vest over an olive-drab T-shirt. A worn, curved-rim ball cap and tricked-out assault rifle complemented the paramilitary look. Unfortunately, the gear did little to camouflage the fact that the guy underneath it all looked like he might be far more comfortable studying a laptop screen and sipping a latte at Starbucks than fighting an insurgency. Nathan leaned back into the room.

"You're in good hands," he said, winking at Keira.

When he stepped back into the hall, the young man extended a hand. "Jeff," he said.

Nathan accepted his handshake, noticing their backpacks stacked against the wall next to the door.

"Nathan," he said, letting go of Jeff's hand.

"I know. Everybody knows."

He regarded the man warily. Exactly what did *everybody* know about him? Enough to convince the Mexican army to loan the CLM a parachute assault force. Fuck. Keira was right. They needed to get as far away from here as possible—even if it meant spending every last dollar in his pocket on the next taxi available. If the town still had taxis. He picked up the two backpacks, sliding them onto his aching shoulders.

"Everything from the vehicles is here," said the man.

"Except two rifles and three helmets."

"That's all they brought by this morning," Jeff said apologetically.

"And where is here, exactly?"

Jeff looked uncomfortable with the question.

"Let me guess. Classified?"

"Sorry. My instructions are to send you that way"—he pointed to Nathan's left—"once you're up and about. I'm sure they'll answer all of your questions."

Nathan peered down the dark, dirt-walled hallway toward a closed door. A compact camera attached to one of the exposed wood ceiling beams pointed in their direction. Nathan waved at the camera before taking in the rest of the area. The opposite end of the passageway appeared to consist of a wall of hard-packed dirt. Their room was the only one in the corridor. He suddenly felt very claustrophobic.

"So," said Nathan, "there a lot of dead ends down here?"

Jeff nodded. "The previous owners didn't complete all their tunnels."

He didn't need to ask who might need to build an extensive network of tunnels underground in Mexicali. He knew the answer, and it was one more reason why they needed to get away from this place.

Nathan picked up their backpacks and slipped back into the room with them.

"What?" Keira said, rising onto one elbow.

He dropped the backpacks onto the dusty floor at the foot of the mattresses and knelt next to her. "I have our packs," he whispered. "I think we should wear our boots and gear at all times while we're down here. I'm pretty sure this is a former drug cartel hideout. We might have to leave very quickly."

She sat up all the way. "Are you serious? We need to get the hell out of here, right now. I can't believe he brought us here."

"I know. I know," he said, putting his hands up defensively. "But we can't just walk up onto the streets. We don't know the situation up there. Give me a little time to figure it out—and get David on board. We can't leave without him."

"I almost forgot about him. Jesus," she said, shaking her head.

"I'll try to find him first. See what he wants to do."

"He won't want to do much, but you have to convince him to leave with us immediately."

"He'll want to bury Alison," said Nathan. "Or make some kind of arrangements to ship her body north."

"I'm grateful for everything he's done, and I can't even wrap my head around Alison's death—this place can't be a secret. Not if the cartel used it at some point."

"I can't pressure him after what happened," said Nathan. "I don't think we'd get very far without him."

"Then you need to be convincing. I'd like to be as far away as possible when Cerberus comes knocking. We're completely trapped down here."

"I agree," he said, kissing her forehead.

CHAPTER 10

Jose Guerrero stared at the wide, flat-screen monitor on his desk, studying the flow of reports filed by his paid contacts throughout Mexicali. He knew their time here was limited after last night's rescue. CLM's relationship with the governing cartel was based on money, and despite the significant amount of cash spent on maintaining the relationship and paying lookouts, the One Nation Coalition had far deeper pockets. It wasn't a matter of *if* the cartel gave them up; it was a matter of *when*. He just hoped the contract with CLM was lucrative enough to buy at least a little time before the cartel flipped on them.

He'd give the final evacuation order later this afternoon. By sunrise tomorrow, the CLM's southern hub would go quiet for the first time in three years. Before that, he wanted Nathan Fisher and his resourceful friend, David, to get a solid feel for the scope and complexity of CLM's efforts. They had to see the bigger picture, from ground zero. Had to see that the CLM stood in a position to better the lives of millions of people across several states and Mexico—and that real people had given up everything to be a part of this.

He'd intended to fully brief them in Cabo, but a colonel in the Mexican army had decided to declare war on a rogue criminal element in Estación Coahuila, effectively sealing off the roads leading south. Bringing them here had been a risky move. He could have tried to reroute the entire escape farther west, into the Baja Peninsula, but changing the plan at such a late hour carried too much risk. Maybe this would work out better, allowing Jose to make his desperate pitch at the source—CLM's southern headquarters.

When he stood up from examining the reports, satisfied that nothing appeared out of order, an unfamiliar face near the southern corridor drew his attention. It was Nathan Fisher, rubbing his chin, taking in the operations center with a neutral look. Jose had hoped he might look a little more impressed. This was going to be a very tough sell indeed.

"No coffee?" said Nathan. "I would have expected a pot of coffee in an operations center."

Jose smiled. At least he recognized it as an ops center. That was a start. "I can get a fresh pot going in the canteen, along with some lunch for you and your family. Come on in."

Nathan took a few hesitant steps into the expansive room. "I think we'll grab a bite to eat at a taco stand on the way out."

"That would not end well for you."

"I'll grab some Imodium at a pharmacy," replied Nathan.

"You'll need something stronger than that on these streets. I assume you've pieced together where we brought you?"

"Mexicali."

"Former heart of the Sinaloa cartel's US distribution system. The Mexicali plaza, as they called it, was the most profitable of the eight Sinaloa border plazas. Nearly everything got through the border station. At one point, a joint DEA/US Customs undercover investigation indicated that forty drug shipments got through the ten-lane crossing for every shipment detected. Now? Nothing gets across, and the city has devolved into a violent, unmitigated shithole. Perfect for hiding our little operation, but nobody goes topside without cartel permission and a serious armed escort."

"Which I presume you can arrange for us—soon."

"Why the hurry?" he said, hoping to get a better gauge of Nathan's situational awareness.

"Do you really have to ask? It's only a matter of time before Cerberus rolls into town and starts waving around enough money to dissolve any of the loyalty you've cultivated over the years. Please tell me you're aware of the consequences of bringing us here."

Very aware.

"I considered those consequences before we decided to rescue you. I knew it spelled the end of our Mexicali stay."

Nathan appeared to consider his words, and for the briefest moment, Jose thought it might be that easy. He should've known better than to get his hopes up.

"I'm afraid I'm going to disappoint you," said Nathan.

"At least hear what I have to say, and if you don't mind doing me a favor, can you convince David to listen?"

"I think he has enough on his plate right now."

"We don't have a lot of time, as you pointed out," said Jose.

"All the more reason to move this discussion elsewhere."

"Give me an hour at the most. I'll get some coffee going and dig up some decent rations. Your wife should be here, too."

"You don't want her in the audience."

"Probably not, but I know how it works," said Jose. "All in or all out. At least that's how my family rolled."

"Yeah? So your family's here, too?" said Nathan, defiantly.

"No. I lost them in the Albuquerque firestorm." Jose quickly mastered the tears before they could surface. It was his parlor trick, leaving nothing for an observer but the slightest pause in his speech.

"Oh. Sorry. I didn't—I can't imagine," said Nathan. "I thought everyone—you're not from California?"

"This is way bigger than California, Nathan. That's what I need to show you," said Jose, glancing at the wall-size maps covered with symbols on the far eastern wall of the room.

Nathan's eyes followed, stopping when they reached the maps. Jose watched as he took them in. They were too far away for him to decipher the strategic or tactical significance of the symbols and markings, but surely close enough for him to feel the gravity of their purpose.

"Let me show you where to find David," said Jose. "Shall we reconvene in fifteen minutes with coffee and hot chow?"

Nathan nodded, his eyes drifting from the wall to Jose. "I can't make any promises," he said.

"I just want an opportunity to explain the bigger picture, and why you're important enough to scrap our location here."

"I'll see what I can do," said Nathan, hesitantly. "Have you tried talking to David yet?"

Jose grimaced. "We were up nearly until dawn burying his wife. I haven't wanted to bother him—but time is running short."

"He buried Alison already?" said Nathan, looking confused. "What happened to the whole proper burial thing you promised?"

"*Proper* takes on a whole different meaning in Mexicali. After a long discussion with David, we decided on a more practical burial service. More private."

"Where did you bury her? Never mind. I don't want to know," said Nathan, shaking his head. "And he was fine with this?"

"He was far from fine with it, but he knew there was no other realistic option. A quarter of the city's remaining population perished in the violence and chaos that followed California's border closure. The funeral industry vanished nearly overnight. It was all they could do to bury the hundreds of bodies produced every day."

"You just dug a hole outside and buried her in it?"

"We have a place set aside for this kind of thing, on the outskirts of city. It was the best we could do under the circumstances."

"And you weren't going to tell me any of this before I walked over and woke him up?"

"He doesn't blame you," said Jose. *He blames me, for not getting there in time.*

"I got him into this," said Nathan.

"That's not how he thinks, and you know it. I believe your father shares the same warrior ethos?"

"I don't like how much you know about me."

"Funny thing is, I'd never heard of you until two days ago."

"Nothing funny about that," said Nathan.

"I suppose not, but you'd be surprised to learn how much has transpired on your behalf between then and now. Your arriving here is just short of a miracle. Let me show you where you can find David so I can explain why."

CHAPTER 11

A hesitant knocking at the door drew David Quinn's attention away from the dark knot in one of the uneven ceiling planks directly above him. The same knot he'd stared at, off and on, for the past few hours, during bouts of consciousness. He was past the point of sleep deprivation, caught between the waking and sleeping world in a form of purgatory, where the certainty of his current situation remained slightly out of focus. Where his wife's death didn't feel real.

Another knock. David's eyes lazily drifted toward the door, wanting nothing more than to continue staring at the ceiling.

"Yeah?"

The door cracked open, a partial face visible but undefined through the slit.

"Can I come in?" Nathan.

"Yeah. Shut the door behind you."

Nathan slid inside the room and closed the door while David sat up—still dressed in a bloodied, dust-caked uniform. Alison's blood. Nathan patted a loosely folded stack of clothing on the battered wooden chair next to the door. Military-style clothing, from what David could tell. He barely remembered the clothes being there. He'd collapsed onto the mattress when they'd removed his hood and showed him into the room.

"They thought you might want to change out," said Nathan.

"I'm good."

Nathan surveyed him and his filthy clothes from head to foot, nodding without comment. They stared at each other for a few awkward moments.

It was all he could do to look at Nathan, let alone carry on a conversation with him. Rationally, he knew he couldn't blame him for Alison's death, but David was still pretty far from sustaining a logical inner monologue. He needed time—and separation—from all of this. He suspected he wasn't about to get either.

"So. What's going on?"

"Jose wants to show us what they're up to," said Nathan.

David shook his head, keeping quiet.

"I'm guessing it's a sales pitch for joining the cause," said Nathan.

"Not interested." And that was an understatement.

"I didn't think you would be," said Nathan, followed by another long pause that Nathan finally broke. "Listen," he said. "We need get out of here sooner than later. This is an old cartel bunker. Probably a holding point back in the day for drug packages that went into the cars and backpacks pouring through the border control station. So this place isn't even close to being off the radar. A little Cerberus money in the wrong hands, and we've got a problem."

The mention of Cerberus cut through the thick fog of guilt and disbelief clouding his mind. David suddenly understood why Nathan was standing there, watching him like that. Nathan couldn't see the crippling storm of self-doubt and remorse clouding David's thoughts. He still saw Captain David Quinn, United States Marine Corps. His family's protector and savior.

The thought buoyed him for a moment before the heavy curtain of reality closed on him. Nathan was one of very few people he had managed to adequately protect and save last night. David put his hands on the sides of his tightly shaved head and squeezed, exhaling deeply. Nathan was thinking clearly. Mexicali was the worst possible place for them to hide. The city was a graveyard waiting to be filled. He had to get a grip on himself.

"Does it look like we can slip out of here?" said David, fairly certain of the answer.

"They have the place locked down pretty tight."

"I assume they have our gear locked down pretty tight as well."

"They delivered our rucksacks, but no weapons or helmets."

"That's no good," said David. "Liberating the rifles and helmets needs to be our first priority. And the satphone."

"They took your satphone?"

"They're operating under strict emissions control security protocols here. I get that, but we can't leave without the phone. That's the only secure link to your dad and mine."

"We were supposed to contact them this morning. They have to be worried out of their minds."

"Maybe. Maybe not. It's quite possible that Major General Nichols, First Marine Division's commanding general, knows our status. We can only hope he reached out to my dad."

"So is that our play? Head north somehow?"

"With an emphasis on the somehow."

"What about going south for a while?"

"Is Jose still offering an all-expense-paid yacht trip to Cabo?" said David.

"I'm not sure. My guess is no."

"We can't go south on our own. We'd draw more attention to ourselves south of the border than north of it. Gringos are persona non grata in Central America after the trade shutdown. South America, too, for that matter. We need to vacate this bunker, pronto, and work on that somehow-head-north thing. I can't imagine they'll loan us a four-wheel-drive vehicle after we politely decline their offer to join the resistance, or whatever they're operating."

"Jose didn't sound very optimistic about our survival prospects on the mean streets of Mexicali," said Nathan.

"That's why we need to get our shit back. A suppressed rifle and night vision–equipped goggles can work miracles after dark," said David, feeling alive again.

"I don't think we're collecting our shit or slipping out of here without either sitting through his sales pitch or raising some serious hell. I say we give him our attention and take it from there. I feel like we owe him that much."

David nodded reluctantly. He couldn't deny the fact they would be stuffed in dark green government body bags, tidily arranged inside a sweltering Yuma air base hangar, if Jose's force hadn't intervened. Or whoever had initially intervened on their behalf. Mexican Special Forces? He'd love to hear how Jose had managed to arrange what amounted to a foreign invasion—if it didn't take too long.

"I'm not opposed to hearing what he has to say," said David. "But we're out of here as soon as the sun sets. We need to be as far as possible from Mexicali when Cerberus gets its first sniff."

"What if they *oppose* our departure?"

David pulled a compact semiautomatic pistol from a zippered compartment concealed behind his tactical vest's ballistic chest plate. "We're leaving tonight. One way or the other."

Nathan glared at the pistol and nodded, a look of discomfort washing over his face.

"It won't come to that," said Nathan.

"Let's hope not."

Chapter 12

Keira checked her watch again and squeezed her legs together. Where the fuck did he go? She needed to use a bathroom but had no intention of leaving her son alone in this room. Owen lay curled up on the mattress, breathing deeply, an olive-drab wool blanket pulled up to his chin. He needed every bit of rest he could get, especially if they intended to spend the night on the road. She couldn't imagine any one of them sleeping in a car again—ever. Not after last night's interstate ambush, and especially not with Cerberus hunting them.

She watched Owen for a few moments, envious of how deeply he slept. She'd passed out as soon as Nathan had pulled the blankets over them last night, but her sleep had been scattered. She'd spent much of the morning awake, sensing that Nathan was plagued with the same problem. Neither of them wanting to disturb the other, or Owen. Of course, he'd barely stirred when Keira and Nathan had gotten up. She wasn't sure that was a good thing.

Their son had shown surprising resilience throughout the entire ordeal, particularly after last night's attack, but he'd witnessed the horrors of combat—up close and personal. Few adults could emerge mentally unscathed from an experience like that. An eleven-year-old? Forget it. She'd briefly concentrated her studies on post-traumatic stress disorder before deciding to pursue a master's degree in cognitive disability therapy, and knew the odds. They'd need to watch him closely for signs of emotional trauma. She didn't want to think about the long-term effects. One step at a time. She glanced at her watch.

"That's it," she muttered, crossing to the door and yanking it open to find Nathan standing inches from her face. "Jesus!"

"Sorry."

"I'm about to piss my pants here," she hissed.

"Got pulled away for a minute," he said, remaining in her way.

Keira glanced past Nathan's right shoulder at the armed man seated behind him. He looked more like one of those bearded hippie hybrid types than a soldier. They were far from safe here. Shit. Before she could say something, Nathan pushed her inside the room and shut the door.

"What was that about?" she said.

"You looked like you were about to say something about our guard—in front of him."

"Not exactly awe inspiring."

"This is babysitting duty. The hard-core crew is probably guarding the entrances and buildings leading to the entrances," he said quietly. "I'm not worried about it."

"You willing to bet our son's life on that?"

Nathan pulled her deeper into the room. "I talked to David. We're getting out of here."

"When?"

"Maybe right after dark," he said, looking at his watch. "Sunset is at 7:49, so we're looking at a few hours."

"That's too long. While we've been sleeping, Cerberus has been looking," she said, a swift urge hijacking her thoughts. "I really have to go to the bathroom."

"The guard outside our room can point you in the right direction. It's easy to find." He shrugged. "Hey, after you get back, I need to leave again. David and I agreed to meet with Jose to discuss our situation.

He's brewing up fresh coffee and preparing some food. I'll bring that to you before the meeting."

"What's there to discuss? We thank them for their help and leave when it's dark. Hopefully sooner."

"It's not that simple. We're in the middle of Mexicali, in a former Sinaloa cartel drug-processing bunker. We can't leave without an armed escort."

"Says who?"

"Jose. The cartel still controls the city. We can't just walk out of town with our backpacks and rifles. We still need their help. How would we get anywhere? The town is locked down by the cartel. Not to mention we're in the middle of a desert."

Now she understood why Jose had called a meeting. She knew their rescue hadn't come free.

"And they need our help, too. Right? If we don't help them, they don't help us. Does that pretty much sum it up? What does David think about our little situation?"

"I don't think it's going to be like that," he said. "We're going to listen to Jose's sales pitch and politely decline whatever he's proposing."

"Really? What if he's not satisfied with that? They went through a lot of trouble to rescue us."

"We'll give him something. Enough to get us across the border safely."

"Like what?"

"I have an idea," said Nathan.

She didn't like the sound of *an idea*, but she had far more urgent things to take care of at the moment. She was about to further soil her already filthy pants. "We need to have a long talk before you sit down with Jose. The less you say in that meeting, the better," she said, breaking for the door.

"Hon," said Nathan, grabbing her hand. "We're gonna be fine. I promise."

She pulled away. "I get the distinct impression that it's not really in our hands anymore. Maybe it never was."

"I'm optimistic about our future," he said as she opened the door.

"Annoyingly optimistic," she said, cracking a faint smile before stepping into the hallway.

CHAPTER 13

Nathan met David in front of a wall-size map of the western United States and northern Mexico. The Marine stared vacantly at the map, sipping coffee from a Styrofoam cup.

"At least the coffee's good," said David.

"Jose said it's from a roaster in Puerto Vallarta. Better than the usual operations center swill. My dad never stopped complaining about it," said Nathan.

David nodded absently, taking another sip. After a few seconds of silence, Nathan continued.

"And God knows it's a massive step up from MRE coffee."

"They put Starbucks coffee in MREs now," stated David, never taking his eyes off the map.

"That wasn't Starbucks we drank during our little camping trip at Pendleton."

"I gave you old MREs," he said drily before nodding at the map. "They're after more than just an independent California."

"That's what Jose alluded to earlier."

"Doesn't change our plan," said David.

"No. It doesn't," Nathan said, reaching out to trace the Colorado River.

Major dams along the river had been circled, extending from the Imperial Dam just north of Yuma, Arizona, to Grand Valley Dam outside Grand Junction, Colorado. An array of unfamiliar symbols accompanied each dam, betraying little about the California Liberation Movement's plans. The Hoover Dam at the bottom of Lake Mead was crowded with symbols, followed upriver by Glen Canyon Dam, a few miles north of Lee's Ferry, Arizona.

Lee's Ferry served as the official demarcation line between the Upper and Lower Basins of the Colorado River, but the Glen Canyon Dam represented the true division between them. Water flowed through Lee's Ferry at the rate allowed by the dam, which sat comfortably inside the Upper Basin. In 2027, at the height of the Basin Water War, First Ranger Battalion, Seventy-Fifth Ranger Regiment had been assigned to protect the dam and the Lake Powell Reservoir from an increasingly hostile and rightfully frustrated Arizona state government.

Water flow into the reservoir and through the dam had continued to decrease in the early 2020s, as more water was diverted into a series of new irrigation canals built into the Colorado side of Lake Powell. Not a problem if the Upper Basin states had limited the use of their federally allotted share of the river water to irrigate their own struggling ecosystem, but when they had started pumping vast amounts of water destined for the Great Plains, you had a big problem.

Especially when the Upper Basin states made a fortune from the water. Colorado, Utah, and Wyoming filled their coffers while draining critical Arizona aqueducts that kept Tucson and Phoenix from drying up and blowing away in the hot desert winds. When Arizona state legislators started talking about sending National Guard troops to seize control of the Glen Canyon Dam, Washington, DC, preempted the move by deploying the Rangers as a deterrent.

That was when Nathan had started looking for a similar job as a water reclamation engineer in one of the surrounding states. He knew better than anyone that Arizona was living on borrowed time. The key was getting out of the state before the general public realized the water situation had crossed the point of no return.

The sound of a chair sliding across the floor behind him drew his attention away from the map. Nathan turned his head to see a stocky, intense-looking man push away from one of the computer stations on the opposite side of the room, where he had met Jose this morning. Nathan had barely given the bearded man a second look a few minutes earlier. Looking at him now, he could tell the guy was important. Possibly Jose's second in command or chief of security.

He wore what Nathan had come to regard as the CLM uniform: high-end, earth-tone hiking boots; light brown or olive-drab cargo pants; fully loaded tactical vest over T-shirt of choice. The T-shirts seemed to be a personal statement, though the man standing behind them wore an unpatterned, light brown T-shirt—like Jose's. He didn't carry a rifle, instead sporting a brown thigh holster. Once again, just like Jose's. He was definitely in a leadership role. For all Nathan knew, the guy could be the head honcho. He had just assumed Jose was the group's leader.

The man met Nathan's glance with steely eyes. He was a whole new tier of badass. Locked into a staring contest, Nathan withstood the withering look, grateful when Jose appeared.

"Gentlemen, this is Baker. He runs the tactical side of our operation," said Jose.

Baker smirked faintly before turning to address Jose.

"No signs of trouble from our contacts. Exterior security reports all clear on the streets. Remote observation teams report the same."

"It's still early," said Jose. "I guarantee it's in the works. Once the price is right, we'll start to notice extra surveillance. Might even get a courtesy call from our *patrón*."

"If he's not the first to sell us out," said the man.

Jose shook his head. "There's too much money at stake. I hope."

How much money could CLM afford to pay to stay here? It couldn't possibly be enough to keep a low-level informant from taking a stack of cash.

The man shrugged. "Only time will tell."

"I'd like to be out of here before time runs out," said David, pivoting on his feet to face them.

"That's the trick, isn't it?" replied the mystery man.

"Nathan. David. This is Jeremy. Former US Naval Special Warfare Development Group. Squadron commander. He runs security for the installation and southern-tier tactical operations."

"Development Group?" said Nathan.

"SEAL Team Six," said David. "Very serious shit."

Jeremy's face didn't betray the slightest response to David's compliment.

"Yeah, he's about as serious as it gets," said Jose. "He directed the assault that cleared Cerberus from their positions overlooking your convoy."

"He dropped in with the Mexicans?" said David.

"There were no Mexicans present during last night's operation," said Jose.

"Everyone keeps saying that," said Nathan.

"That's because it's an important point to clarify," said Jose.

"Uh-huh," replied Nathan. "Just like the CLM isn't running operations out of a foreign country."

"Exactly," said Jose. "Will Keira be joining us?"

Nathan shook his head. "I took her some food and coffee. She doesn't want to leave Owen alone."

"Perfectly understandable." He pointed toward the map. "What do you guys think?"

"I think you're planning on taking out a few dams," said David.

Nathan shook his head as Jose walked between the two of them to stand next to the wall.

"You don't think we can do it?" said Jose, raising an eyebrow at Nathan.

"I know you can't do it. Not without access to the air force."

"The US or Mexican Air Force?" replied Jose.

Was he kidding? Landing a platoon of paratroopers a few miles north of the border was one thing—launching a coordinated air strike against major US infrastructure points was altogether different. He didn't like where this was headed. He was in enough trouble as it stood. Adding domestic terrorism and federal treason to the list could only serve to ensure that neither he nor his family ever lived a normal life again. He had a chance against Cerberus and the trumped-up murder charges in California. There was no going back from what Jose was suggesting.

"If you have access to the Mexican Air Force, why do you need me or David?" said Nathan.

"Because we don't have access to the Mexican Air Force. Even if we did, I can't imagine any scenario in which they would cross the Colorado–Arizona border to hit the Glen Canyon Dam. If they were willing to risk that kind of aggression, taking out the Hoover Dam would make more sense, yes?"

Knocking out the Hoover Dam would undoubtedly benefit Mexico, dumping the contents of Lake Mead into the Colorado River and sending an unrestricted flow toward the Sea of Cortez and the long-dried-out aqueducts in Baja California. It would also overwhelm the smaller dams built along the river south of Lake Mead, quite possibly destroying them. That would be an unmitigated disaster for the Lower Basin states, emptying the reservoirs that fed water into Arizona and California.

Of course, all of this was a moot point. Most of the Colorado River's water never made it out of the Upper Basin. Nathan would take a different approach altogether if he was put in charge.

"You don't seem to like that idea," said Jose.

Jesus. Was he that easy to read? Jose stifled a laugh as Nathan cleared his throat.

"We have no intention of destroying the Hoover Dam. That would be counterproductive for everyone, including Mexico. Most of the water would dump right into the Sea of Cortez—wasted," said Jose. "Control it? Yes."

"If you're looking to restore the Lower Basin to historic levels, you're going to need the Mexican Air Force. Not us," said Nathan. "Glen Canyon Dam has to come down. There's no point in seizing it. If the government doesn't drop the US Army Rangers on your head, I guarantee the Upper Basin states will mobilize their National Guards to evict you, so to speak. Not that it really matters. Lake Powell is at its lowest levels ever. They're diverting too much water upriver."

"It's a compound problem," said Jose.

"That's an understatement."

"We could use your expertise in formulating a plan."

Nathan shrugged. "I don't know what these symbols mean, but it appears to me that you're focusing on the right dams."

David reached for the map, pressing a finger against a point in northern Utah, near the Wyoming border. "This one seems pretty isolated. Why destroy a dam this far north?"

Jose nodded at Nathan. "Care to explain?"

"You're not dragging us into this."

"What's the harm in reiterating what the CLM already knows?" said Jose.

Nathan gave him a skeptical look, then turned to David. "Flaming Gorge is one of the keys to this whole mess. It controls the flow of the Green River, which is the Colorado's main tributary. There's no shortage of water flowing from mountain sources north of the dam, but the Upper Basin Authority diverts a ton of it east, toward the Great Plains."

"Doesn't the federal government control these dams? How fucking difficult is this to fix?" said David.

Jose shook his head. "Very difficult, when some of the nation's wealthiest industrialists have so much to lose if the water starts flowing again. They tend to spend money on these things. Lots of money. Lawmakers on both sides of the aisle in DC have turned their backs on this issue. The US Bureau of Reclamation has ignored Colorado River Compact violations for so long, they've more or less redrawn the water allotments. Even the White House turns a blind eye to the problem. Three administrations, both Democratic and Republican—nothing but empty promises to investigate the issue. This isn't going away by policy. Dams need to come down."

"Uncle Sam isn't going to sit back and let you destroy these dams," said David. "You'd need the equivalent to a Marine combat division, with full air support, to pull this off. Your time and money would be better spent lobbying for more desalination plants—if water is your main concern. Even a public awareness campaign about the water diversion."

"We've been down that road, and it always leads to back to the status quo," said Jose. "Desalination plants are expensive. The state can barely cover the current infrastructure costs of the California Self-Reliance Act."

"Is that new legislation?" said David.

"See? That's the part of the problem right there. The CSRA was renamed the California Infrastructure Improvement Act seven years ago—eight years after the legislation passed it into law. A subtle but effective way of deemphasizing the whole point of the act: to achieve resource and economic independence from a federal government too corrupt to address a serious threat to California's future. Most Californians have forgotten why they overwhelmingly voted in favor of the CSRA in 2020.

"We've been losing the media battle. Doubling the current number of desalination plants will not produce the amount of water needed to both irrigate California's fields and hydrate the population. It'd help, but it'd be a trickle compared to what the Colorado River can supply. If the

Upper Basin cuts the river flow any farther, the state will have to choose between the people or the farms. This is where it gets interesting."

"This is starting to hurt my head," said David.

"It's been hurting mine for more than a decade. Let me break it down for you. When push comes to shove between delivering water to the population and irrigating the fields, the citizens will take the hit."

"I don't think so. Public outcry would win that battle," said David. "People won't go thirsty."

"Really? I think you've been living in your Marine Corps bubble a little too long."

"Excuse you?" said David, setting down his coffee cup on a chair behind him.

"Camp Pendleton has its own desalination plant, which provides an unlimited source of water to the base, while providing both Orange and San Diego Counties with water."

"That's part of Pendleton's community outreach program. It's not exactly a bad deal for the counties."

"Depends on your point of view. It certainly takes the sting out of local municipalities supporting your federal mandated water allotment—which is far higher than, say, the average citizen's. Fifty percent higher, if I'm not mistaken."

David remained quiet.

"And your neighbors can't buy whatever they want, whenever they want, at government prices on base. You might be surprised how water stressed they feel. I'm sure Nathan could shed some light on this. He's spent the past several years working on this problem. Has it gotten better or worse since you started, Nathan?"

"Definitely worse," said Nathan, keeping his focus on the map. "Most families supplement their water allotment with store-bought juices or sodas. Whatever they can get their hands on. Staying adequately hydrated is a challenge, unless you're willing and able to throw disposable income at it."

"And surprisingly few Californians have disposable income these days," said Jose.

"All the more reason why they won't stand for a reduction," said David.

Jose shook his head sympathetically. "They won't know it happened. Decisions like these are made behind closed doors. One Nation Coalition lobbyists have worked hard to push the state's big-picture resource deal making into the secret recesses of the Sacramento statehouse—where money and promises can change hands without public scrutiny. In fact, the details never really see the light of day. From top to bottom, state resource agency operations are highly classified. Can you talk about your job outside the home, Nathan?"

"I'm not really supposed to talk about it inside the home. We all sign nondisclosure agreements."

"The system is like this by design—the ONC's design," said Jose. "Ever hear of Cal Farms United?"

David shrugged.

"It's not a name you hear in the mainstream media or find easily in search engines—*by design*. Cal Farms United owns or represents close to ninety percent of California's remaining agricultural industry, and—surprise, surprise—they are one of the biggest contributors to the ONC. The once beleaguered agricultural industry is a lucrative business now that CFU rigs water distribution and regulates the vast majority of the state's exports. Those poor water-stressed California farmers have no choice but to charge the rest of America exorbitant prices for produce or livestock. Right? And it's not the individual farmer's fault. They're not making a dime more today than they did twenty years ago. CFU takes most of their profits, *graciously* allowing them to stay in business—and feed the greed machine. Trust me when I say this, David. Water will flow to the farms before the people. Ninety-two billion dollars in profit per year guarantees it. Jack Bernal, the head of Cal Farms United, makes the Mexican cartel bosses look like street peddlers. And he's just one of several industrialist kingpins working over the American people. It gets worse."

"I don't know. Sounds a little conspiracy heavy," muttered David.

"I'm not making any of this up. I've spent the better part of a decade investigating the connections between all of these groups, watching it slowly play out. That's the key, you see. This hasn't happened overnight. Californians have been conditioned over time to accept it."

"Did you know all of this?" David asked, nodding at Nathan.

"Not exactly," said Nathan, slightly distracted by the map. "My focus is pretty narrow at work."

"That wasn't always the case," said Jose. "You used to see the big picture. I have a thesis paper written by you at UC–Davis that proves it. I suspect you once cared, too. The tone of your paper is—inflammatory? Accusatory? Both?"

"That was a long time ago."

"They buried your paper pretty damn fast. Classified top secret before it was published. I bet that wasn't a pretty scene."

"I put it behind me."

"Not far enough, apparently," said Jose.

"You figured this out in college?" David asked Nathan.

"Not the Cal Farm United connection."

"It was too early for that," Jose said. "Jack Bernal was still a small-time crook at that point, on the verge of discovering his true place at the big table. Nathan exposed some inconvenient truths about the diversion of water in the Upper Basin, then he had the balls to recommend that the Arizona National Guard seize the Glen Canyon Dam. Your professors at Davis must have swooned over this paper—until the black helicopters showed up."

"Black Suburbans," said Nathan. "I had two hours to sign some serious paperwork to avoid domestic terrorism charges."

"No shit," said David. "Your dad must have blown a gasket."

"He never found out."

"Nobody did," said Jose. "Well, I wouldn't say nobody. Copies survived. You've been on my radar ever since I read it."

Nathan put both hands on the map. "Look, this isn't rocket science. Drop these two dams. Control the Hoover. Water flows to California. I don't see why my paper is a big deal. You need a demolitions expert and a shit ton of explosives, not a water engineer and a thirteen-year-old thesis paper."

"You're not going to take down one of those dams with a demolitions team. The feds will shut you down fast, especially if your tales of corruption are true. At best, you might temporarily disable one of the dams—maybe both of them, if you coordinate a simultaneous strike. Frankly, I'm not seeing the manpower required to pull that off," he said, glancing around the operations center. "Kind of a ghost town around here."

Ghost town. Nathan had been struggling to put his finger on something that had been bothering him since he'd seen the Mexican paratroopers. Now his eyes darted from dam to dam, taking in the scope of Jose's proposed plan. Flaming Gorge Dam was nearly an impossible target; several hundred miles away from any point in California, it had to be a major stretch for the California Liberation Movement. Then he turned to take in the entire room. Empty tables lined two of the walls, leaving only one wall occupied by digital communications gear and Jose's computer station. The fourth wall stood in front of them, covered with maps. This was his fourth visit to the operations center, and in all that time he'd seen only Jose, Jeremy, and maybe two more members of the team. From what he could tell, the center was mostly staffed by security, and there couldn't have more than a few dozen of them.

The numbers didn't add up. None of this added up. He found Jeremy turned in his seat, burning a hole through him with an eerie stare—half grin, half scowl.

Oh shit.

"Something wrong, Nathan?" said Jose.

"You're on your own here," said Nathan, turning his head slowly to the map. "None of this is sanctioned by the CLM."

"It's sanctioned—by a group of us tired of fighting a reactive battle, on the wrong front. Too many in my organization have become so focused on secession that they're missing the bigger picture. Secession won't solve the problem. In fact, it'll probably make it worse. Water liberates California . . . and Arizona . . . and Nevada. This is bigger than California. It has to be."

"Fuck," said David, his hand slinking toward the pistol hidden behind his chest plate. "This is a splinter group? Rogue CLM? We'll take our chances on the streets."

"I wouldn't advise that," said Jose.

"One group hunting us down is enough," David said. "We don't need the CLM after us, too." He shook his head. "I knew this was fucked from the start."

"You did?" said Nathan. "When were you going to mention it?"

"Once we got our bearings—and our weapons. And I wanted some coffee," he said, slowly squaring his body toward Jeremy.

"David," said Jose. "No need to draw your pistol. This is not a prisoner situation."

"Good. Then you won't mind if we depart pronto, like, before Mexicali starts to get really crowded with people looking for this place."

"The rest of CLM has no idea what we have in mind. All they know is that the cartel situation in Mexicali has destabilized to the point that we need to seek a more stable base of operations north of the border. Leaving here was inevitable. No eyebrows will be raised for quite a while. I evacuated personnel not affiliated with my *splinter group* when we learned you'd travel by convoy to Yuma. My original plan involved meeting you on the road soon after you left the base. To have this talk and offer our protection.

"When our aerial surveillance assets detected the Cerberus ambush, I scrambled to get those paratroopers airborne. The Mexicans would not jump until the convoy was attacked. Not my rules. We brought you reinforcements as quickly as possible. Unfortunately, not soon enough."

David's eyes moistened. He swallowed hard, then took a deep breath. Nathan reached out to put a hand on his shoulder, but David shook his head.

"I appreciate what you did, but we're done here," said David, pausing for a few moments before gesturing toward the map. "This is insane, by the way. You'll either get killed or sent to prison for the rest of your lives if you try it."

"That's why we need Nathan's help," said Jose. "And yours."

"How about this: supply us with a get-out-of-Mexicali-free card and a working vehicle. Once we link up with our parents, as far away from here as humanly possible, Nathan will be glad to get in touch with you to fine-tune your suicide mission."

"Maybe it wouldn't hurt to—" Nathan began.

"Negative," said David. "We need to put some distance between this place and your family. You're still my responsibility. And I wouldn't mind seeing the only family I have left before Cerberus takes that away, too."

"We've all lost people to this cycle of greed and corruption," said Jose. "Seeking revenge won't bring them back, but it does occasionally ease the pain. This plan is the most effective way to break a cycle that has ruined millions of lives."

"I need to take care of my own before I even consider diving into something like what you're planning. Nathan needs to do the same."

"Nathan?" said Jose.

He had to tread carefully here. Jose had sounded genuine when he'd said they were not prisoners, but he couldn't imagine him letting them go without making a stronger pitch. Nathan had been through higher-pressure time-share presentations than this. If Jose truly thought he held the key to taking down the dams, he couldn't outright reject the notion of helping in some way.

"Well," he said, "once I get my family somewhere permanently safe—"

"Such a place doesn't exist," said Jose. "Not for long, anyway."

"We have something worked out," said Nathan. "Once we get situated, I'll start by giving a sworn deposition about what I saw at the beach and what's happened over the past three days."

Jose sighed, meeting his stare for a brief moment. "A sworn deposition from a cop killer is meaningless."

"I didn't kill anyone," blurted Nathan.

"We know that. But we're apparently the only ones. Publicly, we can't afford to voluntarily connect with you in any way at this point. That's why Cerberus went the extra mile to frame you for killing a detective. Even David's testimony would be worthless. Trotting him out will only serve to identify him as Pendleton's mystery accomplice, and an accomplice to a cop killer is equally worthless to us in the public relations realm."

"Motherfuckers," said Nathan.

"That's more or less been my personal mantra for the past several years," said Jose.

"I'm not sure how I can help you beyond validating this plan. You have the right targets. You just need to figure out a way to take down both dams."

"We've been stuck at that point for far too long," stated Jose. "And time is running out."

"When I get to safety, I'll try to figure something out."

Nathan knew that sounded terribly weak, if not worthless, but what the fuck did the guy expect? Beyond the fact that Nathan could see no feasible way for Jose's crew to destroy even one of the dams, the thought of compounding his own criminal status by engaging in a blatant act of terrorism gave him serious pause. He couldn't afford to upgrade his fugitive status. Not if he wanted any chance at a normal life for his family. He had to protect Keira and Owen, both short and long term.

"Can I at least provide you with a security escort north through the Wastelands?" Jose said. "I'm not going to pretend this is a selfless offer. I'd like to get you to your destination in one piece."

Nathan was about to accept the offer when David interjected.

"We won't need an escort."

"We won't?" said Nathan.

"No. Too many cars on the road will draw the wrong kind of attention on the ground and in the air. I don't need some disgruntled Border Patrol drone pilot looking to meet his monthly kill quota with the car I'm driving. If you can get us out of Mexicali quietly, we can cross into Arizona farther east along the border. It's more or less quiet at the Nogales crossing, right? That's what our intelligence summary reports indicated."

"*Quiet* is a relative term in Mexico. You could probably get through Nogales without trouble, even at night. Tucson is where it all goes to shit."

"I know Tucson," said Nathan. "We lived there for close to six years."

"It's a little different now."

"We'll be fine," said David.

"All right," Jose said, almost too quickly. "But nobody leaves until dark. We'll work on a way to slip you past the cartel lookouts."

"That's it?" said Nathan.

"That's it. It's in God's hands now," said Jose. "All we can do is pray."

"I didn't take you for the religious type," said David.

"I'm not. But where you're going, I'll make an exception."

Nathan left the room wondering if they hadn't overestimated their chances of successfully navigating Arizona. He'd heard crazy rumors about the Wastelands.

CHAPTER 14

When Jose was certain that Nathan and David had not lingered outside the operations center, he moved a chair next to Jeremy Baker. He took one more look around before nodding. Baker clicked the wireless computer mouse, reactivating the security feed window. The top left-most digital images showed Nathan and David returning to their respective bunk rooms.

"They went their separate ways," said Baker. "Interesting."

"David didn't appear to be in the mood for conversation," said Jose.

"He's a Marine. They don't talk much."

"Or he suspects they're under surveillance."

"Neither of them acted like it earlier. Sorry my people missed the pistol. He's a cautious little fucker, isn't he?"

"*Resourceful* might be a better description. He'd make a great addition to our team, but he isn't close to being receptive. Listen carefully to Nathan's conversation with his wife," said Jose. "He's an open book one minute, totally closed the next. I want to get a better feel for where he stands. I got the distinct impression that he was placating me toward the end of our conversation."

"Are you really letting them head to Nogales alone?" said Baker.

"Alone in a sense. We'll keep them under surveillance. Close enough to respond to an attack."

"Kind of hard to respond to a rocket-propelled grenade attack or a roadside bomb when you're not right on top of it."

"What other choice do we have?"

"It depends upon how important you think this guy might be."

"I honestly don't know yet. I've read his thesis paper backward and forward, but I'm not finding what I really need. He's either purposefully holding back key information we can use, or he doesn't understand the importance of what he has locked up in his head. The guy's still in shock, so getting him to safety and letting him decompress may be our best strategy."

"As long as we can still find him," said Baker.

"Yeah. I have no intention of losing track of Nathan Fisher, or letting any harm come to him."

"Easier said than done. We might have to break a few eggs to get them out anonymously," said Baker.

"We're done here, so break as many as you see fit. But break them quietly. We can't rush our departure."

A message appeared in the bottom corner of the computer monitor screen, grabbing Jose's attention.

"That doesn't look good," he said.

Baker navigated to the messaging application that handled the encrypted reports sent by CLM's network of informants. The system supported direct messages, a function enabled only for the few highly trusted, key contacts in the government, military, or cartel. Only one member of the cartel had been granted this level of access, and he'd just sent a message.

Spydr520: New faces in town with $$$$ and ?'s. Gringos. Want them gone?

The idea was tempting.

"What do you think?" said Jose.

"Disappearing them would buy us the time in the very immediate future, but it could trigger an overwhelming, targeted response. They don't know *anything* for sure. Mexicali is a logical destination from the ambush point, but it's not the only destination. For all they know, we swapped the dune buggies for SUVs in Ciudad Morelos. We could be halfway to Cabo by now. I say let this play out. There's no reason to prematurely draw more of them to Mexicali."

"Sounds good," Jose said, typing on the station's keyboard.

> HoseA: No need to take out the trash yet. Keep a close eye on new faces. Expect more visitors. Will pay extra $$$$ plus unlimited tunnel access to keep our secret.

"We're not blowing the tunnel?"

"They can have it," said Jose. "Without access to our drone feeds, California Border Division will shut his ass down within the week. He has to know there's more to the crossings than meets the eye. He's greedy, not stupid. He won't sell us out unless the Russians get to him. I'm just hoping to buy a buffer until tomorrow morning."

> Spydr520: Consider it done. Anyone who talks is a dead man.

"A lot of good that does us," said Baker. "We need them dead *before* they talk."

Jose nodded.

> HoseA: Much appreciated. Keeping these gringos away keeps business and $$$$ flowing. Keep me posted.

> Spydr520: I'm on it.

"I bet he is," Baker said. "I'll brief the external security team again, and triple our offer to the few independent contacts we have floating around the city."

"Keep an eye and ear on our guests. Their true long-term intentions will determine how we proceed."

CHAPTER 15

Keira tensed when the doorknob clicked, looking instinctively for a weapon. She had the choice between a foldable aluminum shovel taken from her rucksack and a foldable serrated knife she had carried in her back pocket since they'd fled her house in San Diego. She could barely open the knife without cutting herself, so she grabbed the shovel off the dirt floor. It extended her reach and felt heavy enough to hurt badly if smashed down on someone's skull.

Even as she gripped the hollow metal handle, she couldn't believe her thought process had defaulted to cracking someone's head open with shovel. "Welcome to your new life," she muttered to herself as she lifted it high behind her and squared off against the wall beside the door.

When Nathan stepped through it, she lowered the shovel and tried to conceal it behind her leg, but his eyes had already widened.

"Planning on digging your way out?" he said, quickly shutting the door behind him.

"Funny," she said, dropping the shovel.

"Dad!" yelled Owen, shooting past her to hug Nathan.

"Hey, buddy, you're awake!"

"We've been feasting on MREs," Keira said. "I'm developing an unusual fondness for chili mac."

"I thought you liked the brisket?" Nathan said over Owen's head.

"I'm addicted to the jalapeño cheese in the chili mac."

Nathan pulled her into a group hug, holding them tight. After several seconds, he eased up and asked Owen how he was feeling.

"Tired."

"Me, too," said Nathan. "I feel like I've been run over."

"A Javelin missile will do that to you," said his son, eliciting a brief round of laughter.

Keira wasn't sure why she laughed. Probably because their situation defied any sort of logic she could muster—and because she'd never heard of a Javelin missile before one hit them.

"So?" she said. "What's the plan?"

"We're leaving after dark. Sounds like Jose will arrange a way to get out of Mexicali."

"Then what?"

"We head for Nogales. Cross into Arizona and make our way north."

"Alone?" she said, cocking her head.

"No. David's coming along."

"That's not what I meant. Are they going to provide us with an escort?"

"David didn't seem too keen on dragging the CLM along with us. He said we might attract too much attention from Border Patrol drones."

"What does that mean?"

"I'm not totally sure, but he made it sound like the drones might fire on a group of vehicles inside Mexico. Probably drug war related."

"I guess," she said, shaking her head. "Do you think we'll be safe on our own?"

"Jose seemed to think so. He said our biggest problem would be Tucson."

"Tucson? I know it's hit rough times, but how bad can it be?"

"I wish I knew. I haven't talked to anyone there for a few years."

"Everyone we knew left," she said. "Well, at least we know our way around that area. We can avoid the trouble spots."

"Jose made it sound like the whole place was trouble."

"We should try to get in touch with the Marines in Yuma," said Owen. "I bet they'd take care of us."

"I wish we could, Owen," said Nathan, "but the situation is too complicated right now. Our best bet is to disappear until everything gets sorted out."

"Is Mr. Quinn ever going back to the Marines?" said Owen.

"I imagine he will, but for now he's going with us. We're headed north to find Grandma and Grandpa. David's dad is probably with them already. Everybody is hiding for now."

"He doesn't have a mom?"

"If I remember correctly, she passed away a few years ago."

"And now Miss Alison," said Owen, lowering his head.

Keira held her son close, pressing his head into her shoulder. "We're all very sad about what happened," she whispered, squeezing him tighter. "Nothing is going to happen to either of us. We're going to do exactly like your dad said—hide somewhere far away until it's safe. Somewhere with swimming pools."

"Really?" said Owen, pulling his head back a few inches.

"Do you even remember what a swimming pool is like?"

"Not really. Like the ocean?"

"A lot warmer," she said.

"And cleaner," added Nathan. "No trash washing up everywhere."

They hadn't been to the beach for so long, she'd almost forgotten about the continuous flow of plastic refuse assaulting the West Coast. Twice the size of Texas, the Great Pacific Garbage Patch floating between Hawaii and California provided a ceaseless barrage against California's shores, literally covering the beaches after a strong easterly wind or an offshore weather system. Even on a good day, floating debris was visible in small patches beyond the breaking waves of the surf zone, keeping a small army of volunteer beachcombers busy from dawn to dusk.

"Even better," she said. "We'll take you to a lake."

"Have I been to a lake before?" said Owen.

"You have. In Idaho—at Grandma and Grandpa's. You were really little."

"I think I remember that."

She hugged him again, not sure what to say, or if she could say anything without her voice cracking. Her eyes moistened, but they needed to keep Owen as calm and self-confident in this situation as possible. Seeing your parents break down in front of you was not a confidence booster. Nathan looked the same way, rubbing his eyes while Owen's back was to him. The feeling passed a few moments later, and she let her son go.

"So," she said. "What do we do between now and then? We have close to three hours to kill."

"I don't know about you," said Nathan, "but I could eat another MRE and take a nap."

"He's not serious," said Keira to their son.

"He looks serious," he replied.

Nathan had started riffling through the pile of sealed meals, holding one up. "Chili mac. I'm judging by its frequent appearance that it's not a big hit."

Keira snatched the MRE away from him. "Hands off my jalapeño cheese."

A knock on the door froze them all in place. Her eye went to the shovel next to the mattress.

"Come in," said Nathan.

The door opened, revealing the woman she'd seen standing guard the night before and a man she didn't recognize. The woman nodded at them without smiling.

"We brought your weapons and gear, plus some general supplies. Fill your hydration bladders from the water jugs we gave you earlier. I set a few more jugs outside the door if you need them. Stuff any remaining MREs in your backpacks, though I highly suggest you finish those off here. You'll be hungry again in an hour or two, and there's no sense carrying extra weight around town. You have a walk ahead of you tonight."

"How far?" said Keira.

"I don't know yet. You'll be taken to one of our vehicle stashes and escorted to the edge of the town. My guess is they'll take you out Route 2 until you hit the Route 20 interchange. We rarely have trouble out there."

"Is that because you have an arrangement with the cartels or because it's a safer area?" said Nathan.

"Both," she said, neglecting to elaborate.

"How much longer will that arrangement remain in place?" he asked. "You know, with your permanent departure imminent."

What was he talking about?

"Long enough to get everyone out of here," said the woman, unslinging a suppressed rifle from her shoulder and holding it out to Nathan.

It looked like the same rifle he'd used in the desert, except it had been fitted with a suppressor. He accepted the weapon, checking the safety before sliding it over his shoulder. A compact MP-20 submachine gun appeared next, which Keira took out of the woman's hands. It felt unnervingly familiar in her hands after all the time she'd spent with it over the past three days. Another thing she could add to her never-in-a-million-years checklist. She verified that the safety was engaged before placing it on the mattress.

She saw Owen's eyes follow the weapon to its resting place. "Don't touch that," she said to him.

"I need to be able to shoot, too," said Owen.

"Just—don't touch the guns. Please."

She wasn't ready for her son to learn how to handle firearms, though she suspected it was inevitable given their circumstances. In all truth, he probably knew more about guns than she and Nathan combined. He'd acquired quite an education playing video games outside the house. Still, she didn't want him carrying a gun.

"I know how to use one," he pressed. "It's not exactly complicated."

"Listen to your mother, Owen," said Nathan. "And trust me on something. It's far more complicated than you think."

She glanced at her husband and mouthed, "Thank you," receiving a quick wink in return before an unzipped brown duffel bag slid a few feet into the room. Nathan knelt and started digging through the contents.

"You'll find spare mags for your weapons in the bag, along with your helmets. We replaced Ms. Fisher's helmet with one of our own, since we don't have the capability to repair the integrated night-vision system. You'll have to make do with a slightly older-school rig. Still turns night into day, so you'll be fine. We've thrown in some medical kit items and other gear to round out your backpacks. Food and water for your road trip north is already pre-staged in the vehicle. If you can think of anything else, don't hesitate to ask."

"Thank you," said Keira, getting a curt nod from the woman.

"We arrived with an encrypted satphone?" said Nathan.

Keira had almost forgotten about that.

"Captain Quinn's satphone will be returned outside town," said the woman.

"All right," said Nathan. "Thank you. We really appreciate the help. Were you given an exact time for our departure?"

"Nine. Jose would like all of you geared up and waiting in the operations center at eight fifteen, to go over the route and procedures."

"We'll be there," said Nathan.

When the door shut, Keira turned to her husband. "Are they abandoning this place permanently?"

"I need to bring you up to speed on something. Jose sent most of his people north a few days ago."

"How does that make sense?" she said.

When Nathan finished recounting the details of his recent meeting with Jose and David, Keira had a sinking feeling in a stomach that she hadn't thought could go any lower. Jose had gone rogue? This changed everything.

"I think we need to be as far away from Jose and his plan as possible."

"I didn't make any promises," he said. "Our plan is still intact. Meet up with my parents and hide. Whatever David has planned is his own business. If I can think of anything that might help Jose's crew—"

"You can't afford to get involved with him. Our situation is precarious enough, and I don't see that changing for a long time."

"I know. I know. But if I can help from a distance—"

"With all of the technology out there, distance is irrelevant. We have Cerberus hunting us, not to mention every cop in the country looking for you. There's no margin for error. One slipup, electronically, and they could find us," she said, putting a hand on Owen's shoulder.

"Why are the cops looking for Dad?" said Owen.

Keira wasn't sure what to say. A few hours before leaving Camp Pendleton in David's convoy, they'd learned Nathan was a suspect in two murders that he couldn't possibly have committed. They'd decided to keep this from Owen, since he was dealing with enough stress at the time. Things had moved along pretty much nonstop since then. She gave Nathan a nearly imperceptible nod. It was time Owen truly understood what they were up against.

"I don't have all of the details, buddy, but it looks like this Cerberus group framed me for two murders that took place while we were packing to leave. We have to be very careful wherever we go, until I can clear my name."

"Why would they do that?" Owen said. "Why do they hate you so much?"

"I saw something they didn't want anyone to see."

"Like somebody getting killed?" said Owen.

"No. I saw two military stealth boats pull divers out of the ocean close to Del Mar nuclear triad plant about a half hour before something at the plant went wrong. I think the plant was sabotaged by the divers—they snuck into it and purposefully fouled it up—and Cerberus, the people after us, don't want me telling anyone what I saw. Framing me for murder ruins my credibility and puts every cop in the country on the lookout for me."

"Why can't you just promise you won't tell anyone?"

"I wish it was that easy," said Nathan. "I'd gladly make that promise to keep us safe. I just don't think these are the kind of people who make deals like that."

Keira wasn't sure where her husband would take this conversation, or how much her son could process.

"Why can't we go to the police and tell them what happened?" Owen asked. "We can tell them you couldn't have killed anyone. Mr. Quinn could do that, too."

"We can't afford to show our faces anywhere for now. The police would separate us and throw me in jail. They can't protect us from these people."

Keira needed to redirect the conversation. "Owen, honey, we just need to hide from everyone until the authorities can sort it out on their own."

"What if they never sort it out?"

"These things get sorted out, eventually," she said, giving Nathan a quick glance.

Their son looked sadly doubtful. "It might take a little while, buddy, but we'll figure it out. We have some connections through Grandpa that should help speed it along. For now, we're going off the grid, with people we trust. Family."

"We can always have them meet us somewhere south of here," said Keira.

"I don't see any way for my parents to make that trip without drawing the wrong kind of attention. Same for us. David made a good point about Americans not being very welcome in Mexico or Central America. Outside the established tourist areas, we'd come under scrutiny. Possibly be harassed."

"I know. I just like the idea of a little separation from this," she said. "I don't get the impression Jose is going to leave us alone anytime soon. He obviously thinks you're the key to his plan."

"I don't see why," said Nathan. "He knows everything I know."

"That doesn't matter. If he *thinks* you're important, he's not going to let you slip away. You need to keep that in mind until we're safe."

CHAPTER 16

Leeds created a visor with his hand, squinting through his sunglasses at the horizon beyond the runway. A white speck hovered in the distance, just above the shimmering desert horizon. The asphalt runway apron radiated heat in undulating waves, baking his face. He couldn't wait to get back into the air-conditioned vehicles waiting behind them.

"Why are we cooking to death out here?" said Ray Olmos, standing to his immediate left.

"I did a little digging. These guys are hard-core. Jumping out of an air-conditioned SUV at the last minute won't make a good impression."

Leeds watched Olmos take a sip from the hydration pack attached to his vest, shifting the weight off his injured leg. He'd bounced back quickly enough from the mess created by the failed kidnapping attempt outside Nathan Fisher's house, but he was visibly uncomfortable. Leeds had expressed his concerns about bringing him down to Mexicali, but Flagg had insisted, given the complexities of dealing with the Sinaloa cartel.

Olmos had spent twelve years with SEAL Team Four, his entire career focused on operations within Central and South America. He spoke the core Spanish language fluently and was passably familiar with many of the regional colloquialisms and dialect differences among the regions. On top of that, he looked the part. Even Leeds had a hard time arguing with Flagg's logic. Most importantly, Olmos's expertise would allow Leeds to focus on the Russians—arguably the more difficult task.

"Who gives a shit what these mercs think?" said Olmos.

"I do. These mercs give zero fucks about anything but money, and Petrov is paying them a fortune for this job. We're just a means to an end for them. We need to give them the distinct impression that we'll take a few of them with us if they decide we're no longer important."

"You're kidding me, right?"

"Do I look like I'm kidding?" said Leeds. "If you brought pain pills for your leg, I suggest you down a few before they land. You look like a gimp."

"I'm just a little stiff."

"Might as well be missing a leg from their perspective," said Leeds.

"You're serious."

"Dead serious. The initial meet-and-greet means everything. If they sense any form of weakness, they'll test it."

"That's crazy," said Olmos.

"That's the way it works."

"Nice of you to let me know about this a few minutes before they land," said Olmos, shaking his head.

The Gulfstream's tires bit into the concrete runway, briefly screeching before its powerful engines roared into reverse, bringing the elegant luxury jet to a surprisingly rapid stop. The jet taxied onto the apron, the pilot deftly maneuvering the precision machine into position less than forty feet away.

"Here we go," said Leeds, glancing at Olmos.

A quick hiss drew his attention to the rectangular hatch behind the cockpit windows. The hatch lowered mechanically, hinging from the bottom, as an aluminum stairway smoothly unfolded to meet the asphalt. A sun-weathered, hard-looking man emerged from the aircraft, effortlessly descending the stairs with a massive duffel bag. Dressed in desert camouflage pants and a loose-fitting, short-sleeve, button-down shirt, he dropped the bag at the bottom of the stairs and moved swiftly to greet Leeds.

"Arkady Chukov," he said, extending a tattoo-covered arm.

"Nick Leeds. Welcome to Mexicali."

"I understand we have a tight timeline," said Chukov.

"The sooner we wrap this up, the better," said Leeds, glancing over Chukov's shoulder at the team assembling.

The team looked like it had stepped out of a bar fight, and smelled like it, too. Seven amply scarred and heavily tattooed former Spetsnaz soldiers gathered behind Chukov, casting black glares at Olmos.

"My employer tells me you haven't made much progress unearthing our targets," said Chukov.

One of the Russians pulled a silver flask from his vest and offered it to Olmos, muttering, "Vodka," in a heavy accent. *Take him up on the offer, Ray.* Chukov must have sensed his distraction with the unfolding drama.

"Let the boys get acquainted. Do we have a general idea where our targets may be hidden?"

"Mexicali," he said, seeing no change to Chukov's expression. "We've spread enough money around to let the cartel functionaries know they're in for a serious payday if they cough up Fisher. Money loosens tongues down here, along with tequila," said Leeds, nodding at the booze ceremony in progress next to them.

"Piss water compared to vodka," said Chukov, turning to watch.

Olmos took a long swig from the flask, showing no reaction to whatever caustic liquid was surely contained within. When he extended his arm to return it, the Russian sprang forward, launching a fist toward the SEAL's face. Olmos must have anticipated the move. He released the flask and pivoted on his left foot, grasping the Russian's wrist with his left hand and guiding the mercenary's momentum in a downward spiral arc. A quick reversal of the wrist brought the filthy ex-soldier to the pavement, his elbow locked straight and his face pressed into the tarmac. When one of the Russians moved to help his squarely incapacitated teammate, Olmos slipped a compact serrated knife out of an ankle sheath and slid it under the beaten Russian's throat, shaking his head at the approaching mercenary.

"Enough," stated Chukov, raising a hand.

The Russian stopped, melting back into the group. Leeds glanced at Olmos, nodding once. The former SEAL retracted the blade and released the elbow lock, pulling the man up by his wrist. He plucked the flask out of a nearly evaporated puddle and took a swig, holding it upside down in front of the Russian.

"I owe you a refill," said Olmos.

"Keep it, Chicano," the Russian replied, pulling another flask from one of his vest pouches and belting it back.

The seamless replacement of the Russian's alcohol supply didn't exactly inspire the highest level of confidence in the group. They appeared to carry more booze than ammunition. Maybe this wasn't one of Flagg's best ideas. Actually, Leeds was quite certain it was one of his boss's worst ideas, but options had been slim at the time. He'd have to make this work.

"Ray. Get them organized in the vehicles," said Leeds. "We need to get moving."

"Where are we headed?" said Chukov, picking up his bag.

"Safe house in southwestern downtown area. Our contacts report that a convoy of SUVs entered the city around three thirty a.m., headed west on Route 2. They were last seen near Route 5, which cuts the city in half from north to south. We're in a good position to rapidly investigate tips."

"We don't have time for this loosening-tongues business you talk about. Petrov wants the cartel spilling their guts to us now."

"That's not how it works down here. The whole town works for the cartel. If we crack the wrong skulls, we run the risk of turning the cartel against us. Ten of us against thousands of wannabe gangbangers is a recipe for getting skinned alive."

"If we do this my way," said Chukov, "we'll be done before anyone notices the skulls cracked."

"What do you need from me?"

"I need a list of names, organized by rank and affiliation within the cartel. You don't hit anyone too high until you've verified they have what you're looking for. We work through middle management until we identify someone rumored or confirmed to be dealing with outsiders. Gringos in particular. Nobody in the middle gives a shit what happens to the guy next to them. Less competition. We've done this before."

"I can get you what you're looking for. A few low- to middle-range guys. Even a high-level contact—when you're ready."

"I'm ready, Nick Leeds. I'm ready to quit wasting Mr. Petrov's time," he said, walking toward the lead SUV.

Nick met Olmos next to the convoy, patting him on the shoulder. "That was quite a move. How does that leg feel?"

"Like someone slammed a car door on it," said Olmos. "I have you and Chukov in the lead SUV, with two of his guys in the back. Myself and three more trailing in the second, with the final two taking the sedan. Looks like you're driving. None of them seemed interested, and Chukov just took your seat."

"That's fine. I think most of them are too drunk to drive anyway."

Olmos shook his head. "We could have outsourced this to a contract team looking to get on the Cerberus payroll. Plenty of solid crews out there to choose from."

"I made the same recommendation to Flagg, but he felt Petrov's hired guns would be better suited for the job," said Leeds. "I'm starting to think he might be right. Chukov's men look unstable enough to pull this off."

"Without getting us killed?" said Olmos.

"That'll be the tricky part. Knowing when to gently tug on Chukov's leash," said Leeds.

"Good luck with that."

Leeds grimaced. "Get ready to roll. I'll call this in to Flagg and see if he can dig up more names for Chukov to visit."

CHAPTER 17

Flagg typed the last few lines of an update to Ethan Burridge and John Peralta and pressed "Send." That should keep them happy for a while. Long enough to get things back on track and moving in the right direction.

Everything he had typed was true. He'd just omitted the part about going behind their backs with Petrov to tie up the loose ends he'd previously reported eliminated. If all went well tonight, the Russians would close the loop on Nathan Fisher in Mexico, and Riggs would shut the last open door on Fisher's father in Montana, leaving nothing to bite Flagg's operation in the ass.

Almost nothing.

The fact that the California Liberation Movement had taken such extreme measures to protect Nathan Fisher remained more than a bit unsettling. Flagg still couldn't figure out how they had identified him in the first place. The scope and complexity of the CLM's rapidly mounted interest in Fisher suggested a traitor in Flagg's organization, or a higher-level mole at Cerberus. He'd soon have a better idea of what he faced in terms of a leak. The ongoing effort to locate and kill Fisher had been assigned to his most trusted operatives in Southern California. If Fisher narrowly escaped another impossible situation, he'd know the problem originated close to home.

His computer screen indicated an incoming call from Riggs. This could be the breakthrough he had been waiting for in Montana. They had gotten lucky with one of the security cameras inside Starbucks, which had caught the license plate of the Jeep that had dropped off Jon and Leah Fisher.

He figured Nissie Keane had something up her sleeve, but like all of her previous jobs for Cerberus, she refused to give him mirrored access to everything her team could see. She was crafty that way, parsing just enough live data to keep him satisfied they were worth the money, without giving him the kind of full access that might strip away the mysteries of her profession, leaving her vulnerable to replacement. Most importantly, she never withheld the information he paid dearly to acquire. She'd mastered a delicate balance that kept him coming back for more, especially when the job required some distance from Cerberus oversight.

Flagg accepted Riggs's call.

"Do we have a name and address yet?"

"The Jeep wasn't traceable to an individual. It's registered to SusCorps, an LLC located in Billings, Montana."

"Dummy corporation?"

"Sort of. The address on record for the LLC belongs to a company that provides registered agent services."

"A cutout," said Flagg. "We should still be able to get some names from corporate documents."

"Montana doesn't require corporations to list company directors or officers. Miss Keane hacked into their files."

"Of course." Flagg sighed. "Am I being too hopeful to wish for a listing of real estate assets with addresses?"

"No real estate listed. Just vehicles purchased by the corporation."

"How many vehicles?"

"Twenty-two," said Riggs, "plus several boats."

He'd expected to hear two or three. Twenty-two? It sounded like Jon Fisher might have tapped into something a little more organized than a sympathetic Marine buddy with a spare bedroom and a not-so-thrilled wife.

"That's a damned fleet," muttered Flag. "Don't make any assumptions about your security situation up there. Can Miss Keane track any of the twenty-two vehicles? I'm guessing not."

"She's saying no. DMV registration doesn't show a link to any GPS listings. And it turns out that Montana is one of six states that refuses to allow the use of automated license plate–reading technology."

"This is the worst phone call I've had all day," said Flagg before an idea flashed through his head. "Crazy question. Have you run the Jeep's plates for moving violations?"

The ensuing silence answered his question. "Hello?"

"Hold on, sir," said Riggs.

"It's a simple question."

"Fucking idiot."

"I hope that wasn't directed at me," said Flagg.

"No. That was directed at myself. Speeding violation dated July 25, 2033. License information on the citation identifies the driver of the Jeep as Scott W. Gleason of 5190 Clearview Way, Missoula, Montana. Miss Keane is searching for any local links to Mr. Gleason."

"I highly doubt she'll find anything. Gleason and his friends have gone to considerable lengths to conceal their identities," said Flagg. "Have her run all of the license plates for other moving violations. We might find a pattern."

"She's already on it," said Riggs. "I bet these guys are ex-military."

"I guarantee it."

He typed the search string SCOTT W. GLEASON UNITED STATES MARINE CORPS into a custom-programmed Department of Defense and government agency database search engine. The program simultaneously penetrated dozens of personnel databases, anonymously searching hundreds of petabytes of data stored by the government.

Riggs spoke up. "Keane's initial search turned up empty, outside of a driver's license in his name. Do you need his birth date?"

The screen in front of Flagg filled with compiled information, including several photographs taken at various points in retired Marine First Sergeant Scott W. Gleason's thirty-one-year career.

"No. I found him. You're dealing with a retired infantry Marine who spent the latter part of his career teaching at the Mountain Warfare Training Center in Bridgeport, California. Combat tours in Afghanistan. No surprise there. Both Jon Fisher and Stuart Quinn served in Afghanistan during the same time frame, though Gleason wasn't in the same unit. The plot thickens."

"Any sign of Stuart Quinn yet?" said Riggs.

"You'll be the first to know if we get a hit on him, though I'm not holding my breath."

"Sounds like they're getting the band back together."

"It certainly looks that way," said Flagg. He paused a moment, considering how to proceed. "All right. Check out the Clearview Way address very carefully. Use some of Miss Keane's team if necessary. No offense, but your guys don't exactly look like the suburbs types. From what I'm seeing on Google Earth, this is a tidy townhome development."

"Believe me, you'd be better off with my guys. Have you ever seen her team? They look like aliens. We can head over to the Gap and pick up some clothes."

"Just be careful. One pass only. Multiple cameras running so you can analyze the exterior. I see a few opportunities for surveillance nearby, but you'll have to wait for nightfall. You know the drill."

"Got it," said Riggs.

"I want Jon and Leah Fisher alive. I can't stress that enough. Taking Stuart Quinn alive is a bonus, but not required. I'll pay a kicker either way. Thirty percent for everyone involved. Standard rates."

"You say alive would be a bonus," said Riggs. "That means you're *paying* one if we deliver him alive?"

"You manage it without fucking anything up, I'll pay more."

"How much more?"

"I'm not going to tell you. I'll roll a pair of dice after you deliver."

"I hate when you do that," said Riggs.

"I'd rather you pursued the easy money and just took him out, but if a no-shit, zero-risk opportunity arises, there's no reason you shouldn't get paid a premium. He could have information we can use."

"Sounds good," said Riggs, the call ending.

Flagg ran both hands through his thick black hair. Riggs gave him pause sometimes, but he'd never failed to produce results. Same with Nissie Keane, which was why he'd paired the two teams together. If initial reconnaissance of the town house revealed more than the Fishers and their host, he could have a second contract team in Missoula within six hours.

He clicked on a few commands to upload everything he'd found on Scott Gleason to Nissie Keane. She might find something useful in the glut of career information contained in the compiled data.

With the Montana situation moving forward, he turned his attention to the screen detailing the progress made in Mexico—or lack of progress. Hopefully, that was about to change. The Russians sounded just as unsavory as he had hoped, more than willing to ignore convention and spill some blood to appease their paymaster. The Russians would unearth Fisher soon enough.

He'd give the Mexicali drama time to play out before recalling Leeds. He needed Nick to shepherd the next big step in his plan to completely bury any realistic hope of an independent California. The pendulum of public opinion had swung squarely in favor of keeping the status quo favored by his clients, thanks to Flagg's skillful manipulation of events.

It made no logical sense for the California Liberation Movement to sabotage the nuclear triad plant in Del Mar, but throw Nathan Fisher's role in the murder of a police detective and a nuclear plant engineer into the mix, and conspiracy-hungry Californians were off and running. Fisher's bank accounts flush with cash and digital evidence suggesting frequent contact with CLM leaders sealed the deal. Top that with Lieutenant Governor McDaid's assassination, and it was hard to shed a sympathetic light on the only radical group with a reason to kill the blatantly antisecessionist lieutenant governor. Even the blame for Congresswoman Almeda's assassination back in Washington, DC, had started to migrate in CLM's direction.

It was endlessly amusing for Flagg to watch the public respond to the media's foregone conclusions, all influenced if not outright purchased by Cerberus money. Now Californians needed one more push, and Flagg intended to deliver it—just as soon as he took care of a few annoying loose ends.

Chapter 18

Nathan checked the makeshift ballistic vest provided to Owen by Jose's team. Not a bad fit for something put together in a hurry from extra pieces of gear. Nathan pressed against the enhanced chest plate protecting his son's critical organs from small-arms fire, wishing they could have fitted him with one of the liquid-gel vests. Not only was the latest-generation liquid-gel armor lighter, but it also dispersed the blunt force trauma of a bullet strike far more efficiently, cutting down on cracked sternums and internal organ damage.

He slapped the back plate. "Looking good, buddy. Mr. Quinn said this plate will stop a 50-caliber bullet."

"Why can't I have one like yours?" said Owen, pressing against Nathan's vest.

"The gel inserts were too big to work with. They had some extrasmall plates used in concealed vests that better fit your chest. They tried, but the only way to get it to work was to fold the gel packs. Doing that messed with the gel's sheer thickening effect."

"I've seen this stuff on the Military Channel. If something hits it, it hardens. I don't see why they couldn't use it."

"Is that what the two of you watch when I'm not home?" said Keira, who pulled the MP-20's sling over her shoulder like David had shown her.

"The Military Channel is the least of your problems when the guys are hanging out," Nathan said, then turned back to Owen. "It needs to lie mostly flat to function properly. Something about dispersing energy over a wider area. You'll be fine, buddy. We won't need any of this." He grabbed both of Owen's shoulders. "You ready?"

His son nodded, a nervous look passing over his face.

"You, Keira?"

"As I'll ever be."

"All right. Let's do it."

The guard outside their door stood from his chair as they approached and was leading them up the cramped hallway when the door at the end burst inward. The young man dropped to one knee and raised his rifle as David rushed into the corridor, stopping at the sight of the rifle barrel.

"Jesus," said the guard, lowering his weapon and rising to his feet. "You trying to get killed?"

"Didn't they call you?" said David.

"No. Nobody called to say you'd be kicking the door in."

"That's not my problem," David said, gesturing for Nathan to step forward. "We're going right now. Quick briefing with Jose, then we're out the door."

"Is something wrong?" said Nathan.

"Jose didn't say, but considering the fact that they've moved up the timeline by thirty minutes, I'd say something wasn't right."

"Great."

David led them through the tunnels to the operations center, where they gathered with Jose and two serious-looking men in front of a city map. Jose handed Nathan a tattered, compactly folded AAA map.

"I highlighted the route you need to take to reach Nogales. Do not alter the route under any circumstances. Route 2 is generally safe, but the side roads can be a different story."

"What if Route 2 is blocked?"

"Then you'll have to take one of the side roads. Not a lot of choices. Do you want to rethink my offer to escort you north?"

"We're good," David interjected. "What's up with the fire drill?"

"A jet just landed at one of the private strips to the south. The same guys that have been spreading money around the city all afternoon picked up the passengers."

"Passengers?" said Nathan.

"Eight men," said Jose, handing Nathan a digital tablet. "Professional soldiers, by the look of them."

The screen showed a group of deeply tanned, unshaven, dark-haired men carrying overstuffed duffel bags. They wore an uncoordinated array of street clothes, with a few hip holsters visible under loose-fitting, button-down shirts. Their attention was focused on two sharply dressed men standing in front of a three-vehicle convoy.

David pulled his arm to get a better view of the tablet screen. "They're pros, all right. What do you know about the two suits?"

"We've identified the paler gentleman as Nick Leeds. Sources indicate he's former CIA. Special Operations Group. Based on what little we know about the Cerberus operational structure, my guess is he's the operational area's second in command."

"And the other guy's number one?" said Nathan.

"Doubt it," said Jose. "This is just an errand run. An important one, maybe, but not important enough to drag an operational head to this shithole."

"This is a Cerberus team?" David asked. "Kind of rough looking compared to what we've seen so far."

"Not sure. Logic says they're Cerberus, but something is off," said Jose, checking his watch. "We need to get you out of here. This picture is forty minutes old."

"Forty minutes!" hissed Keira. "How far away is the airport?"

"I'm confident this location hasn't been compromised yet. They drove to a location even farther away, so we've got a buffer."

"Still," David said. "Can your team brief us on the way out? I'd like to get moving."

"Give me thirty seconds of your undivided attention, and I'll turn you loose." Jose pressed his finger against a street-level map tacked to the wall next to him. "This is your starting point. You'll—"

"Jesus, I didn't realize we were this close to the border," said David. "What is that, two hundred feet?"

"More or less," answered Jose. "Foot and vehicle traffic are light on Francisco Madero at night, so it's our best option. You'll be in a tunnel for about a hundred feet to get there, and it'll put you out at the back of a vacant lot facing the road. Do exactly as your escorts say. Getting out of that exit might be a little tricky."

"I presume this is our escort?" said David, nodding at the silent duo standing behind Jose.

"Meet Alpha and Bravo. We kept it simple for you. You can tell them apart by the A and B duct-taped to the front and back of their ball caps. No names, just Alpha and Bravo."

David nodded.

Nathan looked them over. Fit, no-nonsense types wearing local clothing over concealed tactical vests. Compact night-vision headsets fitted under their hats. Each carried a short-barreled version of Nathan's rifle, fitted with a hefty suppressor and magnified optical sight. An imposing pair, for sure, but he'd expected a slightly larger group—like an infantry squad.

"Only two of them?" he said.

"We're moving an armed group on foot through a dense urban area. The six of you will attract enough attention. Can we get back to the map?"

Nathan nodded, following Jose's hand.

"Your escorts will determine the best route, so follow them closely. If you get separated from them, head east until you reach Calle H, then turn south. Your destination is located between Calle H and Calle I on

Avenida Marmoleros Sur. Just get yourself to that block and we'll take care of the rest. Two point one miles total."

"Why can't we drive there?" Nathan asked. "It would take us three minutes."

"Noncartel vehicle traffic is rare in Mexicali, especially at night."

"And six people dressed in tactical gear carrying weapons is common?"

Jose smirked.

"Can we get going?" David asked.

"We're going to knock out the power grid for about twenty minutes to cover your movement," Jose said. "You'll be deep into the neighborhoods when the lights return. Power outages are pretty standard in Mexicali. Any questions?"

Nathan turned to his wife and son, who shook their heads. He turned back to Jose. "We're ready."

"All right. Good luck to you and your family, Nathan. I hope our paths cross again. We could use your help," said Jose, extending a hand.

He accepted the gesture, then watched as the man shook Owen's hand and patted him on the shoulder, then grasped Keira's hand firmly. "Keep him out of trouble," he said.

"We wouldn't be here if I had any say in that," she said.

Jose smiled. "It's not too late to reconsider my offer. We can protect your family."

"Man, you're relentless," said David, breaking in. "We're be fine. Thank you for saving the rest of my Marines last night. Good luck with your mission. God knows California could use a break."

Jose raised a handheld radio. "Cut power in nine-zero seconds."

A digital voice responded. "Copy that. Cut power in one and a half minutes."

"Let's go," said Alpha, hustling to a closed door set in the far right corner of the wall holding up the maps. He reached for the door handle, pausing to address the group. "We move single file, in the following order, until we reach our destination or you're given different instructions. This is our default formation: Alpha and Bravo first, followed by Nathan, Owen, and Keira, in that order. David brings up the rear. The three Fishers keep their safeties engaged. Everyone else exits the tunnel cleared hot."

"My son isn't packing," said Nathan, immediately regretting his joke.

"He should. Especially out here," said Alpha, cracking a short-lived smile. "Don't worry. We'll take good care of Mr. Owen. Just stay close at all times, and stay down if the shit hits the fan. Clear?"

"Clear," said Keira.

"Clear," he added.

"The missus beat you to it," said Alpha. "Time to boogie."

He yanked the door open, exposing a mostly dark void, lit sporadically by light green chem lights. The lights barely illuminated the tunnel, serving little purpose beyond proving that the murky abyss indeed continued forward.

"Night vision on," said Alpha, pushing his goggles in front of his face. "Hands grab the person in front of you. Short, quick steps until we get to the exit."

Nathan pressed a hand against the front of his helmet and slid the integrated visor down, suddenly able to see all the way to the end of the shoulder-width tunnel. He turned to his son, who had already lowered his visor.

"Good to go, buddy?"

His son nodded, apparently too excited to use words.

Keira pulled the night-vision goggles mounted to her helmet down in front of her eyes. A faint green glow illuminated her face.

"I'm good," she said, giving him a thumbs-up.

By the time Nathan faced forward again, Alpha and then Bravo had entered the tunnel. He shuffled into place behind the second escort, placing his hand on the man's shoulder. He felt a slight tug on his own backpack. With the chain complete, he moved deeper into the tunnel, keeping pace with the two men assigned to protect them.

Less than a minute later, they reached the end, where two armed sentries hid next to a short stairwell leading upward through the tunnel's ceiling. Alpha continued up the wooden stairs as the rest of the group huddled underneath him.

"Five seconds," said one of the sentries. "Four. Three. Two. One. Lights out."

Nathan watched Alpha put a shoulder into the rectangular metal door at the top of the stairs, swinging it out of the way on silent hinges and instantly aiming his rifle toward a figure on the roof of an adjacent low-rise building. The figure moved frantically, both hands raised to his head as he fumbled with the head strap of his night-vision goggles. A green laser from Alpha's rifle connected with the man's head, immediately followed by two suppressed cracks. The man dropped out of sight.

"Primary overwatch target down. Looking for secondaries," said Alpha, exiting the tunnel with Bravo close behind, the two of them leaving Nathan and his family hunched in place.

A few seconds later, they heard several snaps outside the tunnel entrance, each sounding no louder than a prematurely triggered, empty mousetrap.

"All clear," whispered a voice from above. "Let's go."

Nathan climbed the short, makeshift staircase with Owen and Keira close behind, climbing out of the cool tunnel into a blast furnace of desert air and a patch of dried-out scrub at the back of a rectangular lot. A shoulder-height, chipped stucco wall flanked the right side of the lot to the street, where a crooked chain-link fence extended across the face of the desert weed–infested lot to the corner of the bare, two-story building on their left. A small stain midway down the lip of this building's roof marked where the first cartel lookout had died. Nathan had no idea where the others Alpha and Bravo had taken down had fallen.

David moved past them, his rifle trained on the street beyond the chain-link fence. Nathan flipped his night-vision visor up for a second, curious to gauge the impact of the CLM-induced blackout. The sky beyond the building to their left glowed deep blue, casting a faint twilight hue over the lot. Dark enough.

"This way," whispered one of their escorts from darkness at the back of the lot.

Nathan lowered his visor and followed the men toward a human-size gap in the cinder-block wall spanning the rear of the lot. Automatic gunfire erupted in the distance, echoing off the buildings surrounding them. Nathan stopped and raised his rifle. Another burst of gunfire tore through the night.

"This is a bad idea," he muttered, rubbing the selector switch on his rifle with his thumb.

At the gap in the wall, Bravo glanced back over his shoulder. "This is completely normal for Mexicali. Nothing to worry about."

Nathan and Keira shared a blank look, then he took their son's hand and slipped with Keira through the gap into a long-neglected alley and turned east.

Two point one miles to go—through a city gone mad. *Nothing to worry about at all.*

CHAPTER 19

David trailed Keira by several steps, already drenched in sweat in the stifling heat. His position in the back required him to scan the area behind the group for threats while keeping track of the formation's movement, a juggling act made all the more difficult by the Fishers' erratic progress. The frequent sound of distant gunfire stopped one of them nearly every time, once again halting the group's advance along the empty alley. He understood the family's hesitation and fear on a logical level, but it frustrated him nonetheless. After the first dozen harmless bursts of faraway automatic weapons fire, he had expected them to adjust to their environment.

A prolonged chain of deep thumps resounded through the alley, freezing all the Fishers in their tracks. David turned to face the rear, sweeping his rifle across the alley.

"What the hell is that?" whispered Nathan.

David turned his head and put a gloved finger to his lips before leaning close to Keira. "Probably a 50-caliber machine gun," he whispered in her ear. "Nowhere close to us. Pass it on, quietly."

He resumed his vigil, silently watching the alley until he heard his group resume their advance behind him, their boots softly scraping the ground. He waited a few seconds and then started after them, walking backward and glancing back every so often to track the formation's progress. They proceeded at a fast walk for another minute, until Alpha raised a fist and took a knee, leaning against the graffiti-covered concrete wall that framed the left side of the alley. Bravo nestled in behind him, holding an open hand to the Fishers, who tucked themselves in against the wall a few paces back. David saw the wide boulevard ahead, representing their first passive obstacle. A few moments later, Alpha signaled him forward.

"This is Calle Gaston Salazar," he whispered when David had taken a knee next to him. "Calle D, if you're keeping track of the grid. It's one of the busier roads up here during the day. Sounds and looks quiet now, but we're still going to cross in small groups. I'll go first, by myself, setting up at the corner of that garage. Bravo will bring the family across, with you holding down the fort on this side of the street. Anyone on the street not associated with this group is a priority target. We can't risk detection. Good to go?"

"Good to go," said David, though he was a little surprised by the rules of engagement. *Anyone* on the street? A little extreme. He'd make that call on a case-by-case basis. He had no intention of shooting someone walking home with groceries.

Once the Fishers had been briefed by Bravo, Alpha edged forward along the wall until he reached a twisted, wrought-iron fence extending to the sidewalk. Beyond a few scattered, very distant gunshots, the street was deathly still. Either nobody dared to venture onto the streets at night in a blackout, or the night was just getting started. Either way, he liked what he heard. They had a thirty- to forty-minute transit ahead of them. Quiet was good.

David settled into position behind the Fishers and trained his weapon back down the alley. Alpha had crossed the street by the time he looked over his shoulder to check. The operative crouched next to the one-story garage, swept his rifle in a slow arc from left to right, then summoned Bravo with a hand signal. Bravo led the Fishers in a dead

Steven Konkoly

sprint across the street and past the concealed operative, continuing deep into the alley, where they huddled in a shallow doorway.

David kept his eyes on Alpha, waiting for his turn to cross. A nod from Alpha launched him forward. He was racing across the street when a voice yelled something in Spanish, causing him to slow and level his rifle. A car door had opened to David's right and deposited a scraggly, bald male on the street. David placed the rifle sight's green circular reticle in the center of the man's head, applying pressure to the trigger. *Anyone on the street.*

"Whoa. Whoa. Whoa. *¿Qué pasa, amigo?*" yelled the man, holding his hands above his head. *"¿Estás perdido?"* He had no idea what the guy was saying, but he appeared to pose no threat to the group. The man's head snapped back, a sharp crack reaching David's ear before the body collapsed to the street.

"Get out of the fucking street," hissed Alpha.

David cleared the road and joined the Fishers in the doorway. Alpha slid next to him a second later.

"The cartel has people everywhere—standing on rooftops, hanging out on porches, hiding in bushes . . . sitting in fucking cars. They get paid if they report something useful to the cartels."

"What kind of idiot lookout exposes himself like that?"

"It's a risk we can't take. That's why we shoot anyone on the street that might be in a position to see us. I thought I was pretty clear on that point. This is too important to take a chance."

David had no intention of burning a kid taking out the trash—or letting one of these fuckers do it. This wasn't how Marines operated.

Alpha patted him on the shoulder. "Hey. Don't get wrapped over this. Shaved head. Tattoos on his neck. The guy was cartel, or a cartel wannabe. We don't discriminate. Trust me, that's all you're gonna see out here."

"And if I see something else?"

"Then look the other way. Unless I see a grandma in a wheelchair or a kid riding a tricycle, I'm not taking any chances."

"We're burning through our blackout window," whispered Bravo.

"Copy that," said Alpha, standing up. "You good?"

"Good as I'll get," said David, glancing toward the street. "So we just leave him there?"

"Nobody gives a shit about a lone lookout going down. If they find more than one—that's a different story. But you'll be long gone before anyone connects those dots," he said. "Same formation. Let's go." Alpha and Bravo started down the next alley.

"What was that all about?" Nathan asked David, stopping after he'd led his family out of the recessed doorway and into the alley.

"They popped a cartel lookout down the road."

"It sounded like you two were arguing."

"Come on," David said. "Down the alley." When Nathan had slipped past him, David checked Calle Gaston Salazar one more time. Nothing but a dead man in the street.

Nathan was waiting for him in the alley. "What were you arguing about?"

"The guy they shot was unarmed," David said. "Kind of goes against everything I've ever stood for as a Marine. But I don't doubt they're right. I need to recalibrate fast, or I'm going to get us killed. The guys after us won't think twice about drilling us through the forehead."

"Hey. Your instincts got us this far. If you think something's wrong with these guys, we're with you one hundred percent—no matter what you choose to do."

"I think we're where we need to be," said David, putting a hand on his shoulder. "Thanks for that. Now we better get moving," he said, nudging Nathan toward the others, who'd just slipped out of sight around a bend in the alley.

Following Nathan, David mentally reviewed their progress. Thirty-minute walk? Not likely. They'd be lucky to get to their vehicle within an hour at this rate. They had to cross three more streets before turning south on Calle H, and that's where the real fun started. He'd counted at least fifteen cross streets standing in their way, at least three of them major east-west thoroughfares. A glance at his watch showed they had about fifteen minutes until Jose's people restored the electrical grid. Odds were good that they'd have to cross at least one of those bigger roads with the lights on.

Chapter 20

Nathan raised his night-vision visor to wipe a thick sheen of sweat off his face, frightened to discover that he didn't need the light-enhancing device to see the road ahead of them. They were about to cross the busiest street on their transit, and the whole road glowed orange! How long had they been walking the streets exposed? He glanced over his shoulder, calming down slightly. The portion of Calle H they had just left behind remained dark, only scattered lights poking through the haphazardly boarded windows of the homes lining the street.

Still, the fact that they had approached an illuminated intersection unaware cast serious doubt on their escorts' capabilities. He tapped Bravo on the shoulder, interrupting a hushed conversation with the other operator.

Bravo turned his head and whispered, "What's up?"

"The lights are back on."

They were huddled between a rusted, flat-tired sedan and the crumbled sidewalk on the left side of the road. A tall, pockmarked stucco wall stood flush with the walk. Several feet behind them, a sturdy metal gate sat in the middle of the wall, guarded diligently by David. An unlit Pemex gas station canopy loomed over their corner of the intersection, visible through the palms lining the southern edge of the house.

"They've been on for three minutes," said Bravo.

"Aren't we a little close to the road given the light situation?"

Bravo shifted to face him. "Lower your visor and check the ambient light reading in the top right corner. Should read close to AL12. Your night-vision device measures the available light and displays it as a percentage compared to normal daylight conditions. Under twenty percent is considered dusk—difficult to see without help. Under ten is as good as dark."

Nathan lowered his visor and found the reading—AL11. A second green symbol sat directly below it—DL42.

"What if it goes higher than twenty?"

"If it goes higher than twenty, we toggle between normal and night-vision mode to make a better assessment of our surroundings."

"How do you toggle?" said Nathan, feeling along the lip of his helmet for a button.

"Raise your visor up and down," he said. "Low-tech."

"And how did you know the lights were on?"

"You like questions, don't you?"

"You guys won't always be around," said Nathan.

"Good point. Radio."

"And what if you didn't have the radio? We could be in the road before the ambient light reading raised an alarm."

"Do you see the second symbol, directly below ambient light?"

"Yeah. DL42."

"That's your distant light reading. It measures the brightest detected light levels in your visor's center reticle. DL42 means we will be plenty visible when we cross the road."

"That doesn't sound good."

"It's not. We're coming up with a game plan, which will likely involve running and shooting. I need to get back to that meeting," he said, turning to continue his whispered conversation with Alpha.

Keira pressed up close to him. "What's going on?"

"They're figuring out what to do about the well-lit road ahead."

"Shoot out the lights?"

"It's probably not that simple."

Alpha crawled on all fours around Bravo to a position next to Nathan and Keira, calling Owen and David into a huddle beside the car.

"We're going to shoot out the two closest lights during the next long burst of cartel gunfire, gauge the street for a response, then cross all at once. Dead sprint. You a strong runner, Owen?"

"Yes, sir."

"Good. Because we're not gonna stop at the other side. We have to keep running past the business on Avenida Zaragoza. You don't stop for any reason. Copy?"

"Copy," said Owen, looking up at Nathan.

"He's good," said Nathan, squeezing his shoulder.

"I'm not worried about Owen," said Alpha.

"We're good, too."

"All right. Bravo and I will take covering positions near the street. I'll take the Pemex station gas island. He'll hide behind the low wall on the corner across Calle H. We'll hit the lights from there and wait. When you see me signal, starting running down the middle of the street. We'll join you on the flanks as you pass. David leads the way and covers forward. Any questions?"

"Same ROE?" said David.

"We'll let you know when it changes," said Alpha. "Ready?"

They all nodded and muttered readiness. The two commandos moved to the front edge of the car and knelt, seemingly in no hurry to run across open ground to their positions. They appeared to be listening. Without warning, they burst forward, splitting apart. Alpha arrived at the gas station quicker than Nathan thought possible, crouching behind a thick concrete crash barrier forming a V shape at the edge of the intersection. The second commando slid into position on the ground behind the thigh-high brick wall across the street.

Nathan couldn't see the streetlights illuminating the intersection but guessed Bravo had sighted in on the light beyond the gas station, keeping the wall to his back for protection. When Alpha braced his rifle against the top of the barrier and aimed in Bravo's direction, Nathan knew he was right. Now it was just a matter of waiting for another drunk cartel jackass to fire his weapon in the air.

"Any time now," Nathan said over his shoulder, feeling his son press against him.

They didn't have to wait long. A brief torrent of gunfire ripped through the night—including two suppressed cracks from Alpha and Bravo's rifles. The symbols in Nathan's visor changed. AL4. DL13. Nearly pitch-dark by the car. Still a little light on the street, but safe to cross—according to Alpha. Then again, it had been dark when they shot the cartel lookout in the street a mile or so back. He kept focused on Alpha, waiting for the signal.

Nathan sensed the deep vibration before he heard it, the sensory impact triggering a memory of sitting in traffic. When the next thrum buzzed through him, he recognized the sound, taking a step backward into his son. One of those crazy bass systems idiots liked to crank in their cars.

"There's a car coming," he whispered, checking to see if David was watching the street behind them.

"All clear back here," said David, scanning the street with his rifle.

When Nathan looked back toward the intersection, he saw Alpha's head lower behind the barrier. Nathan had no intention of raising his head any higher to check on the other operative. As the bass thumping got deeper and louder, Nathan flipped his visor up to take advantage of the one visual trick his synthetic daylight, night-vision system couldn't replicate.

The gas station disappeared, slowly rematerializing in the soft glow of approaching headlights. As the bass vibrations grew stronger, the light bathing the right side of the concrete barrier intensified. As the lights turned in Nathan's direction, he pulled Owen to the ground next to the curb, Keira and David dropping low with them. Light poured over the car hiding them, creating a moving shadow as the vehicle thumped past. He held his breath, waiting for the squeak of the brakes or the telltale red glow. He'd emerge gun blazing if the car stopped.

As the bass faded far to the north on Calle H, Nathan lowered his night-vision visor. Alpha had risen into view above the barrier he'd been hiding behind and was motioning emphatically. Shit. He wanted them to cross the intersection right now? There was no other way to interpret the signal. It was time.

"We're going now," said Nathan, pulling his son to his feet. "In three, two—"

"Not in the middle of the street, please," said David.

"Agreed. And we stay together," said Nathan. "Go!"

They ran together, at a swift, controlled pace, toward the intersection. Nowhere close to a dead sprint, because he didn't want his family spread out across the road—plus, his backpack hurt like a bitch when he ran. If his hurt, Keira's hurt. Nathan set the speed, constantly checking on their son's progress. So far, they looked fine.

When they hit the intersection, Alpha and Bravo raced into position on their flanks, matching the pace. A quick glance to his right down Avenida Zaragoza showed it to be empty of vehicle or pedestrian traffic. He never got to look in the other direction. A sustained burst of staccato gunfire boomed nearby, and he heard bullets snapping overhead and buzzing through their formation.

Nathan yanked his son and wife to the dusty pavement as several rounds zipped inches above them. Alpha landed on his back with a thud ahead of them, his fall far from intentional. Just beyond his family, Bravo lay on his stomach, frantically searching in a westerly direction for the shooter. David lay on his back behind them, clutching his left shoulder, rifle useless next to him.

"Is everyone OK?" Nathan said to Keira and Owen.

"I'm good," she said, pulling Owen closer.

"Buddy?" he insisted, receiving a nod from his son.

"Lie on top of Owen," he yelled, deactivating his rifle safety.

A seemingly endless succession of deep booms rippled across the intersection, and Nathan's visor system did something he hadn't noticed before. Small green circles appeared in the direction of the gas station, followed by a new symbol in the upper right corner. GNFR.

Gunfire.

"Where is it coming from?" screamed Keira.

"It's coming from the gas station!" he yelled, lining up the circles with the reticle in his rifle sight. The concrete barrier blocked all but the top quarter of his view of the squat building, but he caught movement in the window on the far right side of the gas station.

"Right corner window!" he said and repeatedly pressed the trigger. The rifle bit into his shoulder as his bullets exploded the top of the concrete barrier and punched visible holes in the stucco around the targeted window. He'd forgotten that his magazines were loaded with armor-piercing rounds.

"Cover me!" yelled Bravo, pushing himself off the ground.

Nathan fired at the top of the window, his rounds blasting the upper edge of the barrier into a cloud of concrete dust. He never saw where the rest of the bullets from his magazine struck. Bravo's rifle chattered, adding to the maelstrom of tungsten-tipped bullets striking the gas station.

Nathan yanked a fresh magazine from his vest and took stock of their situation, which appeared far from optimal.

David had rolled onto his right side, exposing a bloodied wound on his left shoulder. Alpha had turned onto his stomach and begun slithering toward the weapon he had dropped several feet away. Worse yet, they had stopped in the middle of the intersection and were completely exposed in every other direction. Only the concrete barrier at the corner of the gas station had kept the previously unseen shooter from unloading more bullets into the group after they had dropped to the street. He inserted the magazine and rose to one knee, depressing the bolt catch to charge the rifle.

"Pound the gas station!" said Bravo. "I'm going wide left to make sure this fucker's dead." He took off in a full sprint toward the rusted car they had just left.

With a less obstructed view of the entire station now that the top of the barrier had been blasted away, Nathan aimed his rifle scope's reticle just to the left of the window and pressed the trigger, seeing a hole punch through the wall where he suspected the gunman might be hiding. He systematically stitched the building with bullets, focusing his fire on the walls immediately adjacent to the doors and windows. By the time he'd expended the thirty-round magazine, Bravo had reached the far left edge of the building. *Shit. He's going inside?* Nathan ejected the magazine from his rifle and pulled a replacement from his vest. When he was ready to fire again, Bravo had disappeared.

"What's our status?" grumbled Alpha, raising himself to a knee and leveling his rifle toward the station.

"Bravo is clearing the building," said Nathan, scanning the front of the building with his scope. "You all right?"

"Took a hit in the chest. Vest stopped it cold but knocked the shit out of me."

Two pops echoed from the gas station.

"That should be the end of it," said Alpha, pausing for a moment to listen to Bravo's report through his helmet's comm system. "Confirmed. Hold your fire, he's coming out."

Bravo appeared in the center doorway and took off in their direction.

"We stumbled across a cartel sentry station. Two guys, Bravo said. One was already missing half his head. Nice shooting," said Alpha.

"Probably wasn't me."

"Still a nice job. You're cleared hot from here on," he said. "David? You still with us?"

"I'm fine. Grazed my upper shoulder," said David, digging through a pouch on his vest. "Bleeding like a mother, but I'm good. Nathan?"

"We're good," said Nathan.

"Clear the intersection," said Alpha. "After a minute or so of quiet, people will start peering through windows to see what happened."

Nathan lifted their trembling son to his feet, hugging him tight. "We're fine, buddy. I promise."

"I'm scared," he whispered.

"Me, too, but we have to keep going. We'll be safe soon enough," he lied.

Keira stood behind Owen, staring down Calle H in the direction of the route they had taken to reach the intersection. "I think we might have a problem," she said in a raised voice.

Nathan followed her gaze. Several blocks away, a car sat in the middle of the street. Probably the same car that passed them before they tried to cross the intersection. He lifted his night-vision visor, seeing two faint red brake lights in the distance.

"Patch yourself up later, David," said Alpha. "We need to get moving."

Bravo reached them a moment later. "What's up?"

While Nathan watched, the red lights turned white. "Shit!" he yelled, flipping his visor back into position. "They just went into reverse!" He grabbed his son and started to pull him toward the southern side of the intersection, but Alpha grabbed him.

"We can't run. When they see what happened here, we'll have a hundred cartel soldiers on our ass."

"I'm getting my son out of here," said Nathan, pulling free of his grip.

Alpha scanned the intersection. "Safest place is behind the gas station barrier. We'll hit the car farther down the street."

"Headlights inbound!" yelled Bravo.

"Go!" snapped Alpha, pushing him toward the gas station.

The two commandos and David vanished down the street as Nathan's family ran for the gas station. When they reached the concrete barrier, he got his first close look at the devastating power of the armor-piercing bullets. The top of a two-foot-wide, one-foot-thick section had been chewed to jagged pieces by the tungsten-tipped 6.8-millimeter bullets, exposing the metal rebar embedded in the concrete. Glancing at the bullet hole–riddled station, he wondered if the rounds had passed entirely through the building, hitting the homes behind it.

A revving engine drew his attention back to Calle H.

"Lie flat and watch our back," he said to Keira.

She unslung the MP-20 and sandwiched Owen between herself and the barrier, pointing the submachine gun toward the street behind them. Nathan nestled the forward grip of his rifle against an unbroken section of concrete, pointing the barrel over the barrier. His visor indicated a significant, continuously rising change to the distant light measurement. The car was getting close. A rapid discordance of muffled gunshots erupted just out of sight on Calle H where Alpha and Bravo had been heading. When the fusillade ended, the wide sedan appeared between the last parked cars on the street, barreling through the intersection. Nathan tracked the car with his rifle as it swerved nose first into a utility pole on the diagonally opposite corner, launching the driver through the windshield and onto the sidewalk. The car's back end lifted several feet into the air and slammed down, crunching the rear bumper and spraying plastic light cover pieces into the street.

"Empty your magazine into the car!" he yelled.

He and Keira fired methodically, flattening the tires and shattering the few intact windows in an instant. Most of the bullets punctured the doors and trunk area, warping the metal inward as the frames collapsed. Nathan's magazine emptied first. When Keira's weapon finally fell silent, the car resembled a scrap metal chassis, its former shape barely recognizable. Nobody could have survived that. Nathan reloaded and swept the street in both directions for additional threats.

"Uh, I think you got 'em," said David, appearing above the barrier on the other side.

"I just hope I didn't kill anyone on the next block. These bullets are crazy," said Nathan.

Bravo side hopped over the barrier, landing a few feet from where Nathan lay.

"Jesus! That's one way to do it. Everyone in that car was dead before it hit the intersection, by the way," said Bravo.

"I wasn't taking any chances," said Nathan.

"Apparently not," said Bravo, turning to David. "How's the shoulder?"

"I just need to wrap it in hemo gauze to stop the bleeding."

"Wrap it on the run, Marine Corps!" yelled Alpha, rushing up to the group. "We need to clear this area right now. This bought us some time, but every motherfucker around here has a cell phone, with their friendly neighborhood cartel boss on speed dial. They're calling this shit in as I run my mouth. We're jogging from here."

A few seconds later, they crossed the intersection at a slow trot. The backpack cut cruelly into Nathan's shoulders, weighing him down with every step. He hoped Alpha wasn't serious about jogging the rest of the way.

CHAPTER 21

Keira vomited near the corner of Calle H and Marmoleros. It wasn't the stomach-pitching, fire-hose event she expected, but it still sucked. She felt a second wave coming and resumed her position on the curb—legs spread, hands on her knees. For some odd reason, she felt bad about puking on the dusty, oil-stained sidewalk. Her stomach heaved, launching a small mouthful onto the street. Not so bad this time.

Nathan crowded her on the left. "Try to breathe slowly and deeply."

She wanted to push him away. It was a little hard to breathe when ejecting your stomach after jogging more than a mile with a forty-pound backpack. Instead, she nodded from the uncomfortable position and spit a few times, trying to get the taste out of her mouth before standing upright.

"I'm fine now," she said.

"I told you to lay off the chili mac," he said.

She laughed, standing up slowly.

"If you're not puking, you're not trying," said David, crouched on the street several feet away, aiming his rifle down the street they had just traveled.

Car tires squealed nearby, drawing Alpha across the street from a hidden position between two cars.

"Break's over. Jose said there's a ton of radio traffic on cartel frequencies. Give me one more minute, and I'll give you all the time in the world to puke," said Alpha. "We're almost there."

"You said we were almost there ten minutes ago," said Keira.

"Now we're really almost there," he said. "It's just down the street."

"I knew you'd say that," she said, reaching out to her son. "How are you doing, sweetie?"

She knew the answer. Nathan had carried him off and on since they'd started Alpha's forced march after the gas station ambush, Owen spending more time in his dad's arms than on his own feet toward the end. She was amazed Owen had made it as far as he had. The combination of heat, stress, and Alpha's merciless pace had taken a toll on all of them.

"I'm OK," he said. "I'm sorry I made Dad carry me."

"Don't be silly, Owen. Your dad doesn't mind," she said, glancing at Nathan, who moved sluggishly into place behind the two commandos.

She wasn't sure how Nathan had managed to carry Owen. She'd tried to give him a break early in the forced jog before quickly realizing she could carry either the backpack or Owen, but not both. She put him down after taking no more than a dozen labored steps, her legs rubbery after half of them. Nathan carried him the rest of the way without complaining. It made her feel better about their chances of survival. He looked determined and capable—adapted to their new reality. If they were going to survive, she'd have to make the same transformation. They couldn't survive on Nathan's attitude alone.

"A few more minutes, and we'll be in a car the rest of the way. Promise," she added. "Catch up with your dad."

Owen nodded and marched off to join Nathan. She took another moment to catch her breath before falling in line behind the already moving group.

"You sure you're all right?" said David, shuffling in her direction.

"As long as Alpha isn't full of shit about the time, I'll be fine," she said, noticing the tightly stretched gauze covering his lower left shoulder. "How bad is your shoulder?"

"Not bad, but this stuff only stops the flow," he said, gesturing for her get moving.

She took one more deep breath and jogged after her son, hearing another long tire screech somewhere within the neighborhood. How in the hell did they hope to get out of here by car? On foot they could hide, kind of. Surely driving the streets would draw a ton of attention.

One step at a time. They had to get to the cars first.

Her stomach in a tight, painful knot, she lumbered behind Owen, thigh muscles tightening. This would be a shitty time for a leg cramp. Another car engine revved nearby—somewhere behind them—causing her to pick up the pace. Real shitty.

Ahead, Alpha kicked a metal gate, crashing it into the yard next to them.

"Get inside and stay low," he hissed.

They quickly filed through the gate, sliding down the inside of the shoulder-height stucco wall bordering the sidewalk. Alpha pushed the squeaky gate shut and crouched on the other side of the opening, opposite David. The muffled engine sounds grew louder until she heard a worn brake squeal nearby.

"They're at the corner we just left," he whispered, raising his rifle and sliding its barrel a few inches through the closed gate.

Would they see her vomit on the side of the street and put two and two together? She hugged Owen tight as the deep thrumming crescendoed. For a brief moment, the sound level fell, indicating the car had passed, before it started to rise again. Shit. Were they backing up? She let go of Owen and slid the MP-20 into a ready position across her tactical vest.

"Second car," whispered Alpha.

She grabbed Owen again and held him until the second car passed. As the sound of the engines faded, Alpha peeked over the top of the wall. He stared down the street until it fell quiet.

"Two cars loaded with cartel heavies," said Alpha. "They're just cruising around, hoping to get lucky."

"How much farther. For real?" she said.

"You can see it from here. We're headed to an abandoned school on the opposite side of the street. The tall chain-link fence marks the start of the school. We can walk the rest of the way. They won't double back."

She turned to her son. "We're almost there."

"Good. I'm too tired to walk anymore."

"You can sleep the rest of the night in the car," she added.

Somehow she doubted that was true, but she said it anyway. She couldn't imagine sleep would come easily, if it came at all. The kid needed something to cling to.

They filed back through the gate and continued west on the sidewalk. She hadn't thought it was possible, but Avenida Marmoleros took Mexicali's dilapidated motif to a new level. The farther they moved from the US–Mexico border, the worse it looked. Ever-present graffiti. Boarded windows. Cracked walls. Collapsed roofs. Bullet holes. Stripped cars. Trash everywhere. The city was in an unrecoverable state of neglect, plagued by violence and ruled by gunmen.

The fence Alpha had referenced barely qualified as a barrier. Twisted, unraveled sections of chain link clung to bent poles. The school beyond it looked worse. Calling it abandoned was a kind description. *Destroyed* would have been more appropriate. The right half of the one-story building just beyond the fence had collapsed, its flat roof angled steeply into a soccer field littered with piles of metal and wood scrap. The only reason she assumed it had been a soccer field was based on the warped rectangular goal visible beyond the scattered debris.

Alpha led them past the school and into a narrow passage beside a shuttered, graffiti-covered auto-parts business. They passed between the school's chain-link fence—surprisingly intact here—and a head-high wall topped with haphazardly placed coils of rusted razor wire that grabbed at the top of her night-vision goggles if she rose from a stoop.

They continued along the path to the southwest corner of the property, where two figures inside the school yard pulled open a neatly cut section of the fence to admit them. Alpha writhed through the fence first, while Bravo continued on several steps to guard the alley the passage opened on to. Once they'd all passed through the fence, Alpha ushered them through a dented metal door into the building next to the fence.

The room met expectations established by the school's exterior. The walls were covered in graffiti and scorched in several places. Squatters' cooking fires, Keira imagined. A long, cracked chalkboard leaned against the southern wall to her right. The windows on the opposite side of the room had been boarded over but were surprisingly intact. In between the front and back walls lay the remains of a classroom. Broken metal desks and facedown bookcases. The door slammed shut behind them.

"You can ditch the night vision," said Alpha.

Keira lifted the goggles attached to her helmet and squinted as her eyes adjusted to the interior light. She glanced at the intact windows again, then behind her at the metal door, which looked new from the inside. "This room looks like a movie set," she said.

"The whole place has been more or less staged," said Alpha, walking between them to open the door leading deeper into the school.

"Does the cartel know about this?" said Nathan, looking around.

"The cartel knows everything," he said. "But this place is mostly unknown to the rank and file. It's also off-limits by order of the cartel jefe who rents us all of our space in Mexicali."

Keira patted Owen's shoulder. "We can rest here, sweetie."

"No rest for the wicked, I'm afraid," said Alpha. "The gas station scene generated a lot of communications traffic. Jose wants you out of here immediately, before every cartel bozo looking to earn a bonus shows up."

"Christ, we just got here," said Nathan. "We need a break!"

"You can recuperate on the road," said Alpha. "Last time I checked, driving wasn't a physical activity."

"Our car trips haven't exactly been relaxing lately."

Alpha opened the door, revealing a dimly lit hallway. "My mission is to get you to the Route 2 and 20 interchange—alive. The chances of a successful mission decrease every second we spend this close to the center of town."

"It's fine, Nate," Keira said. "I'm fine. I want to get Owen as far from here as possible."

Nathan sighed, then nodded. "All right. Let's go."

The hallway and adjoining classrooms smelled musty and had been stripped bare, explaining the scrap piles spread over the soccer field. Keira now wondered if the school's entire exterior facade had been carefully crafted to discourage investigation, right down to the partially collapsed building.

At the end of the hallway, the Alpha directed them into the last classroom on the left, which contained a surprise. Two metallic gray, midsize SUVs, side by side, facing the wall on the right side of the room.

Keira and Nathan dumped their backpacks onto the floor. Staring at the SUVs, Keira couldn't help asking the first question that popped into her head. "How did you get the cars in here?"

Alpha laughed. "I thought you might ask how we plan on getting them out."

"The answer to one question satisfies the other," said Nathan.

"That it does," replied Alpha. "The wall they're facing is obviously fake. Well, it's a real wall, but it can be pulled down from the outside—when we're ready."

The windows in the doors of the SUVs looked odd. Each was rolled down a third of the way, topped by a thick metal bar spanning the top of the window.

David must have seen the same thing. "What's up with the windows?" he said.

"Retrofitted bullet-resistant glass. We installed a single molded sheet that extends from the metal support bar to the bottom of the door. The entire door serves as a shield. We left the top third open so you can shoot. The metal bar extends into the door frame on each side, keeping the glass in place."

David reached out to touch one of the windows. "What about the front windshield and rear cargo windows?"

Alpha shook his head. "We purchased these off a commercial lot. It wasn't feasible to replace the windshield without some serious modification to the upper chassis. We've bolted a custom-cut sheet of glass behind the rear seat bench, extending to the top of the seat. You're covered from the sides and rear."

"But nothing helping us up front," said David.

"You got the engine block and your tactical armor," said Alpha. "Look on the bright side—you can shoot forward if you need to."

"How bullet resistant are the side windows?"

"Standard-issue, jacketed semisteel-core rifle rounds will not penetrate. When you start getting into the tungsten-carbide stuff, all bets are off. You'll know when something like that hits one of the windows. You don't want to be there when the next one hits."

"Four-wheel drive, I assume?" added David.

"You assume correct. Full spare mounted inside and under the rear compartment, which will be a pain in the ass to access. We packed the compartment tight with the supplies you'll need to get past Arizona. Fuel cans. More MREs than you can stomach. Water. Medical. Six-eight ammo for your rifles. Even a tent and some sleeping bags."

"When did you run these last?" said Nathan.

"I honestly don't know," said Alpha, glancing at Bravo, who shrugged. "The guys you saw outside arrived a few hours earlier and said everything checked out."

"Does it matter which vehicle we're in?" Keira asked.

"Take your pick. For all practical purposes, they're identical."

"In that case, this one looks good," she said, opening the rear door of the SUV directly in front of them.

"Great choice," said Alpha, cracking the first smile she'd seen since they'd met him.

"You'll find a handheld radio in the glove box, tuned to the channel we'll use to communicate between vehicles. My team will lead. You follow closely—less than a half car length. Report anything that doesn't look right."

"The whole city doesn't look right," said Keira.

"Funny. Report any threats, real or perceived, and we'll handle the rest. It's important that you stay close. If a car gets between us, things will get very complicated. With any luck, we'll be at the interchange in twenty minutes. Questions? No? Good. Let's get on the road."

Less than a minute later, they were situated in the SUV according to David's tactical seating plan. Owen sat in the middle of the rear bench, two backpacks separating him from the right passenger door. Keira sat next to him, her assigned field of fire extending from the left side of the car to the rear. Optimally, she'd drive instead of David, freeing their most qualified shooter to occupy the most flexible firing position. Realistically, she didn't trust herself to drive under fire well enough to suggest the switch. Emotionally, she had no intention of leaving her son's side.

Her husband peered back between the front seats. "Ready, buddy?"

Owen gave him a thumbs-up, and Nathan reached back to give him a high five.

"How's Mom doing?" he said.

"Never been better," she said, purposely overdoing a smile.

Nathan nodded sharply and smiled. "I have a good feeling about this."

"You keep saying that," said Keira, her voice trailing off. Nathan's words had rekindled a thought.

"What's up?" he said.

"Maybe nothing, but why would both cars be identically loaded with supplies? We're the only ones going any distance."

"Jose said they were all pulling out and heading north," said Nathan.

"Yeah, but not right now," said David. "And these two guys wouldn't just be taking off on their own."

"I don't know," Keira said. "I just found it odd."

"It sure as hell is," said David, making as if to open his door, then freezing as Alpha's digitized voice squawked over the encrypted hand-held radio.

"Ready to roll?"

David sat back in his seat, eyes narrowed. He shared a dark glance with Nathan and Keira in turn, then shook his head. "Either way," he said, "we can't hang around here. If they stay with us after we get out on the road, we'll deal with it then."

"You reading me?" Alpha pressed. "Ready?"

Nathan picked up the radio and pushed the "Transmit" button. "Affirmative. Lead the way."

"Remember to keep the distance between the two cars as close as possible. We'll turn sharp right coming out of the building, then left in the alley."

"Copy that," said Nathan.

"Start your car. The wall comes down in three, two, one."

As the SUV rumbled to life, the classroom wall in front of them fell like a ramp, crashing into the ground. A thick cloud of dust exploded from the impact, obscuring their view beyond the room.

"That was cool," said Owen.

"Not something you see every day," Keira agreed.

Alpha's SUV pulled forward and stopped on the crashed section of wall. Two figures emerged from the swirling haze, immediately absorbed by the vehicle. The men who'd let them through the fence, Keira imagined.

"Alpha, your brake lights are out," said Nathan.

"All taillights have been disabled," replied the commando.

"What about the front lights?" David asked.

"We'll run with headlights inside the city, so we don't stand out. Once on the outskirts, we run dark."

"Makes sense," David said, turning on their headlights and illuminating the dust cloud.

"Roger. Let us know when to go dark," said Nathan, lowering the radio. "I hope they know what they're doing."

"Me, too," said David. "Because I don't have a better plan that doesn't involve heading south for Acapulco."

The SUV in front of them lurched forward and immediately turned right. David followed, their vehicle emerging from the school into the suspended dust. They crept behind the lead SUV, which faced an open gate to the alley. A few seconds later, both vehicles sped uncomfortably fast through the gate and proceeded disturbingly close to each other down the alley. Keira squeezed Owen's hand, more for her sake than his.

"It'll be all right, Mom," he said.

"You're starting to sound like your dad."

CHAPTER 22

Mexicali flattened into a wasteland of shabby and abandoned road-side business fronts once they turned left on Route 2, headed for the eastern fringes of the city. In the solitary glow of their headlights, it looked uninhabited. Through David's night vision, it looked long dead. A few miles from the Route 20 interchange, the businesses faded away, replaced by long stretches of broken and warped chain-link fence. Behind the useless property barriers, derelict tractor trailers, their tires and engines missing, stood tall over barren lots filled with scrapped cars and piles of junk.

David tapped the brake as Alpha's SUV decelerated and applied it a little more firmly when the rate of closure between the two vehicles didn't immediately decrease.

"Ask him why they're slowing," said David, watching the wind-shield-projected speedometer shoot below forty-five miles per hour.

"Why are we slowing?" said Nathan.

"We have a small situation coming up. Plan on coming to a full stop in five, four—"

"Define 'small situation,'" said Nathan, interrupting Alpha's count.

"Two, one—"

David pressed the pedal hard, bringing them to a controlled stop less than a foot behind the lead vehicle. Flashes erupted from the SUV on both sides, accompanied by the crackle of suppressed automatic fire.

Nathan detached his seat belt and rose to one knee in the front seat, aiming his rifle through the wide slit at the top of the window. "What are they shooting at?" he yelled.

"Left side!" David barked as the SUV rained fire on a sedan facing the highway from behind a shallow, rocky rise, bullets peppering its windshield, stitching it with holes and spraying crimson blotches against the remaining windows. The sedan's doors remained closed throughout the fusillade, its occupants probably either dead or critically wounded by the first volley.

Then Nathan's rifle began popping repeatedly. By the time David's eyes focused on that side, a massive pickup truck facing the highway alongside a derelict building had met a similar fate.

"We're moving again," said Alpha. "That was the cartel's easternmost lookout post on Route 2. They focus on traffic inbound to Mexicali, so it's unlikely they reported our approach, but they would have dimed us out in another ten seconds."

"If you knew they were going to be there," Nathan said, "you think you could've given us a little warning?"

David laughed to himself, shaking his head. A car full of guys Nathan had never met before tonight were risking their lives to escort him through cartel land, and he didn't hesitate to give them shit. What had happened to the gentle scientist who'd climbed on this ride?

"They change location every night," said Alpha, maintaining admirable cool. "Thermal imaging didn't pick them up until the last minute." He chuckled. "We'll try to anticipate your needs better next time, though."

Nathan still bristled. "They knew we'd be hitting those lookouts *somewhere* along here. Their need-to-know attitude doesn't work for me," he said to David. "When it comes to my family's safety—I need to know what we're up against."

"We'll be on our own soon enough," said David.

The lead SUV sped away, David flooring the accelerator to keep up. The highway rumbled underneath them, amplifying the heavy silence. They cruised east at seventy miles per hour, the land on each side of the highway flattening away to desert. After a few minutes, he spotted the overpass marking the Route 20 connector. From there on, they'd have the road to themselves for several hours. If the other car followed, they'd undoubtedly spot it at some point on Route 2.

"We're almost there," said David.

Nathan raised his rifle and peered through its magnified optics. "Looks clear."

The radio crackled. "We're going to range ahead of you to check the other side of the underpass. Just in case. Slow to forty miles per hour—*please*."

"Copy your last. Slowing to forty," said Nathan, then lowered the radio. "Smart-ass."

The distance between the two vehicles opened swiftly, as if the lead SUV had turboboosted forward. It passed underneath the low bridge well ahead of them, pulling off the road just beyond the structure.

"All clear," said Alpha. "Pull in front of us, and we'll get you on your way."

"Be there shortly," said Nathan.

"I don't know whether to be nervous or happy," said Keira.

"Both," replied David.

"Definitely both," said Nathan. "What about you, big guy?"

Owen leaned forward between the seats. "How long until we meet up with Grandpa and Grandma?"

"A few days," said Nathan.

Best-case scenario, thought David, keeping that to himself. Owen settled into his seat without responding. He couldn't imagine what was going on inside that kid's head. Excitement. Fear. Anxiety. Hopelessness. Anger. Probably a toxic mix of everything. But despite the unrelenting hell tossed in his lap, the kid appeared to be coping better than David imagined possible—especially for an eleven-year-old.

His train of thought continued to derail as the underpass grew rapidly in the windshield. Maybe Alison's fertility challenges had been a blessing in disguise, saving him the grief of losing both his wife and the mother of their children. Or maybe he would have delivered the phones and driven off if there had been more at stake. Lots of maybes.

"You gonna stop?" said Nathan.

David overcorrected in response, jamming on the brakes as they passed under the metal bridge, throwing them all against their seat belts and eliciting a round of curses from Nathan and Keira. The SUV barely slowed in time to park a reasonably close distance in front of Alpha's vehicle.

"What was that about?" said Nathan.

"Just testing the brakes," he said lamely. "Sorry to scare everyone."

"Yeah. Well, they work," said Nathan, detaching his seat belt.

Bravo and the two operatives who'd joined them at the school formed a three-point perimeter around the cars, scanning the distance with their rifle scopes while the rest of them huddled around the hood of the SUV with Alpha.

"You still have that map?" Alpha asked Nathan.

For a moment, Nathan looked like he might deliver a sarcastic retort. Instead, he silently dug the road map out of one of his cargo pockets and spread it on the hood. They squeezed together in front of the vehicle to better view it from the proper orientation, including Owen, who stood in front of Keira. Alpha checked his watch before shining a flashlight on the map.

"It's five after ten. Barring any difficulty, you're looking at a seven-hour drive to Nogales. About three hundred and sixty miles. As you can see, Route 2 follows the Arizona border pretty closely until you hit Sonoyta. Do not try to cross the border in Sonoyta, and do not stop in Sonoyta. Do I need to repeat that?"

"What's in Sonoyta?" said David.

"Nothing. It's completely dead—for a reason. Drones out of Yuma have recently started killing anything trying to cross over. The Sinaloa cartel doesn't bother with it anymore."

"Maybe we should avoid it altogether," said Nathan.

"We thought about that, but the only other way is to take Route 8 along the north coast here," he said, pointing at the top of the Sea of Cortez. "That adds close to three hours to your trip and puts you at the crossing well after sunrise. You'll already be cutting it close. The sun comes up early there—around five thirty. Jose thinks you'll attract too much attention."

"A lone car crossing at five in the morning won't attract attention?" said Nathan.

"The city will be wide-awake at eight, injecting too many variables into the equation. Plus, we have no idea when Cerberus might locate our headquarters in Mexicali. When they find it abandoned, it won't take long to connect the dots from there. You need to be across the border before people start keeping an eye out for gringos heading north."

"I see," said Nathan, crossing his arms.

"Keep an eye on the road conditions beyond Sonoyta. You only have one spare tire. And follow the damn map. Jose's route keeps you out of most towns. There's no way to avoid Altar when you turn north on Route 43 here," he said, tracing the route with a finger. "But after that, you're home free until you hit the Hermosillo–Nogales border station just west of Nogales proper."

"Is the border station manned?" said David.

He shook his head. "It's no longer a functioning port of entry. Just a road now."

"US Customs doesn't monitor the border?" said Keira.

"No," he said, giving her an odd look. "They abandoned the Arizona border more than two years ago. New Mexico shortly after that."

"What are you talking about?"

"What do you mean?" said Alpha.

"You're just saying that things are bad on the border, right?" said Nathan.

"No, I'm saying the previous border doesn't exist, for all practical purposes. Don't you watch the news?"

"You don't see this on the news in California," said David.

What Alpha was saying wasn't news to him—he'd read highly classified area reports and situation reports on the cartels' influence along the state borders, though even those reports downplayed the extent of the problem Alpha was describing.

"I don't know this for a fact, but for a while now, we—as in, many Marines—have suspected there's a state-imposed media blackout regarding the true state of affairs in the Wastelands."

"Unbelievable. Even the Texas border is barely functional! El Paso and Laredo go back and forth between cartel and Texas National Guard control on a weekly fucking basis—" Alpha cut himself off.

"We don't have time for this. Bottom line: when you get through the border crossing at Nogales, don't stop. Keep pressing north, but make sure you bypass Tucson. You'll find a local-area map in the glove box to help you with that. I recommend getting off Interstate 19 in Green Valley, several miles south of the city. I can't remember the name of the road. Continental something or other. It parallels the interstate and dumps you on the southwestern outskirts of the city. Stay on the outskirts and sneak your way northwest until you connect with Interstate 10. You'll see what I mean on the Tucson map. You have a second set of license plates on the floor under the front passenger seat. Arizona plates. Ditch the Mexican tags when you reach Interstate 40. That's kind of the east-west demarcation line between cartel and state control. Questions?"

"Lights on or off for the trip?" said David.

"You know the deal with the goggles. Synthetic daylight mode paints a better picture than headlights, but I don't care what the design company says, you're not seeing a true three-dimensional picture. Winding roads pose a problem. Flat runs are fine. From a security perspective, I'd run dark through any towns. If it's still dark when you cross the border, I recommend dousing the headlights a mile out on both sides."

David nodded. "Satellite phone?"

"Thought you'd never ask," said Alpha, producing the encrypted satellite phone given to David by Lieutenant Colonel Smith, his commanding officer. Jose had confiscated it from him before they arrived at the CLM bunker. He handed it over. "Good luck, and play it safe. I sincerely hope all of our paths cross again."

Nathan extended a hand. "Thank you for delivering us safely. I wish you all the best of luck. I can't honestly say I want to see you again, but that's mainly because I'd like to vanish where nobody will find me."

David's eyes moistened when Owen shook Alpha's hand. Just the sight of the seasoned war fighter taking the kid's hand and telling him to watch out for his parents was enough to bring a lump to his throat.

Once they were all in the SUV, David started the engine and waited for everyone to fasten their seat belts.

When Nathan had snapped in and leaned his rifle against the door, he picked up the radio. "Should we return this?"

David shook his head. "We can keep it in power-saving mode, and if they're careless enough to transmit on the frequency, we'll hear it. Never know, right?"

"Right," said Nathan, handing it through the front seats to Keira. "I'll turn this important duty over to our communications team."

"I was going to take a nap. Hopefully sleep through Sonoyta," said Keira, stowing the radio under the back of Nathan's seat.

"Don't worry about what Alpha said," said David. "As long as we stay on this side of the border, the drones won't bother us. I know a Marine drone pilot at Yuma, and they have strict rules of engagement."

What he didn't tell them was that he didn't know any of the CIA, DIA, NSA, Border Patrol, or air force drone pilots housed in the adjacent trailers at Yuma. He eased the SUV off the highway shoulder, picking up speed when he felt all four tires grip pavement. Some things were better left unsaid, especially when they were completely out of your control.

PART III

PART III

CHAPTER 23

Jon Fisher stood next to the single window in the unfurnished den of the Gleasons' town house and peered through the wooden blinds. A front had moved in a few hours ago, obscuring the quarter moon and casting an impenetrable darkness over the neighborhood. Beside a few lights in the upper floors of the nearby town houses, he could barely see across the street. If someone was watching him, there was little chance he would detect it unless they made a foolish mistake. No sense worrying about something out of his control.

He let the shutter blade fall back into place and returned to the kitchen, taking a seat at a round table that nearly touched the back of the family room couch. The town house was a notch or two past cozy, but what did the Gleasons care? They spent most of their time in a pristine, self-sustained community hidden in the hills, returning to society only to hang out with their children and grandchildren. And eat sushi. Apparently that was important to Kim, and Jon had no right to judge. He suspected Leah had agreed to move to their Idaho location as much for the proliferation of Thai restaurants in Ketchum as her love for the scenery.

Jon checked the satphone lying on the table for missed calls. Still nothing. It was well past his natural bedtime, and he was starting to feel a strong pull toward the spare bedroom upstairs. He'd set a few noise traps and retire for the evening in a few minutes. Stu and his son-in-law would arrive in the morning, and he wanted to be fresh for the initial planning session. He figured Stu would want to start driving south as soon as they mapped out a few potential travel routes. Of course, it would help immensely if they heard from either David or Nathan. Driving blindly into the Wastelands, with no guidance beyond "head south," didn't exactly inspire confidence in the mission. He'd undertake it regardless, but they could use some actionable intelligence. Otherwise, they were literally driving to points unknown.

He was thinking about pouring a glass of water to take upstairs when his satphone rang. He recognized the number from the hundreds of times he'd imagined it appearing on the phone's small screen over the last twenty-four hours. Recalling one of Stuart's many surveillance precautions, he stood up and walked toward the bathroom.

"Hello? David? Nathan?"

"Dad, it's me," said his son. "I have Keira, Owen, and David with me. We're fine."

"I'm so glad to hear your voice," he said, closing the bathroom door behind him and running the faucet. "Nathan. Can you give the phone to David for a minute? We heard about Alison. Major General Nichols spoke with David's father earlier today. I should talk with him first."

"I understand, Dad. Here he is."

"Hello? Sergeant Major Fisher?"

"David. We heard about Alison. I don't know if you've talked with your father, but we heard from Nichols, who heard from your Marines. I'm sorry. I don't know what else to say, other than—I'm forever in your debt. And we're gonna make these fuckers pay for this. For all of it."

"Sergeant Major. That's all I needed to hear. If you don't mind, I'd like to leave it at that."

"Copy that, David—and please call me Jon. I haven't been called Sergeant Major in a long time."

David laughed—a good sign. "I'll give Jon a try, but don't hold it against me if I revert to Sergeant Major. What am I hearing in the background, sir? Sounds like static?"

"I'm sitting on the crapper, with the door closed, running the faucet. Don't laugh—it was your dad's idea."

"Can't be too cautious. I'm gonna pass this to Nathan. I look forward to seeing Sergeant Major Fisher and Colonel Quinn back in action."

"Your dad and brother-in-law should be here in the morning. Probably start heading your way soon after that."

"Blake is with my dad?"

"That's what he said."

"He's one badass dude," said David.

"That makes three badasses headed your way."

David laughed again. "All right. Here's Nathan."

"Dad. Great to hear your voice. Is Mom there, too?"

"No. I sent her back to the compound. She'll be safer there. I have Stuart and his son-in-law arriving early. We'll head south to link up with you guys as quickly as possible. What's your current status? We heard some conflicting reports from Nichols."

"I don't know where to start, Dad. We're currently driving to Nogales, on the Arizona–Mexico border."

"Nogales? Where are you now?"

"An hour out of Mexicali. If all goes well on the road, we expect to cross into Arizona just before dawn."

"Is the road safe at night? I thought Mexico was a mess," said Jon. "Are you with this mystery group we heard about?"

"I can't imagine what you've heard."

"Not much. Only that the group literally swooped in by parachute to save what was left of the convoy."

"It gets a lot more complicated, but that's the gist of it. The group that orchestrated the counterambush is a splinter cell of the California Liberation Movement."

"What? What do they want with you? Are you with them right now?"

"We've parted ways, at least for now. They asked me to help them with something that would have undoubtedly worsened my legal situation in California. I told them I'd reconsider after I got my family to safety, you and Mom included."

"They just let you go? Odd move, after going to so much trouble rescuing you."

"I know. There's not much we can do if they're tracking us. We'll ditch the car when it's feasible."

"They gave you a vehicle? You need to ditch it sooner than later. I guarantee it's being tracked."

"They gave us a bullet-resistant SUV with enough supplies and fuel to reach Las Vegas. This beats whatever we can buy or steal on our own. It is what it is for now."

"Sorry to get excited, Nate. This whole thing is crazy. I just want you guys to get back in one piece," said Jon. "CLM, huh?"

"They've been running part of their California operation out of Mexicali."

"Right under the cartel's nose?"

"They've been paying the cartel rent. Like I said, it's complicated," said Nathan. "You want to say hi to Owen and Keira?"

"You bet your ass I do," said Jon. "Put the big guy on the line."

He wished Leah could be here for this. Her stoic Marine-spouse face had been on the verge of crumbling for the past twenty-four hours, wanting nothing more than to talk to her son and grandson. He'd have to call Scott's phone and leave a quick message to let her know they were alive and well. Not out of danger by any stretch of the imagination, but making progress.

"Grandpa?" he heard.

The hardened shell Jon had built over a thirty-year Marine Corps career crumbled at the sound of the tired child's voice. His eleven-year-old grandson was driving in an armored SUV through the back roads of Mexico, with any number of lunatics looking to kill him. It took him a few moments to muster a response.

"Grandpa?" repeated Owen.

"How's my big guy doing? Keeping your mom and dad out of trouble?"

"I don't know about that," said Owen. "We're driving somewhere in Mexico. It's really dark out. I can't wait to see you and Grandma."

Jon paused to wipe the tears running down his cheeks. "I can't wait to see you either. We'll find a quiet, safe place where we can hide out for a while. Grandma sends her love, too. She's been talking about seeing you all day."

"Is she there? Can I talk to her?"

"She's staying in a supersecret compound, kind of like the place I'm going to find for all of us. I'll tell her you asked for her, buddy. That'll make her whole week. How does that sound?"

"Good. Are you coming down to help us? We're on our own now," said Owen, sounding sad.

"I'm meeting with David's father and another very capable man tomorrow morning, and we'll drive as fast as possible in your direction—without stopping."

"David's dad? This David, with us?"

"That's right. Everyone's parents are getting involved in this. That's what families do, and if my calculations are correct, this entire family will be back together sometime tomorrow night. Somewhere in Utah."

"I wish Mom's parents could be there, too," said Owen.

Jon could imagine his daughter-in-law squirming in her seat at the boy's dark, out-of-the-blue statement. He'd never known Keira's parents, who'd died in a freak skiing accident in Whistler, British Columbia, before she'd met Nathan.

"Buddy, I guarantee you her mom and dad are pulling some serious strings with the big guy upstairs for you. Think about all of the close calls you've had. Someone is watching out for you."

"I think you're right," said Owen. "Mom says she wants to talk to you."

"Well, put her on," said Jon. "Hey. We'll pick out a place where you can go swimming. I mean it."

"Really? Warm or cold water?" said Owen.

"Warm. Though I might have to pee in it," he said, getting a laugh from his grandson.

"That's gross, Grandpa."

"I know. Don't tell your mom. Love you, Owen."

"Love you, too. Here's Mom."

Jon wasn't sure what to expect from Keira. They hadn't enjoyed the best relationship, due to the differences in their political opinions, though he'd done his best to keep it civil. Nathan might not agree that he had always succeeded.

"I heard what you said," said Keira.

"I promise I won't pee in the water."

Her voice changed. Quieter and hesitant. "No. The other part, about my folks. Thank you for saying that. He—we both needed to hear that."

"Well," Jon said, "I believe it. And I think about you and what happened to them a lot."

"You've just made up for every disagreement we've had," she said, sniffling.

Jon heard Owen's voice in the background, probably asking her what was wrong. He decided to change the subject. "Keira, what's the real situation there? I don't trust David or Nathan to give me the straight scoop."

"They haven't held much back. We're driving toward the border crossing at Nogales, which may or may not be open to us. Our CLM friends claim it's wide-open. We're not convinced."

"Customs would probably identify Nathan."

"They swear it's wide-open."

"Well, be careful," he said. "It would be silly to get detained there. You're better off hiding in Mexico if it looks shaky. We can come to you."

"If it looks like business as usual at the border, we'll turn back. You stay safe, too. We'll see you sometime tomorrow night if everything goes according to plan."

"Give Owen a hug for me, and save one for yourself," said Jon.

"Thanks, Jon. I'll pass you back to Nathan."

"Hey, Dad. We'll be careful at the border. After that, it's a matter of making our way north without attracting attention from Cerberus or the cartels. Our CLM contact gave us some tips for getting around Tucson."

"I wouldn't be so worried about the cartels in Arizona. The police might be a problem. You're a federal fugitive now."

"Don't remind me," said Nathan. "I don't think the police will be much of an issue, though. They say that most of Arizona is under cartel control."

"I don't know about that. Cartel influence definitely increased after the Southwest Exodus, but they mainly stick to the drug trade. You should be able to slip through."

"We'll be careful either way," said Nathan. "Dad, I need to focus on the road. I'm scanning long-range from David."

"Gotcha. I'll let you get back to work."

"When will David's dad arrive?"

"They think around seven or eight."

"All right. We'll call you at eight to check in. We should be working our way around Tucson by then. Can't wait to see you, Dad. Love you. Pass the same on to Mom."

"I will. Love you, too, Nate," he said, surprised how easily those rarely spoken words came out. "Be careful. Talk to you in the morning."

With the call finished, he turned off the water and returned to the kitchen. Now for the hardest part—falling asleep. Or course, he had a few things to take care of before he settled in for the night. He couldn't afford to let his guard down.

CHAPTER 24

Chris Riggs stretched out in a deep leather couch facing the town house's gas fireplace and mantel, listening intently once again to the seriously problematic recording of Jon Fisher's side of the phone conversation in the unit across the street. The call had no doubt been important, as Fisher had rushed into the bathroom to muffle the sound. And it had worked, running water dashing any hopes that Nissie's surveillance gear might capture something useful.

Riggs knew from the initial greeting that they had Nathan Fisher or David Quinn on the other end of the line. What a missed opportunity! Nearly five minutes of back-and-forth between Flagg's most wanted parties, possibly disclosing their location. This could have been his chance to make an impression on Flagg, maybe convince him to bring Riggs's team, or just him, into the Cerberus fold.

A dangerous idea crossed Riggs's mind. He shook his head. No. Flagg had been clear about what he expected tonight.

But what if he pulled it off?

"Fuck," he muttered.

"What?" said Tex, sitting in the dark at the kitchen table.

"Never mind."

He needed to let it go. Flagg had changed the mission based on his last report. Surveillance of Gleason's town house strongly suggested that Mr. and Mrs. Fisher had gone separate ways. Flagg wanted Riggs to watch and wait. Jon Fisher would eventually lead them to the wife, and possibly Stuart Quinn, who had disappeared from the Washington, DC, area three days ago.

Three of the twenty-two vehicles registered to the cutout corporation associated with Scott Gleason's Jeep had been flagged with moving violations, each driver's license pointing to a different address in Missoula. All owned by former or retired military personnel. Flagg suspected the owners belonged to some kind of survivalist enclave within easy driving distance of the city. Compounds like that had proliferated over the past few decades, especially in the upper Rocky Mountain states. A person could hide forever in a place like that—if they didn't have a Starbucks addiction. Or a lead foot.

Riggs had postponed breaking into the town house across the street until most of the lights had gone out on the street. He hadn't wanted to risk detection by some nosy neighbor peeking out of a window before going to bed. It was still possible Leah Fisher was still around. The infrared laser microphones pointed at the townhome's front-facing windows didn't indicate a second person in the house, but analysis wasn't conclusive. She could've fallen asleep before they arrived. They couldn't know for sure without biometric detection technology.

It didn't matter. All they needed was one of the Fishers.

His dangerous idea just wouldn't go away.

"What if we grabbed Mr. Fisher now," Riggs said, "and extracted whatever information he acquired from that phone conversation? You know they discussed a game plan. Meet-up locations. Routes. They probably told the old man where they are right now. What if they're not even in Mexicali? We could save Flagg a ton of time and hassle."

"That's not our problem," said Tex.

"I didn't say it was our problem. I'm saying we have the chance to take the initiative and solve a problem."

"I don't see anything good coming out of it. We have our orders."

"What if Fisher ditches us tomorrow? Figures out we're tailing him? We got lucky with that license plate. If he disappears we're screwed, and the longer this drags out, the more complicated it's likely to get. We still have Stuart Quinn running around out there, doing God knows what. The quicker we get Fisher off the street the better."

"Sounds like a reasonable pitch to make—to Flagg," said Tex. "Wrap the request into a summary of the phone call Fisher just received."

"Flagg's not going to change his mind based on an unintelligible phone conversation. If I bring it up and he says no, then it's off the table."

"It's off the table now."

"Not if it looks like the phone call might have been a warning to Jon Fisher to get out of the town house," said Riggs.

"But it doesn't look—"

"We say it does. We say we see him moving."

"I don't like where this is headed."

"It's our story," said Riggs, "and it's a good one. We catch Mr. Fisher trying to sneak away."

"What if we can't make him talk? Fisher won't be an easy nut to crack. Not when it comes to family."

"Funny you should use the word *nut*. Reminds me of a few highly effective ways to extract information," said Riggs, pressing his collar-activated microphone.

"No, God damn it!" said Tex.

Riggs slashed a finger across his throat, shutting Tex up. "Ross. Oz. Nissie," he said into the mic. "Change of plans."

CHAPTER 25

The wireless earplug in Jon Fisher's left ear squelched, emitting a continuous, low-pitched chirping sound. The standalone pulse Doppler motion detector he'd concealed facing the backyard patio had registered movement. A higher-pitched chirp activated, creating a medley that alternated between the two pitches. The sensor covering the front of the town house had just been triggered.

Not a coincidence.

Jon peeled away the thick comforter, dropped it to the hardwood floor next to the bed, and swung his boots onto it. He'd lain down on the guest room bed dressed in the same gear he'd worn all afternoon, following the same procedure that had saved his skin a half-dozen times in Afghanistan. Never dress down in hostile territory, no matter how secure you think your perimeter might be. And right now—he was deep in enemy territory.

He removed the earplug and listened to the inside of the town house. Silence. He wondered how they would breach the unit. Quietly, if they had any sense. They couldn't afford to draw attention in a neighborhood this compact. He could assume they'd enter the front and back simultaneously, giving them full visual coverage of the ground level. Once they cleared the first floor, they'd work their way to the stairs, trapping him. If Jon hoped to survive whatever was coming his way, he had to take the initiative.

He grabbed the short-barreled rifle that had been lying next to him and flipped the selector switch to burst, nestling the carbine's stock into the soft body armor covering the front of his shoulder. He'd made the right call keeping Leah at the compound. The thought reminded him of something. He typed a quick message to Stuart Quinn on his satphone and pressed "Send," then silenced the phone. A reply arrived by the time he had crept to the bottom of the stairs.

Jon stared at the words. Stuart was right, but it was going to make some noise.

CHAPTER 26

Concealed from the street by a squat evergreen hedge, Riggs watched Tex manipulate the front door's locks. They were up against a simple doorknob lock and a dead bolt, and the dead bolt appeared to be a standard installation. They should have access to the town house in a matter of moments.

"Riggs, this is Oz," he heard through his right earphone. "Back door is unlocked. No interior locks detected."

"Copy," said Riggs, tapping Tex's arm. "Back door is unlocked. Give us a few more seconds."

"Working on it," grumbled Tex.

Nissie's voice broke onto the net. "I have noise on the ground floor."

"Probably us working the locks," said Riggs.

Tex gave him a thumbs-up, pocketing the tool he had been using to disable the dead bolt.

"No," she said. "I filtered that out. It's something else." She paused. "Shit. I don't hear it anymore. It was two distinct mechanical clicks. Kind of loud."

"Like someone readying a rifle?"

"Different. More hollow."

"Back door," said Riggs. "Did you hear anything?"

"Negative," said Oz.

He knew they couldn't see inside. Like Tex and him, the back door team was crouched below window level to avoid casting any kind of shadow detectable from the interior.

"Talk to me, Nissie," said Riggs.

"It's dead quiet inside now."

"Should we pull back?" said Oz. "We can leave the door open for later."

"Negative. Stand by to breach. Nissie. Confirm that the home alarm system is deactivated."

"For the third time: I have hacked into the system. It will make no sounds, nor will it send a signal to the security call center."

"Just answer the question next time. Is your driver ready to pick us up?"

"Yes."

Riggs hated using Nissie's techs to do anything but type at a keyboard, but he needed everyone on the assault team to hit the town house—and all that gangly-looking nerd had to do was drive a few blocks without crashing off the road.

"I have the SUV running. Just waiting for your signal," added the tech.

"Copy that," he said, forgetting the tech's name. "Nissie. Monitor police frequencies."

"Frequencies are quiet. We'll know if *your* team draws any attention."

He didn't need her shit right now, or ever. Her responses sounded innocent enough, but Riggs had cracked that bitch's passive-aggressive code. When this mission was done, she was going to pay.

"All stations. Prep for breach," said Riggs.

Tex moved to the right side of the door, crouching low on the granite stoop. He twisted the doorknob with his left hand, pushing the door far enough for the latch to clear the strike plate, then nodded at Riggs.

Gunfire exploded inside the town house, dropping Riggs and Tex to the cold stone. Staccato bursts continued as the two operatives slithered off the porch, their rifles pointed at the door. Riggs stayed low, expecting holes to punch through the wood at any moment.

"Back door, report," he said.

"Oz is down hard," said Ross. "I returned fire, but have no targets."

"How bad is Oz?"

"Missing half of his head."

Nissie interrupted. "I have a nine-one-one call reporting gunfire. Nearest police unit is six minutes away."

"Copy that. Start the clock," said Riggs. "Nissie. Are you getting any sounds inside the town house?"

"A low humming sound that started when you gave the breach order."

"I'm going in," said Riggs. "Back me up."

Tex nodded, his face unreadable behind night-vision goggles.

"Ross, I'm breaching the front door. Do not open fire."

"Understood."

Riggs pushed the door with his left hand, keeping the rifle steady as it opened. A light haze hampered his view, millions of suspended drywall particles wreaking havoc with the synthetic image. He tapped his night-vision goggles, switching to the traditional green-scale view, and the image cleared, revealing extensive damage to the back door and the walls surrounding it. Much of the damage looked like it came from the outside, compliments of Ross's extended burst of gunfire.

He moved down the hallway, sensing Tex close behind. They worked in tandem, shifting and clearing the threat angles with their rifles as they moved deeper into the space. The humming grew louder. Riggs approached the foot of the stairs and knelt next to the wall framing the staircase. Two jagged holes above his head reminded him that the drywall provided zero cover. Residential walls and furniture served one purpose in a close-quarters gun battle—concealment.

A nod at the wall told Tex that Riggs was ready to check the stairs. Riggs took a few short breaths before peeking up the stairs with his rifle. Clear to the landing.

The sound from the kitchen stopped, followed by several beeps that identified the source of the humming. A microwave.

"Riggs. I think we're clear," whispered Tex. "Body in the kitchen."

"Watch the stairs."

"Got it," said Tex, shifting to cover the stairs.

Riggs flashed to the other side of the stairwell and looked into the kitchen, seeing a pair of legs splayed on the floor between the refrigerator and the eat-in counter. Jon Fisher, no doubt, but he had to be sure before exposing himself.

"Did Oz enter the house before he went down?" he whispered over the radio net.

"No," Ross replied. "He's out on the patio."

Riggs slid farther to the right, craning his neck beyond the corner of the refrigerator. Shit. Ross had killed Fisher when he returned fire. The man's lifeless eyes stared at the kitchen ceiling, a small bullet hole evident in his right temple.

"Fisher's KIA. Bring the SUV to the street behind the town house."

"OK," the tech responded in a squeaky voice that didn't inspire confidence.

"Ross. I need you in here," said Riggs, stepping into the kitchen with his rifle aimed at the body.

"Closest police unit is four minutes away," announced Nissie.

A light flickered inside the microwave next to the stove. Something had caught fire. He fired a single bullet into Fisher's unprotected groin to be sure the old man wasn't playing dead. His body didn't stir. A thin stream of smoke poured out of the microwave as Riggs stepped over Fisher to take a closer look at the machine. What he found didn't surprise him at all. A melted satphone. His hopes of salvaging any useful information from this colossal screwup were fading by the second.

"Entering the back door," said Ross, appearing a few seconds later. "What the fuck is that smell?"

"He cooked his satphone," said Riggs, kneeling on the kitchen tile next to Fisher. "Tex. Ross. Find a bag or a suitcase. I don't care what you use, but start loading up any files, letters, paperwork. Anything. We need to be out of here in like two minutes."

Riggs searched Fisher's body, finding nothing useful. He had to give the guy credit. Fisher could have done a lot more damage if he hadn't been preoccupied in the kitchen, but cooking the phone had severed any traceable connections to his son, his wife, Stuart Quinn, and this secret compound Flagg suspected.

Tex rushed down the stairs. "I got everything I could find in the closets and dressers—which isn't much. Fisher had a bag full of goodies upstairs. Some kind of survival kit. I got that, too."

"There's nothing down here," said Ross, stepping out of the empty office.

Nissie's smug voice filled his ear. "You just hit the two-minute mark. My guy should be there with the SUV any second."

The hum of a powerful car engine vibrated the house. Riggs lifted his night-vision goggles an instant before a bright light bathed the backyard.

"Mr. Riggs. I'm out back," said the driver.

"We can see you, and so can the rest of the neighborhood. Kill the lights and open the back lift gate." He turned to his team. "We need to move Oz into the Yukon."

While Ross and Tex filed by, Riggs noticed a thin stack of letters on the counter next to the wall, mostly buried under a jagged chunk of drywall. He brushed the mess aside and stuffed the mail in one of his cargo pockets. The dying flame in the microwave beckoned him as he turned to step out of the town house. *Not this time, my friend—but soon.* He envisioned feeding a screaming Nissie Keane to a much bigger, hungrier fire than that one. Something bright and hot and beautiful enough to make up for his long hiatus. No, merely setting some building on fire wouldn't be enough to satisfy his friend.

CHAPTER 27

Keira stared at the glowing, twisted wrecks through her window as their SUV turned off the highway into the sand. Chunks of blackened debris covered the pavement around the smoking heaps, and David wasn't taking any chances on a flat tire.

A flat tire, she thought. It seemed like such a homely, minor concern.

She turned her eyes to the star-filled northern sky. "So much for the rules of engagement," she whispered, not wanting to wake Owen. "Recent attack, right? A few of the tires are still burning."

"Takes them a while to burn," David said. "Besides, lightning rarely strikes twice in the same place."

"Yeah?" she said. "Well, let's just set up camp here for the duration, then."

A low chuckle. Then, after a moment: "I'm willing to bet this was a targeted strike based on confirmed intelligence. The vehicles were headed to Sonoyta."

"*We're* headed to Sonoyta," Keira pointed out, squinting into the dark above them. Not that she had any chance of detecting a stealth drone or, more importantly, ever seeing the missile it fired. They'd be here one second, gone the next.

There was no point in worrying about it, though how in hell were you supposed to do anything else? From the armed drones circling overhead all the way down to the MP-20 she cradled in her lap, it all made her sick—and angry. It was obscene how these machines of war could erase people and families with the pull of a trigger or a mouse click. The thought of some indifferent drone pilot, sipping coffee with one hand and deciding her family's fate with the other, filled her with rage. If she could press a button right now and instantly kill every drone pilot in existence, she wouldn't hesitate, which made her even angrier. She was no different than them now, consumed by the circle of violence that spared none.

"We'll be fine," said David.

"You're stealing my husband's line," she said, noticing that he'd grown strangely quiet since they'd first spotted the destroyed vehicles.

"We can't turn back," Nathan said quietly.

"We can do whatever we want," she said.

"We're less than five miles from Sonoyta. The closest road behind us is two hours back."

"Aren't you a little concerned we might end up like that?" she said, fighting the urge to raise her voice.

Nathan twisted in his seat to look at her. "I'm very concerned, but turning back guarantees we end up like that. We have better odds out here."

"I know you're right. I just can't stand the thought of not being somewhat in control of our fate," she said, peering skyward again. "Somewhere in Yuma, someone not happy about pulling the night shift holds our fate in his delicate fingers."

"Actually, the night shift is highly coveted," said David. "The air-conditioning can't keep up during the day. Night flights go to the senior drone operators this time of the year."

"Terrific," she said.

The SUV drifted left, scraping over and through a field of low-lying bushes before emerging on the highway beyond the wreckage.

"We'll be fine once we get past Sonoyta," said Nathan.

"Oh yeah," she muttered. "Smooth sailing all the way."

"I liked it better when you were sleeping."

"I was never sleeping," said Keira. "Just pretending so I could eavesdrop on you two."

"Probably not the best use of your downtime," David said drily.

"No kidding," she said, stifling a laugh. "How the hell can the two of you drive that long without saying more than five words to each other?"

"We were keeping quiet so you could sleep," said Nathan.

"Really?"

"Not really," said David. "I didn't feel like talking."

"Neither did I," added Nathan.

She grunted, lifting her night-vision goggles to take a short break from the bright image.

"How about our guy?" said Nathan. "He faking it, too?"

"I don't think so. He's been breathing heavy for the past hour."

"You should wake him up before we reach Sonoyta," said David. "Just in case we run into a problem driving through town."

"We're driving straight through it?" said Keira.

Nathan slid the map through the front seats. He'd folded it to show the area around Sonoyta. "It doesn't look like we have any alternative. Route 2 cuts right through Sonoyta, north to south."

"Maybe there's some side road?" Keira asked.

"If it's not on the map, we're not taking it," said David. "I don't want to get lost on a side road in the middle of cartel land."

She studied the map, coming to the same conclusion. "I agree. Without a detailed map of the town, we're better off staying on Route 2. I'll start waking Owen."

Keira nudged him with her elbow, watching him stir for a moment before he sank back into a deep sleep. She wondered if this was necessary. If they were attacked in Sonoyta by banditos, or whatever cartel dirt bags lingered in these parts, she wasn't sure it would matter if he were awake or asleep. If they were forced out of the car, they were probably as good as dead. Then again, he could become a serious distraction inside the car if he woke up disoriented in the middle of a firefight. She raised his night-vision visor and nudged him a little harder. His eyes fluttered open, slowly drifting shut again.

"Owen," she said, loudly.

His eyes flung open, hands reaching for the missing visor.

"It's OK, sweetie. You're OK," she said, gently grabbing his hands.

He calmed immediately, speaking in a sleep-induced slur. "What's going on?"

"We're coming up on Sonoyta, and we need an extra pair of eyes watching the street," she said.

Owen rubbed his eyes. "All right. How long until we get there? I'm thirsty."

"A few minutes, I think," said Nathan. "You have time, buddy."

She loosened the drinking hose attached to the shoulder of his vest and pressed it into one of his hands. He drank deeply while she scanned the empty landscape behind and to the side of the SUV. Low hills rose to the north, the border lying somewhere in between. So close, yet so far. Sonoyta was the only road crossing the border between Yuma and Nogales—and it was denied to them by assholes sitting in air-conditioned trailers a hundred miles away.

When Owen was finished, she slipped the CamelBak hose into the clip sewn into the vest and lowered his visor.

"Looks like we're getting close," he said, pointing toward the windshield.

Scattered roadside structures started to take form in the distance. She guessed the approach to Sonoyta would resemble the road out of Mexicali, only on a smaller scale. Gutted businesses, torn fences, and stripped vehicles. Abandoned, for all practical purposes. As they passed the first building, she knew it would be much worse. The top right corner of the narrow, two-level structure had been destroyed, replaced with a jagged, fire-scored hole extending several feet down each side. She caught a glimpse of additional damage to the back of the building before the SUV cruised past. She'd never seen anything like it.

"Missile strike," stated David solemnly. "Blew out the back wall and left debris in the parking lot."

"Drones?" said Nathan.

"Has to be. There's no competitive cartel activity between Tijuana and Laredo."

"Alpha said the drones killed anything crossing the border," she said. "Maybe they ran out of legitimate targets."

"I don't think so. That's a precision hit. Probably took out an observation post watching the western approach into town. I expect to see more of this as we get deeper into town. This is a good thing."

"A good thing?" she said.

"Yeah. Sonoyta will be clear, as in nobody around."

"Because of the same missiles that could turn us into a—" Keira stopped herself. Without realizing it, she'd violated one of their rules. She'd unnecessarily heaped another layer of fear on Owen. Fuck. A hand patted her knee.

"It's OK, Mom," he said. "We'll be fine."

She shook her head, suppressing a smile. "For the record, 'We'll be fine' does not create a magic force field around us."

"Hey, it's worked for us so far," said Nathan, raising his hand for a high five.

David shook his head, rejecting the high five.

"See? He's afraid of you, too," said Nathan, turning his head toward Keira.

"He should be," she said. "Both of you should be."

"Jesus," hissed David, bringing their banter to a halt. "Look at this."

Scorched vehicles littered the road ahead, some upside down, all of them at odd angles. Gutted one-story buildings lined each side of the street. Beach ball–size holes had been punched clean through their stucco, the patterns framing larger areas of demolition that reminded her of the missile hit they had just passed. Sonoyta was a war zone, and this was just the outskirts.

"Looks like our drone pilots went a little trigger-happy here," said Nathan.

David didn't respond right away. He slowed the SUV, swiveling his head to take in the unfolding scene. "This wasn't drones. The smaller holes look like 25-millimeter cannon fire. Drones don't carry gun pods," he said. "I'd say a helicopter did this. How far away is the border?"

"About a mile and a half," said Nathan.

"Well within Strikefire missile range, but a stretch for helicopter-mounted guns," he said, adding a whispered, "You sneaky fuckers."

"What?" said Keira.

"They crossed the border. Our helicopters were here," said David, easing the SUV past the first charred vehicle. "This truck was taken out by gunfire. Look at the hole in the door."

Owen leaned over her to see.

"You don't want to see this, sweetie," she said, gently pushing him back.

Instead of protesting, her son climbed halfway over the backpacks on the other side of him. She'd grabbed his vest to pull him back when he slid back into his seat on his own.

"I saw a few bodies," he said, his head pointed straight at the windshield.

Keira looked past him out the window and saw more than just a few bodies. She spotted a dozen twisted shapes strewn on the ground between the blasted vehicles, bones clearly protruding through shredded clothing. Scorched faces stared back at her from inside the cars and trucks, her night vision allowing her to see more detail than she wanted. Whatever had happened here had been a complete massacre.

"The bodies look like they've been picked clean," said Nathan.

Keira looked away from the scene, squeezing Owen's hand.

"This happened a few weeks ago. Desert animals did their work already," said David. "Alpha wasn't kidding when he said this place was dead."

She wanted to scream. They were driving an SUV with Mexican plates, in the dead of the night, through a military free-fire zone on the United States–Mexico border, and to top it off, David and her husband were narrating the entire fucking experience.

"Can we just get through this without the commentary?" she said.

"Sorry," said Nathan.

David navigated through the kill zone, coming to a complete stop twice to open his door and verify that they could squeeze through an opening in the packed debris field. Once through, the SUV accelerated toward the center of town.

The rest of the road approaching Sonoyta's business district was free of destruction, the United States military's sledgehammer tactics seemingly confined to the outskirts. After they turned due south into the densest part of town, Keira started to miss the carnage. The emptiness left her unsettled. Her night-vision goggles didn't register a single artificial light source, and the street was completely devoid of parked cars. Sonoyta was a ghost town.

The SUV lurched forward, picking up speed moments after they entered the busiest stretch of downtown road. The windshield HUD read seventy miles per hour, which was excessive for an urban street— even a deserted one.

"You might want to take it easy here," said Nathan, echoing her thoughts.

"Take a look at your ten o'clock," said David.

They looked to their left.

A dark gore stain smeared against the tan stucco wall of an OXXO convenience store marked the location of a slumped body on the sidewalk.

"Drive-by shooting?" said Nathan.

"I don't think so," replied David. "Looked like a single shot."

"Snipers?" she said.

"That's why I'm driving like a maniac."

"There's another one. Right side," said Nathan.

Keira looked too late, barely glimpsing the repeated scene. Snipers on both sides?

"That one had a rifle," added her husband.

"They have this place locked down tight," said David, pushing the SUV up to eighty-five miles per hour.

An earsplitting bang filled the car, creating a moment of pandemonium. Keira instinctively pulled Owen over her lap before David slammed on the brakes, forcing her against her seat belt, then floored the SUV, rocketing them back against the seat. When she looked up, she couldn't see through her window. She started to form words, but a hollow thump vibrated the car, a brief shower of sparks bouncing off the windshield and disappearing.

"Stay down!" yelled David, the SUV veering into the oncoming traffic lane.

Owen tried to raise his head, but she kept him buried under her arms, leaning over his torso. A sharp crack, immediately followed by a shower of glass, kept her locked into position over her son. The SUV accelerated faster than she thought possible, the rough street rumbling furiously underneath them.

"Are you OK?" yelled Nathan.

She lifted her head far enough to see Nathan turned in his seat, partially leaning over the center console. He extended a hand, which she grasped and squeezed.

The SUV shuddered, traveling at breakneck speed for another minute or so before slowing.

"We're out of the town," said David. "Whose window got hit?"

"Mine," said Keira.

"Mom, you're crushing me," protested Owen.

"I don't really care. You're not sitting up until the town is out of sight."

"Describe the window for me," David said.

"Shattered in place," said Nathan.

"Probably took a hit from a military-grade armor-piercing bullet," said David. "You're lucky to be alive."

"I feel like the luckiest girl in the world," she said bitterly. "Is my window useless now?"

"Another bullet like that will go right through, but it should stand up to more conventional rounds for now."

"Should?" she said.

David shrugged. "I've seen this type of glass take a beating long after I would have guessed it was useless, and I've seen it fail miserably under the same circumstances."

"Which situation happened most often?"

"The first."

"Finally some good news," said Keira.

"Want to hear something even better?" said David.

"I can't wait."

"We're still alive," said David.

"Hard to beat that."

"Seriously. One of their bullets grazed the middle of hood. If it had struck the side of the vehicle, we'd still be in town—most likely dead or bleeding out."

"The good news express keeps delivering."

Owen and Nathan laughed.

"What are you laughing at?" she said to her son, at last letting him sit up.

"Watch the glass back there," said David. "I'll stop about ten miles south of town so we can clean that out."

"I'd prefer you didn't stop until we reached Mexico City."

"We're not going to Mexico City," said David.

"Maybe we should be."

Keira was starting to have second thoughts about crossing into the United States at Nogales—or anywhere, for that matter.

Chapter 28

Leeds shook his head as Olmos steered their SUV between the two gaudy, illuminated marble pillars that marked the entrance to La Araña's gated estate. He had to give this Spider guy some credit. Instead of building a mansion on a sprawling tract of land on the outskirts of town, he had declared the drug cartel's equivalent of eminent domain and confiscated something a little closer to the action. The digital maps still listed his estate as a public park. Impressive.

Leeds tensed when a few guards appeared inside the gate and pointed flashlights at the SUV, still wary of the safe passage guaranteed by Chukov. The men kept their rifles and submachine guns pointed away from the vehicle despite the murderous glares directed at the tinted glass windows. They had reason to be angry. He just hoped their fear of disobeying La Araña's orders would trump any drug-fueled vigilante notions. Chukov's team hadn't been subtle when they'd breached the compound. They'd cut a wide path through the guards on their way in.

A massive Mexican wearing a black suit over a stark white collared shirt waved them through.

"Drive slow and steady," said Leeds. "Don't give them an excuse."

"I don't see how this is supposed to work for us. Why can't Chukov go to work on Spider-Man and leave us out of it?"

"Because we need Señor Talamanco's cooperation and blessing, no matter how insincere, to continue operating in Mexicali. If the cartel turns against us, we won't last the hour."

"I'm worried about later," said Olmos. "I can't imagine he's going to take Chukov's stunt lightly. These guys build their reputations on fear and respect. Chukov just knocked him down the ladder a few notches."

"We just need to get through the night."

"I don't know. These guys look hungry. Never know who's got their eyes set on the big mansion."

"I think we can reach a satisfactory agreement with this guy," said Leeds.

"I hope so."

Leeds didn't exactly trust the situation either, but Chukov hadn't left him much of a choice. He'd been just as surprised as Olmos when the Russian's call came through. Somehow Petrov's ragged bandits had managed to infiltrate the cartel boss's compound and capture a man who had, until tonight, respectfully declined any association with Cerberus. Now he was politely requesting an audience.

They were directed to park beside a Range Rover under a carport set behind a line of trees. When they got out, one of two men standing at a thick, black gate set into a tall, brick wall gestured for them to follow. Leeds was pleased to see that neither man appeared armed, as he had insisted.

They followed the men into a lush courtyard. Apparently, the water crisis hadn't reached Señor Talamanco's private gardens.

The guards guided them across the exquisitely manicured grounds, past a brightly glowing pool to a softly lit, open-air dining room attached to the main house. A man Leeds assumed to be Talamanco sat alone at the head of a thick wooden table, casually eating from a plate piled with food. Chukov faced him, seated at the opposite end. Three Russian mercenaries were visible, forming a loose perimeter around the alfresco dining room.

As Leeds and Olmos reached the brick patio connected to the room, Talamanco waved the two escorts away. They disappeared into the gardens, never looking back.

"Welcome," said Talamanco, gesturing to the chairs next to him. "Please join me for a late dinner. My kitchen staff always prepares enough food to feed an army. Little did they know, I'd be entertaining one."

"I'll let you handle this," whispered Olmos, nodding respectfully at Talamanco before stepping to the edge of the room near one of Chukov's men.

Leeds nodded. "I don't normally eat this late, but there's nothing normal about tonight. Thank you."

He'd reached out to pull back the chair next to Talamanco when he noticed the plate was already full. Leeds decided to stand.

"That was my wife's plate. We don't normally eat this late either," said Talamanco, cutting into a steak without looking up. "And we've never had uninvited guests—until tonight."

"I trust Señor Talamanco's wife and children are being treated well," said Leeds, glancing at Chukov.

"With white-glove service," said Chukov.

Talamanco took a sip of red wine. "I assume you are familiar with the term *Mexican standoff*?"

Leeds smirked. "Of course."

"And your friend?" said Talamanco, waving the glass of wine at Chukov.

The Russian shook his head, as if the Mexican's question was a waste of time.

"Then let me put it into terms a Russki might understand," said Talamanco. "It's similar to a stalemate in chess. There is no winning situation for any party involved."

Chukov's expression remained the same. Unimpressed.

"I'm here to break the stalemate," said Leeds. "We can all walk away from this winners."

"All of this was rather unnecessary," said Talamanco.

"We're operating under a strict timeline, and you haven't exactly made yourself available to us today."

"I'm a busy man, Mr. Leeds. I don't have time to pursue petty cash offers made in bars or on street corners."

Leeds tried to conceal his surprise that Talamanco knew his name.

"Don't strain too hard to keep a straight face. I knew who you were within an hour of your arrival, along with Raymond Olmos, former Navy SEAL. I have dossiers on both of you."

Chukov stifled a laugh.

"Don't laugh, Mr. Chukov. Your team has made a name for itself in and around Mexico City," said the cartel boss.

Chukov's face hardened. He placed his elbows on the table, interlacing his fingers. Talamanco put his wineglass down, smiling cordially at Leeds.

"What are you offering to break the stalemate?"

"The lives of your wife and children," stated Chukov.

The Mexican shook his head. "He truly doesn't understand. We're all dead. You. Me. Olmos. Chukov. His team. My family. That's where this negotiation starts. The neighborhood surrounding this place is filled with my soldiers. Word is out. Nobody survives. So, what are you offering for me to sell out one of my best-paying clients?"

Leeds shook his head at Chukov, who had reached one hand below the table and leaned forward. The Russian eased back against his seat.

"One million dollars," said Leeds.

"That doesn't cover one month's rent for the space they occupy—and the protection I provide. The clients in question pay on time and directly enable important aspects of my business. Look around you. The other bosses don't live like this."

"Five million."

"This is fucking bullshit," grumbled Chukov.

"I agree," said Talamanco. "Five is low."

Leeds needed to take a different approach. There was no way Flagg and Petrov combined were going to pay this guy more than $5 million without a guarantee of finding the suspected CLM bunker. Likewise, there existed little chance that Talamanco would accept a handshake that the money would be transferred after a successful mission. He had one more angle that might appeal to the drug boss.

"Is it fair to assume that you've already warned your clients of our interest in their whereabouts? I can't imagine you'd pass on the opportunity to squeeze more money out of them. Maybe let them stress over it awhile and try to initiate a bidding war?"

"The thought may have crossed my mind," said Talamanco, picking up his wineglass.

"I guarantee they know you better than you think," said Leeds. "They're probably long gone by now."

"My people haven't reported anything unusual," said the Mexican before draining the rest of his wineglass.

"Five million right now," said Leeds. "You give us the location. Whether they're there or not, you get the money."

"I don't believe you're in a position to—"

"You have ten seconds to make a decision. Start counting, Chukov. Silently," said Leeds. "I hope he can count right."

"This is crazy," sputtered the Mexican. "We're negotiating."

"Five million," said Leeds, surveying the lush grounds. "Eight Spetsnaz, a former SEAL, and an ex–CIA operative? We won't all make it out, but I like my odds."

Leeds took the bottle of wine on the table and topped off Talamanco's glass, filling a second glass halfway. He raised the half-full glass. "Shall we toast to a five-million-dollar deal?" he said. "How are we doing on time, Mr. Chukov?"

"Two seconds. One and—"

"OK. OK. It's a deal! But I get paid now, and you let my family go," said Talamanco, lifting his overfilled glass.

"You get paid one million now. Two million when we confirm you didn't send us to a long-abandoned drug depot, and the rest when we are safely out of Mexicali. We walk out of here. Your family stays."

"Cash?"

"Confirmed bank deposit," said Leeds. "Only a tourist carries cash in Mexico."

"Funny," said Talamanco.

"And if you decide to go back on your word, for whatever reason—"

"Hey! I said we have a deal."

"I'm just making the terms of our deal clear. If you fuck us over in any way, you'll never eat a nice meal like this again without worrying about a drone raining missiles down on your family."

"I get it," he said. "You have my word."

Leeds clinked Talamanco's glass and took a generous sip.

"Exquisite," he said. He lifted the bottle off the table, gently tilting it to read the label. "Cerbaiona Brunello di Montalcino. Twenty ten," he said, nodding his approval. "I'll have to remember that."

"You won't have much luck finding a bottle. Only six hundred and fifty cases were produced, and most of the vintage has been consumed over the years. It was considered a cult brand at the time. I'll send you a bottle, assuming our financial affairs are in order at the end of the day."

"All the more incentive to get it right," said Leeds, finishing the glass.

CHAPTER 29

When Leeds ducked under a thick wooden beam protruding from the low ceiling, his shoulder scraped the heavy-duty wire mesh stretched against the walls, and the Russian in front of him—and for all he knew, the entire column—halted due to his carelessness. Chukov had forbidden even a hushed whisper on the radio net.

Several long seconds passed before they started moving again.

He hated tight spaces, though he had to admit this tunnel was a huge step up from some of the sketchy holes he'd climbed through in his agency days. Just the thought of the cave system used by Turkish insurgents in the Kizildag hills made his palms sweaty. Regardless of the comparative luxury in construction, he was anxious to break into the CLM's main bunker complex—even if it meant a vicious firefight. Anything was better than this.

He leaned to one side, straining to catch a glimpse beyond the Russian blocking most of his view down the passage. Nothing. Their night-vision goggles were essentially useless in the pitch dark without activating infrared flashlights, which would be detectable by anyone wearing the most rudimentary night-vision gear.

The group stopped again, remaining deathly quiet for another seemingly endless stretch of time, and then the tunnel brightened, exposing an open doorway that led into a low-ceilinged room.

"The place looks abandoned," said Chukov, peering inside the room ahead of them.

"Abandoned for a few years or a few hours?" said Leeds from behind the massive Russian separating them.

"My guess is a few hours. I'm getting residual heat signatures from the lightbulbs hanging from the rafters. Very faint, but it would have dissipated in less than a day. Someone was here," said Chukov. He cocked his head. "Hold on. I'm getting a similar report from the other team."

Chukov had his team split in half, moving through two of the access tunnels identified by Talamanco's street operations chief. The other group's tunnel had originated in the secret basement of a dilapidated funeral home on Avenida Reforma; the route his team had taken had started in the roach-infested closet of a shuttered mechanic shop one street south. A third tunnel existed to the east, emptying into a fire-damaged Chinese restaurant, but the Russian didn't want to spread his team too thin. Talamanco had a small army watching that exit.

"PowerBar wrappers. Crumbs not yet claimed by the rats or cockroaches. I think it's fair to assume this place was recently abandoned," said Chukov. "We're pushing forward."

"Concur," said Leeds. Not that he really had a say in the matter. Chukov was calling the shots down here. Leeds and Olmos were little more than glorified observers at this point.

They filed through the doorway, entering a cramped space featuring a chair pushed against one of the walls and two crude light fixtures bolted to the crossbeams. A hardwired camera pointed toward the doorway they had just left. A sturdy metal door sat half-open under the camera. Aside from the beam cast by Chukov's infrared rifle light, Leeds detected no artificial sources of light beyond the door.

A wider hallway led to a larger central room flanked by folding tables. One of the tabletops supported a sizable flat-screen monitor, its power cord still connected to a surge protector on the dirt floor.

The monitor's connection cable dangled in front of the table, however, taunting them. The rest of the team activated their IR rifle lights and spread out to cover the other entrances. Leeds triggered his light and surveyed what certainly appeared to be an operations center. It wasn't fancy by any stretch of the imagination, but judging by the number of zip-tied cable bundles running from floor to ceiling along the room's frame, this room had been wired for high bandwidth—an indication that it had served as an operational hub.

Rows of chairs faced a wall that had likely held up maps a short time ago. A coffeemaker sat on a wooden table in the corner beyond the map wall, a partially filled carafe nestled into place. Several coffee mugs stood neatly stacked next to the machine.

Chukov stepped up to the coffeemaker, feeling the carafe with the back of his wrist. "Still warm."

Leeds felt the sting of reproach in Chukov's voice. If they'd arrived a few hours earlier, not only would they have fulfilled their contract to kill Fisher, but they could have handed Flagg the keys to CLM's castle.

A light appeared to Leeds's left, drawing all of their rifles to the hallway entrance next to the computer monitor station.

"The other team is coming through," said Chukov, pointing in the direction of the approaching light. "They found six large rooms with bunk beds off that hallway. Four of the rooms were stripped bare. They left everything behind in the other two."

"Let's clear the rest of these passageways and start bagging up anything useful," said Leeds.

"Like what? Empty coffee mugs?" said Chukov.

"Handwritten notes in clothing pockets. A secret journal about life in the CLM. A forgotten thumb drive. Dead phone," said Leeds. "People leave the oddest stuff behind when they're in a hurry. We need to treat this like a crime scene."

"You want to go around sniffing panties? That's your own business," said Chukov. "We get paid to kill people."

"Well, there's nobody here to kill."

"Precisely. I'll give you five minutes. You're on your own after that."

Leeds knew better than to push back right now. The Russian was seeing red. His payday had disappeared, possibly for good, and the blame fell squarely on Leeds's shoulders in his warped, killer-centric mind. Right or wrong didn't matter when you were trapped forty feet below the ground with eight professional murderers. Leeds moved swiftly across the room to grab Olmos before he ran his mouth. He sensed they were one snide remark away from a Mexicali burial.

CHAPTER 30

The crisp digital satellite map of Mexicali blurred as Flagg's head drifted slowly toward the screen. His eyes bolted open, the image instantly crystallizing. He took a deep breath and rubbed his face before standing up. Falling asleep wasn't a luxury he could afford with two field teams on the verge of a breakthrough. He'd dig into the military-grade stimulants reserved for field operatives if he kept drifting off.

He examined the street map again, marveling at the audacity of the cartels. For years they had run an underground drug-packaging station within sight of the border. Probably drove the delivery vehicles right into the mechanic's shop, where they were loaded with drugs and sealed up for the short journey to a distribution shop across the border in Calexico. They probably ran a dozen more operations like this along the wall.

Flagg didn't care about the fifty-year war on drugs. A much more insidious group had taken residence in the former Sinaloa bunker, a faction of radicals far more dangerous to the country than a $200-billion-a-year drug habit. Chump change compared to the damage the California Liberation Movement could inflict on his client's bottom line. And the problem extended far beyond the financial interests represented by the One Nation Coalition. The entire system was at risk if California managed to break free of its federal chains. Even a limited secession would cause a catastrophic ripple effect of states' rights affirmations.

Of course, none of the big-picture impact truly bothered him, as long as he still had a place at Cerberus. A prospect in serious jeopardy unless he started to receive some better news tonight.

He considered calling Riggs. The guy had sent him one inane update after the other all fucking day—then went silent after breaking into the house across the street from Jon Fisher. Maybe he should ping Nissie Keane. She'd gone mysteriously quiet around the same time. He'd just reached for the keyboard when Nick Leeds's satellite phone started tracking on the digital map again. They had just emerged from the bunker. *Please. Please let this be finished.* A call appeared on his screen, which he readily accepted.

"What do we have?"

Leeds hesitated too long, which told him everything he needed to know. It wasn't over. "Nothing," Leeds said. "Looks like they cleared out a few hours ago."

A few hours? He wanted to scream.

"Nothing at all?"

"No electronics. No documents. We bagged up what little they left behind."

"Talamanco made it sound like they were running the space program from that bunker. How could they have disappeared without a trace?"

"Probably slowly evacuated over the course of a few days. We found six dormitory-style bunk rooms. Two looked like they had been abandoned in a hurry. Sleeping bags, clothing, footwear, and other nonidentifying personal effects left behind. The other rooms looked empty, but we found signs of recent occupancy under a few of the bunks and in the usual nooks and crannies. I don't think Talamanco was exaggerating, but I do think his CLM clients have been slipping quietly away under his nose."

"Where does that leave us," Flagg said, "other than five million dollars poorer?"

"I'd leverage Talamanco against the rest of the money. For that kind of payout, he can flex his muscle outside Mexicali."

"There's only one problem with that."

"Don't worry about it. I'll deliver the message personally," said Leeds. "I'm pretty sure Chukov won't mind helping me with that."

Flagg laughed, more at his own predicament than anything else. "That's not the problem," he said.

"It can't be good if you're laughing."

"Talamanco doesn't have any influence outside Mexicali. The jefes controlling territory along the California border don't command any respect from the rest of the Sinaloa. They don't make enough money to attend regular cartel meetings. They pay fees up the chain of command to continue operating their little fiefdoms, and that's about the extent of their connection to the cartel. They're more like franchises. I'll have to widen the net and engage my primary Sinaloa contact."

"Sounds expensive."

"It makes the five million I wasted on Talamanco sound like a bargain," said Flagg. "And my deal with the real Sinaloa isn't negotiable."

"Does it guarantee results?"

"You know better than to ask that," said Flagg. "The only thing it guarantees is an extensive effort to accomplish our goal."

"Extensive or expensive?"

"Both. They'll do whatever, wherever we ask, for a limited amount of time."

"Very expensive," said Leeds.

"I'm conjuring an extensive excuse to justify the transfer of funds as we speak. I'm probably going to charge this to One Nation and label it a onetime security guarantee from the cartel to stay out of our business in the Wastelands."

"You think they'll buy that?"

"They don't have a choice. Everyone on that council had a hand in Congresswoman Almeda's assassination. We had the situation under control in California until they pulled that stunt, and I have no doubt Petrov put them up to it. He can iron out any concerns they have about the expenditure."

"Good luck getting him to cooperate," said Leeds. "The Russians I'm dealing with seem to do what they please."

"Chukov is a means to an end," said Flagg. "I can divert money to our new problem, but I can't divert manpower. People talk. As far as Cerberus knows, and will ever know, the heavy loss of personnel last night was necessary to ensure the results."

"I understand," said Leeds. "Where do you want us?"

"With the Russians at the airport, on five-minute standby. No sense in guessing which direction they took. The Gulfstream can cover more miles in an hour than they can hope to drive in ten on the highway."

"I'll break the good news to Chukov," said Leeds.

"And watch their drinking," said Flagg. "This group has a bit of a reputation."

"Oh, I've been watching them drink since they arrived. Hasn't affected their operational performance in the least from what I can tell."

"They'll get the job done regardless. That's not what I'm worried about," said Flagg. "If they're not killing or sleeping, they're drinking and fighting. Keep your distance at the airport."

"You don't think they'll just take a nap?"

Flagg couldn't tell if Leeds was being sarcastic, and he couldn't take the chance that he might be asking a serious question. "There's no chance of them settling in for the night, and the drinking and fighting a bit more often than not leads to killing. I'd sleep in the aircraft, with one eye open. Probably the most comfortable place anyway."

"Wonderful," said Leeds. "Do I get a hazard pay kicker for working with them?"

"You're overpaid as it is. Check in with me when you get situated," said Flagg, disconnecting the call.

A fit of yawning overtook him. He'd have no choice but to dig into the stimulant supply. Sleep was not on his immediate horizon, or any horizon he could imagine. Glancing at the time on the display, he shook his head. First, time to find out if the $5 million paid eight months ago for "twenty-four-hour VIP access" to his Sinaloa contact had been worth it. He navigated to a contact list on his encrypted Cerberus account and punched the number into his satellite phone. Moments later, he entered a series of numbers that rewarded him with a soothing recorded voice.

"Thank you. You will be called on this phone as soon as the client is available."

Less than a minute later, his phone rang.

"Señor Flagg. How may I help you?"

Worth every penny.

CHAPTER 31

Riggs ignored the phone buzzing on the cheap wooden desk. He was frazzled, trying to walk through every step they had taken since arriving.

They'd kept the silver Yukon used to transport the team to and from Scott Gleason's town house away from the hotel, parking it at a busy highway travel center a few miles north on Interstate 93 when it hadn't been in use. There was no way to connect it to the Travelers Inn.

That truck had been abandoned, with Oz's body, in the garage of a vacant home a few miles from the town house. According to Internet records retrieved by Nissie, the house had been on the real estate market for five months, indicating there was little interest in the home. The vehicle could go weeks undiscovered in that garage.

The minivan used by Nissie's team hadn't left the hotel. No issue there. Only the sedan had been in both places, but he'd kept that exposure to a single daytime reconnaissance pass. The police might be able to identify the vehicle from a street-facing security feed, but the team would be long gone before the car was linked to the motel. He planned on splitting the group up tomorrow morning, moving them to even shadier places near the University of Montana. Nissie's crew might even fit in around there—not that they ever left their connected rooms.

Riggs buried his face in his hands, each buzz of the phone causing his jaw to clench. He'd followed the proper protocols, except for part about obeying Flagg's orders. That was going to be a problem.

"You gonna answer that?" said Tex, his hand keeping up its ceaseless movement back and forth between his mouth and a bag of corn chips. The operative stared through a small opening between the room's shades, his eyes fixed on the parking lot as he ate.

"I'm thinking," said Riggs.

He'd fucked up big-time. There was no way around it. His only option at this point was to fess up and ask what he could do to make it right. He'd obviously start by returning the advance. He could afford to bankroll the team on this one. Work had been steady, and he wanted to keep it that way. A screwup like this could get him blacklisted.

"Do you need me to write out a script?" said Tex.

"Fuck off."

"Hey!" hissed Tex, still staring through the shades. "You dick this up and we could end up dead."

"I got it under control," said Riggs, his hand hovering over the phone.

"You better," said Ross from the doorway connecting the two rooms. His hand rested on the top of his thigh holster, the pistol's retention strap unfastened.

"Really?" said Riggs, nodding toward the holster. "That's the way it's gonna go down?"

"If you fuck this up, it is," said Ross. "You take the call on speakerphone."

"I don't think so," said Riggs, gripping the phone.

Tex shifted slightly, the suppressed rifle cradled in his arms now pointed directly at Riggs's chest.

"You, too?"

"It's nothing personal, Chris," he said. "But I'd just as soon shoot you dead and try to make my own bargain if your conversation with Flagg goes sideways."

"I'll remember this," said Riggs.

"I hope you do. There's a valuable lesson here," said Tex. "Don't fuck over your clients."

Riggs pressed the screen, accepting the call, then hit the speaker-phone icon.

"Mr. Flagg. I was just about to call you."

"You can drop that bullshit right away. I have a fairly good idea of what's happening in Missoula right now. You know how they say that absence makes the heart grow fonder?" said Flagg.

The line went silent.

Tex lifted the rifle's barrel a few inches.

"Yes," said Riggs, his eyes glued to the rifle. "I'm familiar with that phrase."

"Well, in my case, absence makes me suspicious. There appears to be an unusual amount of police activity around Mr. Gleason's town house."

"We had a little problem with Fisher," said Riggs. "There were unexpected—"

Flagg interrupted his planned speech. "Stop. Here's the deal. You just inherited a post office box."

"What? I don't understand."

"Of course you don't," said Flagg. "On top of potentially severing our only link to several key witnesses, you didn't even glance at the scant evidence collected from Gleason's town house."

"I thought delegating that to Nissie's team would be the best use of—"

"Chris," Flagg cut in. "After such a colossal fuckup with Jon Fisher, I would have expected you to have pored over that evidence yourself as if your life depended on it. Because it does."

"I haven't heard from Nissie," Riggs said. "What did they find in—"

"A total of five seconds sifting through the pile and they found a mortgage statement addressed to a post office box at 1100 West Kent Avenue."

"Great. Got it," said Riggs. "We'll stake out the box."

"Just so you completely understand, let me clarify. No matter how long it takes for one of the Gleasons to show up, your team owns this post office box."

"Sure," said Riggs. "What if nobody ever shows up?"

"Then you're all dead men," said Flagg. "And just so I'm clear—I did mean *all* of you. If either of your colleagues decides to cut his losses and make a run for it, I will place a permanent, tier-one contract on his head. The same goes without saying for you. Are we all on the same page, gentlemen?"

Tex and Ross acknowledged Flagg's query with uncharacteristically crisp replies in the affirmative.

"Excellent. Check out of the Travelers Inn at a normal time in the morning, to avoid suspicion, and relocate to the address I've passed to Miss Keane. The location is residential, with a two-car garage. Nissie will have the entry codes. Nice touch ditching the Tahoe, by the way. I haven't completely lost faith in your abilities, Chris."

"Thank you, sir."

"Last thing. I need you to drive to the airport in Helena to pick up two new rental cars. The rental offices open at six a.m., and it's a two-hour trip each way. Plan accordingly. Obviously, this will require at least two of you. One of you will need to stay behind and watch the post office. PO boxes are accessible twenty-four hours a day at this location."

Tex lowered his rifle and silently mouthed an obscenity.

"We're on it, Mr. Flagg," said Riggs. "We're gonna fix this. I made a really bad call back at the town house."

Tex shook his head and rolled his eyes.

"Water under the bridge. All we can do is move forward," said Flagg. "Last thing. Miss Keane's team is off-limits. She didn't reach out to me with any of this."

The satellite phone chirped, indicating that the call had ended. Riggs verified that they were no longer connected, giving them a thumbs-up.

Ross whispered, "Power the phone down."

Riggs removed the battery. Tex and Ross did the same with their phones.

"That went better than I expected," said Tex. "Even though we're still fucked."

"We've been in tougher spots than this," said Riggs.

Ross nodded. "I'm still thinking about shooting you. This PO box thing is a long shot."

"We can work around this if nobody shows up," said Riggs. "Somebody in town knows Scott Gleason."

PART IV

CHAPTER 32

Nathan's helmet knocked against the bullet-resistant window, jolting him awake. The car was drifting to the right over the median, into the leftmost northbound lane. He looked at David, who glanced at him for a second.

"I'm good," he said.

"You were halfway into the oncoming lane."

"There's no traffic on either side."

"That's not the point."

He checked his watch—5:03 a.m. He'd been asleep for around eighteen minutes. He knew that because David had almost driven them off the road at four forty-five. Nathan had sworn to himself that he'd keep an eye on him, but the jolt of adrenaline had worn off much quicker than he'd expected.

"I'll be fine once the sun comes up. The sky is changing," David said, pointing past him.

Nathan raised his visor, not sure how anyone could make that determination looking at a synthetic daylight image, and stared into the darkness. As his eyes adjusted, a thin strip of blue framing the low hills to the east became visible. David was right—about the sun coming up, not his ability to drive. Once they crossed into Arizona, they had to stop somewhere to grab some sleep. All of them. They faced a full day of driving to reach Las Vegas. Probably twice that, with the detours around Tucson and Phoenix.

"We'll stop and rest on the other side of the border," said Nathan.

"I don't think that's a good idea."

"It's better than driving off the road and killing everyone. I'm even thinking we might be better off lying low for the day and heading out again around nightfall."

"We need to keep moving north," said David.

"Who's going to drive? Me? Them?" He pointed at his sleeping family.

"I'll be fine," said David. "What does that sign say?"

Nathan examined the green-and-white road sign ahead. "*Aeropuerto* eleven kilometers," he read aloud.

"We're getting close to the Route 150 connector."

"We don't want to miss that," said Nathan, settling into his seat to watch David.

A few minutes later, barely able to keep his own eyes open, he watched David's head lower slowly. They were definitely finding an out-of-the-way motel on the other side. He gripped the wheel with his right hand and nudged David with the other.

The Marine bolted upright, shaking his head. "Shit. Sorry."

"That's it. You can't keep your eyes open for two minutes," said Nathan, tapping his watch. "I don't think a few hours of shut-eye is going to kill us."

David inhaled and exhaled deeply. "We'll see if we can find a safe place to stop."

A lighted highway sign, spanning the two northbound lanes, appeared in the distance. The sign didn't contain any highway numbers. The left side read RECINTO FISCAL NOGALES III-FRONTERA USA, the other AEROPUERTO-NOGALES CENTRO.

Nathan said, "Stay left and follow anything that reads 'Frontera USA.'"

"How far to the border from the split?"

Too tired to remember the calculation he had made earlier, Nathan had to take the map out again. Fortunately, he had scribbled the distance on the map. "About eight miles. Takes us west of Nogales proper," said Nathan. "I still find it hard to believe the border crossing here isn't manned. If it is, we're screwed."

"I don't think Jose would have sent us here if there was any doubt."

"They drove us into a very dangerous situation back in Sonoyta. What if the United States military's shut down the Nogales crossing and left snipers behind there, too?" David sighed. "Knowing what we know now, I would have routed us south, away from Sonoyta."

Now it was Nathan's turn to sigh. "It doesn't matter at this point. Stay left. Looks like it splits ahead."

The SUV eased into a long, winding curve that took them onto an overpass. An artificial orange-scale glow lit the sky to the northeast, competing with the rapidly approaching sunrise.

"That must be Nogales," said Nathan.

"I'm surprised it's lit up. From the look of it, you'd think nothing was wrong here."

"I read that Mexicali was pretty quiet in El Chapo's days. Before California started squeezing the flow of drugs coming through the border there. A peaceful place, if you can believe that. He kept the violence to a minimum in that city, so it didn't attract attention from either side of the fence. Police officials from Tijuana kept their families there, commuting back and forth on the weekends. Maybe Nogales is the new Mexicali."

"I'm not stopping for a breakfast burrito, if that's your angle," said David.

Nathan chuckled. It was good to hear David crack a joke. He'd been all business since their worlds had collided three days ago. Three days felt like an eternity, and their journey was far from over.

"I'm not that hungry," said Nathan. "Time to wake up the crew."

He reached back and shook Keira's leg. She barely stirred. A second shaking didn't improve the situation, so he pinched the inside of her thigh, just above her knee.

"What the fuck!" she yelled, jerking upright.

Owen mumbled and shifted in the seat, leaning against the backpacks instead of Keira's shoulder.

"I tried to wake you up using more conventional methods," said Nathan.

"What was next, light my pants on fire?" she said, shoving his hand away.

"Sorry. We're coming up on the border."

She rubbed her eyes and squinted, looking around. "The sun's coming up," she said, checking her watch. "How long was I out?"

"Two hours?"

She took a long sip from her CamelBak hose. "I could use about ten more."

"We're going to stop on the other side and get some rest. Nobody is in any condition to drive at this point."

"Is that a good idea? Jose was pretty specific about getting as far north as possible," she said.

"Tucson is less than a hundred miles north, and there's nowhere to stop in between. Alpha made it clear we need to skirt the city, which will slow us down. We need to be sharp if we're taking side roads, and we need to find somewhere to gas up. We're down to a hundred miles until empty. We rest, refuel, eat—hit the road running."

He purposely withheld the part about possibly waiting until nightfall, hoping David would forget he'd said it. He'd let them sleep as long as they needed, even if it meant burning up most of the day. Getting across the border was the important part. Even if the cartel had turned on Jose by this point, they'd be tucked away safe and sound. The more he thought about it, the more sense it made. Nobody would expect them to slow down or stop.

Nathan was so deep in thought—or half-asleep—that he didn't realize David had started talking. "—awake for the past hour," he was saying. "I'd like to keep moving, but I agree with Nate that the risks outweigh the benefits. A quick nap is all I need to recharge. If they have a hot pot or a microwave, we can make some coffee. I have a Ziploc bag filled with Starbucks ready brew in my pack."

"You had me at Starbucks," said Keira.

The first indication they had reached the border came a few minutes later, when the two northbound lanes opened into three lanes separated by parallel running concrete barriers. A long sign suspended over the lanes had been hastily spray-painted white, obscuring the directions separating traffic.

"Any guess which lane we should use?" said David.

"I don't think it matters anymore," said Nathan, checking the map. "This isn't the border."

"Kind of looks like the border," said Keira.

"I know, but we haven't been on Route 150 long enough. Maybe this is some kind of tariff station? Who knows."

They entered the far left lane, which ran for a mile before they reached what looked like an inspection point. A tall pole and beam structure rose across the highway, covered by a wide corrugated metal roof. Underneath, the road widened to accommodate four lanes, none of which contained an inspector station. To their right, just beyond a chain-link fence, a similar structure sheltered narrow booths. From what Nathan could tell, the booths appeared unmanned.

"Looks like we picked the express route," said Nathan as the SUV shot through the middle opening.

"I hope the border is this easy," said Keira.

"I suspect it will be," said David. "This isn't a border anymore."

"All that congressional bickering about losing jobs to Mexico and ending NAFTA, and the cartels open the border to free trade," said Nathan.

"Free trade in drugs," said David. "I don't see any eighteen-wheelers packed with produce heading north."

"We haven't seen a single vehicle, period," said Keira.

"Mexico ships everything overseas now," added Nathan.

A second unlit station appeared in the distance, resembling what tollbooths used to look like on American highways. Nathan raised his rifle and took a closer look. Dented steel barriers protected each reinforced concrete booth. The faces of the booths looked like they had been used for target practice, the paint chipped and concrete cratered in hundreds of places. He saw neither gates blocking their passage nor people in the booths. As the image clarified, he saw the pattern of a faded, spray-painted symbol. *Libre.* Free.

"What are we looking at here?" said David.

"This must be the tariff station. Looks clear."

They crossed into the United States through a similarly bullet-riddled, graffiti-covered, and thoroughly abandoned tollbooth island. The only difference was the sign greeting them at the US Customs station. WELCOME TO THE UNITED STATES had been spray-painted to read WELCOME TO MEXICO.

Chapter 33

Keira peered between the front seats, examining the motel as they turned off Mariposa Boulevard. Nothing stood out as particularly worrisome at first glance. Like the rest of the town, it looked neglected by time. Well worn, but still functional on the outside. An empty shell. She didn't like it.

"I don't know about this," she said. "Maybe we should get back on the interstate and head north."

"David's about to drive us off the road," said Nathan.

"Why don't you drive?"

"I'm not doing any better. We just need a few hours of sleep."

The SUV drifted across an empty parking lot bordering Mariposa Boulevard, headed toward a smaller lot on the other side of the building. The parking area looked to be concealed from the boulevard by a screen of bushes and small palm trees lining the road, but that privacy came with a price. There was only one way in or out of the lot.

"I can drive," she blurted. "I've been napping off and on since Sonoyta. We can find a hotel along the interstate, south of Tucson. It has to be better than this."

"If we could count on just cruising down the freeway, I'd be all over you driving. But if we run into trouble, I need to be behind the wheel. Counterambush driving is its own thing, and I've been through more training than you'd believe," said David, easing the SUV into the small lot facing the motel office. "This actually doesn't look that bad—and the town is quiet."

"*Creepy* is a better word," she said.

"We'll gas up the car, have breakfast, and take a short nap. Back on the road in a few hours," said David.

"This is the last place anyone would look for us," said Nathan.

Her husband didn't sound convinced by his own statement. She could read him well enough to decipher the subtleties of his inflection. Then again, the last forty-eight hours had demonstrated they weren't safe anywhere. There was no reason for Nathan to sound convinced.

David pulled into one of the parking spaces deep inside the lot, facing the two-story main building. To the SUV's left, beyond a wide concrete sidewalk, a row of four tightly spaced motel room doors extended from the corner office to a breezeway that passed through the main structure. She glanced over her shoulder at the opposite side of the lot, seeing that it backed up against a row of tall palm trees. The backs of several businesses crowded the line of trees, separated by a narrow service road.

Even if David could manage to squeeze the SUV between the palm trees, which she doubted, there was no way he could turn onto the strip of asphalt behind the business building. The only way out of this parking lot was back the way they came. Keira decided not to bring it up. Surely both David and Nathan had considered it.

"We'll refuel first, in case we need to leave unexpectedly, then figure out the room situation," said David. "We should probably take a room on the second floor, where we can see the car."

Nathan turned in his seat. "How's Owen doing?"

"Asleep."

"Why don't you get him moving while we refuel."

She opened her door to get some fresh air. As soon as they parked, the temperature inside the vehicle spiked, leaving stuffy, dust-caked air. She hadn't minded the dust while cool air poured through the cabin during their all-night, open-window ride, but now it was intolerable. She couldn't imagine what the motel room was going to feel like. Within a short span of time, the sun would be beating down on the rooms. Whatever the reasoning for stopping, Keira still wished like hell they had kept going. The thought of hiding inside a sweltering, stagnant room for a few hours was repugnant. She was losing it for no reason, she told herself.

While David and Nathan topped off the vehicle, she woke Owen, preparing him for their transfer to one of the rooms. Nathan leaned inside her door while Owen stretched.

"Hey, bud. We're taking a short break here before we get back on the road."

"Mom told me," said Owen, still looking half-asleep. "I'm pretty hungry."

"We'll bring our packs into the room. You can eat whatever you want."

"How are we going to get into a room?" said Keira.

Secretly, she hoped the rooms were locked. Without electricity, they probably wouldn't be able to open any of the doors, even if they managed to find a master key in the office or on a custodian's cart. They could try to kick one of the doors in, but she suspected they would move on instead.

"David thinks they lock in the open position when the batteries in the key-card reader fail," said Nathan. "It doesn't look like this place has had any power in a long time. I'm going to check a few of these doors."

"Be careful."

He nodded before walking toward the row of doors facing the SUV.

"I don't like this place," said Owen.

"Neither do I, but we won't be here long."

"How long?"

"A few hours," she said.

Owen looked genuinely frightened by her answer. "I think we should get out of here. It doesn't feel right."

Keira didn't know how to respond without scaring him even more. Instead of lying, she went with a half-truth and nodded toward Nathan, who stood in front of an open motel room door with a smile and a thumbs-up. He walked to the next room and opened another door effortlessly.

"Your father and David have gotten us this far," she stated assertively. "We'll be fine here."

She pulled him in for a hug, wishing that the motel room doors had been locked. Like Owen, she had a bad feeling about this place.

CHAPTER 34

Jose stared through the windshield at the yellow-orange strip of sky lifting above the horizon. The sun would be up in a few minutes, and he sincerely hoped that Fisher was in Arizona by now. His last report from Alpha indicated they were on schedule to reach the border before sunrise, but you could never tell what might happen in Mexico, or anywhere in the Wastelands, which was why he had opted to bring three armored vehicles west.

They certainly hadn't anticipated what happened in Sonoyta. Their intelligence sources had indicated only that the Sinaloa cartel had given up trying to send shipments through the town, not that they'd been encouraged to do so because Sonoyta had been converted into a helicopter gun range. He was even more surprised to discover American snipers hidden throughout the town. If Jose had known any of this, he would have routed Fisher south, toward the Sea of Cortez, and risked a broad daylight crossing. Sonoyta was supposed to be safe, if you didn't turn north and approach the border. Now the entire town was off-limits, by order of the US military.

What would his Mexican armed forces contacts think of that? Maybe they already knew and didn't care. The Mexican government had long ago quit fighting the cartels. If the United States was finally taking a more proactive stance, Mexico only stood to benefit in the long run. Cartel influence and its associated violence had been a key talking point for US legislators keen on severing major trade ties with Mexico. His satellite phone buzzed moments after the sun peeked over the jagged hills ahead.

"Perfect timing. I was just about to check on our friends," said Jose.

"You're not going to believe this," said Alpha.

His heart sank.

"What happened? How bad is it?"

"No. It's nothing like that. They crossed the border without incident, but—"

Alpha paused.

"But what?" said Jose.

"They stopped at the Motel 6 on North Main Avenue," said Alpha. "Two miles from the border."

"Are you fucking kidding me?"

"I wish I were. We thought maybe they'd come under attack when they turned off Interstate 19, but their car continued at a normal pace. We tracked their transponder to the Motel 6."

"This can't be real. Something is up. Are you sure they don't know you're following them?"

"Not a chance. We stayed two miles back, running completely dark at all times."

"What are they doing right now?" he said, making eye contact with the operative driving the car and shaking his head.

"GPS maps them in the motel parking lot. We're in the lot of an abandoned strip mall just to the northwest. I can see the back of the motel from here."

"What the hell are they doing? Why stop this close to the fucking border!"

"Maybe they're taking a break to refuel and eat. It's a two-story, L-shaped building set back from the road. The inner parking lot is mostly concealed from the road. Not a bad choice for a quick stop."

"I'm concerned they might take a longer break. Quinn made it clear that he needed to be the driver, for tactical reasons. He'd be on the verge of driving off the road by this point. My guess is they're stopping to rest," said Jose.

"I don't like it," said Alpha.

"Neither do I. One of you should head over right now and get a better grasp of the situation."

"I'll head over," said Alpha. "What's the play if this is more than a quick stop for them? We're stretched a little thin here."

"I'm on Interstate 8, halfway between Gila Bend and Interstate 10. That's two-plus hours from Nogales, so you're it for now."

His original plan had been to cross paths on the outskirts of Tucson and offer them help avoiding cartel checkpoints and marauding banditos. He'd instructed Alpha to remove any detailed city and state maps from the glove boxes of both SUVs and provide them with vague instructions to skirt west of Tucson. Without a comprehensive area map or onboard GPS navigation system, their chances of successfully navigating the outskirts were nearly nonexistent without help—which Jose would be more than happy to provide.

"I hope they're just stuffing their faces," said Alpha.

"Me, too. We collapsed the tunnel after crossing back into California. The cartel won't be happy about that, or the fact that we skipped out on our lease. I don't know how far or fast word will spread, but assume the worst. Keeping Fisher alive is our highest priority."

"You really think he's worth it?"

"He better be," said Jose. "Keep me posted."

"Copy that. I'll call you as soon as I'm done checking out the motel."

He lowered the phone, staring into the fiery orange circle slowly breaking free of the horizon. Alpha's team was the only thing standing between the failure and success of Jose's plan. He hoped they would be enough.

CHAPTER 35

Leeds jolted awake from a deep sleep. Olmos was jamming a finger into his shoulder. It took him a few seconds to regain his bearings in the jet's aft cabin.

"What?" said Leeds.

"Flagg's on the line," Olmos said, sticking a phone in his face.

He sat up on the leather couch and took the phone, noticing sunlight through the partially opened window. A quick glance at his watch told him he'd been asleep for about two hours. Olmos backed into the doorway that separated the sleeping compartment from the main cabin. Beyond Olmos, the flight crew hustled toward the cockpit. Something was up.

"Leeds," he said into the phone.

"Taking a nap? That's a good way to wake up dead, with the Russians around."

"They were pretty quiet last night," said Leeds. "Looks like your cartel contact came through?"

"I'm fairly confident they have," said Flagg. "An SUV carrying three adult passengers wearing military-style helmets crossed the border at Nogales around five thirty. They were followed to a Motel 6, where they apparently took a room."

"They still have motels down there?"

"I thought you'd be more surprised by the fact that they stopped at a motel in the first place."

The engines started to whine, powering up from the low-fuel-consumption status they had maintained most of the night.

"Only three confirmed passengers?"

"The kid may have been sleeping, or maybe he didn't survive your ambush. Frankly, we don't know who crossed the border in that car, but this fits the profile—and the vehicle isn't affiliated with the Sinaloa."

"It's the only scenario that fits," said Leeds, leaning across the cabin to raise the shade. Chukov's men were on their feet, slinging their weapons and moving toward the jet's stairs. It was about to get crowded and smelly inside the cabin.

"We'll soon find out," said Flagg. "You should arrive at the airport on the United States side in thirty-five minutes. My contact has arranged for the local jefe to meet you with transportation."

"How much cartel backup can I expect?"

"For the price I've paid, the question is, what do you need?"

"Discreetly placed lookouts, to start," said Leeds. "The sooner the better."

"The guy that followed them is watching their room from the motel office."

"That'll work," said Leeds. "I could use a few dozen men to create a reactive perimeter around the motel. Vehicle based and out of sight."

"I'll make it happen," said Flagg. "Do you want any of the cartel's people directly involved in the attack?"

"From what I've seen so far, Mexicans and Russians don't mix well. I'd prefer to keep them apart when the shooting starts. If the jefe protests, we can use one of his handpicked teams as a direct backup."

"All right. I'll send maps and satellite imagery to your laptop. Start managing Chukov's expectations again. I'd love to take at least one of the adults alive for questioning, preferably Nathan Fisher," said Flagg. "We had a little setback last night in Montana. Our team up there killed Fisher's dad in an unauthorized snatch-and-grab, pretty much cutting off any connection to the wife and Stuart Quinn. I don't want any loose ends out there, especially David Quinn."

The first Russian stepped into the forward cabin, slogging his way toward the back of the plane. Encased in body armor and carrying rifles, he squeezed through the doorway into the luxury seating area.

"Chukov's orders are to kill the Fishers and David Quinn. Period," said Leeds. "You need to take that up with Petrov."

"Just try. I'll pay twenty thousand dollars per surviving adult to each member of the team."

"What about the kid?"

"He won't know anything useful," said Flagg. "I'll be in touch."

Leeds moved into the main cabin to retrieve his laptop. Chukov's mercenaries had absolutely zero respect for personal property, particularly anything that couldn't directly kill someone. One of the brutes had unceremoniously snapped Olmos's wireless tablet in half with his head while Olmos was driving back from the bunker raid. Apparently, Olmos had asked the Russian to verify their return route to the airport from the CLM bunker, and the idiot couldn't figure out that he needed to remove his gloves to use the tablet screen.

He snatched his laptop from the closest table and retreated back through the doorway. With eight seats in the main cabin, he shouldn't have to share space with any of these animals. Wishful thinking. Chukov and his assistant team leader continued toward the back of the plane, ignoring the empty seats.

"Thirty-five minutes," muttered Leeds to himself. "It's only thirty-five minutes."

CHAPTER 36

Alpha walked diagonally across the Mariposa Mall parking lot, passing in front of a defunct PetSmart. All but one of the plate-glass windows spanning the storefront were missing, the broken glass spread over the sidewalk next to the lot. His right hand drifted to his hip as he probed the darkness inside the store for movement. He couldn't assume the business was abandoned. He'd made that mistake on the streets of Mexicali, walking right into an ambush. His chest still ached from the high-velocity bullet stopped by his liquid-armor vest.

Not that he could do much to defend himself from AK-47-toting cartel lookouts at the moment. He'd ditched his vest, helmet, and rifle to avoid attracting attention, staking his life on a concealed semiautomatic pistol. Glancing around at the abandoned businesses and empty streets, he wondered if the ruse had been necessary. Mexicali had a stronger pulse than this place. Nogales, Arizona, appeared to have been ransacked and left for dead by the cartels.

He jogged across Mariposa Boulevard, headed straight for the unlit Motel 6 sign standing tall above the scattered trees and low-lying businesses. The back of the motel was dark. They'd seen no working streetlights on the way into town. Most had been shattered, their remains lying on the pavement below.

Stepping onto the sidewalk, Alpha shuffled briskly past a boarded-up Mexican restaurant. Not even a Mexican restaurant survived? He checked the street behind him out of habit, catching a glimpse of his SUV parked beyond the corner of PetSmart. They had his back. No need to keep looking over his shoulder.

A wide dirt lot separated the restaurant from the Motel 6 parking lot, extending the full length of the motel and ending in a tangle of bushes and browned palm trees. He veered off the sidewalk and crossed the empty lot, heading straight for the corner of the two-story building.

Arriving at the nearest corner, he put his back against the painted cinder-block wall and scanned his surroundings. A boarded-up gas station at the intersection of Mariposa Boulevard and North Main Avenue was visible beyond a dense line of dead-looking palms that flanked the front parking lot. Nothing stirred in any direction he looked. Alpha moved along the wall toward the gas station, stopping at the front corner of the motel. He peeked into the lot, spotting a lone metallic-gray SUV parked at the far end, next to a row of unlit vending machines. He spoke quietly into the miniature voice-activated microphone clipped to the inside of his shirt collar.

"There's no sign of the family or Quinn near the car. They must be in one of the rooms."

"Copy that," said Bravo. "I don't know how much longer we can sit here. A sedan passed west of here, heading north on Interstate 19."

"There's an empty lot adjacent to the motel with some bushes and dried-out palms toward the back. I think you could stash the car there and cover it with dead palm fronds. I'm going to move around the back of the building and position myself somewhere facing the front of the motel. We'll have full coverage that way."

"Do you know which room they're in?"

"Negative," said Alpha. "I'm going to work on finding out."

"Is the office manned?"

"No sign of it, but who knows? Though you'd think the clerk's car would be around here somewhere. All I see is the SUV."

"Can you tell if there's any electricity running to the place?"

"I don't see or hear anything running on electricity here."

"I think the doors default to the open position when the power is out in these places. They may have just walked into a room."

"Then it's fair to assume they'll be here for a while," said Alpha. "At least the inner parking lot is concealed from the street. Not that I expect a lot of traffic. I'm going to head around the back of the motel and see if I can access the office. My guess is they took a room directly in front of their SUV. I should be able to see it from the office."

"Copy. We'll take up a position watching the back parking lot. Let us know if you need a hand."

"Contact Jose and let him know what we're doing," said Alpha.

"Got it."

Alpha returned to the other corner, checking the back parking lot before stepping into the open. He strode past several rooms to arrive at the breezeway that connected the two parking lots. A glance into the opening confirmed he was alone. He crossed quickly, passing a few more doors on his way to the back side of the motel, where he found a beat-up, white, two-door sedan parked in the shade in front of two rusted, industrial-size dumpsters. Either the car had been abandoned here long ago, or somebody had beat his team to the hotel.

"This is Alpha. I have a white sedan parked behind the office."

"Copy. Do you need backup?" said Bravo.

"Negative. I got this."

His attention centered on a scratched utility door next to the sedan, which he hoped might give him unobserved access to the office. He took a black cylinder the size of a small flashlight out of his left cargo pocket and drew his pistol, screwing the suppressor tightly to the weapon's threaded barrel. He let his hand sweep over the sedan's hood as he approached the door and found it warm for a car parked in the shade. Somebody was here. Alpha gripped the door handle and turned slowly.

The knob continued to revolve, locking in place after a quarter turn. Now for the moment of truth. He rested the pistol in the crook of his left elbow, the suppressor flush against the door, and leaned gently into it with his shoulder. The heavy metal security door inched inward, passing the point where an interior door lock would stop it. A quick visual check of the door frame came up empty for a contact alarm.

He pushed the door three-quarters of the way open and slid into a rancid-smelling room. Dozens of torn trash bags littered the floor, their contents spread in every direction. Flies buzzed over whatever fetid bits of food the rodents had left behind. He examined the rest of the room, noting that the few linens left haphazardly folded on the metal shelves had a suspicious brown tinge. Business has been very slow for a very long time.

He leveled his pistol at an open doorway leading toward the front of the building and stepped carefully into a short hallway, noticing a closed door immediately to his right, labeled TOILET—BAÑO.

A single cough from beyond the hallway froze him in place.

A second, rougher cough, followed by a muttered curse in Spanish, erased his fear that his entrance had been detected. He walked into the motel office, finding a dark-skinned, weathered Latino wearing a frayed cowboy hat seated in a rocking chair near the front window. He held a satellite phone in his right hand, the other hand rubbing the stubble on his face. Alpha watched him for several seconds before interrupting his intense concentration on something in the parking lot.

"*Buenos días.*"

The skinny cowboy dropped his feet from the plastic table in front of him and started to stand.

"*Siéntate,*" said Alpha, aiming the pistol at his head.

The man hesitated before easing back into the rocker, his eyes flickering back to the window.

"*¿Cuál es tan interesante por aquí?*" asked Alpha, nodding at the window.

The man started to turn his head to face him.

"*No me mira,*" said Alpha. "*Mira adelante.*"

The man faced forward.

"*¿Cuál es tan interesante afuera de la ventana?*"

"*Nada, señor,*" said the man.

"*¿Nada? No lo creo,*" he said, struggling for the right Spanish syntax. "*¿Ha denuncio esto?*"

The man squinted, his face betraying surprise. "Sinaloa?"

"*Sí. ¿Y tú?*" said Alpha.

"No, señor. I work the night shift," replied the man.

"*¿Hablas inglés?*"

"*Sí.*"

Alpha wasn't sure what to make of the situation. He needed more information.

"This is very important. *Muy importante,*" said Alpha. "Did you report the new check-ins to your Sinaloa contact?"

"There's no cartel here," the man stated, visibly tensing.

"I need to know if you made a call," he said.

The Mexican raised the phone to his ear, prompting Alpha to press the trigger. The single bullet passed through both sides of the skull and blasted the satellite phone out of his hand. The man remained upright for a moment, his head superimposed against a crimson-splattered wall, before his corpse slumped over the right armrest. A thick stream of blood poured from his head, spreading rapidly across the salmon-colored tile.

Alpha stared at the mess on the wall for a moment, replaying the moment. The man hadn't given him a choice. There was absolutely nothing he could have done differently. Only cartel snitches carried satellite phones.

He snapped out of the internal dialogue to assess the situation. The bullet had fortunately embedded in the wall a foot to the left of the window. He couldn't tell if it had penetrated the outer wall, but a bullet hole was a lot less conspicuous than a broken window. He'd caught a break with the blood-spray pattern, too, as the densest splatter was mostly confined to the wall. A few dime-size splotches hit the window, which he could easily wipe clean.

He knelt for the phone, which lay behind the man's foot. He plucked the brain-splattered device from the sticky carpet and held it between two fingers. Son of a bitch! The bullet had gone straight through the phone. He had no way to determine whether the man had placed a recent call.

"Motherfucker!" he hissed, throwing the phone at the wall behind the reception counter.

"You OK?" he heard through his concealed earpiece.

"Yeah, I'm good. I found one guy in the office with a satellite phone," said Alpha. "He tried to call for help. *Tried* being the operative term."

"Fucking cartel is everywhere," said Bravo. "Can you tell if he made any recent calls?"

"That's what the 'motherfucker' was about. I somehow put a hole through both his head and the phone."

"You're shitting me."

"I wish I was," said Alpha.

"That complicates things," said Bravo.

"Kind of. Are you guys in position?"

"Affirmative. I nestled us into the bushes, nose facing the street. We're moving some dead bushes around for concealment."

"I'm headed your way in a minute. I need to have a talk with Jose."

"If this was my show, I'd suggest we grab Fisher, explain the situation, and get them out of here before shit gets real."

"I'm with you, but Jose wants Fisher to have some kind of come-to-Jesus moment that'll get him on board with us."

"We're all gonna fucking *be* there when he meets Jesus, if that dude got a call out," said Bravo.

"No shit. I'll be there shortly."

First things first. He needed to locate Fisher's room, which shouldn't be that difficult. The Mexican's eyes had been glued to something within sight of his window. Alpha slid the rocking chair and corpse within it back several feet and crouched, trying to replicate the man's view out the window. Standing in a thick pool of blood, he stared through the thin, blood-splotched curtain, looking for anything out of place in the windows on the ground floor. Nothing.

He shifted his gaze up and scanned the second-floor windows, his eyes immediately drawn to a thin gap in the curtains three rooms from the second-floor breezeway. Brilliant light from the rising sun bathed half of the window, exposing movement inside the room. *Now we're in business.*

Alpha searched the check-in desk for a room map, finding a coffee-stained copy behind the counter. The Fishers were in room 204. The room directly behind them was 215. He folded and stuffed the sheet of paper in a pocket. He dialed Jose while looking around for anything else that might be useful.

"What are we looking at?" answered Jose.

"That depends. Can I knock on their door and explain the situation?"

"Well, what *is* the situation?"

"The situation is I don't know the situation. The office was manned by a shaggy-looking Mexican with a satellite phone. No obvious cartel branding, but he was staring at Fisher's room hard, and his first instinct was to place a call on his shiny satellite phone."

"Please tell me he didn't make the call."

"He didn't, but I have no way to tell if he'd made an earlier call. I hit his head and the phone with the same bullet," he said, pulling the dead Mexican forward off the rocking chair. The body hit the floor like a sack of cement.

"Why would he take a bullet trying to make a call if he'd already reported the Fishers' arrival?" said Jose.

"Instinct? Panic? This guy didn't look like the best decision maker."

A period of silence ensued, broken by Jose.

"If we pull them out now, we lose Nathan's trust—but keep him alive. If we wait and see, we risk losing him altogether. Or we win big and keep that trust intact."

"We're not afraid of a few Russian mercenaries," said Alpha.

Jose laughed. "You'll be up against more than just Russians."

"It's your call. We can keep an eye out five miles up and down the freeway for any cartel activity, and roust the Fishers out at the first confirmation that they've been made."

"Do it. Pull them out at the first sign of trouble and drive north. We'll run interference on the highway."

"Sounds like a plan," said Alpha. "I'll be in touch when we're in position."

"If anything feels off, get them the fuck out of there."

"Copy that," said Alpha, turning his attention back to the task at hand. He dragged the body into the cramped bathroom attached to the hallway between the office and the utility room and pushed the door closed. Then he stepped into the utility room, closing the door behind him to conceal the blood he'd dragged into the hallway.

"Exiting the back door," he whispered.

"You're clear," replied a member of his team.

After trying one of the room doors facing the back parking lot to confirm that the motel's doors had locked in the open position, he sprinted next door to his team, taking a wide approach to assess their concealment. The vehicle was well hidden by a combination of bushes and strategically placed dead palm fronds. His team was nowhere in sight.

"Quick meeting behind the SUV," he whispered.

The three men materialized from the bushes, converging on the vehicle as he removed his rifle from the front seat.

"Backup is a good two hours away," said Alpha, "and I scrapped our only way to know if the cartel is coming."

"What did you hit first? Head or phone?" said Jackson.

"Didn't matter, smart-ass," said Alpha. "Seriously, guys—we're it for now. We need to come up with a plan to defend, and ultimately extract, the family. Since we're a little shorthanded, we'll have to get creative."

His team nodded gravely. Carlos spoke up. "Should we dig into my carry-on luggage?"

"If you feel like sharing," said Alpha, glad Carlos had insisted on lugging some of his toys along for the trip.

CHAPTER 37

Raymond Olmos strained to follow Chukov's animated pre-mission brief. Olmos didn't speak Russian, and Chukov littered his crude diagram of the Motel 6 with wild, chaotic bursts of arrows, circles, and stars with his black dry-erase marker, but still, Olmos got the gist of it. Two strike teams would climb the stairs facing Mariposa Boulevard, out of sight of the target room, and split up on the second floor. One group would move along the outdoor walkway facing the inner parking lot to stack up to the right of the target door, while the other headed around the backside of the motel to the opposite side of the door. About as simple as it got, outside of planting explosives and dropping the entire motel.

"You," said Chukov, pointing at Olmos. "You go with Griga to the office and find out what the fuck is going on with our cartel contact."

Olmos nodded, scanning the mercenaries for any sign of which one might be Griga. The short, stocky Russian who'd challenged him when they first arrived cocked his head and pointed a thumb at himself.

"Griga," he grunted.

No shit. Olmos glanced at Leeds, who stood in the abandoned community college classroom's doorway with his arms folded. Nick winked, wearing a faint better-you-than-me smile. Olmos silently mouthed an obscenity, broadening the smile.

Without any discernible change in tone or volume on Chukov's part, the briefing ended, and the Russians headed toward the door. Olmos stood in place for a few seconds, putting some distance between him and the team's ritualistic pre-mission head-butting ceremony. Leeds met him just outside the classroom in a graffiti-sprayed hallway.

"You sure you're up for this?" said Leeds, glancing at his injured leg.

"I'm good. We need at least one set of eyes on this," said Olmos. "I don't like it that the cartel guy took off."

"The SUV is still there," said Leeds. "They didn't walk out of Nogales."

"I still don't like it. The dude should be answering his phone."

"He's probably stoned out of his mind," said Leeds. "Anybody stuck behind in Nogales is here for a reason. I'm not exactly impressed with the Sinaloa jefe running the show around here."

"He looks eager enough."

"Tell me about it. I'll have my hands full keeping him in check."

"I better get moving," said Olmos.

"Watch your back," whispered Leeds. "I don't trust these guys."

"Don't worry," replied Olmos. "I don't plan on turning my back on them."

He caught up with the Russians before they reached the end of the hallway. Chukov paused at an emergency exit and spoke to the team in Russian for a few seconds before leaning into the door. Olmos could feel the heat from the desert sun before he reached the door.

The team filed out of the building, forming their assault groups on the move. Griga dropped to the rear of the two groups, never checking to see if Olmos had followed. As Olmos hustled after him, he watched the groups cross the community college's shallow, empty back parking lot and slip into the dusty alleyway between two single-story buildings. Chukov halted the team along the end of the tan-colored building on the left, peering around the corner.

From Olmos's position at the back of the column, he could see the north-facing end of the motel's second floor across the street. The rest of his view was blocked by either a line of bushes and trees on the other side of Mariposa Boulevard or the line of Russians ahead of him. Chukov conferred with the mercenary behind him before the team bolted across the empty street. Olmos wiped the sweat off his brow and followed.

A deep pain radiated the length of Olmos's leg by the time they reached the other side of the road. He'd fallen several paces behind Griga, not that the Russian had noticed, but he caught up when the team paused briefly behind the browned bushes separating the road from the motel parking lot. He knelt on his good leg in the crusty dirt next to Griga, grimacing at the sharp pain in the opposite knee.

Chukov peered through a break in the foliage for a long moment, then gave the team a hand signal and quickly disappeared through the bushes.

Olmos rose to his feet with a grunt and struggled after the Russians. He faced a painful, thirty-yard sprint across a crumbling asphalt parking lot before they reached the northwest edge of the motel, where he hoped to God the pace would slow. He arrived a few seconds after the assault teams had started their ascent up the open stairway. Griga looked over his shoulder, casting a disdainful look at Olmos before stepping around the corner.

Olmos and the Russian moved cautiously past the ground-floor row of motel room doors facing the vacant back parking lot. His leg throbbed, but he had no trouble keeping up with his counterpart now that they'd traded speed for stealth on their final approach.

CHAPTER 38

Alpha shifted in the seat he had dragged in front of the motel room window, peering through the shade. He'd taken the room two doors down from the office for his observation post, risking very briefly exposing himself to room 204 as he slipped inside.

The room's window gave him a full view of the inner parking lot and the rooms that faced it. More importantly, it provided clear fields of fire to engage anyone who directly approached room 204 from either the first or second floor. Jackson covered all of indirect approaches from a concealed location in the abandoned lot near their vehicle.

His team had one partial blind spot, due east of Alpha's room, which he suspected the cartel would avoid, as room 204 faced much of that approach. If the cartel tried it anyway, they'd be forced to maneuver through the pool area and behind the office to reach the nearest stairwell. Jackson had that area covered, too.

Alpha wiped a thick sheen of sweat off his face with a sleeve, exhaling the stuffy motel room air. It was barely seven in the morning, and the place was cooking. Well before noon, it would be a veritable convection oven. If Fisher and company hadn't moved on by then, he might have to knock on their door to make sure they hadn't suffocated. He was fantasizing about cracking the window a few inches when Jackson whispered in his right earbud.

"I have heavily armed foot mobiles crossing Mariposa. Minimum of four. Looks like they stopped in the foliage break between the northern entrances. All other approaches look clear."

"Copy that," said Alpha. He didn't want to jump the gun on this, but success in situations like these often came down to seconds, and there was no way to tell how long it would take get room 204 moving. "Time to wake up our friends."

"Initiating contact with room 204 and prepping the breach," said Bravo.

Alpha stared over his rifle sight, his attention focused on the thick clump of bushes barely visible beyond the northeast corner of the motel while he let his peripheral vision passively scan for movement to the east. He couldn't effectively engage anything in that direction from the window, but if his eyes detected movement, it would influence his plan to evacuate Fisher from his room.

The bush moved, and Alpha lowered his face into the magnified sight. A man dressed in paramilitary tactical gear, carrying a compact rifle, pushed through the leaves and disappeared from sight behind the edge of the motel.

"Contact. Moving from Mariposa to north face. Just caught a glimpse, but looks like one of the mercenaries that landed in Mexicali yesterday," said Alpha. "Use the back door for extract. Jackson?"

"Copy back door," said Bravo.

"I counted nine total. They disappeared behind the north face," said Jackson. "Fuck. They're moving again. I have two men, ground level, heading south along the motel, and three men, upper level, heading in the same direction. No sign of the other four."

Alpha had a good idea where they'd turn up. He aimed the green reticle of his rifle sight at the far end of the second-floor walkway and was rewarded by the appearance of a pair of hands easing a rifle around the corner, holding it in the open for a few seconds. Alpha guessed the rifle's sight was integrated wirelessly with the mercenary's goggles or a standalone device, turning it into a remote camera. When the rifle vanished, the four remaining mercenaries emerged, heading toward room 204.

"I have four men, upper level, heading toward the target room. Expect the two groups to meet outside the target room. Lower group may be headed around back to the office. How are we doing with the extraction?"

"Everything is ready," whispered Bravo. "I just can't get any of them to answer the damn satphone. I can hear it on the other side. I'm gonna pound on the wall."

"Negative," said Jackson. "You got three hostiles moving past your room in a few seconds."

"Hang up the phone," said Alpha. "If you can hear it ringing, the Russians will hear it, too."

"What the fuck else can we do?" said Bravo.

"I have an idea, but if it doesn't work, we open the back door anyway."

"That could end badly," said Bravo.

"It'll end worse if we don't."

Chapter 39

Nathan held the satphone away from his body like it might explode. None of them recognized the number, and David could somehow tell that the call did not originate from another DTCS (Distributed Tactical Communications System) encrypted phone. Someone other than Nathan's dad or David's dad had somehow acquired a highly classified number. Nathan had let it ring for over a minute while they scrambled to get their gear ready for a quick departure. When it finally stopped, an eerie silence descended on the room. Keira peeked through the opening in the shades, moving them slightly with her hand.

"Get away from the windows," said David, shouldering his backpack.

"We need to see what we're getting into," she said, staying next to the window.

"You want to take a sniper bullet?"

"They don't know where we are."

"They will if you keep moving that shade," said David.

"Hon. Let's stay away from the windows," said Nathan, kneeling next to Owen. "You ready to roll, buddy?" he said, checking his son's slightly oversize helmet to make sure it was snugly attached.

"Yep," he said, nodding bravely. "Who do you think called?"

Nathan shook his head. "Probably a wrong number."

His son didn't look convinced, which didn't come as a surprise. Passing off lame answers on Owen was becoming increasingly difficult. He'd been through enough by this point to know the difference between the hard truth and one of their increasingly less frequent "don't worry about it" answers.

"Just stay down," said Nathan.

He headed toward the small table next to the television to retrieve his backpack, freezing in place when a muffled voice broke the room's silence. Keira and David ducked, backing away from the window. With the room completely still, the voice sounded louder, but it came from the desk. Seemingly from his backpack. Nathan pushed his pack aside, finding the radio they'd used to communicate with Alpha's vehicle while driving out of Mexicali.

They had kept the handheld in standby mode for the entire trip, just in case their CLM escorts had decided to follow them out of town and neglected to change frequencies. Unlikely, but they had nothing to lose by monitoring the frequency. Nathan's shoulders dropped a little. It was entirely reasonable to think that Jose had their satellite phone number. He'd been in possession of their phone for most of yesterday. He was probably just checking in.

Nathan swiped the radio off the desk.

"Fisher. David. This is Alpha. We know you're in room 204. Please answer this. It's life or death. I'm not fucking around."

Keira joined her son between the two beds. David aimed his rifle at the door, slowly backing away from the front of the room. Nathan answered the radio.

"How did you find us?"

"No time for that. Listen carefully and whisper. Cerberus found you. They're stacking up on both sides of your room as we speak. If you want to live, here's what I need you to do. Take one of the mattresses and place it against the back wall of the room next to the bathroom, then get everyone into the bathroom. Do it fast. Do it right fucking now."

"Got it," whispered Nathan, turning to his family. "Owen. Keira. Get into the bathtub. Now."

They scrambled to the bathroom with their gear, while David helped him lift a mattress off one of the beds. Within seconds, they'd jammed the queen mattress against the wall, its disheveled sheets and bedding partially draped across it. The instant they'd finished, David yanked him into the bathroom.

"I know what they're doing," said David. "Give me the radio."

When Nathan handed it over, David pushed him toward the bathtub. He leaned over and grabbed Keira's hand. She lifted her head high enough for him to meet her eyes under the lip of her helmet. He nodded at her.

"It's gonna be fine," he said.

"You always say that."

"Lie flat," David hissed.

Nathan let go of her hand and patted Owen's helmet before pressing flat against his rifle on the floor next to the tub.

"This is David. We're ready for you to breach."

"Copy that," said Alpha. "We have to time this perfectly, so you won't get a warning. I need you up and on your feet fast after this goes down. Out."

David crouched next to the tub. "Plug your ears, keep your mouth open, and breathe shallow. Like this." He mimicked how he wanted them to breathe for a few seconds before lying next to Nathan on the dusty linoleum tile.

"What're they planning?" whispered Nathan.

"Something loud," said David, pausing. "Something soon."

Nathan plugged his ears under the helmet and waited.

CHAPTER 40

Olmos strained to keep up with Griga, who had picked up speed once they passed the breezeway leading to the inner parking lot. Whipping after him around the southwest corner of the motel, he found his counterpart in a full sprint down the service alley. The Russian had already cleared half the distance between the corner and a white sedan parked in front of two trash dumpsters. Olmos dashed after him, jolts of pain shooting down his leg.

The Russian ran between the car and the building, abruptly stopping at an unmarked metal door next to the sedan and reaching for the doorknob. *Jesus. Don't just open the door!* He stifled the urge to yell a warning. When the Russian opened the door and disappeared inside with one fluid motion, Olmos threw himself into a crouch against the building. When a few seconds passed without an ear-crunching explosion, he bounded forward toward the door.

A fetid stench hit him as he raised his rifle and stepped through the open doorway. Griga stood directly ahead of him in the hallway before an interior door, his hand on the doorknob. He turned to Olmos, and their eyes met for a moment. Olmos shook his head.

Griga's stolid expression slowly transformed into a thin smirk. Olmos backed out of the room and hid most of his body behind the exterior door frame, leveling his rifle at the door just beyond Griga. The Russian pushed the door open a few inches and announced his presence in fluent Spanish. Sunlight from the front office poured through the thin crack. He opened the door another inch and repeated his announcement. The widening vertical line of sunlight remained unbroken. Nothing stirred inside the office.

Griga muttered and shook his head, shoving the door open and sliding through the doorway simultaneously. Olmos caught a glimpse of a blood-splattered wall beyond the short hallway a fraction of a second before the Russian's body blocked his view.

"No!"

The Russian disappeared in an explosion that blasted Olmos into the car behind him. He slammed into the front of the passenger side door and crumpled to the ground, where he lay on his stomach for a few seconds—until pure survival instinct took over. He needed to get out of this alley. Ears ringing and still unable to draw a breath, he tried to push himself up onto the pavement, only managing to lift the left side of his body. When he turned his head against the pavement to see why his right arm didn't respond, he identified the problem right away. His arm was missing from the elbow down.

When a second, more distant explosion rattled the ground, Olmos took the only option currently available to him. He squirmed into the smoldering office.

Chapter 41

A deep, crunching sound rattled the bathtub, which Keira mistook for her sign to get up. She'd just begun to lift her head when a deafening blast shook the tub like an earthquake, showering them in drywall fragments. Sprawled atop Owen, she kept the tips of her fingers pressed against her ears underneath the helmet and her elbows grinding into the nonslip surface of the tub above her son's shoulders until she felt a strong tug at her backpack, followed by a burst of automatic gunfire, which caused her to stiffen and resist the pulling.

"We have to go!" yelled Nathan, his face inches from hers.

She forced herself to climb off Owen and out of the bathtub. Pulling Owen to his feet, she allowed Nathan to drag them toward the bathroom door, which stood at an angle against the wall, blasted from its hinges. Eyes stinging from the dust and explosive residue blasted into an aerosolized powder, Keira gripped her son close to her as they passed through the door. A thick cloud of smoke masked the desperate struggle being waged in their motel room. Two figures knelt behind a flaming, doubled-over mattress, firing sustained bursts from their suppressed rifles into the thick haze obscuring the front of the room.

Nathan pushed her through a scorched, man-size oval hole blasted in the back wall of the motel room a few feet away from the bathroom door. She emerged in a mirror-image room that didn't look any better than the one she had just left. A figure dressed in body armor squatted next to her, aiming his rifle at the room's open door.

"Clear the hole!" he yelled, pulling her deeper into the room.

She recognized the voice as one of the operatives who had helped them escape Mexicali. The man pulled the rest of her family through the jagged breach, ushering them to the front of the room, where he put a hand on her husband's shoulder.

"We're heading down the breezeway stairwell and then across the back parking lot," he said, pointing through the clearing smoke at a row of palm trees beyond the door. "No matter what happens, you get to those trees. I got a man waiting for you there. You do what he says."

"Get them fucking moving!" yelled a frantic voice from the other side of the hole.

A bullet snapped through the wall next to the hole, thunking into the window frame a few feet away from Keira.

"This is Bravo. I'm moving the Fishers," he said, before turning to Keira. "You ready?"

She nodded nervously, flicking the selector switch on the MP-20 to semiautomatic without taking her eyes off Bravo. He patted her on the shoulder.

"We'll be on the road in thirty seconds," he said, disappearing through the door.

CHAPTER 42

In the moments leading up to the office explosion, Alpha licked his cracked lips and watched the mercenaries outside room 204. One of them had nearly finished taping a linear explosive charge along the room's door. The group's leader crouched behind the man setting the explosives, pointing his fingers at the door and moving his mouth. Alpha wanted to kill the leader first, but the circumstances leading right up to the moment he pulled the trigger would determine where to send the bullets.

"Jackson. What's going on with the office?"

"Two men moving cautiously . . . hold on. They picked up the pace," said Jackson.

"Bravo?"

"Ready."

He needed to make a decision in the next few seconds. The team leader looked impatient, and Alpha couldn't let them detonate their breaching charge.

That's it. He was cutting it too close.

"Jackson. Focus your fire on the two men in the alley. The assault team is almost done with the door," said Alpha. "Bravo. Stand by to detonate your charge."

"The first guy just reached the office door," said Jackson. "A few more seconds, and they'll detonate the charge."

"We don't have time. They're about to blow the door to room 204," said Alpha, moments away from giving Bravo the order to blast a hole between the back-to-back motel rooms.

"He just pushed the door open and walked inside," said Jackson. "Looks like they're in a hurry to clear the office."

That's because their team leader was rushing the job. The man planting charges on Fisher's door was at least ten seconds away from finishing. Alpha would count down from five and then give Bravo the order to blow the hole that would provide the Fishers their escape route. That was as close as he was willing to take this. Ideally, the two men in the office would trip the charge first, momentarily disorienting the mercenaries stacked outside room 204. Whatever happened, he couldn't allow them to blow the door.

"Bravo," he said, "detonate on my count. Five."

"The second guy just entered the office," said Jackson.

"Four. Three."

"Second guy just backed out," added Jackson.

"Two. One."

The windowsill shook violently from the antipersonnel mine detonated inside the office a few rooms away from Alpha, cracking the window in place and blocking his view.

"Breach. Breach," yelled Alpha, moving away from the window as a second explosion thundered.

He pulled his room door open to see glass raining down on the Fishers' SUV. All of the mercenaries on the second-level walkway turned away from the window, crouching or kneeling in protective positions. Alpha pressed his rifle into the door frame and centered the reticle on the leader's head. His finger was a few pounds of pressure away from vacating the man's skull when Alpha caught something in the far left side of the sight's field of view and shifted the reticle onto a mercenary detaching a grenade from his tactical vest. The rifle bit into his shoulder, planting a three-round burst of tungsten-carbide bullets in the middle of the mercenary's back. A bright red spray hit the wall behind the man before his body collapsed to the deck. Alpha quickly searched for the leader, not finding him before bullets started to fly in his direction.

The team's return fire was inaccurate, but that would change rapidly as the seasoned mercenaries shrugged off their initial confusion. Needing to delay that as long as possible, Alpha flipped the selector switch on his rifle to automatic and started raking the men on each side of the motel room with gunfire, careful not to send any bullets directly into room 204. The mercenaries on the walkway screamed in Russian as his bullets tore through muscle and bone, splattering the motel facade with gore. One of the men raised his rifle above the edge of the walkway with two straight arms and fired blindly at Alpha. A few of the bullets ripped through the door frame and walls, causing him to drop flat onto the floor. It was only a matter of time before one of them got lucky.

"I have them pinned down on the walkway, but not for long," said Alpha. "Start angling your fire through the adjacent rooms."

"Copy," said Carlos.

The wall behind the outstretched rifle on the second-floor walkway exploded outward, as the bullets fired by the team inside room 204 ripped the Russian's arms apart. Jagged holes stitched across the walls and doors of the adjacent rooms, keeping the rest of the mercenaries pressed to the walkway.

Alpha decided to take advantage of the cross fire to make his escape. Despite the appearance of a slaughter on the balcony walk, he knew better than to assume the Russians were done. One mistake could pin him in place long enough for the Russians to gain the upper hand, or bring the entire Sinaloa cartel down on him.

"Alpha moving to SUV," he said over the radio net.

"Copy. We're pulling out. The Fishers have been moved to the other room," said Carlos, the sound of gunfire echoing in his transmission.

"They should be at the stairs already!" yelled Alpha.

He fired a long burst at a partially visible head to the left of room 204, not sure if any of his bullets connected. A second burst discouraged another attempt to locate his position. With all of the Russians momentarily seeking cover, Alpha bolted out of the room and dashed toward the breezeway, plucking a fragmentation grenade from a pouch attached to his vest as he ran. He pulled the pin and released the lever, counting to three before he lobbed it toward the upper-level walkway. The grenade exploded just as he entered the breezeway, spilling chunks of concrete and splintered pieces of the wooden railing onto the asphalt parking lot behind him. A body tumbled over the side, crunching head-first on the concrete parking lot bumper two spaces down from the SUV.

"This is Bravo. I'm moving the Fishers," he heard in his earplug.

"About fucking time," said Alpha. "I want Carlos and David with me."

"Everyone is moving," said Carlos.

A bullet snapped off the stucco wall next to his face, peppering him with stinging fragments. He caught movement in his peripheral vision and crouched, a second bullet striking the wall where his head had just been. Alpha found the sharpshooter standing next to a building across the parking lot and blasted a pinkish-red mist into the air behind the Mexican's head. While bullets hissed and snapped through the breezeway, pinging off the stucco above and behind him, he replaced his rifle's mostly empty seventy-five-round drum with a thirty-five-round magazine.

"Move faster, or the Motel 6 is gonna be our Alamo!"

Chapter 43

Bullets snapped through the breezeway, chipping stucco and buzzing off the cement. Nathan hung over his son to shield him as he fought to determine the source of the gunfire. Alpha crouched next to a wall near the end of the short corridor, shooting furiously at targets Nathan couldn't see. He pointed his rifle in Alpha's direction and yelled over his shoulder.

"Does he need help?"

"Keep moving!" replied Bravo, sounding distant.

Nathan spun around, finding his family at the back of the motel with Bravo. He'd started to run after them when David and another CLM operative appeared at the top of the stairs.

"Go! Go!" yelled the operative, emphatically gesturing for him to catch up.

Nathan reached Owen and Keira before they left the highly questionable safety of the breezeway for the empty parking lot. His panicked mind saw the lot as an endless, open kill zone.

"Are you sure the back is safe?" he yelled, hovering over Owen.

A bullet ricocheted off the staircase railing behind them with a loud metallic crack, instantly smacking into the wall on the other side of the corridor. The Fishers flinched, reflexively dropping into a crouch and pressing against the wall next to them.

"The safest place for you is anywhere but here," said Bravo, another bullet zipping past, this one causing the operative to flinch.

Nathan put a hand on Owen's shoulder. "Ready, buddy?"

His son nodded, wincing from another ricochet.

"Here we go," said Bravo, stepping into the open.

They got halfway across the parking lot before bullets started chipping away at the brittle pavement around their feet. Bravo stopped and turned to face the parking lot entrance to their right.

"Keep going!" he said, firing a short burst at a gunman taking cover behind the far corner.

Running with his son, Nathan threw an arm around Owen's shoulders, placing himself between the new threat and his son, while Keira pulled tight to Owen's other flank, creating a compact human shield around him. A sustained burst of suppressed gunfire erupted from the bushes ahead of them, rustling the branches and leaves, immediately followed by a scream to Nathan's right. He turned in time to see a man holding a rifle drop to his knees in the middle of Mariposa Boulevard and face-plant into the street. The bushes rattled again, and a second man tumbled to the street, landing near the first.

When the Fishers reached the edge of the parking lot, the operative who'd been covering them emerged from the dry foliage to guide them to the vehicle. They wove through the bushes to arrive at an SUV identical to the one they had driven out of Mexicali. Bullets started to hiss through bushes, one shattering the left side of the SUV's plastic front grille underneath the dead palm fronds, another spiderwebbing the top right corner of the windshield. The operative opened the front passenger door, beckoning for them.

"Let's go!" he shouted, a bullet thunking into the bullet-resistant door.

Bravo burst through the bushes behind them, causing Nathan to spin and aim his rifle.

"Three targets to the front!" yelled Bravo, continuing past him to the SUV.

A volley of bullets tore through the bushes, several striking the open doors and windows. Bravo fired his rifle over the top of the door, while Nathan's family crawled into the backseat.

Nathan spotted three men running across the dusty lot. The lead gunman twitched before tumbling to the ground, undoubtedly a victim of Bravo's bullets. Nathan aimed his rifle at the second man, leading him with the sight reticle like his father had taught him. A controlled press of the trigger dropped the man in a bloody heap. The third shooter dived behind a thick clump of bushes and held his rifle in the air with both hands, firing wildly. Nathan drew down on the brown shrub, centering his reticle between the two arms, and pressed the trigger twice in rapid succession. A red geyser of blood erupted, soaking the shooter's arms before they collapsed.

When he turned around, Bravo was in the front seat, reaching for the door handle. They locked eyes for a moment, the operative nodding his approval. The car started moving forward before Nathan reached it, picking up momentum. He grabbed the luggage rail above the door and swung both feet into the backseat. Keira pulled him in by his vest just as the door hit the trunk of a palm tree and slammed shut. Bravo twisted in his seat.

"Keep your son as low as possible," he said, pointing into the rear foot well. "That might not be a bad place for him right now."

A bullet hit the center of the windshield, glancing off the top of Keira's helmet. Nathan pulled Keira down over Owen, covering both of them with his arms. He examined her helmet, finding nothing more than a shallow graze mark.

"Contact, one o'clock!" yelled Bravo, stitching the windshield with fully automatic gunfire. "Need a little help here!"

Keira sat up, snatching the MP-20 leaned against her door.

"Stay down with Owen!" said Nathan.

"I don't think that's an option right now!" she yelled, jamming her rifle through the opening between the bullet-resistant glass and the top of the door.

I guess not.

CHAPTER 44

David reached the bottom of the stairs just as Nathan and his family bolted across the parking lot. He didn't like the idea of separating, but Carlos had tried to explain the logic on their way out of the room. They needed an even distribution of operatives and capable shooters between the vehicles. If David went with the Fishers, it threw off the number of operatives in each car. That was about all he got out of his new counterpart during the desperate scramble to escape. It wasn't until David's feet hit the ground that he processed the implications of Carlos's explanation. He grabbed the operative as bullets struck the stucco next to them.

"We're getting in that SUV?" said David, craning his head as far into the corridor as he dared to see if the vehicle was still intact.

"That's our only ride out of here," said Carlos, shaking himself loose of David's grip. "If it still works."

Alpha glanced in their direction from his position several feet closer to the inner courtyard.

"Looks good so far!" he said. "Cover me!"

David followed Carlos down the breezeway, breaking off when they reached Alpha. He sprinted across the corridor, bullets following him into a dark vending machine vestibule, where he crouched and peeked around the cinder-block wall, spotting two men advancing down the sidewalk between the parking lot and the rooms. He fired at the first gunman, striking him twice in the chest and dropping him to the concrete.

The second gunman emptied his rifle in David's direction and tried to take cover behind one of the metal beams supporting the upper-level walkway. Unfortunately for him, the beam didn't completely shield his body. David's first bullet, an instinctive center-mass shot, ricocheted off the thick steel beam protecting part of the man's torso, but his second struck the man in the shoulder, spinning him into the open, where David's third and fourth shots knocked him onto his back.

"Clear to the north!" said David.

"Lots of hostiles east!" said Alpha. "Moving!"

More men appeared at the far end of the parking lot, headed toward the north end of the motel. David held his fire while Alpha exited the breezeway, then squeezed off a few shots at the distant targets.

"David! Get to the SUV. Backseat," yelled Carlos from Alpha's previous position covering the east.

David bolted from the snack room, heading diagonally across the sidewalk for the SUV. Alpha was crouched next to the open driver's side door, firing east toward a gas station service center. When David reached the parking lot pavement, Alpha slid into the driver's seat and pulled his door shut. David opened the rear driver's side door and instinctively took over for Alpha, firing at targets of opportunity to the east.

"Get in!" yelled Alpha, revving the SUV's engine.

David slid into the backseat, closing the door and turning in his seat to continue firing at the approaching cartel soldiers. One of the front car doors opened and slammed shut.

"Let's go!" yelled Carlos, and the vehicle lurched into reverse.

Several metallic clunks echoed through the cabin.

"Motherfuck!" yelled Carlos.

When David looked over his shoulder, he found multiple holes had been punched through the roof. Carlos aimed his compact rifle upward and created twice as many holes before blood spurted from the top of his shoulder, streaking the partially cracked windshield. Sticking the barrel of his rifle out of his window as Alpha threw the steering wheel left to point the vehicle straight at Mariposa Boulevard, David was ready when the SUV screeched to a halt with his weapon aligned with the walkway directly in front of room 204. He fired a quick burst at the only head visible, seeing it snap back from the impact of the bullets.

Tires screeching, the SUV launched forward and raced through the parking lot.

"Contact. Right side!" yelled Alpha.

Carlos responded slowly, blood still gushing from his collarbone area. Given the bullet's angle of entry from above, his wound could easily be fatal without immediate treatment. David moved to the opposite side of the rear bench seat and stuck his barrel through the window slit, searching for the target Alpha had called out and finding him, sprinting from the service station to a thick palm tree at the edge of the parking lot. Both Carlos and David fired short bursts into the man's chest, crumbling him to the pavement.

David continued firing at anything that moved to their right, while Carlos shifted his aim through the partially missing windshield.

"Contact. Dead ahead," said Carlos, firing the rest of his magazine. "Reloading."

A torrent of hollow metallic thumps and sharp cracks reverberated inside the SUV as the front and right sides of the vehicle absorbed and deflected dozens of bullets. A warm stream of bright red blood sprayed across the back of David's neck, drawing his attention to the front seat. Carlos's head tilted left at an odd angle, blood pumping out of the right side of his neck. Alpha was crouched forward in the driver's seat, the front lip of his helmet pressed against the top of the steering wheel. A half dozen or more cartel gunmen ran wildly through the bushes ahead of them, firing on full automatic.

"Turning left!" said Alpha.

David quickly changed rifle magazines and readied for the turn, while Alpha grabbed Carlos's rifle with one hand and jammed the barrel through the passenger side window. When both rifles were in position, Alpha eased the SUV into a shallow arc, putting the mob on David's side of the car. They worked the rifles back and forth, firing short burst after short burst into the gunmen. Caught in the open, less than thirty feet away from the SUV, the cartel group was obliterated by the 6.8-millimeter broadside.

David pulled his weapon inside the vehicle and aimed over the backseat through the rear lift gate window, witnessing the impact of their mobile firing squad. The gunmen lay in a motionless, tangled heap of bloodied bodies behind them.

He started to pull another magazine from his vest when Alpha yelled, "Contact. Left! North face of the motel!"

With no time to reload, and the clear plastic side of the inserted magazine indicating fewer than five rounds remaining, David flipped the selector switch to semiautomatic and searched through the window for targets. He located three men clustered together, firing wildly at the second SUV in the abandoned lot west of the motel. David's first bullet missed, striking the wall above one gunman's head and drawing their attention—and bullets. As rounds smacked the glass and thudded into the door frame protecting him, he switched the rifle to automatic and waited for the car to pull even with the group.

"What the fuck are you waiting for?" yelled Alpha.

He pressed the trigger, hitting the closest gunman in the sternum with the last bullets in his magazine and sending the man standing behind him careening back against the wall. The second man bounced to the concrete, and the first fell on top of him.

"Oh," said Alpha. "That."

David's armor-piercing bullets had easily sliced through both men. As the remaining gunman ran for the east side of the building, David reloaded for the next round of threats.

Alpha drove across the back parking lot, barreling through a row of low bushes to pull into formation twenty feet behind the SUV carrying the Fishers. David switched sides, ready to blast away at any vehicles or gunmen in their way. The SUV in front of them skidded into a high-speed turn on Mariposa, its wheels quickly gripping the pavement and catapulting them west on the four-lane road. Alpha followed, fishtailing their truck before regaining full control.

Once the SUV steadied on Mariposa, David checked the road behind them. A few armed men stood in the middle of the road firing at them—rapidly shrinking away.

"Clear in back," said David.

"We're far from clear," said Alpha. "Check Carlos."

He didn't have to spend more than a few seconds assessing the operative's condition. The bullet that had entered through the right side of his neck had punched a hole straight through the back, likely severing his spinal cord. Blood pumped weakly through the entry wound, his heart fading. David didn't think the hemostatic bandages or bullet plugs would make a difference at this point, but gave it a try—the least he could do for someone willing to step into harm's way on his behalf. David started to open the individual first aid kit pouch attached to the side of his tactical vest.

"Forget it," said Alpha. "He's gone."

There was no point in arguing. Even if they could slow the bleeding, which he seriously doubted, Carlos would die long before they could reach a medical facility capable of treating his wounds.

"I'll pull him in back," said David.

"No. Hand me his seat belt. He's better off strapped in the front seat."

"Keep him from flying around in a crash?"

David pulled the seat belt latch across Carlos's body until Alpha could reach it.

"That and he's one more layer between you and a bullet," said Alpha, clicking the seat belt into place.

"What's the plan?"

"Simple as it gets. You watch the back. I got the front."

David knelt on the rear bench seat, nesting his rifle against the headrest. Still nothing behind them. "I meant the bigger plan," he said. "You didn't stumble on us by accident."

"The bigger plan is getting you somewhere safe," said Alpha. "And no, it wasn't an accident. We've been following you since Mexicali with a tracking beacon. Jose wasn't confident in your ability to survive on your own. Turns out he was right."

A yellow pickup truck with oversize tires swerved onto the road several intersections behind them, followed by three or four sedans.

"We have company," said David. "What's the more immediate plan?"

Alpha craned his head back to look, muttering a curse and leaning on the gas. "Drive north on Interstate 19 and try to reach Jose before the cartel reaches us."

"How far away is he?"

"A little over thirty minutes. And I expect we'll run into a roadblock or two ahead. This should be fun."

David loosened a few spare magazines in his vest, readying them for the inevitable battle they'd fight to get out of Nogales.

CHAPTER 45

Nick Leeds ran down the strip mall sidewalk toward Mariposa Boulevard. He'd lost contact with Olmos after hearing two explosions, and the volume of gunfire suggested that Chukov's mercenaries had stumbled on more than just a roomful of weary travelers.

He paused next to a boarded-up window at the edge of the strip mall and knelt. Automatic gunfire erupted from a group of cartel gunmen hiding behind the corner of a gas station, answered by suppressed weapons fired by shooters somewhere in the parking lot.

More gunfire crackled out of sight to the west, and Leeds risked a look around the wall. Two gunmen lay in the middle of Mariposa, past the back parking lot exit, their executioners concealed. Tires screeched from the inner parking lot directly across the street, followed by a long burst of gunfire. A dense row of bushes lining Mariposa blocked his view of the exchange.

He considered sprinting diagonally across the street to a row of thick palm trees lining the service station entrance, but decided against it. He was pretty sure tungsten-carbide armor-piercing bullets could penetrate a mature palm trunk. No point in finding out the hard way.

He scanned the area around the service station, looking for El Pedro's obnoxious pickup truck. *Where the hell did that idiot go?*

The Sinaloa jefe, his only conduit to the cartel teams stationed around the motel, had bolted into the parking lot outside the community college after the first explosion. Squawking excitedly into his handheld radio, the Mexican had hopped into the bright yellow, lifted-chassis beast and driven off without him.

Heavy footsteps pounded the concrete behind him. He turned to see several heavily armed Mexicans sprinting toward him on the strip mall sidewalk. Leeds yelled in broken Spanish, trying to warn them about the pitched gun battle going on in the motel parking lot, but they brushed him aside and ran headlong into the street.

"Shit," he muttered, pausing for a few seconds before leaving the cover of the building to follow them.

When Leeds reached the middle of Mariposa, the cartel soldiers disappeared through the bushes, leaving him alone on the street. Glancing up and down the wide, empty boulevard, he got the distinct impression that he had made a mistake. A sharp hiss to his immediate right confirmed it. Leeds dived to the pavement and aimed his MP-20 toward the bushes. Several snaps passed overhead, mixed with agonizing cries on the other side of the dense foliage line. The sound of a revving engine and crackling tires joined the lethal medley, convincing Leeds to crawl as fast as possible to the curb.

He pressed the length of his body parallel to the eight-inch-high concrete lip, resting the MP-20's hand guard on the top of the curb. Leeds lay motionless, hearing a short burst of suppressed gunfire a few seconds later. The shots sounded farther away, but he had no intention of leaving his concrete shield to investigate. The Mexicans who'd run recklessly into the motel parking lot had been slaughtered.

Two identical silver SUVs, matching the description of Fisher's vehicle, screeched onto Mariposa from the empty dirt lot behind the motel and turned west, away from Leeds. A few cartel gunmen ran into the road shooting from the hip, having no effect on the SUVs.

An unnatural silence enveloped the street for a few seconds, suddenly shattered by the approaching sound of El Pedro's obnoxiously overpowered and unmuffled pickup truck. Leeds scrambled off the street as the yellow monstrosity rocketed out of the motel parking lot, followed by a *Mad Max* fleet of souped-up sedans and SUVs.

Leeds brushed himself off and listened, hearing a few moans and cries from the direction of the motel. Figuring it was safe enough to approach, he leveled the MP-20 directly in front of him and moved carefully through the bushes. He found what he expected on the other side—six men sprawled on the pavement, riddled with holes and bleeding out. A few limbs stirred here and there, the men connected to them groaning.

He moved on, scanning left to right. Two more bodies by the northwest corner of the motel. A bloodied pair under the walkway, halfway down the building. A lone corpse lying in one of the parking spaces toward the far end of the lot.

What the hell had happened here? Where were the Russians?

As he moved deeper into the parking lot, the fate of Chukov's team came into focus. The balcony walkway next to room 204 had been devastated. Splintered sections of scorched railing clung stubbornly to the walkway's buckled frame. Hundreds of bullet holes stitched across blood-streaked doors and walls. A rifle barrel protruded over the edge, a lifeless head resting facedown behind the weapon's scope. From what he could tell, the Russians had been caught in a lethal cross fire reinforced by grenades. Judging by the volume of fire directed at the walkway, he didn't expect to find any of Chukov's team alive—not that he cared one way or the other.

His first priority was to find Olmos. Leeds had no intention of leaving him in this dump, dead or alive. He walked toward the office, analyzing the extent of the damage. Windows blown out, door intact. Minimal scorching on the curtains. He suspected the use of a directional charge, like a claymore. The real devastation would be found on the side facing the alley.

Two rooms down from the office, light gunfire damage to the walls and frame around an open door suggested an ambush position—a shooter hidden in that doorway would have an unobstructed view of the Chukov's team as they closed in on the Fishers' room on the second floor. Dozens of shell casings on the sidewalk outside the room reinforced his theory.

He opened the chain-link gate next to the office and moved past the empty pool to reach the alley. The scene behind the office was no more encouraging. The side of the car facing the door was riddled with evenly spaced, symmetrical fragmentation holes—characteristic of directional antipersonnel mines. If Olmos had been inside the room when the mine detonated, there was no way he could have survived.

Leeds approached cautiously, keeping a close eye on the far end of the alley. He started to breathe shallowly when he reached the dumpsters. The odor hanging in the air was excruciatingly rancid. The dumpsters were locked, so he guessed that the nauseating smell originated from the office.

The wide bloodstain between the building and the car escaped his attention until he was a few feet away from the door. Olmos? He aimed the MP-20 into the dark room beyond the opening and leaned slowly to the left.

"*Hola,*" said Leeds. "*¿Está alguien en casa?*"

"'Hello. Is anyone home?' Jesus, Nick. You need to brush up on your *español,*" said a familiar but very weak voice.

"Ray," said Leeds, "I'm stepping into the doorway." Caution was in order. Olmos sounded like himself, but if he'd lost the amount of blood the stain on the ground suggested, he could be delirious.

"I won't shoot unless you look like you're going to cut bait and run."

"I wouldn't leave you in this shithole." Leeds neglected to mention that he would have jumped in the bed of El Pedro's truck to pursue Fisher if the cartel boss had stopped for him.

"You might change your mind when you see what you're getting into."

Leeds stepped inside the sweltering room, immediately spotting the remains of one of the Russians through the haze. Or at least he assumed the tangled mess of ripped flesh and limbs deeper in the room had been one of the mercenaries, as he knew he'd heard Olmos's voice, and only two men had entered the office.

He found Olmos sitting on top of several spilled garbage bags, his back against the exterior wall. Leeds triggered the flashlight attached to the MP-20, immediately understanding what Olmos had meant. His right arm ended in a bandaged stump just below the elbow, a brown belt tightened around the lower part of his bicep. A bright red morphine auto injector lay on one of the trash bags next to him. The ex-SEAL had taken the initial measures required to keep himself alive—for now. Olmos held a pistol loosely in his left hand.

"You didn't happen to see my arm out there?" he said, barely holstering the pistol.

"Can't say I did," said Leeds. "Let's get you out of here." He pulled Olmos up by his good hand and wrapped the wounded man's arm around his shoulder. "We'll get you to a hospital. Petrov's Gulfstream can reach San Diego in forty-five minutes."

"What about the Russians?" he muttered.

"I don't think Chukov will be needing the jet anymore. I'll arrange a hearse for that idiot."

"What the hell happened out there?"

"Pretty much the same thing that happened in here," said Leeds, guiding Olmos into the alley.

"The whole thing was a setup?"

"I don't know for sure, but I saw two SUVs speed out of here, both matching the description of Fisher's. Whoever was in those vehicles left a big mess behind."

"Identical SUVs?" said Olmos.

"One had more bullet holes in it, but that was the only difference I could see."

"Sounds like a setup."

"I'm not crossing out any theories at this point. All we know for sure is that the cartel description of the SUV that crossed the border and stopped at the motel fit the right parameters. Enough for Flagg to send us."

"Flagg's gonna go ballistic when he hears about this," said Olmos.

"Flagg has nobody to blame but himself," said Leeds, then realized what he'd just said.

Olmos gave him a puzzled look.

"Forget I said that. His problems are way above our pay grade," said Leeds. "We do what we're told and hopefully live to collect a healthy paycheck—which reminds me of something. Mind if I set you down on one of the lounge chairs next to the pool for a minute?"

"As long as you're not having second thoughts about getting me out of here," said Olmos in a serious tone.

Leeds looked him in the eyes. "I'm not leaving you here. I just need to check on something."

After leaving Olmos on the pool patio, he jogged down the sidewalk in front of the office toward the breezeway staircase. The corridor walls revealed dozens of bullet holes. Spent bullet casings littered the ground. A group of CLM operatives had held this ground for a while. At the top of the stairs, he peeked around the corner, seeing a ripped curtain and broken glass lying in front of a nearby room. He was willing to guess that the room sat directly behind room 204. This was starting to look more and more like a planned ambush the farther he explored.

Leeds turned and approached the inner parking lot. He needed to be careful here. If any of the Russians had survived the ambush, they might lie in wait, ready to kill anyone that approached. Things had gone badly enough for them to suspect a double cross. He didn't want to give them an excuse to kill him, something Leeds suspected they would be glad to do regardless.

A quick glance down the walkway toward room 204 told him that none of the Russians had made it into the target room. They had all been killed or mortally wounded, leaving no reason to get any closer. He'd let the Arizona sun finish them off.

"Leeds," someone croaked.

He risked another look, careful not to expose more of his head than absolutely necessary. Chukov sat up against the door immediately adjacent to room 204, pushing a bullet-riddled body off him with his rifle as he rose. Leeds couldn't tell if the blood covering the Russian's torso was his or the corpse's. It didn't matter.

"Get me the fuck out of here," hissed Chukov.

Leeds leaned around the corner with the MP-20, sighted in on the Russian's head, and fired a single bullet through his right temple. Scanning the rest of the bodies sprawled on the deck, he identified a few more that looked like they could be revived with proper medical care. Three headshots later, Leeds was certain there wasn't a hospital in North America that could save any of them. He didn't want any of the mercenaries surfacing to demand payment. Flagg could put Petrov's money to much better use in the cartel's hands.

Automatic gunfire rattled in the distance, reminding him that their welcome in cartel territory had probably expired.

CHAPTER 46

"Roadblock ahead!" said Bravo, striking the shattered-in-place windshield in front of him with the stock of his rifle.

The safety glass on the windshield's passenger side crumbled from the sharp blows, covering the dashboard with hundreds of milky-blue particles. He repeatedly hit the glass in front of the driver with the rifle until he'd cleared most of Jackson's view.

From the backseat, Nathan stared through the open windshield at the wall of vehicles blocking the intersection that led to the Interstate 19 northbound on-ramp. Behind them, the yellow pickup truck and a sizable swarm of cars and trucks had closed more distance. Bullets started to ping off the SUV's metal frame, causing Nathan to flinch. They were absolutely screwed.

"Point all guns forward, through the windshield," said Bravo, leveling the barrel of his rifle at the rapidly approaching roadblock.

"We can't shoot a hole through them," said Nathan, leaning forward and pressing his rifle against Bravo's headrest.

"We don't have to. On my mark, concentrate your fire on the two rightmost vehicles," said Bravo. "Keira, I need your gun, too!"

His wife scooted toward the middle of the backseat, above Owen, and rested the MP-20 against the right side of the driver's seat. Keira looked deadly focused on the task at hand, never glancing away from her gun sight. Jackson, the driver, managed to wrangle his rifle into position to the left of the steering wheel, moments before David's SUV raced from behind them into place along their left side.

"Fire!" said Bravo.

Spent bullet casings ricocheted everywhere inside the SUV as the four suppressed weapons sent a maelstrom of armor-piercing bullets toward the right side of the roadblock. The effects of the barrage on the two vehicles were immediate. Windows shattered, tires flattened, bullet holes punctured the doors, and the gunmen standing behind the cars disappeared. The fusillade ended after several seconds of frenzied shooting, the barrels of their weapons smoking.

"Hold on!" yelled Bravo.

With the cartel's rightmost vehicles disabled, the SUV suddenly veered off Mariposa Boulevard into a sandy field, where it drove at full speed around the blockade. David's vehicle mimicked the turn, staying between the Fishers' SUV and the convoy the entire time. Instead of turning back onto the road, the drivers continued through the low grass and scattered brush, heading directly for the middle of the I-19 on-ramp.

"Reload and cover your sectors!" said Bravo.

Nathan replaced the spent magazine, then turned to help Keira.

"I got it," she said, releasing the bolt catch and charging the submachine gun.

"You watch left and forward. I have the back and right," he said.

"I know my sectors," she said, nestling into position against the door.

Nathan glanced down at Owen, who lay on his back crammed between their backpacks in the foot well. "You all right down there?"

His son gave him a thumbs-up.

"We're almost on the highway, buddy. Smooth sailing from there."

"Big bump coming up!" said Bravo.

Seconds later, the SUV hit the on-ramp's raised shoulder and they were briefly airborne before slamming down onto the ramp. Then they were accelerating smoothly toward the northbound lanes of Interstate 19, the wind pouring through the missing windshield.

Nathan looked behind them and saw David's SUV locked into a blocking position three car lengths behind. Back on Mariposa Boulevard, the cartel roadblock started to move, leaving behind three of the six vehicles that had been spanning the road. The yellow pickup swerved into the field, barely missing one of the sedans from the road-block. By the time the SUVs merged onto the empty interstate, he'd counted more than a dozen vehicles in pursuit.

"How far away is our backup?" said Nathan.

"Thirty minutes," said Bravo.

"This is going to be a long thirty minutes."

Bravo twisted in his seat, staring past him at the dust cloud racing toward the on-ramp. He nodded grimly. "Reach in back and pull the tan duffel bag into the backseat. It should be right behind the seat. We still have a few surprises left."

Nathan struggled to drag the heavy bag out of the cargo compartment and heave it onto the seat between him and Keira. Owen sat up in the foot well to examine the bag behind him.

"You might want to be a little more careful with that," said Bravo.

Nathan unzipped the bag, spreading the sides wide.

"Holy shit," he muttered.

For the first time since they'd left the motel room, Nathan was starting to believe they might make it. Bravo reached into the bag with his left hand and removed a stubby, matte-black grenade launcher.

"Whoa!" said Owen.

"Whoa is right, kid," said Bravo. "There's only one catch."

Keira spoke. "Our son isn't shooting that thing, if that's where you're going."

Bravo laughed, handing the grenade launcher to Nathan. "No. Your husband gets the honor. You know how to work this, right?"

"I've fired the M320 on base with my dad's battalion. This looks the same."

"That's because it is, except it fires a smaller grenade. Everything works the same, except you aim a little differently. The 30-millimeter grenade has a flatter trajectory. More of a point-and-shoot situation than a lob-and-pray job."

"Sounds easy enough. You said there was a catch, though."

"The only effective way to use it in our situation is out the back," said Bravo.

"You mean fire it through the rear window from here?" He didn't like the sound of that at all.

"No. No. These grenades don't have a safe distance arming mechanism like the 40-millimeter version. One bump in the road and you'd blow the back of the vehicle out."

Screw this. Nathan tried to hand it back to Bravo, who shook his head.

"It'll be fine!" said Bravo. "I just need you to climb on top of the gear in back and shoot from the back window."

Nathan looked into the packed rear compartment, trying to envision what that might look like. Every conceivable scenario left him exposed to gunfire on all three sides.

"There's no bulletproof stuff back there!" said Nathan.

"You'll be lying flat with your helmet facing the rear. Small target," said Bravo. "And you can nestle into the gear."

He examined the contents of the compartment again. Was he kidding? "Half of this is filled with gas cans! Not to mention any high explosives you dragged along."

"None of that will explode," said Bravo unconvincingly. "Hey, nothing is better than liquids for slowing down bullets."

Nathan shook his head in disbelief. He couldn't be serious.

"You better get in position," said Bravo, gesturing at the cluster of vehicles in the distance. "I don't think we can outrun them."

He was serious.

Chapter 47

Leeds tore out of the Motel 6 parking lot, turning the tricked-out sedan right onto Mariposa Boulevard. With the roads empty and the traffic signals dead, he faced, at most, a ten-minute trip to the Nogales airport. Ten minutes too long. He cut through the service station on the corner, shaving a few seconds off the drive—anything to get him onto the Gulfstream jet and into the air quicker. He had no idea when the car, or its suddenly deceased owner, would be missed.

The car bounced on its hydraulic shocks and settled onto North Main Avenue, rapidly accelerating south. Leeds eased off the pedal when the speedometer read seventy miles per hour. He could barely see past the three spiderwebbed bullet holes in the windshield above the steering wheel without leaning over the center console.

"This is one sweet-ass ride," said Olmos, reclined in the front seat. "Too bad you fucked it up."

Olmos was no doubt referring to the brains and blood splattered across the backseat and rear window. He'd given the cartel guy a choice. Not much of a choice, but he could have walked away with his head intact and retrieved the car from the airport later in the day. Instead, he'd gunned the engine and tried to drive through.

"Keep an eye on the road for me. I can't see shit," said Leeds. "And I need to call Flagg."

"You haven't called him yet?" said Olmos. "I thought you'd gone to breakfast after you left."

"Sorry to keep you waiting," said Leeds, pulling out his satphone. "It's an eight-mile walk from here to the airport, in case you're curious."

"Just messing with you," mumbled Olmos, sounding less coherent than when Leeds first found him.

"Keep an eye on the road," said Leeds, dialing Flagg's number.

Olmos sat up, squinting drunkenly at the road ahead. "You're clear as far as I can tell. How far to the turn?"

Leeds switched the phone to speaker and put it in a cup holder so he could focus on what little he could see of the road.

"Less than a mile," replied Leeds. "We're looking for Route 82."

Flagg's voice interrupted them.

"The fact that your phone is moving seventy-three miles per hour down a city street toward the airport, and the two of you are bickering, leads me to believe that we had a problem at the Motel 6."

"A big problem," said Leeds. "Chukov's entire team is dead, along with a dozen or more Sinaloa."

A few seconds of silence passed, drawing an uncomfortable look from Olmos. Not an easy feat, given his opioid-fogged state.

"How did the two of you survive?" said Flagg.

"Sorry to disappoint you," said Leeds, wondering if he might be better off taking the jet to Mexico City and disappearing.

"No. I'm genuinely curious—well past the point of sarcasm here. Wasn't Olmos with the Russians?"

"He was a few steps away from absorbing several dozen steel balls. They planted a claymore, or something very similar, in the motel office."

"'They'?" said Flagg. "The Fishers? David Quinn?"

"Olmos lost an arm. I'm getting him to the jet. He'll need immediate medical attention when we get to San Diego, if that's not too inconvenient. We're on speakerphone, in case you're curious."

"I don't care if we're on speakerphone, Nick. Ray's a big boy. Shit like this happens in our line of work," said Flagg. "He'll get the best treatment available when you land in San Diego. Until then, I'd like to get a better handle on exactly what the fuck happened in Nogales. Are we done venting?"

Leeds squeezed the steering wheel, his hands turning pale. Olmos elbowed his shoulder, drawing his attention. "I'm good," he mouthed silently. Leeds nodded, taking a deep breath before continuing.

"I'm better now."

"All right," said Flagg. "Let's start over. Who is this nebulous 'they' you mentioned?"

"That's the problem. I have no fucking idea at this point. Two identical silver SUVs left the motel parking lot, blasting away at anything that moved. Maybe a total of eight occupants."

"Matching the SUV spotted crossing the border?"

"Yes. That's what doesn't make any sense. El Pedro was insistent on the report description," said Leeds. "And you should see the motel. I don't think Chukov's team lasted more than a few seconds. They were torn apart by a well-coordinated cross fire. Whoever did this had people hidden around the motel."

"And they booby-trapped the office," interrupted Olmos.

"So it was an ambush," said Flagg.

"Had to be," said Leeds. "I wouldn't be surprised if Talamanco tipped them off."

Olmos elbowed him again, whispering, "Turnoff for 82."

Leeds nodded, slowing for the upcoming turn.

"Any way the local cartel could have been directly involved?" said Flagg.

"I think it's unlikely," said Leeds. "The cartel took a beating."

"Where is El Pedro now?"

"Last I saw, he was in hot pursuit of the two SUVs."

"Sorry to bring up an indelicate topic in front of Ray," said Flagg, "but why aren't you with them?"

"They left me in the dust long before I found Ray," said Leeds. "I got lucky with this car. Had to create a roadblock with dead bodies to get one of the cartel stragglers to stop."

"All right. I need to get on the line with El Pedro and my primary cartel contact. It sounds like the Mexicans are our only hope at this point."

"If it's any consolation, Petrov can take the money he saved on Chukov's contract and contribute it to the effort."

"Oh, he's going to open his wallet. They all are," said Flagg. "I'm taking a different approach with this, based on what happened in Nogales. I'm going to tell the ONC council that we received a tip from one of our cartel contacts that some gringos were smuggled over the border in Mexicali on the same night as the Marine convoy ambush. Further digging suggested the presence of a CLM covert operations group operating out of the city, moving back and forth into California through a series of tunnel systems. I'm bringing the Fishers and David back to life. Basically saying that they somehow escaped the ambush and were spirited away by CLM."

Leeds was stunned by the idea. It made sense. Quinn and Fisher had so far demonstrated an uncanny ability to slip out of Cerberus's grasp, and there was no reason to think it couldn't have happened again, especially with CLM on their side.

"You could use this to justify escalating hostilities against CLM, and accelerate the timeline of our California operations," said Leeds. "I don't think this would be a tough sell, especially with Petrov's tacit support."

"I could pitch this in my sleep. How does this sound?" said Flagg. "It's obvious that the secessionist movement has progressed far beyond a grassroots political movement. The days of organizing rallies and pressuring voters has yielded to hijacking police drones and fielding special operations teams. If we don't take broad, decisive steps today to combat their shift in tactics, we risk losing everything. Pull out your wallets."

"Not bad at all. Here's a question, though," said Leeds. "Aren't they already paying a small fortune for Cerberus's services?"

"Things have drastically changed over the past few days. CLM is up to something on the California border, and they just ambushed a Cerberus team in Nogales."

"I'm not following," said Leeds.

"I didn't report all of our casualties from the Marine convoy attack. I had a feeling those lost bodies might come in handy to explain my sudden interest in Mexico. I'll report that a four-man team, led by Olmos, was ambushed while investigating a lead in Nogales. Is Olmos capable of verifying that story?"

"I'm sure he won't have a problem with that," said Leeds.

"Good. With enough money, One Nation, through Cerberus, can order carte blanche from the menu. They can put a nationwide price on Fisher's head. All of their heads. Lock down the CLM movement in the Wastelands and beyond. This allows us to refocus our efforts on California, where the real battle will be fought."

"What if Fisher, or any of them, slips through the cracks?" said Leeds.

"With the cartel on the job, they'll be dead within a few hours of surfacing," said Flagg. "I don't think a cop killer will pull at any heart-strings. Neither will a Marine deserter with ties to CLM activists. Not before they succumb to unnatural causes."

"Sounds like a welcome shift in strategy. We're coming up on the airport," said Leeds. "You don't think Petrov will have a problem with us borrowing his jet, do you?"

"I'll call Petrov and square away the jet," said Flagg. "And don't get comfortable after you land. I need you at the Mojave site as soon as possible. That will be the next domino to fall."

"That's a big domino."

"We need something big right now," said Flagg, then disconnected the call.

Leeds craned his neck, looking past the hangar buildings for the white jet that would deliver them from this hellhole.

CHAPTER 48

David studied the line of cars massing a few hundred yards behind them, trying to guess the cartel's new game. Up until a minute or so ago, they had sent one or two cars forward at full speed, trying to ram their SUV off the road. He'd been able to repel each attempt by focusing long bursts into each vehicle, until the approaching cars swerved off the road with a presumably dead driver or dropped back after absorbing casualties.

Only one of the dozen or so vehicles sent had made it far enough to hit the SUV, nearly knocking them off the road. He'd emptied a full ammunition drum into the truck when it tried for a second hit, stopping it dead in the middle of the highway. The swarm of vehicles opened to let it through their ranks, closing up as soon as they had raced past. Now he sensed a different strategy forming.

"I think they're getting ready for a mass attack," yelled David.

"I'm surprised they waited this long," said Alpha. "How are you doing for ammo?"

"I used the last drum on the pickup that hit us," said David. "I'm set for magazines."

He'd replenished his tactical vest with spare magazines from one of the duffel bags pulled from the cargo compartment, stashing the rest throughout the backseat area. Any magazines he couldn't stuff in a cup holder or door had been dumped onto the seat. Running out of ammunition would not be his problem. Putting it to effective use against a coordinated attack was the challenge.

Each magazine held thirty-five rounds, which he could burn through in seconds, requiring him to pause for a few seconds to reload. With all of the vehicles advancing simultaneously, he'd be lucky to knock two or three of them out of commission before they overwhelmed the SUV and moved on to overtake the Fishers' vehicle. Maybe these crazies were smarter than they acted, luring him into expending all of his higher-capacity ammunition drums before the big attack.

"Switch to three-round bursts," said Alpha. "Take one vehicle down at a time."

"Got it," he said, flipping the selector switch to burst.

Dozens of cartel gunmen simultaneously leaned out of the windows and stood up in pickup truck beds behind them and began firing on full automatic. Bullets pinged against the back of the SUV and cracked past the side windows, some rattling through the cabin.

"Here they come!" said David, pressing his rifle's fore grip against the seat back.

Before he stared firing, the SUV veered left, and for a fraction of a second, he thought Alpha had taken a ricochet to the face. When he looked over his shoulder to check, he saw the Fishers' SUV drop rapidly into place next to them.

A puff of white smoke left the back of the adjacent SUV, trailing away behind them as the Fishers' SUV rocketed ahead of them again. David turned his head toward the approaching swarm in time to see the chrome grille of a black lowrider pickup truck explode. The truck instantly swerved right and decelerated, barely clipping the back end of a red sedan before disappearing behind the swarm.

"Direct hit!" yelled David.

A white SUV raced from the back of the pursuing pack to take the lowrider truck's place. One down. Too many to go.

David fired, concentrating his bursts on the raised yellow pickup in the middle. The pickup took several hits across the windshield before it slowed and tucked behind the front line. He switched to the adjacent sedan, placing his first burst into the glass directly in front of the driver. The vehicle swerved left into the void left by the yellow pickup, dropping out of formation.

Two down. And the cartel had closed two-thirds of the gap. This was about to get interesting.

Alpha changed lanes again, letting the Fishers' SUV fall rapidly into place next to them. Another puff of smoke sailed toward the advancing horde, followed by a crunching detonation at least twenty feet behind the farthest cartel vehicle. Shit. Fisher had gotten lucky with his first shot. A dozen bullets slapped into the back of the adjacent SUV before it sped forward again, leaving David's vehicle to absorb the brunt of the cartel's fusillade.

They were about to take more than bullets. A white truck veered diagonally from the left side of the formation, heading straight for the SUV.

"Speed up and turn right!" yelled David.

The truck drifted quickly into his rifle sight, taking two successive bursts to the windshield, which failed to stop the rapidly closing vehicle. He pressed the trigger until the magazine was empty, then braced for impact. The truck slammed into their rear right corner, violently jarring them forward. David was knocked backward against the front passenger seat, dropping his rifle in the foot well. By the time he'd retrieved it, the white truck loomed in the rear passenger side window, at least three gunmen aiming rifles into the SUV.

"Hang on!" said Alpha, slamming on the brakes.

The white truck zoomed past, exploding a moment later from a grenade fired by Fisher from the back of the lead SUV. Alpha kept on the brakes, sending them straight into the swarm. The cartel drivers reacted instinctively to the unexpected maneuver, swerving desperately out of their way. They scraped down the side of the shiny yellow pickup truck, dropping back a dozen or more car lengths before Alpha hit the accelerator.

David reloaded his rifle and leaned through the space between the two front seats, aiming through the front windshield. "Looks like that fucked them up."

"Not for long," said Alpha, speeding back into the group.

The semiorganized formation broke apart, more than half of the cars decelerating. David fired several bursts, spread between the slowing vehicles, as Alpha swerved past them to reach the Fishers' SUV, which led a small cluster of cartel cars by a mere car length. Their surprise move had only delayed the inevitable.

"How far out is Jose?" yelled David, reloading.

"I don't know!" said Alpha, ducking when a bullet struck the top of the steering wheel.

Another bullet hit the top of the dashboard and ricocheted into Carlos's shoulder, splashing David's face with the dead man's blood.

"What do you mean you don't know?" he said, snapping off bursts into the yellow truck's rear window.

"He's close!" said Alpha. "Left side! Left side!"

David shifted to the window behind Alpha and began emptying the magazine into a car that had sped next to them. Dozens of bullets answered, thumping against the ballistic glass and protected door. A few passed between the front and back doors, striking the driver's seat back and exploding into the cabin. If David had been at the opposite window, he would have taken a few of them in the back. At this point, it was only a time before a cartel bullet found its mark.

"We can't keep this up much longer!" he yelled, slapping a new magazine home.

"We don't have a choice!"

I guess not. David returned to the window, searching for the car he had just riddled with bullets. The scene around them had changed dramatically in the past few seconds. They were sealed in on the left. A quick glance behind them and to the right revealed the same problem. They were boxed in.

"Get down!" screamed Alpha, sending David diving flat onto the backseat.

The highway on both sides of them exploded, lifting the back of the SUV into the air. When the vehicle slammed down on the road again, it didn't bounce hard off the road like he expected. It slammed flat into it with a heavy metallic crunch and screeched as metal ground against concrete until the SUV slowed to a stop.

"Holy shit," muttered Alpha.

David lifted his head far enough to look through the front windshield. The shiny yellow pickup truck drifted slowly across the right shoulder of the northbound lanes, continuing its trajectory until it came to a sudden, brutal stop against a short, stout tree.

Nathan's SUV was stopped on the opposite side, a little farther down the highway. A white puff of smoke appeared in its rear lift gate window, followed a sharp detonation that engulfed the pickup truck.

"Holy shit is right," said David.

"Take a look behind us."

David peeked over the seat back. The shattered, smoking remains of six automobiles lay scattered across the highway several hundred feet back. He stared at them for a few seconds before he noticed that the entire back quarter of their own SUV was missing.

"Uh . . . we seem to have a problem."

"And I smell gas," said Alpha, opening his door in a hurry.

"I'm pretty sure the gas tank is gone, if that's what you're worried about."

Alpha opened his door and helped him out, then walked ahead of him to the back of the SUV, where he stopped and shook his head. David saw it, too, when he joined him: the jagged metal edge where the back had been torn away. Smooth, evenly spaced symmetrical holes riddled the frame.

Nothing either SUV might've done could've produced these results. Jose must have placed a line of claymore mines across the highway and detonated the mines in the adjacent lanes.

"Your boss is fucking crazy," David said.

"More like a fucking asshole," muttered Alpha under his breath.

"What?"

"Nothing," said Alpha, an unsettled look on his face.

David looked at him for a moment before glancing back at the shredded metal. A few of the claymore mines' steel balls had struck within a foot of the rear passenger door. It finally fully hit him. "Jesus," he mumbled.

"Yeah," said Alpha, patting him on the back. "Let's get out of here."

CHAPTER 49

From the side of the interstate a quarter mile north, Jose scanned the ambush point with his rifle scope, seeing nothing he could classify as a remaining threat. Some of the vehicles caught in the detonation had tumbled across the median into the southbound lanes, and others had careened into the desert brush on the other side. Judging by the damage done to the cars in plain sight, he wasn't at all concerned about survivors.

He shifted the magnified view to the lone SUV several hundred feet beyond the first piles of wreckage. Carlos sat lifeless in the front passenger seat, head hanging forward over his bloodied vest. Judging by the dark color of the blood covering the headrest and door window, Jose assumed that Carlos had been killed long before they reached the ambush point.

David Quinn and Alpha stood next to the rear of the disabled vehicle, examining the damage. Alpha patted Quinn on the back, and they both started jogging in the direction of the other SUV and Jose.

Jose was confident the two of them had put it together after a look at the condition of the back of the SUV, given the depth of their familiarity with claymores. They'd also know it would have been impossible to remote-detonate the mines and guarantee their safety. It had been pure chance that Quinn and Alpha had survived.

In a few minutes, he'd have to face the men he'd essentially sacrificed to keep Fisher safe. Until then, he had work to do. They were still hundreds of miles inside cartel-controlled territory, with zero confirmed information regarding what to expect from the Sinaloa in terms of a wider response.

Cerberus had no shortage of money to throw at the problem, so they should assume for now that the Sinaloa would make a real effort to find them. With Tucson less than thirty miles north, they needed to reach the first of the Green Valley exits within no more than ten minutes. Moving west on the side roads out of Green Valley would give them a shot at avoiding the primary cartel lookout points. Of course, if Cerberus threw serious cash at the cartel bosses, they could face a cartel snitch at every intersection from here to Las Vegas.

He jogged across the highway to Jeremy Baker, who had just dispatched a two-person team to check the yellow pickup truck. The rifle grenade fired by the surprisingly resourceful Nathan Fisher appeared conclusive, but nobody was taking any chances.

"Jeremy. Get in touch with Vegas station and have them deploy a scout team to clear Route 93. Ideally, I'd like to know if that route's viable by the time we reach Phoenix."

"That might be a little tight."

"We can go twenty miles past Phoenix on Route 60 before making a hard decision, so they have some leeway."

"Maybe we should default to the western route and head up through Havasu City. The closer we move to California, the less cartel activity."

"I'm worried about the dust storm moving in," said Jose. "The western route adds close to three hours to the trip."

"We'd be moving away from the storm."

"Until we turn north. This one is going to sweep well into California. If 93 is clear, I want to shoot straight up from Phoenix. We should be able to reach Kingman before the storm hits. I'd feel a lot better about getting stranded in Kingman than along the side of the road."

"I'll get Vegas station moving," said Jeremy, glancing south on the highway toward Quinn and Alpha. "You're really going to make them run the whole way?"

"I'm hoping they'll be too tired to punch me in the face when they get here," said Jose.

"I don't know, they look like they're in pretty good shape."

Jose shot him a sideways glance.

"Hey," Jeremy said. "You made the right call. Mission comes first. Neither of them is a stranger to that concept."

"I know, but it doesn't make it any easier to face them," said Jose. "Or the rest of the crew."

"They understand the stakes, or they wouldn't be here. The crew believes in you. Believes in what you're trying to accomplish," said Jeremy. "If you think Fisher is the key to our mission, then protecting Fisher *is* the mission."

"I wish he was a more willing key."

"He'll come around," said Jeremy, taking out his satellite phone.

Jose hoped so. He'd staked everything on it, effectively setting in motion a series of irrevocable events. Money had changed hands. Promises had been sealed. Costly equipment had been purchased. They wouldn't get a second shot at this.

He walked about thirty feet north along the highway toward the battered SUV that had kept the Fishers alive. Through the dusty, bullet-chipped rear passenger window, he caught a glimpse of Keira leaning her head back. He presumed she was holding Owen, since he didn't see the boy outside the vehicle. Hugging him fiercely, he imagined, after what they had been through this morning.

The SUV looked barely serviceable. He wished there was an easy way to get the two of them out of the line of fire. Maybe he could charter a private jet to fly them out of Las Vegas to any destination they chose—so long as it was without Nathan.

Jose approached Nathan and Jackson, who were busy emptying the cargo compartment.

"Why are you off-loading?" said Jose. "We're leaving immediately."

"You might want to ask Bravo."

"Where did he—" started Jose, hearing a curse from the unobserved side of the vehicle.

He stepped behind them and glanced around the back of the vehicle. Bravo held a lug wrench firmly with two hands, loosening the rear right tire.

"Can the tire go another twenty miles?" yelled Jose.

Bravo didn't stop turning the wrench. "I have no idea how they lasted this long."

"They?" he said, not liking the sound of that.

"Both rear tires are fucked. Didn't you notice? If I turn the engine on, you can hear the onboard compressor working overtime to keep the pressure at the minimum. The run-flats were designed for one or two holes, not twenty."

"How long to change them?" said Jose, kneeling next to him.

"Twenty minutes? Maybe faster if we get everyone involved. They're a little more complicated because of the self-inflation system."

"We don't have twenty minutes. Transfer everything to the other vehicles. Including the spare."

"You have room for seven more passengers?" said Bravo, dropping the wrench to the road.

"We'll have to make it work," said Jose, standing up to locate Jeremy.

He spotted him in the brush next to one of their hidden cars on the other side of the highway, speaking on his phone.

"Jeremy!" he said. "We need to pack everyone into the three remaining vehicles. This one is a no go!"

Jeremy nodded brusquely, continuing the call for several seconds before putting the phone away. "Vegas station is sending two cars south. It'll take them close to four hours to clear the entire route to our decision point north of Phoenix."

"We'll probably arrive at the same time, if we don't run into problems. The back roads around Tucson or Phoenix will take some time," said Jose. "I want to be on the road in under two minutes."

"We can make that happen," said Jeremy before turning to speak into his headset.

Vehicle engines roared to life all around them. Jose returned to Nathan.

"Nathan, is everyone all right?"

"A bit banged up, but considering the circumstances—yes."

"Excellent. I'm glad to see our modifications held up against heavy gunfire. We're not out of the woods yet."

"Where are we headed?" said Nathan, eyeing him skeptically.

"Vegas," said Jose. "That's our new base of operations."

"Yours or CLM's?"

"Both, eventually."

"I presume you didn't choose Vegas for its inexpensive real estate?"

"What can I say?" said Jose. "The Hoover Dam is my new favorite tourist site."

Nathan cracked a grin and extended his hand. "I owe you a second thank-you, even though you followed us."

Jose shook hands with Nathan.

"Just a precaution, and a lucky one at that. We can talk about this in detail during our four-hour, partially air-conditioned drive north. Right now I have to take care of a few things before we take off," he said, turning to help the team reorganize the cars.

"One last thing," said Nathan.

Jose stopped and faced him. "Yes?"

"David rides with us."

"Sure," said Jose. "If he doesn't mind driving."

"I'm sure David won't mind driving, especially if it improves his chances of staying alive."

The mild-mannered water reclamation engineer was even more perceptive than he'd imagined. Nathan's car would be the most protected vehicle in the convoy.

"You're critical to our plan, Nathan," said Jose.

"So is David. You need to consider him just as important if you want my help. We ride together."

"Very well," said Jose. "Get your family ready to move. We have a tight schedule. The New Dust Bowl has spawned another dust storm, and it's headed this way."

As if on cue, a sudden blast of warm wind swept across the highway, flapping his checkered shemagh scarf. Jose searched the partially cloudy sky east of the highway, bothered by the unexpected gust. The horizon revealed nothing unusual, the storm still a few hundred miles away. He reminded himself to check the weather again once they got moving. Weather patterns across the Wasteland states had become hopelessly unpredictable over the past decade, and micro dust storms had been known to rise up in advance of the massive New Dust Bowl events. Getting stuck this deep in cartel territory during a sandstorm would be a problem.

The sound of dragging footsteps drew his attention south, to the two men who had risen from the ashes of their sacrifice down the freeway. Jose rubbed his chin, absorbing their tired looks as they approached. He started to speak but was cut off by Alpha.

"Don't you dare apologize for making the right decision," said Alpha, bending over to put both hands on his knees.

David grabbed his as well and looked up at Jose, breathing heavily. "I'll take an apology."

"No, you won't," said Alpha, standing up to gulp some air.

"You weren't in the backseat," said David. "Statistically, I was far less likely to survive."

"I'm just glad the odds worked out in your favor," said Jose.

"Me, too," said David.

PART V

PART V.

Chapter 50

Stuart Quinn pressed "Send" on his satphone, trying Jon's number one more time before Blake drove them into the subdivision where he had been staying. Stuart didn't like risking the exposure, but they had to investigate. The call went to voice mail again.

"All right. Let's get as close as we can without drawing attention."

They slipped into the neighborhood.

"It's the second left after this turn."

"Got it," said Blake, easing them through the stop sign onto Hillview Way.

Stuart's hopes sank as soon as they straightened onto Hillview. A marked police car coming from the opposite direction turned where they were headed, followed closely by an unmarked car. Neither vehicle stopped at the intersection.

"I think we should pass on the drive-by," said Blake.

"Agreed," said Stuart, reaching into the backseat to retrieve his laptop.

Hopefully, he still had access to the Homeland Secure Data Network through his current job at the Joint Intelligence Task Force. His sudden request for vacation hadn't raised any eyebrows as far as he was aware, but he couldn't make any assumptions with Cerberus involved. They appeared to have a knack for framing people.

A disturbing thought crossed his mind. He'd just assumed that nothing had gone wrong with his job back in DC, since his encrypted phone could still access the DTCS satellite network. One of the first things they would do if his security clearance had come into question was sever his connection to the network—unless they wanted to track him. He shook his head. Now he was being paranoid. Or was he?

Blake drove them past the turnoff into Jon's friend's subdivision, both of them glancing uselessly into the neighborhood. The town house in question was a few streets removed from the entrance.

He opened the laptop and synced with his satphone, typing in a series of passwords to authenticate his access. He was connected to his JITF portal moments later.

"I'm in," said Stuart.

"Try to access something sensitive," said Blake.

"I'd rather not raise any red flags while I'm on *vacation*."

"You always access the classified portal when you're fishing?"

"I've never been fishing in my life," said Stuart, navigating through the JITF system to the Homeland Secure Data Network. "But I do like to make sure the neighborhood is safe when I rent a place."

"Dare I ask?" said Blake, craning his head to take a look.

"This is classified," said Stuart, turning the screen away from him.

"Really?"

"Just fucking with you," he said, turning the screen as far as he could and typing. "I'm checking the Joint Fusion Center's Assessment and Analysis Network."

"Uh-huh," mumbled Blake. "Sounds like hocus-pocus."

"It kind of is. They take everything, from everywhere, and combine the data to identify incidents of interest and emerging threats. It's shared across law enforcement and intelligence agencies."

"Social media surveillance?"

"That's a small part of it," said Stuart, typing search parameters for Missoula.

Stuart clicked "Submit," hoping the search would come up empty. He wasn't surprised by what he saw, but it still cut through him like a knife. Several data points intersected to confirm that Jon Fisher had been killed at the town house. He didn't say anything, fighting back the tears welling in his eyes.

The first point originated on social media from a neighbor reporting multiple gunshots. Several 911 calls immediately followed. The digital transcripts of those calls were already available. The most damning evidence came from the Missoula Police Department's executive summary of the responding officer's findings. By state and federal law, they were required to submit the summary within thirty minutes of the first officer's arrival. The summary identified the victim by driver's license and retired military ID card as Jonathan Fisher, pronounced dead on the scene by paramedics with a gunshot to the head. Significant bloodstains found on patio, along with bullet pattern, indicated a two-way shootout, with a possible second victim. *At least he got one of them.*

"I'm really sorry, Stu," said Blake.

He took a deep breath, his grief flashing to anger—and back. All he could do at the moment was nod in response to Blake and let the reality of Jon's death sink in while they drove toward the university area. After a few minutes, he felt level enough to talk without exploding.

"They'll go after Leah next."

"How do we stop them?" said Blake.

"We need to find out if the town house leads back to Jon's friend," said Stuart, scrolling through his phone for a number Jon gave him. He pressed "Send," hoping like hell Jon's friend would answer.

"Billings Lumber."

"Jon is dead. My name is Stuart Quinn. I'm the friend that was driving into town to meet him this morning. If you're sitting near Leah, please step outside."

"Everyone's still asleep here. How did you get this number?" said the man.

"Jon gave it to me in case something happened. I don't know your name or where you are."

"Then I should probably hang up and dispose of this phone."

"They killed him at your town house," said Stuart.

"There's no link between the town house and our community."

"Are you one hundred percent sure? They found the town house pretty quickly."

"I think I'm going to hang up now."

"Please don't. Please don't. I need you to think of anything that could possibly lead them to you. Anything," begged Stuart.

"Nothing points in this direction."

"Do you keep mortgage statements in the town house? Bills? Any paperwork?"

"Mail gets sent to a PO box. Sometimes I leave stuff in there, but the address on record at the post office is the town house. No link to our community. Nobody knows about this place. It's unincorporated."

"But they found the town house, which means they identified you, not Jon. How did they do that?"

"I don't know, and I don't care."

"You need to care. This group won't stop until they find Leah. They'll either kill her or use her as a hostage to leverage Nathan," said Stuart.

"Then they're going to be at this for a long time, because we don't exist."

"They found *you* somehow!" said Stuart, then suddenly pieced a theory together. "Jon used his laptop at a Starbucks to access his home security feeds."

The man was silent.

"If they ran a trace on his remote access session, they could have identified the store's IP address. That's why he asked you to pick him up so quickly."

"I'm listening," said the man.

"What if they caught your Jeep on one of the store cameras and grabbed a license plate?"

"The Jeeps are owned by a corporation held in Billings. No identifying information."

"You have a driver's license, right?"

"Using the town house address. I keep a notarized letter in the Jeep, from the corporation, granting me permission to use the Jeep. It's the only copy."

"It sounds airtight," admitted Stuart.

"That's because it is."

"I've been working within the intelligence community for too long to believe anything is truly airtight. We're missing something. They found the town house."

"And that's as far as they'll get. Unless somebody physically follows me here, there's no way to track us to the community, and nobody followed me back. We designed this place to be sure of that."

Jon had felt safe leaving Leah there. Maybe Stuart should leave this alone.

"Mr. Quinn?" said the man, his voice suddenly sounding hollow.

"Yeah?"

"I did get a speeding ticket about two years ago. I remember being a little nervous because I had to give him my driver's license. Could they have gotten into the system and pulled the address from the citation?"

"Yes," he said. "They could have done that very easily."

A long pause ensued, as Stuart processed every scenario he could imagine through to determine if the trail ended there.

"How deep can this group dig?" said the man.

"Deep. If your shit isn't hidden behind a lettered agency firewall, they can find it."

"Then we have a problem. I'm not the only lead foot in here that keeps a place in town. If the group chasing the Fishers can access our corporate records—"

"I'm sure they already have."

"Then they'll have a long list of license plates to run, and I guarantee they'll uncover a few more addresses in town. All of our vehicles are registered to the same corporation."

"Shit," said Stuart.

"Shit is right. I'm gonna have some seriously pissed-off neighbors. They'll be watching those locations, too."

"Not right away, probably," said Stuart. "It'll take a little time to move additional teams into place. They'll start right away with something less manpower intensive—which presents us with an opportunity."

"How's that?"

He'd formed the idea as soon as Jon's friend had mentioned the PO box. "They'll start by watching the PO box. That would be my play," said Stuart. "It's a direct link to the second half of their objective."

"Why would I show up at the post office, or anywhere in town, if someone was murdered at my town house?"

"Normally you wouldn't, but if you want to put an end to this once and for all, you'll show up this morning."

"Say again, over. Your transmission was garbled. Or did I just hear you suggest I walk into a trap?"

"We want you to lure them *into* a trap."

"'We'? I was under the impression you were working alone. How many of you are there?"

"Two," said Stuart.

"Two?"

"If we do this right, that's all it will take."

"What if you get it wrong?"

"We won't," said Stuart.

"And how does this make everything go away?"

"Because we're going to burn their operation here to the ground. It's the only way to stop a group like this. You have to make their continued presence here too costly to pursue, and I plan to charge them a fucking premium if they try to stick around. I just need to use you as . . . uh . . ."

"Bait?" said the man.

"I was looking for a more appealing term."

"Like what?"

"*Bait* pretty much sums it up."

"When do you want to do this?"

"Within the next few hours," said Stuart. "We should meet to discuss the plan. You pick the place. Bring the Jeep, or they might suspect something is off."

"I don't want them tracking the Jeep back here."

"You need to ditch the Jeep, sooner than later," said Stuart. "I hate to break this to you, but every vehicle in your community needs to be replaced. Repainted, at the very least."

"Damn," he said. "I'm really up shit creek here."

"Well, if it's any consolation, you did the right thing for Jon and Leah, which means you've made a new best friend."

"I'm gonna need one. I'm about to lose the friends I have here."

"Don't count them out yet."

After they'd finalized arrangements to meet and ended the call, Blake turned to him.

"So. What's the plan?"

"I don't know yet," replied Stuart.

"Oh boy."

"Oh boy is right."

CHAPTER 51

Riggs straightened in his seat. A tan Jeep Wrangler had just appeared on Oxford Street, approaching the western parking lot entrance. From his vehicle's position in the diner parking lot, directly across the street from the post office, he had an unobstructed view of all customer approaches to the building.

"Wake the fuck up!" he hissed, shaking Tex's arm.

"Chill out!" said Tex. "And keep your hands off. I'm getting sick of your shit."

He'd completely lost the team's respect. Tex never would have back-talked him like that before last night's debacle.

"You want to spend the rest of your life staking out this parking lot? Look," said Riggs, nodding toward the entrance.

The Jeep turned into the lot, proceeding slowly toward a spot near the entrance.

"License plate matches," said Ross, passing a pair of binoculars between the front seats.

Riggs took the binoculars and focused on the man driving the Jeep as he eased the vehicle into a space to the left of the entrance doors and got out. It was Scott Gleason.

"It's him," said Riggs, opening his door. "Man, we got lucky. This might work out better than the original plan."

"Sure. If you consider never working in the industry again a better plan."

"You'll be fine. There's always work for the sheep."

"What the hell does that mean?" barked Tex.

Riggs shook his head in disgust and slammed the door shut. Screw that guy. Ross, too. Neither of them had ever put together a team and run an operation. They just did what they were told and collect their split. A glorified getaway driver and a trigger puller. That's all either of those two worthless assholes could put on his résumé.

He reached into his coat pocket and removed the thumb-size tracking device he'd tested an hour earlier. The tracker utilized both the city Wi-Fi and cellular networks, in conjunction with GPS satellite signals, to find and transmit its location.

Riggs walked across the diner parking lot, timing his approach so he arrived at Kent Street, directly in front of the post office entrance, at the exact moment Gleason disappeared inside. His casual walk turned into the lazy jog of someone crossing a street with light traffic. He had timed the trip between the post office door and Gleason's box when the place first opened.

He fast-walked across the post office lot, slipped between the tan Jeep and the car next to it, and knelt next to the rear tire well. He reached his hand high under the chassis, just behind the well, moving the tracker until he felt the magnet stick. He pulled on the device and tried to wiggle it side to side, but it was firmly attached. Rising to his feet, he glanced through the Jeep's back windows at the post office door. All clear.

Riggs had just crossed Kent Street when Gleason emerged from the building, carrying a small package and a few envelopes. Riggs had really hoped that the box had been empty. The only foreseeable wrinkle in their plan occurred if Gleason decided to take the envelopes to his town house. Discovering an active homicide investigation into the murder of his good friend would undoubtedly delay Gleason's day, and theirs.

In the end, though, it wouldn't matter. With the tracker in place, he'd eventually lead them to Mrs. Fisher.

When Riggs got back to the SUV, Tex wouldn't look at him. He glanced over his shoulder at Ross, disturbed that he had to prompt him for information.

"The signal's looking good," said Ross, looking uninterested for someone whose life depended on tracking that signal.

Shit. They'd had a little confidential discussion while he was gone. His problem had just gone from insubordination to mutiny. The only questions were how and when.

"All we can do now is wait and see where he takes us," said Riggs.

Neither of them asked a follow-up question or made a suggestion, which sealed it. They had no intention of finishing the job. They'd move against him this morning, at their first clean opportunity. They'd probably try to leverage Gleason's location for some kind of guaranteed truce with Flagg. Maybe he'd made a mistake by cutting Nissie out of the electronic loop. The tablet in Ross's hands was the only device linked to the tracker. They could kill him now and try to negotiate with Flagg.

Gleason's Jeep backed out of its space and back to Oxford Street, disappearing the way it had arrived.

"We'll stay a few blocks behind them. Farther on the open road," said Riggs, reaching his hand over the seat for the tablet. "I'll do the honors."

Ross didn't look happy to hand it over, but refusing outright or putting up a fight would have been too obvious. Tex just stared through the windshield as he drove, pretending to pay no attention to the little power play that had just gone down. Now they couldn't drive him into the woods twenty miles in the opposite direction and shoot him in the head. God forbid if they had to be creative and think on their feet. He caught Tex glancing at Ross through the rearview mirror. Riggs would have to play this one perfectly to survive.

Fifty minutes later, after an uneventful trip east of Missoula on Interstate 90, Gleason's Jeep exited the highway in Drummond and headed south on Highway 1. Three minutes later, their SUV arrived at the Drummond exit. The off-ramp dumped them onto the state highway, which ran flat as far as he could see on the southern horizon. Farther south, gentle hills rose on both sides of the road.

His operational instincts told him to tell Tex to pull over to the side and give Gleason a few more minutes to open the gap. They'd traveled twice the distance on the highway that the Jeep covered in the same time on this road. His survival instincts reminded him that stopping in the middle of nowhere with two mutineers was undeniably bad for his health, so he didn't say anything. He couldn't see the next car south of them, anyway.

About fifteen minutes later, the Jeep turned right onto an unmarked road two miles ahead of them. He switched the tablet to satellite overlay, seeing a Jeep path intersecting the highway at the point where the tracker departed the road. They had passed dozens of similar paths since leaving the interstate. That was pretty much all they had seen, beside a few one-story homes and trailers set back from the highway. This was about as isolated as it got. He could definitely picture some kind of survivalist camp up in the hills.

"They just turned off the highway onto an unmarked trail," said Riggs. "Slow us down a little."

The SUV decelerated without any acknowledgment from Tex. Riggs widened the map view, trying to gauge the distance from the highway to the edge of the hills. He estimated two miles. They'd probably have the camp a few miles back from that. Maybe farther. He'd have to be careful with Tex and Ross once they turned off the highway. Ready at a second's notice to strike first.

When they turned onto the Jeep trail several minutes later, he scanned ahead of them with the binoculars. The trail ran down a gentle slope for a quarter mile or so, passing through a stand of low-lying trees before rising again. A simple, timber ranch gate spanned the trail just below the top of the brush-covered rise.

"Looks clear," he said, passing the binoculars to Tex. "There's a gate just below that rise out there. We'll pass through and take a look from the top. See if we can get closer without being spotted."

That would be the end of the road for Tex and Ross. He'd open the gate and shoot them dead when he returned to the truck after closing the gate behind them. They wouldn't expect him to make a move this soon. Tex nodded, handing the binoculars to Ross.

"Sounds like a plan," said Ross, returning the binoculars.

Enjoy your last few breaths, gentlemen.

Tex stopped the Jeep farther from the gate than he'd expected. They were at least three times the distance required to swing the gate inward. Looked like this was it. They'd probably try to shoot him as they drove through. He'd have to make his move before that. Probably as soon as he walked the gate over to the side. Drill Ross full of holes first, then Tex. He wouldn't have the best angles, but it would have to work.

"I'll close the gate behind us," said Riggs. "Meet you on the other side."

"Yep," said Tex.

Riggs stepped out of the SUV, taking the MP-20 clipped to the side of the foot well with him, and walked toward the gate. He'd gotten three-quarters of the way when he heard a door open. Spinning to face his attackers, he recognized his mistake instantly, unable to stop his hands from lining up the wrong target.

Tex was behind his open door, his pistol pushed through the open window but not yet fully aimed. Ross's absence could only mean one thing. The operative was covering him from inside the vehicle, in case Tex wasn't fast enough. Before Riggs could pull the trigger, Tex's head jerked sideways, a fine red mist exploding over the top of the SUV. Almost simultaneously, Riggs's view through the windshield disappeared, replaced by another bright red spray, and the rear door window behind Tex's still upright body exploded outward.

Riggs stood still, instinctually knowing that he'd die if he moved. A sound drew his attention to the right.

"That's right, not a muscle," yelled a voice, freezing him in place. "Now release the weapon. Just drop it."

Riggs did what he was told. An older man wearing a brown ball cap and casual street clothes rose from a thick clump of bushes less than thirty feet from the trail. He pointed a suppressed, short-barreled rifle at Riggs's chest.

"Kick the weapon to your left," the man said, walking slowly toward him. "And put your hands on your head."

"How did you know I was following you?" said Riggs, kicking the MP-20 several feet to his left.

"You weren't following me," said the man. "You were following my friend, who drove to the hills to find us a nice quiet place to talk."

"You're that Quinn guy."

"In the flesh," he said.

"Who fired the other shot?"

"I'd rather talk about the tense little drama that just unfolded. Looked to me like you had a little disagreement with your friends," said the man, walking behind him.

"You could call it that."

"I was half tempted to let the whole thing play out, see who was still standing at the end. But with my luck, you'd have all shot one another dead. What's your name?"

"Chris."

"Chris. Here's the deal. You killed a good friend of mine, and you were plotting to kill another good friend of mine."

Riggs briefly considered trying to explain that Jon Fisher's death had been a mistake, but dismissed the idea. There didn't seem to be a point. There was no way Quinn was going to let him live. His road had come to an end.

"It wasn't personal," was all he could think to say.

"It never is for people like you," said Quinn, reappearing on his left side to snatch the MP-20 off the ground, then disappearing behind him again.

"You're going to kill me," said Riggs.

Quinn didn't respond right away.

"Yes, Chris. I'm going to kill you," he said. "Eventually."

A shock radiated from the middle of Riggs's back to his limbs, locking his body with rhythmic pulses of agonizing pain. He fell forward, twitching. The pain lasted a few seconds, quickly subsiding. As it dulled, he felt a tug at his right hip. Shit.

"Back on your feet, Chris. There's no easy way out of this for you."

He struggled to his feet, his legs weak. "Let me guess," he said. "I can tell you what I know right now and get a clean, painless death, or I can hold out and get a painful death."

"That about sums it up, Chris, but here's something to consider. We're not going to start by slapping you around, waterboarding you. I've been in this business for more than thirty years, and I find the buildup phase to be a huge waste of time."

He didn't like the sound of this at all. Maybe there was a way out of this. "I can give you the man that hired me."

"At Cerberus?"

"Yes. At Cerberus."

"But you don't work for Cerberus," said Quinn.

"I do work for them."

"As an independent contractor."

"No. I'm—"

"You just said 'the man that hired me,' Chris. If you're not getting your health insurance through Sentinel, there's no way you can give me the man that hired you. He's a voice on the phone. An e-mail. A text message."

"We can work something out."

"Chris. Listen to me. Nothing can save you. You have to accept that."

"I don't want to die."

"Nobody wants to die," Quinn said, "but everyone wants the choice between—say—passing away in his sleep or burning to death in a house fire. Right? I'm giving you that choice. Quick and painless, or endless and painful."

"That sounds like a poem."

"I might put that in my memoirs," said Quinn. "So what will it be?"

Strangely enough, Quinn's words had put him at ease. Looking back at the morning, he could see that his fate had been decided long before arriving here. All roads led to his end. In light of what he did to Quinn's friend, he was lucky to get a choice.

"Quick and painless."

"You have my word," said Quinn. "After we verify the accuracy of the information you provide."

"Always a catch."

Chapter 52

Stuart Quinn dialed his son's satphone again. He'd called five times since they'd left Riggs in the not-so-gentle care of Scott Gleason and one of his buddies in the hills a few miles beyond Highway 1. He was starting to get worried. David should have answered at this point, regardless of the situation, or at least sent him a quick text. When this call went to voice mail, too, he left a brief message.

"Hey, bud. It's Dad. Give me a call as soon as you get this, or text me if you can't call. I need to talk to you about something," he said, hanging up and sending a text with the same message.

"Nothing?" said Blake.

He shook his head and took a deep breath. If anything had happened to his son, he'd reconsider his promise to Riggs, regardless of what they found inside the motel.

"He's probably just busy," said Blake.

"That's what I'm worried about."

"I meant focusing on the road and staying out of trouble."

"I know what you meant," said Stuart, nodding at the motel beyond the windshield. "What do you think?"

"The place is empty. I think we just kick the doors in at the same time and get it over with," said Blake. "Sounds like our target shouldn't be too hard to identify."

"Don't count on it."

One of the room doors they planned to kick down opened, and a woman resembling Nissie Keane's description stepped outside. She pulled the door shut and walked to the metal exterior staircase in the middle of the motel. Moments after disappearing beneath the stairs, a white stream of smoke drifted up through the steps.

"Is that her?" said Blake.

"The right side of her head was shaved. Tats up her neck. Sure as shit looked like her."

"Riggs said they all looked pretty fucked up."

"But we agree she's a she?"

"I saw tits."

"Keane is the only female in the group."

"Then that would have to be her," added Blake. "This would be a painfully easy snatch-and-grab—"

"If we didn't need all of her gear, too. At least it'll be quieter than kicking the doors in."

They crossed the Albertson's parking lot and walked straight into the motel's lot. They approached Keane just as she took a final drag on her cigarette and tossed it to the cement next to the stairway. She'd just stood up and taken a few steps toward her room when she noticed them. Her eyes went wide at the sight of Blake's weapon, quickly narrowing into slits. For a moment, Stuart thought she might run, which would seriously complicate matters. Blake raised the suppressed MP-20 a little higher.

"I knew that idiot would land us in deep shit," she said, her shoulders slumping. "We had nothing to do with his little stunt."

"That little stunt killed a good friend of mine," said Stuart.

"Oh . . . shit."

"Oh shit is right. You have a room key?"

She nodded, her eyes never leaving the suppressed weapon.

"Slowly hand the key to me," he said.

Keane reached into the front pocket of her ripped jeans and took out the key card, extending it as far in front of her as possible. She was trying really hard not to get killed, which gave him an idea. He took the card and gave it to Blake.

"How badly do you want to survive this little encounter?"

"Very badly," she said. "This is just a job. They pay well."

"I can think of less dangerous jobs."

"This is the first time we've had a problem like this."

"There's a reason for that," said Stuart. "Cerberus fucked up with this one, and not just this op. They're taking hits like this from here to Mexico."

"I'm not aware of any other ops."

"I don't suspect you are—or you'd never have returned Flagg's message."

She tried not to react to the name, but Stuart had been doing this for years. He could read a face.

"Let's circle back to my friend," he said, drawing a pistol from a concealed hip holster under his jacket.

"I'll tell you whatever you want to know," she said, raising her hands in front of her. "I don't give a shit about Flagg or whatever Cerberus is. I do the work because it pays."

He turned to Blake. "Try not to damage any equipment."

"I won't," he said.

Blake lowered his weapon to a concealed position along his right side and walked toward the room she had recently left.

"Where's he going?"

"Nissie . . . may I call you Nissie?"

She nodded.

"Are you emotionally attached to anyone in that room?"

"What?" she said, looking past him nervously.

"Do you hang out with any of them on weekends? Visit one another's families? Have a physical relationship with any of them?"

She shook her head, frustrated. "No. This is a fucking side job. I don't know any of them outside of this kind of work. Why do you care?"

As soon as she asked the question, her face changed. She understood.

"I have a job you might be interested in, unless you think someone in those rooms could do a better job."

She shook her head. "I was thinking of going solo after this job, anyway."

"I can't guarantee the pay is better."

"Pay isn't everything," she said.

Stuart glanced over his shoulder and nodded at Blake, who was waiting outside the door.

"I think I'm going to throw up," she said.

"Just keep your hands in sight. I don't have the time to find a new hacker."

When the key-card reader beeped behind him, she started to breathe through her mouth. He watched her wince every time Blake's gun fired a suppressed bullet inside the room. Three times in rapid succession.

"You've never been this close to the end result of your handiwork, have you?" said Stuart.

She shook her head, still breathing rapidly.

"Let's take a look. You can grab whatever gear you need," he said, motioning for her to walk.

Blake walked out of the room, without the backpack he had brought with him, when they got to the door. "I'll take care of the motel office and get the car."

"Drag whoever's in the office into the grass across the parking lot. Just in case the fire gets out of control," said Stuart, examining Nissie's reaction.

She looked distressed by his order.

"He's just going to knock them out and move them where they won't catch fire," said Stuart, gesturing toward the room. "Shall we?"

She hesitated, taking increasingly reluctant steps toward door. When it became obvious that she'd gotten as close to the unpleasant reality of her work as her own resolve would allow, he pushed her into the room. She'd thank him for it later. He expected her to emerge from the room with a fresh perspective on her line of work, and a desire to make some amends. At the very least, he wanted to show her where she was headed—if she didn't cooperate.

CHAPTER 53

Stuart paced the soggy ground in front of the two dirt graves, his thumb frozen above the "Send" button on his satphone. He didn't want to make this call, but he didn't have a choice. He owed it to Jon. Blake stood behind the dirt mounds, guarding Nissie. Stuart walked away from the graves, his fingers pressing the button after several paces. Leah answered almost immediately.

"Stuart?"

He'd sent Scott and his friend back to their secret compound two hours ago, after killing Riggs. Scott had called him as they'd pulled up to his house, asking Stuart to call back in five minutes. He'd get the phone to Leah.

"Leah. I have some bad news," said Stuart, his fist clenched. He walked away from the graves toward the edge of the green clearing.

"I knew something had happened when Scott took off with one of his friends this morning," she said. "He's really gone?"

"I'm afraid so. It happened late last night, before we got here. I don't know what to say, Leah."

"Have you told Nathan?"

He took a deep breath. "I haven't been able to get through to them today. When I do, I'll—"

"How long has it been since you've heard from them?"

"I know that Nathan talked with Jon last night, maybe around eleven? He got to talk with Owen, too," said Stuart, his voice cracking.

Leah didn't respond for several seconds. He could hear her sniffling. She sobbed between words when she returned to the conversation.

"That's a long time not to hear from them."

"It's longer than I'd like, but they had a solid plan. I expect to hear from them soon. You'll be the first to know."

"Thank you, Stuart," she said. "Thank you for everything you and David have done for us."

"I wish I could have done more."

"You've risked everything for us. You and David. Don't you dare blame yourself for what happened. This falls squarely on Cerberus's shoulders."

"I'm going to take care of Cerberus," said Stuart. "I'll expend my last breath making sure they pay for this."

"Just get our boys and their families back safely," she said. "That's the number-one priority right now."

Families, plural, she'd said. Jon hadn't told her about Alison's death. Stuart didn't blame him. The news would only have added to her anxiety. There was certainly no reason for him to reveal Alison's death now.

"I'm working on that. We're heading south in a few minutes," said Stuart. "If all goes well, they'll reach Las Vegas soon and give me a call. I may have them drive up to Salt Lake City. The roads in between are safe enough."

"Please call as soon as you hear anything."

"I will," he said. "Stay safe, Leah."

"I'm in good hands here."

"I'm very sorry about what happened to Jon. He was like a brother to me."

"I know he was, Stuart," she said. "I don't want to hold you up any longer. You have a long road ahead of you."

"I'll be in touch," he said, ending the call.

Stuart stood still, staring at the mountains to the west. He could see why Jon and Leah chose to live out here. You felt a sense of peace and majesty wherever you looked. Maybe when all of this had settled, he'd take a serious look at the upper Rocky Mountain states.

Blake and Nissie stood up when he walked back.

"Time to go," he said, glancing down at the freshly packed dirt. Two shovels lay on the ground next to the graves. "Wipe the shovels down again," he said. "I don't want to get anyone at the compound in trouble over a partial fingerprint."

Blake nodded and headed to the SUV for the gear. Nissie watched him leave, quickly shifting her attention to Stuart. She was terrified of them, which was exactly how he wanted to start their relationship. Fear was a powerful motivator, and more importantly, a mighty deterrent. He had big plans for Keane, but first she had to demonstrate that she was 100 percent on board with her new contract.

"You ready for a road trip?" he said.

"Do I have to wear these the entire time?" she said, turning and extending her hands to expose the black zip ties binding them together.

"Until I'm convinced that you won't try to kill one of us or make a run for it, you get to wear plastic."

"Haven't I already proven myself? You have the keys to the kingdom thanks to me," Nissie said. "Flagg would kill me if he knew what I gave you."

"Flagg was going to kill you anyway. He's in damage-control mode right now, which isn't his area of expertise. Guys like that are only comfortable running smooth operations. When things go bad, they turn to scorched-earth methods, burning everything and everyone in the process."

"Like the motel you burned down?"

"You can thank me for that whenever you're ready. Not every day you get a fresh start in life."

"I wouldn't exactly call this a fresh start."

"Better than a fresh grave," he said, nodding at the ground.

She didn't look amused by the comment. "You owe me some new metal."

"What? You mean, like, in your face?" Stuart asked. "You'd look a lot better without all of that shit poked through it."

"And through the other parts," added Blake, who had returned from the van with a towel and spray bottle to wipe the shovels clean.

"I bet you enjoyed that," she spat. "Fucking pervert."

"Clit and tit rings ain't my thing, sweetie," he said, tossing the bottle and towel at her feet. "Not into tatted skanks either."

"Wipe up your own fingerprints," she said, kicking the plastic bottle at him.

"This is going to be a fun trip," said Stuart.

"He started it," she said.

Blake shook his head. "Do we really need her?"

"We do, and I prefer that you wipe down the shovels. I'm not familiar with Miss Keane's work ethic yet, and I'm not willing to put more of our friends in jeopardy over a sloppy cleaning job."

"Got it," he grumbled, swiping the bottle from the grass.

"And you," he said, addressing Nissie. "Keep your nose clean during the ride to Vegas, and I'll treat you to all the metal you can poke through your face, or wherever. Deal?"

"That was the plan, anyway, but I'll take what I can get for free."

"Might be the only payment you receive for this job."

"I'm not doing this one for the money," she said quietly, with a touch of defiance.

"Good," he said. "Neither are we."

CHAPTER 54

A hot gust of wind whipped across the two-lane road, rattling pebbles and dust against the SUV while Nathan emptied the last of the fuel from one of the red plastic containers into the gas tank. Owen stood next to him, blocking as much of the wind as his small frame could manage.

A second, stiffer blast of wind drove another sheet of rock and dust into them.

"Hey, bud. Why don't you get inside? It's getting crazy out here. I'm almost done, anyway," said Nathan, patting his shoulder. "I appreciate the company."

"Are we gonna make it before the storm hits?"

"I don't know." Nathan looked over his shoulder at the rapidly disintegrating horizon. "I think this is one of those microbursts Jose was talking about. The big storm is still a few hours away."

His son started toward the passenger door.

"Owen. Get in on the other side. The door might slam shut on you, and your mom might not be too happy getting a face full of sand."

"OK, Dad." On his way around the front of the SUV, Owen high-fived David, who carried a rucksack taken from the car ahead of them.

"Nathan. I found your pack. They must have stuffed it in the lead vehicle," said David, stopping a few feet away from him. "Are you sure you don't have the satphone in your vest?"

"I'll check again. The last time I remember seeing it was in the Motel 6. I think I put it down to pick up the radio. I honestly can't remember what I did with it. Everything moved at light speed in the room."

"I thought maybe Keira grabbed it," David said, "but she checked all of her stuff."

Nathan nestled the gas can into the back of the SUV, while David found a place for his pack. He checked the pockets of his tactical vest again, not finding the phone.

"Dammit," he said. "I should've stuffed it in my pocket when I grabbed the radio."

"I should've been tracking it," said David. "That was the first time the phone wasn't in one of my pockets or hands since Colonel Smith gave it to me. I need to check in with my dad. They have to be worried."

"They should be halfway to Vegas by now."

"So should we," said David. "I hope this isn't the main storm."

"I don't think it is. We'd see it building on the horizon. You ever been in one of these sandstorms?"

"A few times in Afghanistan. It's pretty insane. Day turns to night. Scary enough when we were under cover on base, but out in the field? Like a nightmare."

"We left Tucson after getting hit with five in one summer," said Nathan. "Big ones, too. Air quality goes to shit for days."

"Let's get moving. I can tell Jose is nervous about our progress," said David, grabbing the lift gate.

He shut it, and they both walked down the driver's side to get into the SUV. When Nathan closed the rear door, he still felt the warm wind blowing through the vehicle. The permanently open, bullet-resistant windows funneled the desert air and a steady flow of sand through the car. That was the only drawback to Jose's bulletproof-car design. They couldn't close the windows, rendering the SUV's air-conditioning system effectively useless. The backseat had AC vents built into the center console, which kept them from dying of heatstroke, if accompanied by generous amounts of water. Warm water. Because everything in the car had warmed to body temperature or higher.

"Start the car and kick up that AC," said Nathan.

"Life support systems activated," said David, turning the ignition.

Owen chuckled. He'd really taken to David, which made Nathan happy. His son needed all the friends he could get right now. So did Nathan.

"Jose. How are we looking?" said Nathan, leaning forward between the seats.

Jose was busy listening to his satphone and scribbling on a notepad.

"Sorry," said Nathan, sitting back.

"One second," said Jose, saying something into the phone before putting it down. "All right. I just spoke with Vegas about the weather situation. This is one of several microbursts that have popped up between Tucson and Flagstaff ahead of the wider storm. We'll be dealing with high winds the whole way."

"What about the big storm?" said Nathan.

"It's moving fast. Getting to Kingman will be tight. We're about two hours out."

"Easy for two hours to turn into three out here," said Nathan.

"It's really a straight shot from here. We'll intersect with US Highway 93 in about thirty-five minutes. We take that all the way to Interstate 40. If we can get to 40, we're good to go. The road is regularly patrolled by the Arizona National Guard and heavily armed militia groups aligned with the state. The cartel is not welcome up there. It's kind of the unofficial cartel demarcation line in Arizona."

"And the route is clear?" asked David.

"That's the only good part about falling behind schedule. The scout teams reported no unusual cartel activity between Interstate 40 and our upcoming highway intersect point. I'm tempted to send them through again instead of waiting for us."

"It's not a bad idea," said David. "Thirty minutes gives us plenty of time to make an adjustment if they run into trouble."

"All right. I'll send them ahead and have them wait for us at Interstate 40. They have extra supplies."

"Good, because we're running low on water," said Keira, drinking from her CamelBak hose.

"A few more hours, and we'll be out of this mess," said Jose, sounding exhausted. "I know the ride sucks."

"Jose," said David, "can I borrow your phone for a second, to check in with my dad? He has to be pretty worried by now. I told him we'd call first thing in the morning. I think we left ours behind at the motel in all of the confusion."

"You want me to drive?" asked Jose, handing him the phone.

"No. I'm just gonna check in and give him a quick update," he said, pressing the numbers.

"You forgot the eight after the four," Nathan pointed out.

David paused for a moment before starting over. "I think this heat is frying my brain."

Nathan put his hand in front of the AC vent. The faintly blowing air felt warm. It wouldn't start to cool down until the car was moving.

"Dad. It's David," he said. "Everyone is fine. We ran into a little trouble, but we're on the way. How is everything on your end?"

David paused to listen.

"About two hours from Kingman. We're not going to make it to Vegas tonight. There's a massive sandstorm moving in. I'll call you when we've settled in for the night. I gotta go."

He nodded a few times. "I really have to go, Dad. See you soon."

David ended the call and handed the phone to Jose. "We're good."

"They're all right?" said Keira.

"Sounds like it. They'll get into Vegas around midnight," said David, putting the car in gear.

The SUV in front of them rolled forward, David following closely.

"We have a nice setup in Vegas," said Jose. "Very secure."

"I thought the city was a cartel-free zone?" said Nathan.

"You won't find marauding bands of cartel soldiers shooting up the streets, but they can still flex their muscle in Sin City. It's not as safe as the primetime commercials boast, but for the average tourist? Hard to find a cheaper room with that many amenities."

"I'd like to push north, out of the Wastelands," said Keira. "Our luck has been consistently bad down here."

"Vegas is the perfect place to turn your luck around," said Jose.

"You sound like a craps dealer," said Keira.

"What's a craps dealer?" said Owen.

"Someone that sells bullshit," said Keira. "Sorry, buddy."

"Hon," said Nathan, shaking his head discreetly.

"Sorry," she said, taking a sip from her CamelBak. "The heat must be getting to me."

He stole a glance at her, receiving shrugged shoulders and her patented "What?" look.

"It's been one of those weeks," said Jose. "Just keep an open mind when we get to Vegas."

"I'd consider a trip to the moon to get away from this," said David, clearing the uncomfortable air.

Owen laughed again.

"I think you have a future as a stand-up comic," said Nathan.

"As long as we can clone a few hundred Owens."

"Sounds like a *Twilight Zone* episode," said Jose.

"I love *The Twilight Zone*," said Owen.

"They still show those?" said David.

"You can stream them for free."

"I didn't know that," replied David.

"My son watched all of them. He'd binge-watch them with his sister," said Jose.

"Where are they now?" said Owen.

Nathan tensed. He remembered what Jose had shared with him in Mexicali—his family had died in the 2030 Albuquerque firestorm. He guessed that Jose had been out of town on business or working in another part of the city at the time of the fire. The fire's death toll had eclipsed that of any US natural disaster to date. Half the city had burned to the ground within an hour as a massive forest fire, fanned by hundred-mile-per-hour winds ahead of a historic New Dust Bowl storm, had swept down from the Sandia Mountains. More than a hundred thousand had died in the firestorm, and hundreds of thousands more were hospitalized with burns.

Albuquerque ceased to exist as a functional city after that. The Albuquerque fire started the great migration out of the Southwest. Within a year, several million residents of New Mexico, Arizona, and southern Colorado had fled. A year after that, the term *Wastelands* was coined by the media. The term was fitting. With the people gone, the Southwest wasted away.

"They're in heaven with their mom," said Jose, staring straight ahead.

"I'm sorry," said Owen.

"No. Don't be sorry, Mr. Owen. They're with their mom. That's what matters now."

Nathan looked at Keira, who wrapped an arm around Owen. That was all that ever mattered.

CHAPTER 55

Stuart Quinn lowered the phone and muttered an obscenity. He hadn't been able to do it.

David had been pretty adamant about hanging up—but no, that was just an excuse. He just couldn't tell him about Jon.

Why have it hanging over their heads for the entire drive, though? What good could come from that?

No. More excuses.

"You made the right call," said Blake. "They need to focus on getting to Vegas in one piece."

"What do you think, Nissie?" said Stuart. "Would you want to know your father had been murdered if you had a long drive ahead of you—with more murderers trying to kill you?"

"I'm sorry," she said. "I don't know how many times I need to say it."

"Save your breath. You'll never convince me by saying it," said Stuart. "I need to see it."

"I don't even know what that means."

"You will," he said. "For now, it means you play nice."

"I am playing nice."

"I didn't say you weren't."

A few miles passed on Interstate 15 before Blake broke the silence. "Where are they now?"

"A few hours out of Kingman, but it sounds like they're racing a sandstorm."

"If they can stay ahead of it, they'll be fine," said Blake. "Kingman is safe, mostly."

"Nowhere is safe," said Stuart. "Not until we put Cerberus out of business."

A thought came to him. Major General Nichols had mentioned that his Marines could be running patrols through western Arizona by tonight. Kingman was in northwest Arizona, where David's battalion might be in a position to lend a hand. It was worth a call to the general to pass that information along. He started to dial the number.

"For what it's worth," said Nissie, "you did the right thing. I wouldn't want to know."

She looked like she might start crying behind her thick black eyeliner. There was more to Nissie Keane than met the eye. Something dark, tragic. He just hoped it would work in their favor—and not blow up in his face.

PART VI

PART VI

CHAPTER 56

Sergio Morales sat deep inside an abandoned restaurant along Highway 93, drumming his fingers on a sand-covered table. The wind battered the outside of the rickety building, the old timber frame creaking and groaning with each powerful gust. The constant airflow through the restaurant's main salon did little to ease the sweltering heat. A satellite phone and digital tablet lay in front of him. To his right sat Jorge, who closed a laptop and shook his head.

"The drone's down," said Jorge. "Sorry."

Sergio hadn't expected it to last very long with the storm this close. An expensive sacrifice. The RQ-16 Whisper represented the latest in short- to medium-range military drone technology, and his boss wouldn't be happy to hear that it was out of commission.

"What was their last location?"

"Approaching the town of Nothing."

"Nothing? For real?"

"Not kidding," said Jorge.

Sergio shook his head. At least the people who named that town had a sense of humor. Nothing was right. He touched the tablet screen and used the digital mapping application to make a few quick calculations. Their target was now roughly twenty-six miles away, putting them at the primary ambush point in twenty minutes, maybe more depending on the road conditions.

The dust storm had intensified at an alarming rate over the last half hour, arriving ahead of predictions. At this point, his crew would have to weather the storm in Wikieup. He didn't see any way to avoid it. The closest inhabited town was Congress, and that was halfway back to Phoenix. No. They'd get to spend the next several hours hiding from the wind in Wikieup, another nothing town.

The front door banged opened, ushering in a swirl of sand and wind. Three men wearing red bandito scarves and sunglasses stepped into the restaurant. Sergio motioned them to approach. The guard watching the parking lot from the outside reached inside and closed the door. Sergio's team leaders trudged to the table through the deep layer of sand covering the floor.

"Good timing," he said, standing up. "They're about twenty minutes out."

"You sure you want to go out there, boss?" said Marcos, one of the team leaders.

Marcos shrank from Sergio's sharp look. Under normal circumstances, a question like that might have earned him a bullet, but today Sergio genuinely believed his loyal subordinate meant no disrespect. US military drone strikes had risen steeply over the past few weeks, particularly in western Arizona. The worst of it was down south, but they'd recently lost a few high-ranking members of the organization on the northern roads. The fear was real, not a symptom of cowardice. Still, it didn't help his reputation to hide inside while his soldiers took all the risks. That kind of caution led to resentment.

"They wouldn't risk one of their cowardly drones in this weather," he said, gathering the tablet and phone. "Is everything set?"

The team leader assured him that nothing would get through the ambush point.

"Perfect. I need to make a quick call. Marcos, I'll meet you at your observation post."

"It's an honor, boss," said the team leader. "You can fire the first RPG."

"I would like that," said Sergio. "As long as everyone else is firing at the same time. It's been a while since I've used one of those."

The men laughed for a few seconds before excusing themselves to leave. Sergio dialed his own boss, who was probably watching the storm arrive from his air-conditioned mansion on the outskirts of Phoenix. Rank had its privileges. Hopefully in a year or so, some of that privilege would find its way into Sergio's pockets. He was getting tired of driving through the desert, shaking down his Wastelands fiefdom.

"It's done?" asked a digitally altered voice.

"Twenty minutes or so. I'm heading out to personally oversee the ambush."

"I'm counting on you, Sergio. There was a big fuckup this morning down in Nogales. El Pedro was killed."

He hadn't heard any of this. "Killed? By the organization?"

"No. No. He was killed on the highway, trying to run these people down. Don't take any chances."

"We're not taking any chances. I have enough firepower to stop an army battalion in its tracks."

"Good. Call me as soon as it's done. How is the storm out there?"

"Coming in fast," said Sergio. "We'll be stuck here for a while."

"That's a smart call. This is one of the biggest I've seen in a while. Phoenix is completely dark right now. Power is going down everywhere. Make sure to call me."

"I will, jefe."

His boss didn't ask about the drone, though he surely knew it had gone down. This told Sergio that their targets were extremely important. He pocketed the phone and grabbed the assault rifle leaned against the table, then nodded at Jorge. "Let's go."

Stiff gusts of wind pelted him with sand as they jogged toward a rusted-out school bus parked perpendicular to the highway in a gas station parking lot. A half-dozen derelict cars lay in the desert scrub next to the lot, many of them hiding cartel gunmen. An RV park entrance across the highway, flanked by several gutted mobile homes about thirty feet back from the road, housed a second team. The third group was spread out to the immediate north, manning heavy machine gun positions hidden in the brush on both sides of the road. Nothing was getting through this gauntlet.

The bus's folding door opened when they arrived, revealing Marcos in the driver's seat. Sergio pushed his goggles onto his forehead and stepped inside, surprised to find that it was mostly sheltered from the weather. A few broken windows on the side let in air, but the bus wasn't filled with sand like the restaurant. He had just found his new headquarters for the night.

Marcos led them to the back of the bus, which faced the highway. From the backseats, they had a nice view to the south, despite the rapidly decreasing visibility. A colossal wall of sand, stretching as far as he could see in either direction, loomed thousands of feet over the eastern horizon, in stark contrast to the blue skies and scattered clouds to the west. They'd be digging out from this one.

"Crazy, isn't it?" said Marcos, gesturing to the sand cloud. "I hope they get here before this hits. A storm like this might stop them on the road."

"That's why I picked this shithole town. They'll see it on their maps and slog it out to get here, no matter how bad it gets."

"That's why they made you the boss," said Marcos, pointing at him.

He didn't like the way Marcos said that, and he certainly didn't appreciate the finger pointed at him. They hadn't made him the boss—he'd earned the position. Maybe Marcos's question in the restaurant hadn't been so innocent. He'd deal with this later. Marcos pressed a finger to an ear, listening to a transmission over the radio net. Sergio had forgotten about his earbuds. He reached into a pocket on his tactical vest for them, but the conversation had ended by the time he'd stuffed them in his ears.

"What's up?"

Marco pointed south, down the road. "Same car that passed through a few hours ago is on the way back."

"Scouts," said Sergio.

"Must be. They didn't see shit on the way through. Everyone was out of sight."

"They wouldn't come back through if they saw anything, so we should be able to take them by surprise. Hit them with RPGs. I don't want them warning off the others."

"You want to do the honors?" he asked, lifting an empty RPG-9 launcher from the seat behind them.

"No. I'd like to make sure we hit the car on the first try," said Sergio, pressing the "Transmit" button on his vest. "Team leaders, I want you to coordinate a simultaneous RPG strike on the car coming through. Use it as practice for the convoy."

"Binoculars?" said Marcos, holding a pair out for him.

"I'll use my rifle," said Sergio, unslinging it and aiming south.

Through his magnified sight, the road came in and out of view between billows of sand. The vehicle appeared, headlights announcing its presence long before the rest of it materialized. When it reached the first SUV on the opposite side of the highway, trails of smoke raced forward from hidden positions on each side of the road, simultaneously slamming into the car an instant later.

CHAPTER 57

Jose stared at his phone, puzzled. From what he could tell, the satellite network hadn't disconnected the call. He had full coverage, so he assumed that the scout team was in the same situation, unless the storm had somehow hampered the signal. From what he knew about satellite communications, he didn't think that was the case.

"Pull over," he said over the radio net.

"What's up?" said David, following the lead vehicle to the shoulder of the road.

"I just lost contact with Ranger. There was no interference or signal bleed. They were there one second, gone the next."

"Dead battery?" said David.

"They know better," said Jose. "And they have a backup."

He activated his tablet and examined the satellite map. The scout team had just reentered Wikieup, twenty-two miles away. They had cleared the town two hours ago, but a lot could change in a few hours.

He saw a few options. The most prudent would be to turn around and connect with Interstate 10. He should have taken Jeremy's advice on that one. They could have holed up near the California border and waited for the storm to pass. The only problem with backtracking was that they would undoubtedly get caught in the storm before reaching the interstate, running the distinct risk of having to pull over and ride out the storm even deeper in cartel territory. The closer they got to Interstate 40, the better.

Zooming in on the area around Wikieup, Jose noticed some possible side roads to the east. If they could sidestep Wikieup and get back to Highway 93, they could drive blind to Interstate 40 if they had to. GPS road mapping was accurate enough to keep them from driving off the road, if they didn't push their speed.

"Jeremy, I just lost contact with Ranger," Jose said. "What do you think about trying to skirt around Wikieup? I see what looks like a partial state road leaving the highway south of the town," he said over the net.

"I see it. Route 159 . . . turns into Cholla Canyon Road?"

"That's it."

"That would get us around and put us about five miles above Wikieup. Might be a rough road, though. I don't get the impression road maintenance has been a priority up here for a long time."

"I'd prefer a rough ride to another gunfight," said Jose.

"What about the river running along the road? Should be hard packed like cement."

"Should be, but we can't afford to get a vehicle stuck. I'd rather crawl along Cholla Canyon Road."

"Copy that. I'll input the route and make sure we can find the turnoff. Visibility will be shit by the time we get there."

Jose glanced out of the side window at the towering wall of sand. They really didn't have much time before it enveloped them. The best they could do was get off the highway and move as carefully as possible.

"All drivers stay as close as possible to the vehicle in front of you," he said. "We can't use headlights."

"We can pop a few IR chem sticks and tie them to the license plates," said one of the drivers. "Night vision will pick those up through the dust."

"All right. Make it happen. Back on the road in thirty seconds," said Jose, turning to David. "I got ours."

Jose fought against the wind to open the door, sand and pebbles blasting him when he stepped outside. The door slammed shut without his assistance. He walked to the back of the SUV, knelt behind the license plate, and removed a chem stick from his vest. Nathan appeared next to him, shielding his eyes from the blowing sand.

"I got this," said Jose, taking a small spool of parachute cord from a pocket.

Nathan knelt next to him. "I'm a little concerned about riding this out in the vehicle. We have no way to keep the sand out. It's already hard to breathe."

His concern wasn't trivial. Jose had just been too preoccupied with the route and communicating with the scouts to address it. "We have some N95 respirators in the medical kit. I wish we had some heavier-duty breathing gear."

"The respirators will help for now. I'm more concerned with later. This storm could last several hours."

"Once we get off the highway and find a safe place to stop, we'll work on plugging all the cracks. It's the best we can do," said Jose. "Let me finish up here and grab the med kit."

Nathan nodded. "Do you really think the scout team got hit?"

"I don't know," said Jose. "Wikieup is the only town with more than one or two buildings on Highway 93, so it would be a logical place for an ambush—especially with the storm heading in."

Jose cut a section of cord and looped it through the end of the chem stick, tying it to the license plate holder.

"You forgot to crack it," said Nathan.

Jose laughed. "A lot of good that would have done us." He took the plastic tube in both hands and bent it until he heard it snap, mixing the IR-emitting chemicals. To the naked eye, nothing appeared to have changed.

"My dad used to bring home boxes of them when I was a kid," Nathan said. "We gave them away as party favors at my birthday parties. He could be cheap like that."

"I bet you were pretty popular with your friends," said Jose, standing up.

"Not really. All the other parents did the same thing. I didn't go to school off base until ninth grade."

Jose smiled. "I'm looking forward to meeting your father," he said, patting his shoulder.

As soon as they'd shut the car doors, the convoy rolled forward, quickly picking up speed. Jose distributed the respirators, keeping his in the center console so he could talk over the radio net without sounding garbled.

By the time they reached the turnoff fifteen minutes later, the sky had darkened to the point where he could barely see the outline of the SUV in front of them. Brake lights glowed weakly from time to time, illuminating the sand blowing between the vehicles. Jose reached into the foot well and pulled his helmet off the floor. He knew from experience that everything was about to go pitch-black. With the helmet tightened in place, he lowered the night-vision goggles and found the chem light on the rear of the first SUV, which burned brightly through the sand.

"Can you see him turning?" asked Jose.

"Barely," said David, tapping the brakes.

"You have at least twenty feet separation. You're good. Start easing us over in four. Three. Two. One. Start the turn. I'll tell you when to straighten out."

Their SUV followed the lead vehicle onto Route 159.

"Right here," said Jose. "What can you see now?"

"Brake lights. Kind of."

The storm had swallowed them.

CHAPTER 58

Keira adjusted her son's mask and held him tight. The inside of the SUV was faintly illuminated by the dashboard, the outline of David's head barely recognizable through the dust suspended in the air. Judging by the rising tension between David and Jose over the road conditions, she suspected they were about to stop.

"Do you hear that?" said David.

"What?" said Jose. Keira hadn't heard anything either.

"Sounds like explosions—and gunfire. I can't tell the distance."

She didn't like the sound of that. A quick glance over the seat didn't reveal anything unusual. The rear vehicle hadn't been visible for several minutes. Keira assumed if they were under attack, she'd see gun flashes. Same with the lead vehicle. Still invisible.

"I can hear it, too," said Nathan.

"I don't hear it," said Jose. "All units. My driver reports possible gunfire and explosions. Distance unknown. Can any of you confirm?"

"This is lead driver. Affirmative. Lots of gunfire to the west."

"Confirm. Multiple explosions," said another operative.

"Copy that," said Jose. "Let's stop here to assess the situation. Jeremy, see if you can identify a place to pull over and wait this out."

"Already on it," said Jeremy.

"I'm gonna get out," said Jose. "Try to pin this down better."

"Are you sure that's a good idea?" said Keira.

"If we can't see them, they can't see us," said Jose, opening the door and triggering the dome light.

So much for nobody seeing us, Keira thought. Nathan reached up and turned it off as a fresh load of sand and debris swirled through the cabin.

"Close the door, please!" she said.

When the door slammed shut, the wind settled—but Keira didn't. "This is ridiculous! Owen is wheezing!"

"No, I'm not, Mom," their son protested.

"Well, I'm having a hard time breathing," she said. "So you are, too."

"There's nothing we can do about it, honey," said Nathan, stroking her sand-covered face. "We'll be fine. When the storm passes, we'll cruise right up to Vegas."

Keira tried to let his gentle touch calm her, but she'd built up an emotional head of steam. "I feel like this is my coffin," she said, straining to hold back a full breakdown. "All we do is go from one coffin to the next."

"Honey," he said, leaning his helmet against hers. "This is probably the safest place in the world right now. Nobody can see us. Not even with night vision."

The front passenger door opened, blasting them with hot air and dust as Jose jumped in.

"What's happening out there?" said David.

"Sounds like a battle going on in Wikieup," he said, sounding concerned.

"Who are they shooting at?" said David.

"I don't know," said Jose. "It doesn't make any sense."

That was the last thing she wanted to hear right now. While Jose barked orders over the tactical net, Keira felt the cabin shrink and darken. The warm windows drew closer. She had to get out of here.

"We need to get out of these vehicles!" she yelled, surprised by her voice.

Shit. She was coming unglued. *Calm down.* She had a thought and started laughing quietly.

"Are you all right?" whispered Nathan, probably worried that she'd gone from screaming to laughing without any kind of transition.

"I think I'm fine. Kind of," she said, stifling a laugh.

"What's so funny?"

"I just told myself to calm down and take a deep breath, but I can't really take a deep breath with this mask on, or the dust floating around. Good thing I don't have allergies," she said, laughing again.

Nathan laughed. "I've had to stop myself from telling you to breathe deeply like five times already."

"This is unbearable," she said calmly.

"I couldn't agree with you more, but—"

"We'll be fine," she said.

"I'd kiss you, but I'm pretty sure that's logistically impossible wearing all of this gear."

"They probably design it that way."

Jose interrupted the moment. "We're moving about three hundred yards down the road. Jeremy thinks we can slide into the riverbed at that point and shelter under a raised riverbank."

"Has anyone checked the river?" said David, beating her to the question. "It may not rain often, but it does still rain out here."

"We'll check it out when we get there," said Jose. "Hang in there, guys."

The SUV slowly rolled into the pitch blackness, on what promised to be the longest three-hundred-meter trip of Keira's life.

CHAPTER 59

Nathan strained to catch the slightest glimpse of the SUV ahead of them, intermittently rewarded with a dull red glow that faded as quickly as it appeared. Jose and David communicated quietly, their urgent back-and-forth conversation inspiring little confidence in the backseat. He glanced out of the passenger door window, seeing nothing but a faint reflection of his own silhouette. Someone could be standing three feet from them and he'd never know.

The SUV jolted to a stop, the already strained conversation in the front seat taking on a more desperate edge. He squeezed Keira's hand.

"We can't just sit here," hissed David.

"I'd have to send a team on foot to scout the approach, and they can't see more than a few meters in front of them. It's too risky."

"This road isn't exactly a secret," replied David. "They obviously knew we were coming up 93, which means they had a lookout somewhere south of here. It won't take them long to figure out we didn't backtrack to Interstate 10."

"They won't know we're here until they're right on top of us," said Jose.

"We won't know they're here until they're right on top of us!" said Nathan. "I can't see a damn thing, even with night vision."

"Jeremy said we can set up observation posts next to the road, fifty yards in each direction," said Jose. "It'll give us enough time to spring an ambush."

"You're going to send people out in this?" said Keira. "I thought you said it was a bad idea."

"If they stay close to the road, they can find their way back," said Jose.

"It'll work. We did it in Afghanistan," said David. "The insurgents always tried to hit us during the sandstorms. With our thermal imaging gear, it turned into a turkey shoot."

"We don't have that kind of gear, so we'll have to rely on the element of surprise for our advantage."

"You'll have to station the teams uncomfortably close to the road," said David. "They may only get a chance to hear the vehicles pass."

"Jeremy has a few ideas to help with that," said Jose. "I think it's time we started to block the window openings. We might be here awhile."

Jose said something to David, and the car stopped.

"Did he just turn off the car?" said Keira.

"We can't keep it running," said Jose. "We've sucked way too much dust through the engine filter already."

"What about circulating the air?" she said. "I can barely breathe as it is."

"The best we can do is leave a few cracks open to let the air flow through," said Jose. "We can't risk a mechanical failure."

The car seemed to Nathan to get warmer immediately after David shut the engine off. This wasn't going to work for Keira. Maybe they would be better off hiding outside, in the lee of the riverbank, sheltered from the wind and sand. The air quality couldn't be any worse than inside the SUV, and the cartel wouldn't be able to find them. They could tie a rope or some kind of line to the vehicle. If the storm cleared, or Jose decided to leave in a hurry, they could find their way back.

Nathan was about to make the suggestion when a powerful spotlight cut through the sand choking the air behind them, illuminating the cabin. He twisted in the seat, seeing the silhouette of the rear SUV in the bright light.

No time for a committee decision. He fumbled for his rifle with one hand while feeling for the door handle with the other. With the handle in his grasp, he turned to Owen.

"Buddy. Grab on to my vest and don't let go no matter what. We're leaving," said Nathan, flinging open the door. "Keira. We're going."

"Nathan!" yelled Jose. "Get back inside!"

He stood on the road and slung the rifle over his shoulder, feeling behind him for Owen. Once he had a solid grip on Owen's hand, he started to walk forward into the darkness. Jose continued to yell, along with David.

"Keira!" he said over his shoulder.

"I'm with you. Right behind Owen," she said.

Nathan moved quickly away from the SUV, slowing down when the yelling started to fade. He had no idea how far away the riverbank might be, or if he was heading directly toward it. The road had twisted back and forth several times since they'd left the highway. A quick look over his left shoulder told him that the spotlight hadn't followed him. They were out of the line of fire for now. That was all that mattered. Jose's vehicles might be bullet resistant, but he'd heard the deep crunch of explosions in the distance. Not even the Marine Corps fielded rocketproof vehicles. He knew that firsthand.

"Nate. Where are we going?" said Keira.

"Anywhere but back there," he said, stopping for moment to check on his son. "How are you doing, buddy?"

"I'm scared," said Owen. "I don't like this."

"Here's what we're going to do," he said. "We're gonna find the river and hide along the riverbank, out of the wind. We'll be safer there."

"Nate," said Keira. "I don't hear any shooting back there."

Nathan searched the blackness, already unable to see the vehicle they'd just escaped. The rear vehicle was barely visible in the spotlight's beam. He did find it odd that a battle hadn't broken out on the road. Maybe they could wait here for a little while.

The spotlight swung in their direction, penetrating the sand and scrapping any thoughts about staying in the open. He pulled on Owen's hand, urging them toward the river.

"Let's go," he said. "Away from the light!"

Nathan took a several dozen carefully planted steps before feeling the ground slope away. The light still pointed in their general direction, but it didn't have the power to reach them through the swirling murk.

"I think I've found—"

His son bumped into his back, knocking him off balance. He teetered awkwardly on the edge, letting go of his son's hand before he fell. Nathan skidded through gravelly sand before his right foot hit something solid, tumbling him forward onto his side. Mercifully, his descent ended there, with no discernible injuries.

"I think I found the riverbank!" he yelled. "Get on your hands and knees and crawl backward down the ledge."

"Nathan!" Keira cried. "I hear voices up here!"

"Hurry up!" he said, scrambling up the slope to reach them.

"We're trying!" said Keira.

He felt a smaller boot, which he guessed was Owen's. "Is that you, buddy?"

"It's me, Dad! They're getting closer!"

"Who's getting closer?" yelled Nathan.

His wife screamed, "Get your hands off!"

"Keira!"

His wife's yelling stopped too quickly. Nathan held on to Owen's boot with his left hand, trying to unsling his rifle with the other. He'd just managed to wiggle the rifle free when his son's foot was yanked away.

"Owen!" he screamed, aiming the rifle into the darkness. "Owen!"

Shit. Shit. Nathan had nothing to fire at, not that he would shoot if he did. What could he do? He could only think of one way to proceed. To know for sure whom he was taking down. He dropped the rifle, pulled the serrated combat knife from the sheath on his belt, and began clawing his way up the riverbank.

He stayed quiet when he reached the top, listening for signs of struggle. Nothing. He was edging forward with the knife held in front of him when a pair of strong hands grabbed his wrist, immobilizing the knife, while another pair wrestled him to the ground from behind.

"Nathan!" said a vaguely familiar voice. "God damn it, Nathan. Chill the fuck out. We're on your side. Keira and Owen are fine."

"Where are they?" he said, fighting to shake free. "Who are you?"

"It's Sergeant Graves. I'm kind of hurt you didn't recognize my voice."

It all came back to him in an instant. Graves had operated the armored vehicle's countermeasures systems when they had been attacked by Cerberus on Interstate 8.

"I remember," said Nathan, letting go of the knife.

The grip on his hand released as soon as the knife hit the ground.

"Where are Keira and Owen?"

"They're close," said Graves, pulling Nathan to his feet. "We didn't know how you'd react, so we kept them quiet."

Nathan sat up. "You could have just announced your presence. Would have been a whole lot easier."

"We could barely see your outline with the thermals. Cantrell didn't want to risk the possibility of you shooting first and asking questions later."

"Staff Sergeant Cantrell? He's here, too?"

"At your service," announced a nearby voice. "I have your wife and son right here."

"I can't see any of you," said Nathan.

Someone bumped into him.

"Dad?"

"Hey, buddy. You had me worried there for a minute."

"I thought Mom was dead," said his son. "I thought you were dead, too."

He grabbed Owen and hugged him. "We're fine, Owen. Just like I promised." He felt Keira's arm on their son's shoulder. Nathan pulled her in tight and held both of them for a few moments.

"You all right?" he whispered in her ear.

"As long as we don't have to get back into that SUV."

"I had something a little more robust in mind," said Cantrell. "Let's get you and your family inside my vehicle. David should be there already."

"Clean air?" said Keira.

"Purified. Filtered. Smells like the mountains," said Cantrell.

"Sounds good to me," she said.

They started back, following the spotlight like a beacon.

"Staff Sergeant," said Nathan. "How did you find us?"

"A little birdie told us you took a detour."

"You have an informant in one of the SUVs?" said Keira.

"No. Nothing like that. I can't really talk about it," said the Marine.

"Did you come through Wikieup?" said Nathan.

"You didn't hear us?"

"Jesus," replied Nathan. "Sounded like a small war going on out there."

"That's just what it was. The cartel had at least fifty guys out there waiting for you with RPGs, heavy machine guns—all kinds of crazy shit. Everything but thermal-imaging scopes. We put them down pretty quick."

"Good," said Owen.

"We'll drive through again and mop up anyone that survived the first pass. You're welcome to control the gun turret, Owen. Just like a video game," said Graves from somewhere to their immediate left.

"Yeah. That's not going to happen," said Keira.

Interestingly, their son didn't protest.

"You all right, bud?" said Nathan, squeezing his hand.

"I just want to go home," said Owen in a quiet voice.

"Me, too," said Nathan. "When we get to Las Vegas, we'll work on finding a new home."

"I don't want a new home."

"I know, sweetie," said Keira. "But we can't go back to California right now. We'll make our new home big enough for Grandma and Grandpa. How does that sound?"

"And a pool," added Nathan.

Chapter 60

David crouched in the rear compartment of the Marine armored vehicle, leaning against one of the automated harness systems and taking deep breaths of the purified air, forcing it out of his nose to clear his nasal passages. The effort was futile. He'd taste this dust for days.

"Good to see you again, Captain!" yelled Corporal Reading.

He was seated in the vehicle systems operator position, behind the driver, operating the turret remotely with a joystick. The center screen embedded in the back of the driver's seat displayed a slowly panning thermal image of their surroundings. No wonder they'd been able to find Nathan so easily. They had probably tracked him with thermal imagery all the way to the river.

"Back at you, Reading," said David. "What have you been up to for the past few days?"

"The usual. Riding around the desert."

"Did you get Artigas back to his family?"

Artigas had been killed during the ambush along Interstate 8 a few nights ago. A 50-caliber sniper bullet had essentially decapitated him, dropping his headless body into the AL-TAC during the ferocious firefight that followed their crash.

"We got him on a plane back to Pendleton before the battalion towed a new vehicle out to Yuma. They sent us out right away."

The Enhanced Counterinsurgency Platoon had lost a third of its Marines in the ambush on Interstate 8. They were one of the tightest groups of Marines that David had ever served with. The archetypal band of brothers. He'd been too distracted with Alison's death to properly absorb the greater impact of the night's loss on the platoon.

"Sorry about Arty," he said. He was sorry about all of them. "Is this the rest of the platoon?"

"No," said Reading. "We got absorbed into the rest of the company. Cantrell kept me and Graves together."

"And decided to babysit your asses, too," said David.

"Shit. You gotta keep a close eye on Graves, man. He's all shifty down there, looking at his screens."

"He's a shifty mother, that's for sure," said David. "I heard he's mean on the remote trigger, though."

"Aww . . . you didn't, sir," said Reading. "You didn't go there."

"Just repeating what I heard. I'm sure the Marine Corps isn't planning on outsourcing the turret gunner job."

"I can't shoot what I can't see. They need to give me some thermal imaging up here."

"I don't know. Sounds like they outsourced you already," said David.

David was back in his element—where he truly felt he had always belonged. The temptation to stay here was overwhelming. The Marine Corps had been his calling, until a 50-caliber sniper bullet had altered his life by taking Alison's.

The rear hatch mechanism clanged, activating a series of powerful blowers. When the door swung open, most of the sand and debris was blown clear of the opening.

Nathan helped Keira and Owen into the cramped compartment, lifting himself inside behind them. Staff Sergeant Cantrell poked his head in through the hatch.

"Captain Quinn, I need to debrief you before we head out," he said, disappearing into the darkness.

That didn't sound good. He wasn't sure why, but it felt contrived to pass muster in front of the Fishers.

"Be right back," said David. "I hear the Fisher kid is pretty good at video games. He might be in competition for the turret job, too."

"A young Marine in training! I can live with that!" said Reading.

"He's not going up in that turret," said Keira.

"I was just kidding," said David, squeezing by Nathan and his family.

When David dropped to the road behind the AL-TAC, he shut the rear hatch and pulled the locking mechanism down to reactivate the cabin's pressurization system. He wished he could see the look on Keira's face when she took her first breath of purified air. She had been on the verge of a complete meltdown in the SUV. The rest of them hadn't been too far behind her.

"Staff Sergeant?" he yelled, edging around the vehicle.

"Right here," said Cantrell, activating a flashlight a few feet away from him. "I have Second Lieutenant Gedmin with me. We're part of First Platoon now."

A second light pierced the sandstorm, illuminating Jason Gedmin's face.

"Hey, Jason. You inherited some shit-hot Marines," said David.

"They keep reminding me," said Gedmin.

"They tend to do that. Might be their only flaw."

"It's good to see you, David. Details were kind of sketchy about what happened on the way to Yuma," said Gedmin. "I'm really sorry about Alison."

David sensed a hesitation. Like Jason, he wanted to say more. He didn't want to go down that road every time he talked with one of the Marines. It wouldn't be healthy for him right now.

"Thank you," said David, hoping that would be the end of it.

"David," said Gedmin, "Staff Sergeant Cantrell made an observation while bringing Mr. Fisher and his family back from the river."

"Yeah?"

"I don't know how to say this without sounding callous."

"We're well past the point of pulling any punches here," said David. "What is it?"

"He doesn't know that his father is dead," said Gedmin.

David was pretty sure he'd misheard the lieutenant's statement. Whether it was the last thing he expected to hear, or it simply didn't make sense given the recent call to his own father, Gedmin's words skipped by without making an impact.

"What was that?" said David.

"Colonel Smith called the lieutenant over satcom about ninety minutes ago and told him that Nathan's dad had been killed. That's how we found you. Your dad called Major General Nichols to let him know that you'd be out this way. He told Nichols the bad news at some point. Nobody was sure if you or Nathan knew. Apparently not. Nathan thinks he's meeting up with his dad in Vegas."

"Are you sure? I talked to my dad about two hours ago," said David. "He didn't say anything."

"Colonel Smith was very specific about the details," said Gedmin. "Nathan's father was killed in Missoula at a friend's town house. Your dad and brother-in-law killed the team responsible for his death. Nathan's mom is safe."

"That's why they were late getting out of Missoula," muttered David.

"Smith diverted us from the Lake Havasu area toward Highway 93. He even used one our ELINT drones to find you. They picked up a conversation over an encrypted handheld frequency that led us here. Just so happens the quickest way to 93 was through Wikieup. Bad news for the cartel. Good news for you."

"Yeah," muttered David. "Good news and bad news."

"Sorry," said Gedmin.

"No. You guys saved our asses. I'm the one that should be sorry. I appreciate you sticking your necks out like this."

"It's our pleasure, sir," said Cantrell. "I just wish we could have rolled through the same motherfuckers that hit our convoy, instead of those cartel rats."

"Me, too," said David. "I'll tell Nathan. Give me a little space."

"No problem," said Gedmin. "One other thing. I'm uncomfortable bringing these mercenaries on board the AL-TACs with their weapons. Can you smooth that over with them? I'd be happy to store all of their gear externally."

"Jason. Do me a favor. Cut them a break. This is the same group that saved what was left of my ECI platoon on the interstate. They've been fighting and dying for us since then. You can trust them."

"I can live with that," said Gedmin. "I'll get them loaded up."

"Thanks again, guys," said David, waiting for them to disappear before opening the back hatch. He took a flashlight from his vest and waved it inside. "Nathan. Jose needs to ask you some questions about our meet-up in Las Vegas. Shouldn't take more than a minute."

When Nathan's feet hit the ground, David guided him away from the door and closed it. He aimed the light upward, between them, illuminating their faces.

"Where's Jose?"

"Jose isn't here," said David.

"What?"

"Nathan. I have some really bad news," he said. "Your father is dead."

Nathan didn't say anything at first. He looked down at the light before shaking his head slowly. "What about my mom?"

"She's safe."

Nathan nodded slowly. "How did it happen?"

"He was killed at his friend's town house by Cerberus. My dad and Blake took out the team somehow."

A heavy gust of wind blew a thick patch of sand against them, momentarily blocking most of the light. When Nathan's face reappeared, he was staring at David, his face registering no expression.

"We're going to bring the rest of them down, right?" he said, an edge to his voice.

David was taken aback by the question, though it should have been the easiest for him to answer. He stood there, the wind and sand pelting him for a several moments, before gripping his shoulder.

"I swear it," said David.

Nathan's stoic facade started to crumble. He patted David on the shoulder and turned toward the faint outline of the vehicle next to him, then stopped and turned back. "Don't say anything to Keira or Owen," he said. "I'll give them the news once we're tucked safely away in Las Vegas. They've been through enough."

"We've all been through enough," said David, grabbing the hatch lever. "I'm sorry about your dad, Nathan. My father spoke of him like a brother."

"They *were* brothers as far as my dad was concerned," said Nathan, hitting the side of the hatch with his fist. "Best friends until the end."

David extended a hand. "Until the end."

"Until the bitter end," said Nathan, gripping it firmly.

CHAPTER 61

Mason Flagg opened his laptop and connected to the jet's encrypted server, settling in for the ninety-minute flight to Aspen–Pitkin County Airport. He navigated to a secure e-mail system and checked for an update from his Sinaloa contact.

The last message he'd read prior to leaving the Point Loma operations center for the flight had confirmed that a convoy of three vehicles matching descriptions from Nogales had passed the last turnoff on Highway 93, heading north onto a long stretch of lonely road. His contact had assured Flagg that his problems would disappear on the highway, despite possible interference from a dust storm of "biblical proportions." At worst, Fisher and company might not make it to the ambush site before the storm hit, pulling off the road to let it pass. A short delay to the inevitable, the Mexican had said. Flagg would believe it when he saw the three cars burning. The past ninety-six hours had conditioned him to refrain from making *any* assumptions about the fate of Nathan Fisher.

A new message waited, time-stamped nearly an hour ago. Dammit. He hated using this message drop system, but the Mexican had insisted. Apparently, talking on a satphone had become the number-one cause of death among high-ranking cartel members over the past few weeks. From the sound of things, the United States military had implemented continuous air coverage missions over cartel hot spots. Fully armed stealth bombers cruising at high altitude above each designated area, waiting for target coordinates provided by sophisticated electronic intercept platforms. One minute, Cartel Joe was discussing the latest armored Range Rover models with a buddy in Mexico City; the next minute, forensic scientists were scraping his remains from the side of a two-thousand-pound smart bomb crater.

Flagg could appreciate the security concern, despite his annoyance with logging in to get updates he had paid millions of dollars to receive. He clicked on the message, encouraged to see that the convoy was less than thirty minutes away from reaching what had been described to him as "a gauntlet of firepower."

Don't get excited. The message had been sent close to an hour ago. Thirty minutes had passed since he should have received a message confirming the ambush's success. OK—twenty-five. He could understand a small delay. Flagg started to type a message but stopped. The suspense was killing him.

He pulled out his satphone, which he'd already linked to the aircraft's onboard system, and dialed Javier's number. The phone rang twice before his contact answered.

"I figured you'd call," Javier said. "We haven't heard from the ambush team since they last reported. Nobody can get through to them. It's possible they are having communications problems because of the dust storm."

"Satellite communications should remain mostly unaffected," said Flagg. "How soon can you get a team out there to investigate?"

"They still have blackout conditions in Phoenix. I can't get a team out there until this passes."

"Do I get a refund if your people failed to neutralize the target?"

Javier didn't respond immediately.

"I didn't think so," said Flagg. "For that kind of money, you can send someone out immediately. If the ambush failed, I need to know that before I meet with my clients."

"Let me see if we can send one of the lookouts near Interstate 10. They should be within an hour's drive of the site. Probably twice that with the storm."

"Don't let me hold you up," said Flagg.

"I'll be in touch," said Javier, disconnecting the call.

You better be.

Flagg had hoped to walk into the Ethan Burridge's mountain lair with some good news on the Fisher front but had resigned himself to proceeding without it. The hunt for Fisher had become a stale distraction. At least that's how he planned to sell it. If Fisher had somehow survived the ambush on Highway 93, it was time to permanently outsource the problem to an organization with no traceable ties back to the One Nation campaign. This would allow Flagg to refocus on California, where the tide of public opinion had resoundingly turned in One Nation's favor. The latest polls indicated a seven-point rise in the percentage of Californians supporting the status quo over any form of state secession. Flagg would never admit it in front of the council, but Petrov's rash decision to kill Congresswoman Almeda might have inadvertently triggered a landslide shift in the way Californians viewed the issue—shepherded by Flagg's targeted damage-control efforts.

Almeda's murder had been squarely blamed on the secessionists after the lieutenant governor had been killed less than one day later. It was the only logical conclusion, given the lieutenant governor's public antisecessionist stance. The failure of the Del Mar nuclear triad plant further complicated matters for the California Liberation Movement.

With public opinion swinging rapidly in their favor, Flagg had decided to accelerate one of Cerberus's cornerstone projects—the Mojave Block option. In a few short days, they would deal a killer blow to California's self-sustainability movement. The catastrophic loss of the Sheephole Valley Solar Electric Station to an earthquake would call into question the long-term viability of California's renewable energy plan. The Sheephole site wasn't the only solar farm located in an active fault zone. Rolling blackouts across much of Southern California would serve as a constant reminder of the fragile state of California's green energy infrastructure.

If the Cerberus-instigated destruction of the solar farm didn't extinguish the last serious vestiges of the secession movement, the council would have to consider a far more direct approach: open season on the California Liberation Movement and all of its supporters.

Flagg didn't think it would come to that. He wasn't even sure the council would approve the shift in strategy. Petrov would be on board, but that's only because the Russian was no stranger to scorched-earth campaigns. More than four hundred ranchers, farmers, and local or state politicians had been murdered in northern Texas, Kansas, and eastern Colorado during AgraTex's two-year northbound expansion. Flagg didn't think the rest of the council could stomach a similar campaign of intimidation, extortion, bribery, and murder in California, especially on their own dime. He hoped the Mojave Block option put an end to it, once and for all.

CHAPTER 62

Leeds closed the door to the air-conditioned trailer and descended the short platform of stairs, scanning the flat, brown landscape. A stiff wind swept across the site, loosening a thin film of dust from the hard desert floor. He walked to the end of the trailer, still shielded from the blowing sand, and took another look at the operation.

Two mobile drilling towers loomed in the distance, surrounded by dozens of oversize support rigs. Tanker trucks arrived and departed daily to maintain the high-pressure flow of water and chemicals into the horizontal fracking well. The flow of traffic in and out of each site represented the only security risk to the remote operation, drawing a minimal amount of attention from locals.

The land was private, so most in-person inquiries had been discouraged with a visit from one of their security teams. The few locals who had persisted in sticking their noses too far into their business had been buried where they'd never be found again. From what Leeds could tell, nobody had strayed close enough to any of the sites to spot the drill rigs, which had arrived in the middle of the night five weeks ago. That continued to be their primary security concern. The tall rig structures would draw the wrong kind of attention. Not only was fracking prohibited in California, but there was no shale deposit under these shifting sands. His satphone buzzed.

"Miss me already?" said Leeds.

"Not really," said Flagg. "How does it look out there?"

"Bleak. Flat. Not much of an improvement over Mexico."

"At least nobody is shooting at you."

"Not yet," said Leeds. "Everything appears to be proceeding as planned. All but one of the wells I've visited are between ninety-seven and ninety-nine percent finished drilling the horizontal fracture. After that, it's a matter of opening as many fissures as possible and putting our faith in the surveys and seismic calculations."

"It'll work," said Flagg. "It better work. How does the security situation look?"

"Buttoned up. The place could hardly be more godforsaken."

"I'm more interested in the human factors."

"The rig managers report happy campers so far. I'm not sure how that's all going to play out when they start opening fissures without extracting anything, but the number required to operate each rig will be drastically reduced at that point. Some of these guys are going to put two and two together when the ground shakes. That's inevitable."

"We have our own people on each team," said Flagg. "We should be able to identify and manage any problems."

"I don't think we'll see too much of that. They signed draconian nondisclosure agreements, reinforced by generous, progressive payouts—starting after the work is completed. Any pangs of conscience should be tempered by the prospect of losing most of their money."

"And their lives."

"Too bad we couldn't put that into the contract," said Leeds.

"Unfortunately, that tends to scare away the talent. I anticipate some unpleasant cleanup work when they realize they've triggered an earthquake, but nothing security can't handle—under your direct supervision, of course."

"And you really need me to babysit this until it happens?"

"We can't afford any security issues, internal or external. I know it's boring as hell out there, but we're looking at three to four days at most. This is by far the most important thing on our plate right now. I'm headed up to brief the council on what they can expect from this phase of the operation."

"It sounds like I got the better end of the deal," said Leeds. "Any news on Fisher?"

"I'm not hopeful about the cartel grabbing him in Arizona. He's a loose end we'll sweep up later."

"Sounds like you've been rehearsing that line."

"In the mirror," said Flagg. "Keep me apprised of any concerns out there, regardless of how insignificant they may appear. I want our external security teams to monitor closely for electronic transmissions. The few who managed to smuggle in satphones will start to use them when we pressurize the wells with no apparent intention to collect natural gas."

"Don't they already know there's no shale deposit here?"

"You'd think, but who knows," said Flagg. "I want those satphones confiscated as they're detected. Things might need to get a little rough at that point, to make the rules clear."

"I'll handle it."

"That's why I have my highest-paid operative sitting in the middle of the desert," said Flagg. "I need to let you go. I have to practice my speech a few times."

He pocketed the phone and jogged to the tan Range Rover, getting in the passenger side. A man dressed in a desert camouflage and light tactical gear sat in the driver's seat, ready to drive him to the next drilling site. Leeds nodded apathetically, and the SUV rolled across the hard-packed desert floor.

CHAPTER 63

The column of armored vehicles stopped next to a small parking lot overlooking the Hoover Dam. From his seat in the back of the AL-TAC, Nathan could see the tops of the dam's Art Deco–style intake towers through the rear passenger window. A line of oversize white SUVs blocked the rest of his view. Heavily armed men and women stood around the vehicles. He presumed this was the rest of Jose's Mexicali contingent.

"We're here," he said.

"All right," Keira said, rubbing her eyes and yawning after the fitful sleep she'd stolen during the four-hour ride. He still hadn't told her about his dad. Later, when they'd settled into whatever dank space that awaited them, he'd find a way to break the news to her alone. Together, they'd decide whether to tell Owen the truth or make up some excuse for why Grandpa had stayed behind. Nathan leaned toward postponing the news.

He hoped they were close to their final destination for the day. Jose hadn't been very specific about the location of the Las Vegas station. For all Nathan knew, it could be in an abandoned mine shaft thirty miles north of the city. As long as it had a place for him to lie down, he didn't care.

"Owen," he said, poking his son's knee.

His son sat slumped in the seat harness, his head tilted forward at a painful-looking angle. When Nathan's first attempt to rouse him from a catatonic sleep went nowhere, he reached across the compartment and shook Owen's shoulder, getting a slurred response.

"We're here, buddy. Time to go."

"Where are we?" said Owen, squinting at him.

"The Hoover Dam."

"Vegas, baby!" yelled Sergeant Graves in a rare display of excitement.

"Woo-hoo! Fucking Vegas!" added Corporal Reading.

"Jesus," muttered Keira. "Don't you guys ever power down?"

"No, ma'am," said Graves, holding up an energy drink. "Not with this coursing through our veins."

"I'll take one of those," she said, catching a can flipped at her from the driver's seat a few seconds later. "Thank you," she said, cracking open the can and taking a drink. "Want some?"

"I'm good," said Nathan, getting up to help Owen out of his seat harness.

Keira knelt in front of her seat and peered into the front of the vehicle. "This group looks a little too polished to be Jose's crew."

David nodded. He had been watching them through the window next to his seat. "I recognize a few of his operatives from Mexicali, but not the rest," he said. "The shiny new Suburbans don't fit at all, though. This isn't Jose's style."

Staff Sergeant Cantrell leaned his head between the front seats. "The lieutenant just cleared us for the handover. Your man Jose gave him the green light."

"Then that's it," said David, reaching over to Graves in the seat next to him. "See you guys on the other side." He shook hands with the Marine, patting him on the shoulder. Corporal Reading bent down far enough to reach David's hand.

Nathan waited for them to finish their brief good-byes before thanking them again for saving his family. With the last round of farewells behind them, Nathan helped his zombielike son out of the vehicle. A blast of pavement-baked air waited for them in the parking lot, forcing him to take short breaths until his nostrils adjusted to the extreme temperature. The sun was low over the hills beyond the dam, but it still had to be more than a hundred degrees outside. He could feel the heat radiating off the black asphalt.

"I feel like my boots are going to melt into the parking lot," said Keira, shielding her eyes from the sun.

"They might if you don't keep them moving," said Nathan, scanning the row of five identical white Suburbans.

Jose stood next to the third SUV, talking excitedly through an open window. A Marine Nathan didn't recognize jumped out of the lead AL-TAC, grabbing Jose's attention. They nodded at each other, shaking hands a few moments later.

Staff Sergeant Cantrell turned to Nathan's group. "That's it. Handoff complete. Remember, we're only a satphone call away. You need, you ask."

Nathan stepped forward. "Thank you, Staff Sergeant. I can't tell you how much this means to us. To me."

Cantrell paused, looking uncertain how to respond. Nathan had forgotten that the Marine knew what had happened to his father.

"I think I know," Cantrell said. "You take care of that family of yours, and this guy." He pointed at David. "The Marine Corps would like to get him back in one piece."

"Hopefully sooner than you think, Staff Sergeant," said David, shaking his hand.

As the three armored vehicles rolled away, Jose stepped in front of their group.

"I'd like to introduce you to someone," said Jose, nodding into the SUV next to them.

The door opened, and a man in his late fifties stepped down from the vehicle. He had wavy, grayish-brown hair and smooth, tanned skin and moved with an age-defying, athletic grace. Dressed in a gray suit and light blue shirt, without a tie, he looked like he'd just stepped out of a business meeting.

"Nathan, this is Richard Breene, our key benefactor," said Jose. "None of this would be possible without him."

Nathan wasn't sure what Jose meant by that, or why they were being subjected to a meet-and-greet out in the open at the Hoover Dam. He recognized the man's name but was too wiped out to put the pieces together.

Breene stepped forward to shake his hand. "Welcome to Las Vegas, Nathan," he said. "I heard about your trip—from start to finish. I think you've earned a break. I look forward to getting to know you better."

"Well—that's nice, I guess," he said, laughing at himself. "Sorry. I'm a little frazzled right now."

"No. I'm the one that should apologize. I kind of hit you out of the blue with this. I was just very excited to meet you."

"Well, we appreciate you picking us up, and I do recall hearing your name, I just can't seem to jar my memory loose right now," said Nathan. "Let me introduce you to my wife, Keira, and my son, Owen. And last but not least, David Quinn."

Breene took them all in, nodding in what appeared to be a genuinely friendly manner before shaking their hands.

"Has your son ever seen the Hoover Dam in person?"

"No, he hasn't," said Nathan. "We haven't taken many trips out of San Diego since we moved to California."

"Well, let's correct that before we get out of this refreshing heat," he said, guiding them between the SUVs to a stone wall overlooking the reservoir side of the dam.

The first thing Nathan noticed was the drastically low water level in the reservoir. He'd seen pictures on TV and the Internet, but looking at Lake Mead with his own eyes delivered a gut punch. The white bathtub ring around the reservoir extended hundreds of feet down its reddish-brown rock walls. This was what "dead pool" looked like up close. He wondered when water had last flowed downriver through the dam.

"Wow. I didn't realize it was so deep," said Owen. "This is really cool."

Keira glanced at Nathan nervously, then went back to scanning the rocky hills behind them. He was thinking the same thing. This wasn't the time for sightseeing.

"It looks deep because the water is so low," said Breene. "Kind of tricks your depth perception. When the reservoir is at its average historical fill level, you'd be looking across a lake. You can see where the water level ought to be—at the top of the white line."

"It's really low," said Owen.

"If you can believe it, the water almost came up to the first concrete ring around the intake towers."

"How long ago was that?"

"Way before you were born," said Breene. "Possibly before your parents were born."

"It was 2002, the year I was born. I never saw it," said Nathan. "Mr. Breene, I don't want sound unappreciative, but do you think we can get out of the open?"

"I'm sorry," he said. "It's ghastly hot out here. I apologize."

"It's not the heat," said Nathan, looking around them. "We feel a little exposed out here."

"Of course." He gestured toward the idling SUVs. "Though I assure you the area is secure."

"Based on our experience over the past few days," said Nathan, "I can guarantee that my concept of *secure* differs drastically from yours."

"I don't doubt it," he said. "But I still think you'll find my vision of security more than adequate."

Breene whispered into his collar, then motioned behind them. Nathan turned to face the tall rock formation, seeing a two-person team rise into view near the top. Movement on a few different high points within his field of vision unveiled several teams situated in multiple overwatch locations around them. From what he could tell, all appeared heavily armed.

"We have the area locked down hard," said Breene. "I have over a hundred people guarding the dam at any time, with more in reserve."

"Guarding the dam?" said Nathan. "Isn't that the federal government's job?"

"I took that responsibility off their hands a few years ago," said Breene.

Nathan looked at Keira, who did her best to hide a worried face from the group. He knew her well enough to know that she was thinking the same thing. *Something isn't right here.* David didn't look alarmed on the surface, but that didn't mean anything—the Marines had issued him the same stoic poker face Nathan had seen countless times on his own father.

"I don't get it," said Nathan, directing the comment at Jose. Whatever was going on here, Jose was on the hook for it, as far as Nathan was concerned.

"Richard bought the dam from the Bureau of Reclamation two years ago," said Jose.

"*Bought* the dam?"

"The bureau still regulates the flow of water through the dam," said Breene.

"What flow?" said Nathan.

"Exactly. That's a big part of why they were eager to sell it. Not to mention the fact that the hydroelectric plant hasn't produced power in over five years. Running the dam costs the bureau close to ten million dollars per year, an expense they more than offset by selling electricity to local consumers. Without the water to run the hydroelectric plant, the dam is a financial albatross. And we both know that these water levels aren't rising any time soon. Even if the drought reverses itself."

"You actually own the entire dam?" said David.

"Not exactly. I own the hydroelectric power rights, which are essentially worthless at this point, in exchange for assuming full responsibility for the costs of maintaining and operating the dam. I also paid the bureau a onetime fee equal to the amount of money they've lost on the dam since hydropower generation started to decline."

"But they've been losing money on the dam for more than a decade," said Nathan.

"It was a big check," said Breene.

Nathan was starting to understand the bigger picture and how all of the players were intertwined, including him. He remembered now. Richard Breene was a self-made California real estate mogul, worth more than $20 billion, according to *Forbes*. The value of his empire had skyrocketed over the past decade along with the price of California real estate.

Breene's involvement with Jose and the CLM was intriguing. He had been conspicuously absent from the public secession debate, probably because it didn't matter to him what happened. The state was overpopulated, and the people had to live and work somewhere. California real estate was a guaranteed investment. So why would Breene jump into a losing purchase like the Hoover Dam? Nathan had a solid idea why.

With the full flow of the Colorado River restored to the Lower Basin, Lake Mead would fill to maximum capacity, and the Hoover Dam would conservatively generate close to $50 million in electricity per year on the California market alone. Given the gift of unlimited water and electricity, Las Vegas would be reborn. Nathan wouldn't be surprised to learn that the billionaire had invested heavily in the currently valueless Las Vegas and greater Nevada real estate markets in recent years. Breene's net value would skyrocket, possibly making him one of the wealthiest people in the world. The relationship between Jose and Breene was more a marriage of convenience than anything—very convenient for both of them. Nathan couldn't suppress the sly look forcing its way across his face. Breene saw it and smiled.

"It's a win-win situation for everyone involved," said Breene. "Including each of you."

Keira looked uncomfortable with Breene's comment. David's face remained stoic, but Nathan knew what he was thinking.

"As long as we lend a hand?"

"It's not like that, Nathan. Regardless of your ultimate decision, you, your family, David—whomever you wish to protect—is welcome to stay in Las Vegas, under my protection, until this mess is sorted."

"If you think the Hoover Dam is secure, wait until you see Mr. Breene's fortress in the hills," said Jose. "You'll be safe there."

The decision to help Jose bring down the Upper Basin dams wasn't solely Nathan's to make, and he was in no condition to make a rational choice. Revenge superseded logic. Nathan would discuss his possible participation in Jose's plan with Keira before telling her about their father's murder. He needed one of them thinking clearly about their future.

"*We're* going to need some time to consider this," he said, looking at Keira.

"Take all of the time you need. But first, let's get you out of the heat," Breene said before motioning toward one of the white SUVs. "You get the vehicle all to yourself."

"Mind if I drive?" said David.

Breene grinned. "I understand your privacy concerns, but I'd feel more comfortable with my security team in place."

"We're reasonably capable of protecting ourselves," said Nathan, shifting the rifle slung over his shoulder.

"So I've heard," said Breene. "The SUV is all yours."

They settled into the same seating arrangement used for the ride between Mexicali and Nogales—David behind the wheel next to Nathan in the front passenger seat, Keira and Owen in back.

"This might be the last true bit of privacy we have for a long time," said David.

"I'm glad you thought of it," said Keira, leaning up between the front seats. "I bet we were under surveillance back in Mexicali."

"I wouldn't bet against you," said David.

The lead vehicle in the convoy took off, followed closely by the next vehicle in line. A few moments later, they accelerated in pursuit.

"I don't want to rush this decision," said Nathan, "but we may not have a very long ride."

"I can stop us at any time," said David.

"I'd prefer you didn't. I like the sound of this fortress, or whatever Jose calls it."

"I don't want to get stuck there," said Keira. "We can use it as safe harbor for now, and lie low until our trail goes cold. The sooner we meet up with your parents, the better. Breene's place doesn't exactly sound low-key."

David gave him a furtive look, which didn't go unnoticed.

"What?" she said.

He wasn't ready to break the news about his father's murder to her. Not under a compressed timeline, and especially not in front of Owen.

David stepped in. "While we were getting in the car, I warned Nathan that you wouldn't want to stay here for long."

"I just think we'd be better off somewhere a little more discreet, and a lot farther away," said Keira. "An off-the-grid survivalist compound sounds pretty appealing right now."

If this was her decision, that was fine. They'd stay at Breene's place long enough to identify a secret location where they could hide longer term. While they waited here, Nathan could share with them classified information that he had purposely kept out of his thesis paper regarding the dam system—information about weaknesses in the dam's structural integrity and how best to exploit the weaknesses. He saw no harm in that. If Jose succeeded in bringing down the dam with his help, it would go a long way toward avenging his father's death.

He wanted to be more involved, even see one of the dams fall, if possible, but his primary responsibility would always be Keira and Owen. He couldn't allow himself to lose sight of that, no matter how badly he wanted to take down the One Nation Coalition.

"You're being awfully quiet," Keira said, prodding Nathan with a finger.

"Sorry. Everything's catching up with me," he said, squeezing her hand. "I just want to curl up with you guys and fall asleep."

"You won't get any argument from either of us," she said and leaned back in her seat next to Owen.

Nathan turned and found his son staring out of the tinted window. "What do you think about all this, buddy?"

Owen turned away from the window. "I just want to go home, wherever that is now."

Nathan glanced at Keira, who answered their son.

"We're doing everything we can to make that happen, sweetie."

Nathan nodded in agreement, wondering how closely his concept of *doing everything* matched Keira's.

"This will all be behind us before you know it," he said, smiling at his son.

David looked at him, raising an eyebrow.

"One way or the other," added Nathan.

ACKNOWLEDGMENTS

To the usual suspects—you know who you are.

To the Thomas & Mercer team—Jacque, Gracie, Sarah, Lauren, Timoney, Sean, and the rest of the crew. I can't thank all of you enough for making this publishing process a fun and fantastic experience. I'm beyond excited about what we've accomplished together for the Fractured State series.

To my readers—just knowing you're out there still blows my mind. Thank you for your loyal readership and enduring support.

ABOUT THE AUTHOR

Steven Konkoly is a graduate of the US Naval Academy and a veteran of several regular and elite US Navy and Marine Corps units. He has brought his in-depth military experience to bear in his fiction, which includes the speculative postapocalyptic thrillers *The Jakarta Pandemic*, *The Perseid Collapse*, and the Fractured State series, of which *Rogue State* is the second installment. Konkoly lives in central Indiana with his family.